GENERAL WRANGEL

General Wrangel and his young son Peter with French Marshal Franchet d'Espery sail for Constantinople in 1920 on board French cruiser.

GENERAL WRANGEL

Russia's White Crusader

Alexis Wrangel

To my late wife Theodora,
without whose help and encouragement
this book would not have been possible.

ACKNOWLEDGMENTS

I owe the idea for this book to my late wife whose help, patience and encouragement inspired me to research and write until the manuscript was complete, shortly before her death.

To Lieutenant Colonel Prince Leonid Lieven MBE — my deep gratitude for his generous gift: a most competent research in the files of the British War and Foreign Offices, newspapers and libraries.

To the secretaries who read my most illegible handwriting and wrote and rewrote the manuscript: Mrs. Cheryl Mellar and Mrs. Dolores Coogan — my sincere appreciation.

It is to Mr. George Blagowidow that I owe the original concept of this biography, and his Hippocrene Books, Inc., its publication.

Lastly to all those who contributed, some a line, others a whole manuscript of reminiscences, a grateful thank you, though many are no longer here to hear it.

For information, address Hippocrene Books, Inc.,
171 Madison Avenue, New York, NY 10016.

ISBN 0-87052-130-6
Printed in the United States of America.

Contents

Preface

TO THE READER a biography written by the son may seem prejudiced. In fact there are only two kinds of totally unprejudiced people: the complete cynic and the complete imbecile. In this book the reader will hardly find the first. As to the second, it is to be left to his discerning evaluation.

Much is said these days about human rights. Alas so much abused worldwide. In this story the reader will find much shocking brutality. Though not condoned it should be viewed in perspective of time and circumstance. Civil wars represent the acme of ferocity; the exception, perhaps, the American Civil War. But there no social or religious elements clashed and the war on both sides was run by generals, members of the same "Club," West Point. Wisely they restrained their troops from excesses of barbarity. The Russian and its successor the Spanish civil wars let human ferocity reign unchecked: The toll of death, torture and bestiality defy all imagination.

Reading the memoirs of Gen. Wrangel, a former Soviet general had this to say: "He was too liberal, too clement to his enemies. Perhaps that is why he lost!" — a remark that the Western world should interpret and heed.

The author has attempted to make this book a mosaic, the reminiscences of those who fought or worked with Gen. Wrangel, from the lowly private to the chief of staff. Their composite picture is livelier and probably more accurate than the post factum studies by historians. What they saw and felt through the smoke of battle and the vicissitudes of defeat and exile are a "living" part of this biography.

September 1986
Brownstown Lodge

Introduction

SOMETIME IN THE LATE EIGHTIES there was a party at the Wrangel estate near St. Petersburg. It was to be a masquerade party for children, and young Peter Wrangel was decked out as the devil, complete with horns, a forked tail, and a huge red tongue which popped in and out of his mouth. Anxious to test out this costume among the unsuspecting, Wrangel slipped out of the garden and into the fields where peasants, men and women, were cutting hay. The sudden appearance of the devil threw them into consternation: The girls screamed and fled; the men, after an instant of panic, crossed themselves and, scythes high, rushed at the devil. Seeing that this was no joke, Peter Wrangel turned and sped for home with the peasants at his heels. Handicapped by the devil's long tail, Wrangel would have been cut down before he could explain; the men were gaining on him. The young boy reacted instinctively and quickly; he turned and charged the peasants. This counterattack was too much for their superstitious minds; they backed off and Wrangel ran again. This maneuver allowed him to reach the park gates and safety. There at last everything was explained to the excited mob which rushed in behind him. . . .

Could this presence of mind, this sudden countercharge, have been a portent of greater things some thirty years later? For then General Wrangel's Cossack divisions would charge, and charge successfully, formations of infantry armed with all modern arms — cannons, machine guns, rifles. His cavalry corps maneuvering against fortified positions would take a city, defeating a whole Red army, and mass formations of mounted men would, for the last time in history, deploy and reap victory on a field of modern warfare.

1

The Wrangels

SOMETIME IN THE THIRTEENTH CENTURY a German knight set out from his family domain in Lower Saxony* and headed east to join the knights of the Teutonic Order,** who, under the pretext of converting the Baltic pagan tribes, were (with the pope's blessing) carving out feudal fiefs in the East. Prominent among the conquerors was King Waldemar II of Denmark. In his feudal census *Liber Census Daniae* there is mention of a Dominus Eilardus, lord of a village called Uvarangele. The first real mention of a Wrangel is in a document dated 1277: Dominus Henricus de Wrangel; the knight took his name from the village, his fief. This Wrangel was killed in a battle against the Lithuanians in 1279 in the campaign led by the Grand Master of the Teutonic Order, Ernest von Rasberg. The Wrangel family, though, eventually prospered over the years of fighting and conquest, and towards the end of the Teutonic Order's rule in 1561, it possessed seven knightly holdings — the second largest feudal estate in the Baltic. After all those territories became part of Sweden, a census made in 1681 revealed the Wrangels to be the most powerful family, with fourteen knightly holdings — twice as many as the richest family.

A family history is a mosaic; individuals make up the overall picture. Those individuals may be brilliant or dull; some may be successes, some failures, others nothing at all. The Wrangel mosaic is particularly rich in the individuals that make it up; over the seven hundred years of its existence it produced: seven field marshals, seven admirals, forty-one generals, four bishops, two ministers, three professors, one horse master and one art critic. These individuals served

---

* This knight could have been from the Lewenwolde family of Velzen, whose coat of arms is identical with that of the Wrangels.
** The Teutonic Order (a monastic order) moved into the former Baltic provinces in 1237. Livonia was a church state and the Vatican used it as a base from which to spread its influence into Russia for the forceful conversion of Orthodox Christians to the obedience of Rome. The second object was commerce, to control the Dvina estuary and thus Russian trade.

their countries as Swedes, Germans, Russians, Dutch, and even Spaniards.*

Nationalism, as we know it now, is a product of the French Revolution. Before that upheaval the aristrocracy served whom and where it saw fit; changes in master fluctuated with wars, events, heritages, and sometimes whims. Whereas now a change in passport is viewed with suspicion, if not considered outright treason, in those less bureaucratic days a man could battle for the French king and have estates in Austria, leave the French to fight for the Spaniards, return to the French, and so on, without ever having his name besmirched with the label of traitor or turncoat. Mercenary was then no disparaging term.

One of the Wrangels, Fabian (1651–1737) started his military career in Sweden, then served in France where he was made a captain, went on to serve in Holland as a lieutenant colonel and in Spain as a colonel; he was made a general by the Bourbon king, Philip of Spain. He then changed his mind and fought for the Hapsburgs, and fought successfully against his former masters, was a companion of Marlborough, received a count's title, and ended his career as a field marshal and Governor of Brussels, where he left for posterity the Wrangel coat of arms on the walls of Brussels' city hall.

Another Wrangel who attained fame was Field Marshal Karl Gustav. A student of shipbuilding and seafaring in Holland, he became a Swedish general at the age of twenty-four and at twenty-eight commanded a Swedish army in ·the Thirty Years' War. He beat the Danish fleet in the battle at Fehman, 1644, and in 1647, as a companion of the French marshal Turenne, defeated the Imperial forces at Zusmanhausen. He was made a field marshal, received a count's title, and went on to fight in the war against Poland and Denmark, taking among other trophies the "Hamlet Castle" of Kronborg. Among the many titles and honors awarded to him was the Chancellorship of the University of Greifswald. In those days war booty was legitimate, and Karl Gustav amassed enough of it to build the castle of Skokloster, the "Blenheim" of Sweden; he now lies buried in the castle's church.

Looking further on through the pages of history, we see no less than seventy-nine Wrangels (see Loewenhaupt's book *Karl XII: Officerare*) serving in the Swedish army of Charles XII in his incessant wars. Of these seventy-nine, thirteen were killed in combat (three in the battle at Poltava, where Peter the Great in 1709 wiped out the Swedish army) and seven Wrangels died in captivity.

But already at the end of the eighteenth and beginning of the nineteenth century we find Wrangels in Russian service, there again rising to prominence.

---

* Count Fabian Wrangel was last Spanish Governor-General of the Low Countries.

Baron Carl Wrangel (1800–1872) fought in the Russo-Persian war of 1826–1829, then was for many years involved in the conquest of the Caucasus where he commanded a famous regiment, the Erivan Grenadiers, in whose ranks served at one time no less than nine Wrangels. Defeating the Turkish army at Natshim in 1854, Carl Wrangel took the Turkish fortress of Bayazet. During the Crimean War he defended Sebastopol against the allied French, British, Italian, and, Turkish forces.

The seas also saw Wrangels distinguish themselves not only as naval officers but also as explorers, colonizers, and scientists. Ferdinand Wrangel (1796–1870), after whom Wrangel Island, Port Wrangel, Wrangel volcano, and even Wrangel Indians are named, started his career as a young naval officer, sailing in the bark *Kamchatka* in its world circumnavigation. From 1820–1824 he led an expedition charting the coasts of northeast Siberia. From 1825 to 1827 he sailed again round the world as captain of the bark *Krotkij*. Naval director of the Russian-American company, he based himself in Sitka, Alaska, and remained at that port for five years, during which he explored Alaska's interior, charted Alaska's waterways, and tried to interest the government of Russia in Alaska's potential riches — in vain, however, for to his chagrin Alaska was sold to the United States.

Ferdinand Wrangel was an honorary member of both the Russian and French Academies of Science. His son, also a naval officer and explorer, was later Professor of Oceanography and Meteorology at the Russian Naval College. During the long and strenuous conquest of the Caucasus (it took the Russians sixty-odd years to complete the conquest), another Wrangel rose to military prominence — Alexander (1804–1880). Like his relative Carl, he also commanded the Erivan infantry and fought through all the campaigns, sieges, trials, and tribulations which cost many thousands of Russian soldiers their lives and culminated with the capture of the legendary Caucasian chief Shamil in his supposedly impregnable mountain fortress of Gunib. Alexander Wrangel was in on "the kill," his grenadiers having scaled the walls of the "impregnable" fortress.

Turning from Russia to Germany, we see Wrangels prominent in military service and active in Prussia's many wars. Outshining all his German relatives, Field Marshal Friedrich (or as he was known to Berlin's citizens, Papa Wrangel) had the distinction of winning Prussia's highest military decoration, the *Ordre pour le Merite*, at twenty-two years of age and of commanding an army at the more than respectable age of eighty. But he was best known for liquidating without bloodshed the 1848 revolution which nearly toppled the Prussian monarchy. He did this with courage, diplomacy, and wit. At one critical moment, while walking among the excited populace, he was seized by revolutionaries who decided to hang him from a lamp post. As they were about to do so, Wrangel remarked: "Try another lamp post; this one is rusty and may break!" The crowd roared approval and saved his life. At eighty-six years old and a field marshal, Friedrich volunteered for the Franco-Prussian War of 1870; it took the King of Prussia all the persuasion he knew to restrain the eighty-six-year "young" soldier.

To those readers who believe in heredity, the above enumeration of martial prowess among the many generations of Wrangels needs no explanation for this biography, but those who do not believe may also have a point: Peter Wrangel had a father who was anything but a soldier. A humanist, a rebel, a dilettante, an art connoisseur, he was at the opposite pole of his line of stalwart ancestors who lived by the sword.

Peter Wrangel's father, Baron Nicholas Wrangel, was born in 1847 during the stern reign of the Russian czar Nicholas I. At that time, of the civilized countries only two retained slavery — the United States of America with its Negro slaves, and Russia with its Russian slaves. Nicholas's father, a retired officer and rich landowner, ruled his estate and family in the spirit of the time with an iron hand; he was feared as much by his servant slaves as he was by his children. Nicholas's mother had died when he was a very small boy. By all accounts she was a very beautiful woman, and strange as it may seem for a Russian aristrocrat, her grandfather had been a Negro slave.

The Turkish sultan had presented Peter the Great of Russia with a young Negro. Noting the boy's intelligence, the Emperor sent him to school and then to France, where he studied military science, was received at the French court, had many women admirers among the French aristocracy, and even presented a couple of those ladies with illegitimate children, black, to their embarrassment. Returning to Russia, he served in all the wars of Peter the Great and rose to the rank of a full general. He married a Russian, and among his descendants was the famous poet Pushkin, whose negroid features spoke eloquently of his background.

As a small boy (he had four older brothers and three sisters), little Nicholas Wrangel was brought up by an old slave nurse, was bullied by his older brothers and sisters, and was nagged by an elderly aunt. When he was old enough to start his studies, he was taught by tutors, as was then the custom in the households of the nobility. His studies suffered, however, when Nicholas fell into a state of depression; the tutors complained and his father uttered dire threats. Goaded to despair, the boy tried to commit suicide by throwing himself out of a second-floor window. For weeks he hovered between life and death, nursed by the old nurse and his youngest sister; when he recovered at last, he found a different climate. His father, profoundly shocked by what had happened, repented and went to the other extreme, offering Nicholas the free choice of his education and further life. Nicholas went to Switzerland where he lived and studied in a private *pension*. Geneva was then swarming with Russians, but Russians of a different kind — revolutionaries, Marxists, nihilists, anarchists. Besides their political fervor (though they quarreled and bickered constantly among themselves), they had one thing in common; this was dirty and dishevelled attire, a phenomenon also seen today among segments of rebellious youth, whether European or American.

Nicholas Wrangel was curious and frequented their circle; he met the great revolutionary Bakunin, but he was not convinced. Their behavior, quarrels, and squalor repulsed him, so he turned to other, more interesting people. He met Alexandre Dumas; Princess Pauline Metternich, who was then the toast of Vienna; and also the Prince of Wales, the future Edward VII. At that time Prince Edward was taking every occasion possible to escape from London and the stifling atmosphere of his mother, Queen Victoria. One day Prince Edward and Nicholas Wrangel were coming down the marble stairway of one of the most fashionable brothels in Paris; one of them slipped, and both tumbled — the result a broken leg for Nicholas and broken ribs for the Prince.

On another occasion Nicholas gambled in Monte Carlo and lost; as he was coming out of the casino on his way to the hotel to send home a cable asking for money, he met another young Russian, a Prince Galitzin. "What are you doing here?" he asked. "I have lost all my money and am off to send a cable home," answered Galitzin. "Let us then send one telegram for both and have one more fling," replied Nicholas. They went back and stopped the table — gold louis in all their pockets and their top hats filled with them to the brim.

After graduating as a Doctor of Philosophy, Nicholas Wrangel returned to Russia and went to work for the Ministry of the Interior. He was appointed aide to the Governor of Poland. Poland, after its unsuccessful insurrection, was being ruled by Russia with an iron hand. Oppressed as he had been as a small boy, Nicholas took sides on all occasions with the oppressed Poles; this did not endear him to the authorities, and after some sharp encounters with his superiors, he resigned. After a short service in the Horse Guards, one of Russia's most prestigious regiments, and a still shorter service as a justice of the peace, Nicholas Wrangel decided to become a businessman. As a director of several companies, he invested much of his personal fortune and lost even more. His business affairs had taken him to the provincial city of Rostov on the Don, and in the meanwhile he had married. Typically, his bride Maria was not an aristocratic heiress but an orphan. Daughter of an impoverished officer, she had, besides good looks, a considerable intellect and was deeply interested in politics and social reform. Disillusioned with politics, Nicholas took to what was not only a hobby but also a vocation — art collecting. In this he excelled, gathering over the years paintings, porcelain, and historical objets d'art of all kinds. Towards the end of his life he wrote his memoirs, *From Serfdom to*

Bolshevism * — there he criticized all: the emperors and the revolutionaries, the Christians and the Jews, the government officials and the anarchists. The only entity which escaped was the regiment of the Horse Guards in which he had done his military service; but then, several generations of Wrangels had served there, and it was to him somewhat like a good club. "Two prisoners looked through the prison bars —one saw the mud and the other the stars." Of Nicholas Wrangel one could say that he unceasingly chose the mud. Yet those who knew him loved him. He was a perfect gentleman: cultured; kind; scrupulously honest; courteous to all, high or low, and particularly the low; witty but gentle — perhaps one of the last models of a dilettante gentleman of the nineteenth century. . . .

---

* *From Serfdom to Bolshevism: The Memoirs of Baron N. Wrangel 1847–1920.* London: Ernest Benn Ltd. 1927.

Swedish Field Marshal Karl Gustav Wrangel distinguished himself in the Thirty Years' War.

Skokloster, the "Blenheim" of Sweden, was built by Karl Gustav Wrangel.

Swedish Field Marshal Herman Wrangel of Salmis (1585-1643) was the father of Karl Gustav Wrangel.

Above left: *Admiral Baron Ferdinand Wrangel, explorer and navigator, was last governor-general of Alaska.*

Left: *Ferdinand de Wrangel was one of many Wrangels who gained prominence in Russian service.*

Above right: *Prussian Field Marshal Frederick von Wrangel was known to Berlin's citizens as Papa Wrangel.*

Baron Nicholas Wrangel, renowned Russian artistic personality, was the brother of General Peter Wrangel.

Baron Peter Wrangel was born August 28, 1878, the oldest of three brothers.

2
Childhood and Youth

BARON PETER WRANGEL WAS BORN AUGUST 28, 1878, the oldest of three brothers. The youngest, Wladimir, died tragically of diphtheria as a very young boy, to the great sorrow of the parents and brothers, for they were a very close-knit family. The mother saw carefully to her sons' education. The boys grew up in a very liberal, cultured atmosphere and went to civilian schools in the provincial town of Rostov on the Don, where their father's business had taken the family. Nicholas Wrangel was at that time on the board of several coal companies and had become interested in gold mining in Siberia, so he thought it would be a good idea if one of his sons became a mining engineer. As the younger son was artistically inclined (he later became a talented and distinguished art critic), the eldest son, Peter, was commandeered to the School of Mines in St. Petersburg, to which city the whole family moved, as Maria Wrangel wanted personally to supervise her son's education. Peter Wrangel was then, and remained throughout his life, a dutiful son; he studied diligently, and evidently brilliantly, for he graduated first in his class and was awarded a gold medal. Before setting off for the wilds of Siberia, he had, however, to do his military service, as all other Russians did, except those who were physically unfit or single sons who were exempt as sole supporters of their family. In those days of "benign" warfare, before the advent of gas, germ warfare, atom, and hydrogen bombs, and other mediums of mass destruction, peacetime soldiering, at least for the educated — hence, privileged — class, was not too strenuous and at times rather pleasant.

For the Wrangels, military service meant the Horse Guards, the "Family Regiment." Of this regiment and his service in it, Peter Wrangel's father wrote in his memoirs as follows:

"The Horseguards and the 'chevaliers-gardes,' which in the eighteenth century formed a single regiment, had always been the two smartest corps of the Guard. Only the cream of the nobility served in them, and to be admitted to them was considered a favor. The late Emperor Nicholas I and his son Alexander II headed these regiments and generally wore their uniform, while most of the Grand Dukes were their officers.

"They did me the honor to admit me. Our uniform or, to be exact, our uniforms, for we had many of them, were splendid. We had a tight-fitting red tunic with gold braid for the Court balls, a green one with blue trousers for the town balls and a green military frock coat for dinners and calls. Service dress consisted of a white cloth tunic with gold braid, top-boots coming up to the knees and a gold-plated cuirass and helmet; on the crest of the helmet was an Imperial eagle with outstretched wings.

"Mounted on splendid horses with flowing manes and tails, the men looked like an army of mounted giants. I forgot to say that both men and horses were huge.

"In spite of my age and my philosophy, when I first saw myself dressed like this, I was ready to follow the example of my new comrades, who were less modest than myself, and take myself, not for what I really was, but for a superior being, a demi-god, a hero of the Middle Ages. And, as can be imagined, my immediate circle looked on me differently too. Even my valet, whose services I had never made use of when dressing before, fussed about me in a possessive way, strapping me up and pulling me about. The first day I appeared in unform my porter gave me a bow almost to the ground and my old coachman, a steady and sensible man, set off at a terrific pace as if the devils were after us. And the police sergeants, instead of taking him by the collar and laying information against him, stood at attention. Undoubtedly an officer in the Horseguards was a personage.

"In the spring we set off, headed by the band, for the camp of Krasnoe-Selo, where the Guards, both cavalry and infantry, stayed during the summer. The officers lived in little cottages which only contained two small rooms. I kept one for myself, in which there was hardly room to move, and gave the other, which was still smaller, to my old valet. Like everybody else, I only took my siesta there, and hardly ever slept there at night. The day was spent partly on horseback and partly in the mess, a vast barrack consisting of a single high hall which served as dining-room, library and reading-room all at once; the arrangement did not worry the readers, since the library consisted of various sporting journals, which somebody always lost the first day they arrived, and of the official gazette, which nobody ever read. As for books, there were none. No, I am wrong. One of the officers possessed a novel by Paul de Kock, which everybody thought delightful. But it already had been read and re-read and most of the pages were missing.

"At dawn we were already in the saddle, and would come in about one o'clock in the afternoon dead tired, have a hasty lunch and go to sleep until dinner, which was a real Balthazar's feast, copiously washed down with champagne.

"Our chef was the famous Dussaux himself.*

"In the evening we went to the theatre, or perhaps we went off to St. Petersburg, where we would have a good time, and we would only return to camp just in time to avoid being arrested.

"An intellectual would probably find such an existence very distasteful, and in the long run I agree with him. But nevertheless a soldier's life has a charm which cannot be understood by those who have never taken part in it."

During Peter Wrangel's early soldiering, life in the Horse Guards had not changed materially; true, one could no longer take one's personal valet on maneuvers and one had to pass examinations to get a commission, but otherwise the life of a "privileged" soldier was not exactly a bed of thorns.

Having spent years at hard and dreary studies in the School of Mines, Wrangel plunged headlong and with enthusiasm into the game of soldiering. He entered the army September 13, 1901, was made sergeant by March of 1902, and was an officer candidate on July 15, 1902. Life in the Horse Guards appealed to him so much that he decided to take the required examinations and apply for a permanent commission in the regiment. After the School of Mines the educational requirements for the examinations at the Nicholas Cavalry School were no great obstacle and a year of good soldiering added to the ease of passing the examinations.

As in the case of all Guards regiments, one could only be accepted as an officer in the Horse Guards by the ballot of the regiment's officers; no outside "pulls" could secure the commission. One evening before the ballot Wrangel and his friends celebrated his promotion. It must have been quite a party, for on returning home and passing the senior colonel's residence, Wrangel drew his sword and neatly decapitated a row of young trees planted around the lawn. The colonel, Prince Troubetzkoy, was a humorless martinet; besides, he liked his trees. And Wrangel was blackballed.

Wrangel had a quality which served him truly all his life: He never looked back, never regretted the past; he always looked ahead. Though undoubtedly chagrined at not joining the regiment, he departed reconciled to his new life as an engineer in far-off Siberia.

It is hard for us at the end of the twentieth century to visualize life in a small provincial town in Siberia at the turn of the century. Whereas a Concorde now flies us from Paris to New York in three hours, eighty-five years ago it took that long for the traveler in a horse-drawn carriage or sled to reach the nearest village — in the summer, under clouds of mosquitoes: in the winter, buried

---

* A famous French chef.

under several layers of bearskin rugs in temperatures thirty degrees below freezing, the sled at times even being pursued by hungry wolves. Hospitality replaced entertainment; food and drink superseded intellectual pastimes, and they were available in enormous quantities. The Siberian villages were rich; the land had much to offer in natural resources, and those peasants who had turned their backs on Russia and headed east, as American pioneers had gone west, were rewarded with a richer, if at times harder, life.

A Siberian recalled: "Arriving at a friend's house by sled in winter, one threw off the bear rugs and frozen stiff entered the hall, closed off from the main living room to keep out the cold. There you removed your fur coat as the host brought you a tumbler of vodka. It might as well have been water, for cold as one was, one did not feel it even going down a frozen throat. As wines traveled poorly in those extreme temperatures, meals were washed down copiously with vodka and liqueurs made from berries picked in the woods in summer and served in lieu of highballs as after dinner drinks."

Siberia also had its type of "Texas millionaire." Arriving one day at a rich merchant's house, the young engineer Wrangel was astonished to see a room composed of one rotund mirror of immense proportions. To his amazed question the owner proudly announced that he had bought it at the World Fair in San Francisco.

"But how did you get it here?" asked Wrangel.

"Nothing simpler; by ship to Vladivostok and then here in winter on a sled drawn by a dozen horses."

"And how did you get it into the house?"

"We didn't — we built the house around it."

Just how long Wrangel would have endured such a life or how it would have affected him, we do not know, for an event occurred which changed his life and shaped his destiny — the Russo-Japanese War.

The Russian high command looked on a prospective conflict with Japan as on a colonial war, and at first it was thought that the Siberian-based troops would suffice. Later, according to a revised plan, six reserve corps were to be added, and finally, a supplement of two active corps (X of Kiev and XVII Moscow) was contemplated. By the end of the war Russia had concentrated thirty-eight infantry divisions and twenty-one cavalry regiments, mostly Cossacks. Russian intelligence sadly miscalculated both the size and the quality of the modern Japanese army. Russia paid dearly for this mistake. Even then it would have been possible to win the war were it not for the lamentable leadership by generals whose military aptitude had been dulled by twenty-five years of peacetime soldiering since the Russo-Turkish War of 1877.

From the Guards and line regiments which remained in Russia many officers volunteered for combat duty in the Far East; from the Horse Guards regiment alone fifteen officers and twelve men went to join Trans-Baikal Cossack[1] regiments or volunteer units formed from Moslem Caucasians. Among those who went was reserve lieutenant Baron Peter Wrangel.

Wrangel had always been a dutiful son; his literary-minded mother had encouraged him to write, and much like his contemporary, Winston Churchill, he had a gift for the pen. From the theater of operations he wrote long letters home, describing his adventures and sharing his observations. Years later, unknown to him, his mother edited the letters and forwarded them to the magazine *Istorichiskiy Vestnike* (Historical Review), which printed them. To his amused embarrassment Captain Wrangel received two-hundred and forty roubles for his literary efforts.

Besides their literary value, these articles show great powers of observation, a feel for the life of a combat officer, and an ability to get along with the rank and file, a quality which subsequently Wrangel developed to the maximum.

LETTERS FROM MANDCHOURIA (excerpts)

"On April the 2nd the train carrying our echelon, the 5th Squadron of the 2nd Argun Cossack Regiment, was approaching the town of Laoyan.

"The regiment had been assembled in the town of Nertchinsk and had proceeded to the railways station Mandchouria in columns of two squadrons each, arriving there March 26, after a fourteen-day march.

"We marched twenty-five to seventy versts* per day (with two rest periods of twenty-four hours each) in wonderful warm weather and over rolling country sparsely populated by Cossacks and Mongols, nomads occupied exclusively with horse breeding. On the march we saw their felt yurts (tents), camels, and big herds, 100–150 head of horses. Mongolian ponies are extremely hardy and well proportioned, among them many pacers, especially prized by the Mongols. The herdsman sits on the best horse in the herd, one with particular abilities in speed and hardiness. When a potential buyer points out a prospect, the herdsman dashes forth and lassoes it. Our officers bought several ponies, paying seventy-five to one hundred roubles per horse.

"After three days rest at the station Mandchouria we entrained and proceeded on to Laoyan.

"As we moved along the basin of the river Liaoche, the countryside changed; it became richer and more typically Chinese. The plain was under agriculture, so intensely cultivated as only the Chinese know how and quite foreign to the Russian concept. It was early spring and patches of green rarely broke the brown evenness of ploughed fields. Chinese villages flashed by with

---

* One verst is approximately one kilometer.

their thatched or tiled roofs, surrounded by mud-brick walls; sacred groves and temples with ornate horse figures on the rooftops. Wild ducks swam about on the many ponds and lakes, oblivious of the train passing by. Occasionally we saw here and there massive Chinese coffins standing forlorn in open fields (the Chinese do not bury their dead). Some of those coffins were new, others weather-beaten and decayed with human bones strewn about. ... This picture of death among the gay spring countryside jarred particularly the unaccustomed eye. Parallel to the railway line there was much movement: Chinese peasants, clad in blue trousers and blue coats and wearing conical straw hats, passed in an incessant stream; sometimes one saw a colorful two-wheeled, mule-drawn cart occupied by brightly made-up Chinese women with ornate headdresses gleaming with a myriad of pins; at other times we passed heavy carts drawn by small, powerful, mostly grey horses, and big, good-looking mules, driven with much cracking of whips and shouts of EE . . . EE from their teamsters, dirty, ragged, barefoot, whose sun-tanned, bronze-colored bodies shone through the many holes in their ragged blue shirts. In the immediate vicinity of Laoyan we saw an endless line of those carts, often under military convoy, conveying food and fodder to the military depots. Some supplies came down the river Liaoche, in a mass of junks and barges . . . the nearer we came to Laoyan, the more we felt the rhythm of army life.

"On the railway platform a noisy and colorful crowd; officers from all units, Red Cross nurses, foreign correspondents, Chinese . . . here is the information center of life in Laoyan; here reports and rumors are gathered from units in the field, more often than not either false or grossly exaggerated. In the railway dining room, a deafening noise, smoke, the clatter of plates, everyone shoulder to shoulder, not an inch of free space. Outside a mass of Chinese rickshaws and soldiers holding the horses of officers inside the buildings. A mile away are drawn up the trains housing the Commander in Chief and the Grand Duke Boris. Near the station a small town of administrative buildings occupied by different staffs; further, almost at the walls of the Chinese town, a series of wretched shacks, shops kept by dubious 'Eastern type' shopkeepers, two pathetic hotels and a night club *Chateau de Fleurs* exhibiting 'international girl singers.'

"The Chinese town is surrounded by a deep moat and high walls with gates. The main street lined with Chinese shops with signs painted on boards nailed to carved and gilded posts, shoe shops advertising their presence with huge boots in lieu of name; masses of diverse goods — Chinese saddles with silk trappings, patch quilts, fur rugs, Chinese drugstores, blacksmith shops. A mass of coolies, salesmen of all sorts of foodstuffs in open-air stands, street barbers, even an outside theater. The street crawling with the most diverse crowd; Chinese carts, rickshaws, army vehicles, soldiers of all kinds, Chinese businessmen in small black hats and colored embroidered tunics and huge black pigtails; women in blue coats and trousers, their pigtails wrapped around their heads, their faces grimy and suntanned ... all this mass flows along, stumbles into each other, shouts and proceeds each one on his business. The bright colors, the noise, movement, the shouts of hawkers, and the music of wandering minstrels, all this hits you with an impact as you enter Chinese towns. You just don't know what to look at, everything is so new, so exotic ... but time to head back, to unload our horses. ... Our squadron has been assigned to a village three miles from town ...."

"The weather is fine, the leaves are turning green; it has become so warm that I have moved to a tent and sleep naked covered with a blanket and my burka [Cossack cloak]. We know nothing about our future movements. Rumor has it that we must undergo a rifle-firing course, supposedly mandatory for all reserve Cossacks. Not only are most of the Cossacks excellent marksmen, but they are all veterans of the Chinese campaign,* hence this order can only be wondered at, the more so as there is a shortage of cavalry in action which greatly reduces our reconnaissance potential.

"During our march I became acquainted with the Cossacks. In their mental development, initiative, know-how, and resourcefulness they are vastly superior to our regular army soldier. Astounding in their ability to orient themselves at all times. Once he has gone a certain way, the Cossack will invariably know the route again, whether in deep fog or in the dark of night. I once mentioned this to one of the Mongol Cossacks in my troop. 'When you go somewhere,' he said, 'look back often; as the road will look to you over your shoulders, so it will appear on the way back and you will never go wrong.' I was often to remember his advice and thank him mentally for it. The Trans-Baikal Cossack is extremely hardy, never downcast, is a good chap, and develops a positive relationship with his officer. He is more negligent in his military bearing and outward discipline than the regular soldier, but in view of the specialities of his military service, one can hardly expect it of him; however, once given an order, you can rely that he will carry it out exactly and sensibly. As a cavalryman the Trans-Baikal Cossack is below average; his care of the horse is negligent or better said nil, and one can only wonder at the hardiness and ruggedness of the Trans-Baikal pony, able to carry on in at times extreme, difficult conditions. The Trans-Baikal horses are mostly under fifteen hands and, although no beauties, are extremely hardy and rugged. I think that under careful selective breeding they can provide the basis for an excellent Cossack mount. In the Trans-Baikal region there exist several breeding farms of

* Chinese campaign refers to Boxer Rebellion, 1900.

thoroughbred Trans-Baikal half-breds and the horses I saw there were excellent. The English thoroughbred added an inch or two to the Trans-Baikal horse while considerably improving the gaits, while at the same time detracting nothing from its ruggedness and hardiness. It seems desirable to work further on the improvement of the breed . . ."

"We received our orders April 16 to march on to the village of Shakhe twenty miles from Laoyan where we have to go through a rifle-firing course. It is really maddening to sit here while news of constant engagements and cavalry raids keep reaching us. I keep on with my studies of the typically Chinese town of Laoyan; today I lunched in a Chinese restaurant, and although to our European palate some dishes seem repellent, as for example rotten hard-boiled eggs and sea worms, I forced myself to eat all the courses, some twenty in all, served in small doses in equally small porcelain dishes. There were: a soup from swallow nests, reminding me somewhat of oxtail bouillon, roast duck and chicken minced, a delicious shashlyk of pork with a strong soya sauce, raviolis with pork stuffing, an aspic of octopus, sea weed, other vegetables of sorts, candied fruit, etc. Between courses we were served a weak, highly sweetened tea in micro-scopic cups and warmed up 'hanshin', a Chinese vodka of equally disgusting taste and aroma. We ate with chopsticks, with which the Chinese manage most dexterously, catching the food and stuffing it in their mouths. For us Europeans this was much more difficult.

"After lunch I visited an opium den. On entering, one is immediately overwhelmed by the sweet and intoxicating smell of opium. On couches along the walls lie the smokers; they rest on thin, dark blue, cloth-quilted pads, leaning on pillows of the same material. Next to each smoker is a lamp on which he warms up the thick paste of opium, rolls it into a ball and puts it into a long pipe. The smokers inhale the sickening sweet smoke of opium, making a strong gurgling sound. The faces of the majority of the smokers look haggard; their eyes shining — a feverish look. The fat owner of the establishment stands in a corner near a small table and lethargically prepares pipes for his clientele. . . ."

"The countryside of northern Mandchouria is not attractive; bare cliffs only partially covered with scant vegetation, mountain ridges with small villages of two to three houses resting in the valleys below, many small, swift-running streams.

"Although it was spring time, the scarcity of bird life was startling — bird songs to which we Europeans are so accustomed to hear in spring were not to be heard. Only in the valleys watered by rivers were more prosperous villages to be seen; they seemed gay partly due to the number of cherry trees which were now in full blossom. We entered the village of Tsai-Khe-Gay in total darkness, and having wakened the owner of the local store, an old Chinese, we settled down for the night. Having no news from our army for over two weeks* and hoping to hear some news of our units, I tried to strike up a conversation with our host, in pidgin Russo-Chinese, a language which we used in talking with the local inhabitants.

" 'Khodia, Luskna dgega doon Khodi.' (Hey, Friend, are any Russians about?)

" 'Ibina Turenchen, Pao-Pao, Lusua Lamailo — Lavian Khodi.' (The Japanese are shooting in Turenchen, the Russians are beaten and retreating to Laoyan.)

" 'The bastard is lying. — Do you hear that, captain? He says we are retreating.' I can hardly restrain myself.

"We take a bite of cold chicken, drink some tea and turn in. During the night a storm sets in; it rains, the wind howls — I cover my head with the burka [Cossack cloak] and go to sleep.

" 'Get up, your Honor!' My orderly wakes me. It is cold and damp inside; rain patters on the parchment covered windows. Outside a rumbling noise, as if of endless carts and vehicles rolling along the road.

" 'They say we have been beaten,' continues the orderly. 'We are retreating to Laoyan, hear! Listen to the artillery rolling along. There are also many wounded passing by.'

"As if stung, I jump up and rush out. The captain is standing at the gate, hatless, talking to an infantry officer in a burka and rain-soaked fur cap, mounted on a small grey pony.

" 'You mean we had to leave our guns.'

" 'Yes, alas, the enemy was too numerous; besides our losses were enormous.'

" 'How big our losses?'

" 'Well, just in the 11th Regiment we lost nine hundred men; some companies had all their officers as casualties.'

"My God, is this really true? Is it possible that we have been defeated? Abandoned guns, wounded, and killed left on the battlefield? The little Jap, only yesterday a small pathetic figure, has now crossed the Yalu, forced our retreat to the north, taken our guns, captured our wounded. Yes, so it is! We see the broken-up guns, the decimated rifle companies, these small groups of casualties, heads and arms swathed in bandages trudging along in their water-sogged overcoats . . . the heart stops beating, tears moisten our eyes; we just don't want to believe.

"Without uttering a word the captain and I went back into the house. Sul-

* Wrangel was sent as escort to a general staff officer on a topographical survey.

lenly and hastily, as if wishing to run from the horrid truth, our Cossacks were saddling up.

"Silently, forsaking our morning tea, we set off towards Lanshanguar. Our patrol moves in column of one along the road under a thin drizzle. We pass gun teams, transport wagons, army Red Cross carriages filled with wounded. Sullen, ashen faces, heads swathed in pink bandages stare at us from under sodden army coats. On both sides of the road trudge wounded. Some, utterly exhausted, lie down in the dirt, or drink prone from the puddles the dirty yellow water. . . . I order the patrol to dismount and pick up the more severe cases. But a few steps further others turn up, equally distressed; they look at us feverishly with despairing eyes begging for help — no food —no medical help in two days — just slogging along the muddy road . . . I turn away as I cannot help.

"As we reached Lanshanguar the rain stopped and the sun appeared suddenly from the clouds. The village a veritable chaos; masses of officers; from H.Q. staffs, artillerymen, infantrymen, some in overcoats, others in weather-beaten leather jackets — all talking loudly while eating in an impromptu restaurant established in a shack run by an enterprising Greek.

"On a neighboring hillside, the Red Cross tents. There medical officers and nurses work relentlessly, patching up the wounded arriving in an endless stream from the south. Some wounded sit silently leaning against the mud-brick walls; others lie on the wet grass awaiting their turn. But lo, we hear a sad chant and a group of soldiers carry a stretcher; they cross over a bridge spanning a small stream in the direction of another hill where loom white crosses. There lying on the stretcher under the grey army coat is a dead soldier, one of those wounded who walked a hundred miles to find a final rest so far from home. . . ."

"We did not have to wait for action. On the day following our arrival to Saimadze, General Rennenkampf decided to reconnoiter in the direction of Kindeian, about sixty miles southwest from Saimadze. The Japanese had driven Cossacks from the Argun Cossack regiment out of the town; one dead Cossack had to be left behind. At 0900 two Cossack squadrons and one mounted reconnaisance detachment under the command of Capt. Prince Karageorgievich* set out for Kindisian. In the village of Kindeian another squadron of the Argun Cossacks stationed there on outpost duty was to join us. Prince Karageorgievich's unit was to occupy the mountain ridge of Shao-Go twenty miles north of Kindisian, and to send out a scouting party into town to check for enemy presence and if such were there drive the enemy out of town.

* Yugoslav Royal Family.

"We set off on a hot, sultry day. The road lay through craggy passes over which towered cliffs almost devoid of vegetation. We kept on crossing fast-flowing streams and stoney river beds. Poverty-ridden villages of two or three houses nestled here and there among the numerous waddies and valleys. Shaggy dogs and dirty black pigs roamed aimlessly around the houses.

"The peasants, dark-skinned and ragged, came out to greet us, offering the Cossacks cold water drawn from their deep stone-faced wells. Poor, helpless people; tomarrow they will greet the Japanese dragoons with equal servility, trembling for their last possessions, if not for their lives.

"We rested for one hour en route in the village of Aianiamin and reached the Shao-Go ridge which was found clear of the enemy. Prince Karageorgievich ordered me to form a scouting party and head for Kindisian. I called for volunteers; many answered and having selected ten, I started off at 1700. We had no small-size maps and I used a sketch drawn by Captain Tutchev of the 1st Argun Regiment who had once been in Kindisian. A Cossack from my troop, Pereboev, was to serve as interpreter; he had learned a little Chinese during the Chinese campaign.*

"We moved at a walk, carefully looking ahead and following the course of a partially dried up mountain stream. All our inquiries from the local inhabitants were answered with 'Pudjidao' (I don't know); however, an old, half-blind peasant working around his half-demolished hut finally told us that on the day before eight mounted Japanese had stopped by and had requisitioned his last living hen. It was evidently an enemy scouting party. It was getting dark; darkness sets in quickly in these parts. I sent forward two Cossacks on grey horses riding point, but soon even they were hard to see. A valley opened up before us and we could see the lights of Kindisian; a couple of miles separated us from the town. It was evident that there could be no large enemy force in the town as otherwise they would have had pickets on the ridge. As it was no longer possible to approach the town in secrecy, I dismounted the detachment on the ridge and with Pereboev started to walk as quietly as possible in the direction of the town. As we reached the valley the cold humid air made us shiver. We were in total darkness and the stillness of night was broken only by the far-off barking of dogs and the murmur of water in the mountain streams. It was frightening; our hearts beat faster and we kept anticipating the challenge from a Japanese sentry and a shot at point-blank range. . . . A dark semi-ruined town wall loomed ahead of us. . . . Rifles in hand, we crept along the wall, listening to every sound and peering into the darkness until our eyes hurt. All was quiet . . . the wide, shop-lined street was peacefully asleep. In a house next to the city

* Boxer Rebellion, 1900.

gate a light shone and we heard Chinese talking; a mule brayed and a dog barked. . . .

"Mission accomplished, we reached Kindisian and found it free of enemy. We walk back quickly, joking and reliving our experiences. On the ridge the Cossacks are waiting, worried by our long absence. Today we covered sixty versts; to Shao-Go there were still twenty to go, so having gone on for six versts, I halt in a small village to feed our horses and drink some tea. One of the Cossacks had a duck tied to his saddlebags and a good hot soup rewarded for our toils. After two and a half hours we move off and reach at dawn our sleeping bivouac at Shao-Go. On the eve General Rennenkampf and the rest of the forces had arrived and I report to him directly. I find the General up as always at 5 a.m. Dressed in a yellow linen shirt, the Saint George Cross pinned to the collar and his brown leather jacket unbuttoned, the General is drinking tea, sitting on a bench and dictating in his loud abrupt voice, an order to his chief of staff. Energy and strength radiate from his corpulent but massive figure. . . ."

"I often wonder at the Cossack's ability to pack things in his saddlebags; in a way he reminds me of the circus conjuror who takes out of his top hat chickens, rabbits, and finally an aquarium with fish in it. . . . Look what you find in a Cossack's saddlebags: Chinese slippers, Chinese tobacco, a sickle to cut fodder, a package of Chinese buscuits packed in wax paper. Hanging from the saddle you may see a couple of chickens or ducks and at times a suckling pig. The Cossack is particularly fast when it comes to chow time. Hardly has the command to dismount been given and already water is boiling and the Cossacks settle down to tea or soup. On the march I enjoy riding behind the squadron to observe. As we enter a village, one or two Cossacks unobtrusively break ranks and turn into a farmyard. Chickens come flying out, a pig squealing dashes from under the gate . . . as the squadron rides out of the village, order is quickly restored and only flying feathers testify that today's soup will taste good. I must say that until now I have never heard of complaints about any pilfering; by that I mean pilfering of objects, not food or fodder, which they consider legitimate prey. I remember how outraged my sergeant had been when he saw me pay the Chinese during foraging. 'What are you paying them for — we are not taking their goods!' he would say, considering my expenditures as simple extravagance. In this respect the Cossack will not spare his officer. Cans of food which we saved for emergency rations disappeared in no time. My troop commander saved two bottles of red wine for a special occasion. One day, to his dismay, he found the bottles empty, although the bottles were unbroken and still tightly corked.

" 'Where is the wine?' he asked severely. 'We don't know, your Honor; however, it looks as if it has leaked out,' answered the imperturbed orderly. A lengthy and thorough examination revealed that the bottles had been drilled through from the bottom. . . . True, once he has got onto something, the Cossack will invariably share it with you even if he himself was starving . . . and starving we are, men and horses; it has been three days since we ate meat rations and we have to be content with corn loaves baked in soya oil. To me this soya oil is so repulsive that even starving I cannot face it. My orderly bakes me these corn biscuits with water. We drink tea with no sugar; even the dark Chinese sugar is nowhere to be found. The last two days we fed the horses from the thatched roofs; a couple died of colic. If we stay here long, we shall lose all our horses."

SOME WEEKS LATER
"We reached the village of Aiamin and settled in bivouac along a stream. After the last few strenuous days we were happy to rest, sleep, and get cleaned up. The Cossacks shod their horses, washed and mended their wear; the horses rested and chewed contentedly their bag. But we did not have the chance to rest much longer. On the 15th a report reached us that the enemy was attacking in the direction of Shao-Go. The outposts were held by the 2nd Squadron of the stalwart Captain Shundeev; ours, the 5th Squadron, was sent as reinforcement. We moved off at a trot. At the foot of the ridge we met a mounted messenger.

" 'Where to?' our squadron commander hails him.

" 'Message to the detachment commander, your Honor!

" 'What's going on?'

" 'The Japs are attacking hard — our troop commander has been wounded.'

"We dismount and, leaving the horses below, ascend the ridge. There lie our men. Scattered behind rocks, the Cossacks lie and fire evenly at the lines of the attacking enemy.

"Captain Shundeev, limping along (he has a light leg wound), stands and corrects the firing. 'Take a platoon and occupy that little village below us — I have another platoon there, but it is not enough.'

"We run down the ridge again, mount up and trot to the indicated village. The small, four-farm village is situated at the mouth of a defile with a stoney road leading to it. If the Japanese aim to outflank us, that is where they will come from. But so far nothing is seen. Behind us the firing intensifies. But suddenly around the bend in the road appear eight riders. Slowly, at a walk, as if feeling their way, they move towards us. Our Cossacks crouch low behind a stone wall, eyes glued to the approaching enemy, hands nervously gripping their rifles. The enemy has halted — has one of our men betrayed his presence by a careless move, or does instinct tell them that something is wrong? I command, 'Fire.'

"A volley rings out and a horse crumples; the rider whose leg is caught under the dead horse struggles to free himself . . . free at last, he dashes for safety.

"Bang — Bang, shots ring out; the Japanese somersaults and lies still on the road, arms outstretched. The Cossacks are delighted.

" 'Good boy — you bowled him over like a rabbit!' But from the ridge on the right bullets come flying, pinging against the stone wall. My sergeant, Peshkoff, drops his rifle and ducks below the wall, but he is up again, tearing open with his teeth his medical kit and proceeding to bandage his left hand. 'What's up Peshkoff? Got hit?' 'Just a finger blown off,' he answers calmly and resumes firing.

"The enemy seems to be working around our right flank. We can see his lines on the far ridge.

"I send off my report to the commander. Our mounted squadrons are retreating along the Aiche valley. Time for us to move off, too. I order: 'To the horses!' and we dash off taking the maximum cover from the stone wall. The Japanese increase their fire; their bullets ricochet all over the wall. We retreat in deployed formation and join up with the squadron of Captain Melikoff, also deployed and slowly retreating. From behind we hear a loud boom — the shrill whine of an approaching shell . . . a white cloud as shrapnel bursts overhead, raising dust as it splitters over the field. . . ."

"What strange people, the Chinese; during the firefight at the village of Aianiamin, as my Cossacks were shooting, taking shelter behind the stone wall, a young Chinese woman was working in the middle of the yard; she was driving a small grey donkey who operated a primitive mill. Bullets whined and ricocheted on the wall, but she went on quietly about her work.

" 'Look at that reckless girl!' the Cossacks exclaimed. No, this was no recklessness, rather a complete and unshakable belief in fate, in something higher but unfathomable, which independent of our will governs our lives. As our squadron moved off and the Japanese fire slackened, I turned around to look at the Chinese woman. She kept walking and it was hard to realize that but a couple of minutes before, death had hovered over her. . . .

"On the 18th we moved towards Saimedze and at noon had ascended the Feichulin rocky ridge where we met outposts from the 3rd Squadron of our regiment. No enemy was expected and we settled down to bivouac on a small field. Picket lines were drawn, fires lit, and the Cossacks settled down to tea. A group of officers gathered near a small Buddhist temple and, taking some snacks from our saddlebags, sat around talking.

"Suddenly a volley ripped the air, followed by rapid fire . . . bullets whizzed by, pinging against the roof and walls of the temple and raising dust clouds on the field. The Japanese had found paths leading up to another ridge among the many dominating ours and had put our bivouac under murderous fire. It is hard to describe the ensuing panic. Everyone ran; horses broke from the picket line and dashed about, knocking down tents, trampling people, and with torn reins and saddles askew rushed for the woods . . . the men, losing their heads, ran in all directions, searching safety from the murderous fire, some behind the temple walls, others in the wood or in an overgrown ditch . . . packs, tents, rifles, lay trampled and broken all over the bivouac area . . . all the while men and horses fell dead or wounded . . . a few cool heads were hopelessly trying to restore order. General Lyubavin had jumped on a horse and rode around calling to the men. A few officers tried to gather men from their own squadrons. Captain Shuljenko, commander of the mounted sapper unit, had managed to collect most of his men and, running in the enemy direction, deployed his unit and opened covering fire; he was followed by the 3rd Squadron which being on duty had not unsaddled their horses or laid aside their arms, hence was not quite so taken by surprise.

"The sentry stationed by the regimental colors fell, both legs shattered. The master sergeant Agep Turkin seized the colors and, surrounded by a small group of Cossacks, bore the colors to safety.

"At the first volley I could not even figure out from which direction the fire came. Hearing someone cry out, 'Officers to their squadrons!' I run towards the bivouac, looking for my men: But what I see is chaos! Men of the Argunsk and Nertchinsk regiments run ning in all directions, some leading their horses, others without their horses but rifle in hand, still others with no rifles. Horses, mules, dead and wounded, in one huge confusion. Bullets seem to come from all directions . . . at last I saw the officer candidate Ivanov from my squadron; he is leading a wounded horse and carrying three rifles, which he has picked up. I grab the rifles and shove them into the hands of the first three unarmed men I see, ordering them to stay by me. I see Sergeant Derevnin, mounted and followed by a group of Cossacks, riding towards me. 'Stay together, boys, all together,' he shouts, threading his way towards me. I manage to gather about thirty men and lead them to the road. The divisional chief of staff Colonel Rossiysky meets me. 'How many men have you got? Take them and occupy that hillock — let the horse holders move towards the village of Guardi. Cover us and retreat when you hear the signal!'

"With about twenty men I run in that direction. On the way I meet Captain Anitchkoff riding a palomino pony, pipe in his mouth, riding at a walk, unconcerned by the whining bullets: He calls out in his basso profundo voice for his men to follow. 'Where are you going?' he asks. 'I have been ordered to occupy that hill.' 'Take my men, you don't have too many.' I take his men and deploying them, open fire at the ridge opposite me. In the wood below rapid firing is heard; it is the 3rd Squadron. From my position I can see well the bivouac area: It is now empty except for the corpses of men and horses . . . two horses stand forlorn, heads down with broken legs; lying everywhere are tea kettles, saddles, combat jackets . . . far below me I see the rest of the detachment retreating in confusion. Cross country, on both sides of the road, mounted and on foot are hurrying to catch up.

"The Japanese have stopped firing; the 3rd Squadron has also stopped shooting. Way below I hear the bugle calling recall. We get up and walk through the wood down into the valley. The wood also is full of dead horses and abandoned equipment. In one spot I see a dead grey pack horse. It is lying with neck stretched out under an officer's yellow leather pack. I recognize the horse of our regimental medic Dr. Semitchov. On reaching the road I meet Lieutenant Colonel Zabotkyns of the Nertchinsk regiment. He has gathered a group of Cossacks, mostly orderlies from the supply train, and is also catching up with the retreating detachment; he is wounded and has tied his arm with his revolver lanyard. Soon, further down, we meet again Colonel Rossiysky. He and a group of officers and men are walking back towards the bivouac to pick up the dead and the abandoned equipment. We join him and walk back to the ridge. Widely deployed, we walk through the wood examining each hole and each bush, searching for a wounded or dead comrade. We find none in the wood and only at the bivouac site itself we see five dead, their bodies still warm, their glazed eyes staring into eternity.

"Watching carefully, the Cossacks have spread out, picking up weapons, saddles, tents, and kettles. Somehow we pile all this stuff on three scared horses we have managed to catch, and preceded by five stretchers bearing our dead comrades, we find our way in darkness to the village of Guardi. It is drizzling—our hearts are heavy with sadness. Near the village we find our bivouac in much disorder. Fires light up the figures of Cossacks moving about: The troop commanders are making a roll call; the Cossacks are sorting out equipment. In a small, dirty hut the wounded are patched up. Right there, next to the bivouac, a mass grave is being dug for the five dead lying covered by tent cloths.

"I have often read and heard about panic, but this was the first time that I had to witness it. Having lived through it, I realized its enormity, almost impossible to overcome. . . . In those moments animal instincts seize a man and turn him into a herd beast, ready, like some flock of sheep, to dash headlong into river or precipice. I saw undoubtedly brave men completely lose their heads, unable to make any decision, and Cossacks whom I had seen joking joyfully under fire, now panic-stricken, herded together near the temple wall, or running with no weapons into the wood.

"Those who have lived through horrible moments of panic will remember it to their deaths. In those minutes only men endowed with unusual will power and able to dominate the mass can manage to stop the all pervading flight. . . ."

"Our unit must really look odd to the casual observer. After three months of ceaseless wanderings and combat in this mountainous region the officers' and Cossacks' clothing has taken a heavy toll. Wornout parts of our apparel have to be replaced by local means, at which the Cossacks are most adept. Just the other day I observed a Cossack riding in with a message from outposts. He rode a big grey mule (the casualties in horses have been heavy: in one action alone on the 18th more than sixty horses had been killed or wounded and to alleviate the shortage we had to requisition mules from the Chinese); the mule was saddled with a regulation Cossack saddle. The Cossack wore a Chinese cap with earflaps, his legs clad in Chinese shoes that had been sewn onto his boot leggings. A red shirt and dark blue breeches made up his bizarre attire. But he is only one of many, and accustomed as we are to such eccentricities, no one pays any attention. . . ."

"We had been on outpost duty on the right bank of the Taidzihe river, keeping in touch through mounted patrols with our units on the left flank and with the western detachment of General Samsonov. Furthermore, we sent out daily patrols up the Taidzihe river up to the village of Sao Syr at the intersection of the roads leading to Tsian-Chan and Saimadze, both towns strongly held by the enemy. Lately our patrols had been much interfered with by bands of Hunhuz,* whose activity had expanded and who now dared to attack even individual squadrons on patrol duty. True, they were unable to inflict heavy casualties and, as soon as fire was returned, fled to mountain refuges where they could not be reached by our cavalry. However, they had a great nuisance value, constantly harassing our outposts and interfering with our communications. The Hunhuz were in Japanese pay and, during our reconnaissance forays against the enemy, acted in conjunction with them, mostly on our flanks. According to our spy reports there were about two thousand of them, in bands of two hundred each, armed partly with Winchesters and partly with our rifles taken by the Japanese from our dead and wounded during the battle of Shahe. The overall command of these bandits was in the hands of one Tia-Fu, a young overlord, who had dominated this region for several years. He was renowned for his cruelty. Evidently, not satisfied with the scant Japanese pay, the Hunhuz plundered the Chinese, operating primarily in the no-man's-land between the Japanese and us; whole villages went up in smoke and their population massacred. We tried several times to follow those bands, but as soon as they sensed our approach the Hunhuz either dispersed among the mountains out of our reach,

---

* Chinese bandits.

or simply withdrew behind Japanese lines.

"On the 10th of December, late in the evening, I drew up the draft for the order of the day (I was acting adjutant at the time), and having despatched the mail, I went to sleep. The Chinese bench was heated by charcoal; it was hot and my head was heavy from the coal smoke. Thoughts came rambling through my head: pictures of home so different from our present situation. The Cossacks on sentry duty had lit a fire outside and it cast a red light on the parchment-covered windowpanes. I could hear the low murmur of Cossack conversation; a mouse scratched somewhere in the darkness. Little by little drowsiness overcame my weary eyes and sleep took over my tired body.

" 'Something funny going on at the outposts,' said Obolensky. 'It has been a good twenty minutes that we keep hearing volleys; at times they stop then resume.' 'It doesn't sound like our firing.' I dressed and came outside with the Prince. It was a clear, moonless night. The stars seemed particularly bright. In the still, dry, frosty air all sounds were clearly audible. Everything quiet. The fire crackles and one can hear the horses slowly munching on their bags. A dog would bark occasionally in the sleeping village. . . . Then suddenly the stillness would be broken by a volley, then another and yet another. It was clear that the shooting was at our outposts and that it came from a greater unit than our platoon out there. We had a squadron on daily outpost duty: Three platoons went out; one remained behind in reserve with the squadron commander in the village of Gaolindze. The nearest platoon from where firing was heard lay about two miles away and it was obvious that, if no message had reached us within twenty minutes, something extraordinary was happening. The squadron on duty that day was the 5th, commanded by Prince Massaloff, and at the nearest outpost was his subaltern officer, Lieutenant Count Benkendorff. We woke up Massaloff and he decided to wait no longer but move on with his reserve platoon.

"With sleepy faces the Cossacks emerged from the peasant huts, quickly slinging their rifles and adjusting their ammunition. Girths were drawn up as the horses were led out of the farmyards. Burly silhouettes of Cossacks in their padded jackets and fur bonnets striding their short, coupled, small shaggy ponies loomed for an instant against the fires' background and disappeared quickly in the night's gloom. You could only hear the clatter of hooves on the frozen ground and the short sentences exchanged by the Cossacks. 'Attention! Mount up! Columns of threes. Trot.'—the commands and then the rhythmic pattern of hoofbeats receding into the night and heard far in the distance. . . it was all quiet again at the outposts.

"Obolensky and I walked out to the village outskirts. The gloom of night engulfed us. Millions of stars twinkled on the endless sky. The walls lining the village street with their massive metal-studded gates, the strange figures on the tiled rooftops, the carved pillars of the Buddhist temples, all these assumed fantastic silhouettes in the half-light. The fast-flowing stream which flowed through the village was not frozen over and rumbled dull over its stoney bed. All was still in the dry, frozen air; all nature seemed locked in heavy winter sleep.

"But suddenly in the direction from which we had heard the volleys a red glow spread over the horizon. It seemed that some conflagration had spread over a large area, and again several volleys rang out sharp and clear in the frozen air; then everything reverted again to deep stillness.

"We heard the clatter of horse hooves and from the darkness loomed up the mounted silhouettes of Prince Massaloff and his orderly. 'The damned Hunhuz have assaulted a village and are plundering the inhabitants. Look, they have set the village on fire. . . these impertinent bastards right under the nose of our outposts!'

"I got up late and, having washed myself from a pail of water brought to me by a Cossack, sat down to morning tea. I could hear the lively talk of the Cossacks in the yard, getting ready to set out on forage duty. In the house, behind a screen I heard the Chinese owner clicking his counting beads. An orderly walked in—'Sir, the regimental commander asks for you.' I put on my tunic and walked over to the colonel's quarters.

"The colonel was sitting cross-legged on a Chinese settee; near him on a small table were a blackened tea kettle, a cracked enamel jug, and small pieces of sugar on a small Chinese saucer. Opposite the colonel stood our Chinese interpreter "Andrew"; with mimic and grimaces he was busy explaining something in 'pidgin.' An interesting type, this Andrew—tall, lean man with a pockmarked face, a small shaggy pigtail, dressed invariably in a dirty grey silk gown, wearing a black skull cap topped with a red coral bead. Andrew has been six months with our unit as interpreter. His past was veiled in mystery; we know only that he had served several years as a 'boy' with an officer of the Siberian rifle regiments and had been with him during the Chinese campaign. Lately he had busied himself with small commerce of one kind or another in Kuanchendzah.

"Clever, mean, and extremely greedy, Andrew despised his own people and, using to the maximum his privileged position as interpreter, cheated and bullied his compatriots, who repaid him in undisguised hate. Andrew's supreme wish was to make enough money to settle down after the war and open a brothel. With all these negative qualities, Andrew was no coward, and, egged on, no doubt by commercial motives, never hesitated to penetrate into enemy lines and bring us important information. This intelligence was invariably reliable and Andrew's presence, notwithstanding all his defects, was much appreciated. Andrew's conversation with us was carried out in 'pidgin,' a jargon mixture of Russian and Chinese. This talk was reinforced with gesticulation and awful grimaces during which his small slant eyes were in constant and nervous movement.

" 'Listen to what he has got to say,' said the regimental commander. Andrew nodded his head vigorously and, looking with apprehension at the closed door, whispered intensely. According to him, the Hunhuz had attacked last night a small village near our outposts, had plundered and burned it, killed the village headman and kidnapped his daughter, a reputedly beautiful girl whom Tia-Fu had decided to marry. Having sent off his band to Sao-Syr, Tia-Fu and four of his friends had taken the girl to a small village 3–4 miles from our outposts and settled down to celebrate his marriage in a house belonging to an old Chinese, also an ex-Hunhuz. The village was to bear the costs of the wedding under threat of dire reprisal. All this was told Andrew by two Chinese, who had fled from the sacked village. They swore that Tia-Fu and his accomplices would be easy prey, distracted as they were by the wedding feast; they themselves, however, feared to take us there, scared as they were of Tia-Fu's dreadful vengeance. We had no need of guides, as the region immediately adjoining our outposts was well known to us, and to find that particular village was no problem.

" 'Send out an order immediately to all squadrons except the one on duty; three men from each squadron to assemble at headquarters; take them along and see if you can catch these scoundrels,' said the colonel and less than an hour later we were on the way, having left the two Chinese under guard with the warning that they would be shot if their information was proved to be false.

"Our small patrol trotted along in a column of threes, the hoofbeats echoing loud on the frozen ground, the rested horses moving smartly along. The Cossacks, who had been briefed on the mission, joked cheerfully. 'Wants to get married, eh? We'll get him on his honeymoon.' 'Just so long as the Chinese don't have time to warn him.'

"Andrew rode next to me on his grey pony with a clipped mane, saddled with a Chinese saddle on which Andrew swayed as he belabored the thin ribs of his horse with his soft Chinese boots. A long, open valley, now bare of snow, stretched on both sides of the road bordered by craggy hills; on the ridge to the right we could see black dots—our outposts strung along the hills. On the way we rode by sacred groves and small villages of two or three farms. These villages, plundered, pathetic, and deserted, seemed somehow in a dead slumber. Rarely would a shaggy dog dash across the road or one would catch a glimpse of a peasant in his grey coat and felt hat with earflaps. Here was our last outpost located in a small village at the foot of a ridge. Horses with different colored coats stood saddled in the yard, the Cossacks nearby at their tea. The blue smoke of their fire rose straight up in a thin spiral. On the ridge itself, near a small Buddhist temple, stood our picket. The sentry watched sharply the valley below, where far away one could catch the glimmer of the swift running Taidzihe river. All was quiet. We led our horses, slipping, stumbling and falling down the steep slope, and, sending out scouts, moved on.

"Andrew was getting worried; he kept on questioning the few Chinese we met on our way: See soon; Lanche lee (two miles), he told us.

"We pushed on our horses and soon came upon a small village nestled in a hollow: three or four farms which seemed as deserted as those we had previously passed. Sending out an observation post to the nearest hillock, we galloped up to the village. The seemingly empty village was actually full of life. Music came from it: the rhythmic thumping of a drum and the scratching sound of a Chinese fiddle. The gates of one house were adorned with red bunting and long red Chinese scrolls hung down the gateposts. The music came from inside the house. The Cossacks quickly surrounded the house and I quickly went in accompanied by four Cossacks. Our arrival stopped the music. The scared musicians crowded in the hall; there were six of them, some with drums, others with fiddles or three-stringed guitars. A table was set the length of the whole living room, and the table was covered with a whole variety of dishes and sweets. . . . About twenty Chinese were crowded together at the other end of the room, looking scared at the unwelcomed guests. Among them we saw several men well dressed in colored silk gowns.

"At my shout of: 'The owner!' an old, half-blind Chinese with a goatee came forth; evidently much shaken, he kept bowing and muttering: 'Shango capitana, good friend, Ta-tode capitan' (good officer, good friend, great officer). . . . At this moment a big young Chinese man dressed in a grey silk gown and hat jumped from the crowd; before we could react, he had knocked out a window frame with his shoulder and jumped out. Outside we heard shouting: 'Halt—grab him . . . we got you!'—men running and the sound of a struggle.

"Having posted sentries at the doors and windows with the warning that we would shoot if anyone tried to escape, we started to search the house. With what pleasure the Cossacks turned everything upside down looking in the Chinese trunks, peering into every nook and cranny. Every new object of interest raised loud exclamations—Look, your Honor, rifles, six of them . . . and miserable ones too—wonder how they managed to shoot at all! Look, lad, one of our saddles, looks like from the artillery. . . .

"We found six old rifles, all of different makes, a saddle, an officer's field pouch with a compass, a soldier's shirt with traces of blood. To our query how these objects came there the owner just shook his head and kept on muttering 'Pudjidau' (I don't know). He had lost all composure and was at a loss what to say in his defense.

"Having told the Cossacks to keep a sharp watch over him, I went outside. The Cossacks there had had time to search all the sheds and barns and had found five Hunhuz horses, all under Chinese saddles, with long, bright-colored saddle cloths. Thin, looking worn out and with sore backs, the Chinese horses looked small and pathetic even next to our Trans-Baikal ponies. A group of Cossacks had surrounded a young Chinese dressed in a grey silk gown whom the sergeant held securely by his pigtail. Andrew fussed about, yelling at the top of his voice. The Cossacks were commenting on their capture.

" 'Look how he is dressed—all silk. He must be the gang chief.'

"I walked up and scrutinized the prisoner. It was the same man who had jumped out of the window as we came into the house. I recognized him instantly.

" 'Shima Minze' (What's your name), I asked sternly. 'Tia-Fu,' he answered, looking me straight in the eyes.

"So that is the mighty and dreadful Tia-Fu who had so long eluded us, the cruel monster whose name had become almost a legend among the surrounding Chinese villages! I looked him over with interest. He was a typical Mandchou, about thirty years old, tall, lithe and powerfully built. His long, hairless face was rather handsome. The skin of his face and hands was fine and clear. A hooked nose and a small, tight-lipped mouth gave his face a willful and cruel appearance. But it was mostly the eyes which struck one: cold eyes with an almost metallic glint. Looking at them one felt vaguely uneasy.

"Tia-Fu was dressed in a grey silk gown and trousers. Over the gown he wore a silk jacket padded with lynx fur with clasps of silver filigree. On his head was a small cap edged with mink fur and ornamented with a few colored beads.

"Having understood that he had nothing to say in his defense, Tia-Fu remained silent to all my further questions.

"The sun was setting. Any moment an enemy patrol could appear or even a large band of Hunhuz; I ordered to get going with no further delay. Having mounted the Hunhuz on their horses which the Cossacks took on a lead line and having mounted the old owner on a requisitioned mule, we set forth followed by the cries and wails of the owner's family who followed us to the edge of the village. The west glowed in the red of the setting sun. The tall crags glistened like silver in the last rays of sunlight. Dark purple shadows cloaked the deep valley. Far away where flowed the swift-running Taidzihe river fog was rising. The temperature dropped quickly and the air seemed particularly sharp and clear. We rode in silence, hurrying our horses in order to reach our outposts before total darkness.

"Rarely did a Cossack drop a short remark. The prisoners were also silent, brooding over their hopeless fate.

"We reached the ridge. The half-ruined Buddhist temple and the sentry standing nearby were silhouetted sharply against the last light of sunset. We rode up the ridge and I rode on ahead of my patrol to report to the commanding officer. Soon news of Tia-Fu's capture spread through camp, and as the patrol rode in, officers and soldiers crowded in the headquarters yard, all anxious to have a look at the captured Hunhuz. A crowd of Chinese stood at the gates, looking in awe at the dreaded Tia-Fu. The latter still remained silent and impervious to all questions; his cold stoney look revealed no traces of fear or indecision. The other Hunhuz swore by all the gods that they were innocent, good Chinese. Our commander ordered them to be held under guard and to send them in the morning to corps headquarters.

"We no sooner sat down to eat when we heard outside a hue and cry. We went out and saw a crowd of Chinese who on seeing our commander prostrated themselves, wailing and crying. It turned out that these were inhabitants of the village of Gaolindze; they had heard of Tia-Fu's capture and had come over to beg our commander to execute the Hunhuz forthwith, fearing lest they escape and then wreak dreadful vengeance on the population which had betrayed them. It took us much pain to calm down these bizarre favor-seekers. . . ."

"A warm July evening attenuated the unbearable heat of the day. Evening shadows came down on the broad valley of the Kau-he river; the shadows crept into the waddies and mountain clefts and gradually rose to cover the craggy ridges. One after another, stars lit the sky until it shone with millions of silver specks. The pale disk of the moon rose; its silver blue light covered the rocky ridge, driving before it into the valley the receding gloom of night. All is quiet. Tired after the day's heat, nature slumbers and silence is broken only by the murmur of the mountain stream, and once in a while by the rustle of leaves moved by a sudden light breeze.

"Our bivouac sleeps; it is in a deep valley near a small hamlet of three farms. White tents break the darkness of night. Smoke rises from burning out fires. Horses munch lazily their hay; occasionally a horse irritated by its neighbor on the picket line whinnies angrily; mumbling unintelligibly in his sleep, a soldier echoes it.

"A shape rises; its silhouette sharp against the white background of the tents, it moves towards the road; another shape follows, then another; as if rising from the depth of the earth, these figures move towards the silver light ribbon of the road. Adjusting their rifle slings and ammunition pouches, volunteers move out on a dangerous mission.

"We had been receiving urgent requests from army headquarters for prisoners, or at least for weapons, insignia, or equipment, which would help identify the Japanese units operating against us. These requests had been induced by reports from spies on the appearance of new enemy formations and much importance was being given to clarifying this circumstance. Unfortunately, the Japanese, always extremely careful, were now doubly so; their forward units remained very passive and cavalry patrols moved out supported by strong infantry units. We had tried several reconnaissance missions but to date had not been able to achieve any success. Worried at last by our restless activity, the Japanese decided to move their outposts further forward in order to keep us under close surveillance.

"Our outposts had noticed yesterday men digging trenches on one of the ridges closest to us. As darkness fell, the work party had returned to its lines and it was highly probable that they would return again the next morning to resume their work. Our commanding officer had decided to call for volunteers to move up to that ridge and prepare there an ambush. To give cover to our volunteers, two squadrons of Don Cossacks and a machine-gun detachment of the 8th Siberian Cossacks were to move up under command of Lieutenant Smetzky of the Guard Hussar regiment. The mission was a risky one; the ambush being laid within rifle range of the Japanese lines could easily be detected from their outposts and retreating for us would be under heavy fire. Danger did not seem to deter our troops for there were more volunteers than needed. . . .

"Talking in low tones the group gathers on the road. Each one realizes the difficulty of this mission—somewhere deep down the nagging thought keeps whispering, 'Maybe I shall not get back; maybe it is for the last time that I see my friends who are staying behind, hearing their voices!'

"Well, Godspeed! March—heads are bared and crossing ourselves we move off. A narrow stoney path winds its way uphill. The silhouettes of our party move on in moonlight casting dark oblique shadows on the road. We have left our swords behind, a hindrance to movement in the mountains; the men carry only their rifles. Used as we are to months of mountain warfare, we move on swiftly and come soon to our pickets hidden behind the ridge in a small grove. Among the trees we can see the burly silhouettes of Cossacks and horses awaiting our arrival.

" 'Nothing new on the enemy!' says the picket commander. 'Take care; they may have left hidden sentries behind.'

"We work our way up the ridge, peering carefully ahead. The valley sleeps with its scattered hamlets among the tall Gaolian grass and its monotonously murmuring river; slumber reaches up to the high, barren ridges with thin, scant growth of bushes and numerous waddies. Somewhere far below in the valley a red light blinked, for a moment breaking the night's monotony, blinked and vanished. . . .

"We walk past our picket; we start down the ridge. We creep noiselessly, gripping our rifles and trying with all might to see what is ahead of us in the darkness. Carefully weighing each step, we move on. A heap of stones, a bush, take on strange shapes at night and make us imagine the presence of an enemy. Sometimes a loose stone rolls down, jarring our taut nerves. But here at last is our ambush site; a stoney ridge covered with bushes. Far below us is the wide valley of the river Kau-he, emerging out, the mandarin highway; to the right of us a deep waddy stretching to another ridge occupied by the Japanese and looming menacingly over us. Closer to us and separated from us by another deep waddy lies the hill where the enemy was observed keeping an outpost during the day. Around, everything reminds us of the enemy's presence; moonlight reveals in light patches the freshly dug clay of trenches; empty cigarette packs and pieces of Japanese newspapers lie on the trampled grass.

"The Big Dipper lowered itself to the horizon; the stars grew dimmer and the sky got a shade lighter. We must not waste time; we must orient ourselves and camouflage our men. Our volunteers are all experienced; each one picks his place, some hiding in the trenches, some behind bushes or heaps of stone. Within half an hour everyone is in place and the ridge seems as empty as it had been before our arrival. Hugging the ground and covered with branches, our men lie still. So still that even breathing seems noisy—under each bush and behind each rock a pair of eyes glows feverishly.

"Nature is awakening from its restful slumber; night shadows recede and the grey silhouettes now take definite form. Opposite us, no further than two thousand yards, is the hill where the enemy sends out a daily picket. The hill looks like a large tit and is bare of vegetation. We can now see two huts made from branches where the picket takes shelter. Way below us we can see a Chinese village on both sides of a fast-flowing creek. Down the sole street are a dozen grey houses surrounded by mud-brick walls, with yards cluttered with barns and sheds. A thick fog rises like smoke from the riverbed. A pheasant calls somewhere close to us; a second answers him, then a third. The first rays of the sun illuminate the high rocky ridge of the Japanese positions. Through binoculars we see details of the heavy trench fortifications that the enemy has erected. Another lower ridge leads down towards the tit-shaped hill where the enemy puts out a picket.

"I take out my notebook and start sketching the enemy positions. My work is interrupted by the nervous whisper of Lieutenant Vykrestov lying next to me. 'Look, the Japanese!'

"Under the slanting rays of the rising sun nine horsemen ride towards us along the ridge. Through binoculars I can observe: the small bay horses with their cropped tails, the horsemen in khaki uniforms with caps and neck covers. Sunlight glistens occasionally on the metal scabbards of their swords. . . . This must be the picket we have been waiting for. The horsemen disappear in a dip; a few minutes later two small figures on foot appear at the foot of the hill. They walk up slowly, step by step carefully examining everything around them. We lie glued to the ground; our hearts throb painfully. What if they see us? They will start shooting and all our work has been in vain!

"No, everything seems normal. Having observed nothing unusual, the Japanese halt on top of the hill. One of them waves the others on and soon four small figures appear on the crest. The other Japanese stayed evidently behind, holding the horses. A sentry is posted and the others sit down in the branch shelters. We can see them really well through the binoculars; one has leaned over and is fixing something on his boots; another one is squatting and is telling something with much gesticulation.

" 'They have not seen us—we camouflaged ourselves really well,' whispers Lieutenant Vykrestov.

"After the first moments of excitement, I resume my sketching. Down in the valley life is stirring; the village has awakened; one can see the blue jackets of the Chinese. A peasant trots out of the village, bearing on his shoulders a pole with a basket at each end. Another drives two donkeys loaded up to their ears. At the edge of the village several black pigs wallow in the dirt. A peaceful scene bathed in the warm rays of the July sun. But this idyl is suddenly broken by the appearance of several Japanese infantrymen. The khaki-clad figures walk swiftly towards a small farmhouse lying in a waddy outside of the village. They seem to be questioning the owner who waves in the direction of our outposts. The Japanese walk on, one behind the other up a small winding path— their yellow khaki uniforms appear and disappear among the green bushes. They climb the ridge opposite us and separated from us by a wide valley. They are now on our level but about one to one and a half kilometers away. Again, tense moments of worry. . . .

" 'They have seen us—look, two are heading back,' Lieutenant Vykrestov anxiously whispers at my side.

"The two Japanese stride down, back into the valley. We watch anxiously, trying to guess their intentions. Now they are down in the valley and on the road. They walk briskly, but in no hurry, talking as they go. Now one has stopped to question a Chinese working in the field; the other stands by.

" 'No, they have not seen us. Had they done so, they would have hurried on.' I share my thoughts with Vykrestov, not daring to hope that all is well. The two Japanese disappear around the road bend and all is quiet again. Now the sun is beating down mercilessly upon us. Our mouths are dry and immobility makes our bones ache. Nothing new from the enemy side. The Japanese on the hill have climbed into their shelters and only the sentry can be seen. I take out my watch.

" 'What time is it?' whispers Vykrestov.

" 'Soon eleven—I guess they will not come today!'

" 'Pity with all our good camouflage.'

" 'Anyhow we must wait until darkness before getting back; otherwise we shall suffer needless casualties.'

"A light rustle in the bushes and a loose stone rolling down the hill interrupt our whispered conversation. No further than thirty yards down the slope a Japanese soldier appears, appears so suddenly that it seems as if he just popped up out of the ground. We can see him down to the smallest detail; a young, hairless face with slant eyes and a large flat nose, his cap with a grey linen neck flap, his ammunition pouches of yellow leather. He stands still; having spread the branches of a bush, he peers at the mass of vegetation ahead as if sensing some danger. Forgetting everything about us, we stare at him with bated breath. Our hearts throb painfully; a spasm grips our throats; our eyes glow feverishly. A tiger crouching in the jungle thus awaits the herd of antelope moving to a water hole.

"Again leaves rustle and a second Japanese appears some ten yards to the right—this one older, heavy-set with a bristly moustache. Slowly both Japanese move forward, carefully pushing aside branches and peering intensely ahead. They must be the point—behind them moves the work party to continue with its trench diggings. Slowly, slowly the Japanese walk towards us; now we can see every crease in their uniforms, every buckle of their ammunition pouches. They are now only a few steps away.

"But suddenly the young Japanese's eyes meet those of one of our men lying in ambush. A sudden spasm of fear contorts his face. Crouching like a cat ready to jump, he turns towards a bush—'Bang' cracks a shot, and the soldier, throwing up his arms, doubles up and falls on his face. 'Bang Bang'—shots ring out and the other Japanese, who has turned around, crashes heavily to the ground. Several of our volunteers jump up and rush forward to strip the dead of their arms and ammunition. Below in the bushes a loud sharp command and rapid fire comes our way. The detachment behind the Japanese point has quickly deployed and opened fire. We also get fire from the hill above us. Bullets are whistling about and ricochet loudly against the stones, snipping branches and leaves on their way. Some Japanese on the ridge to our right give us flanking fire. Neglecting them, we fire straight ahead trying to give cover to our volunteers and let them have time to strip the dead of their arms, ammunition, and especially identification tags, which every Japanese soldier carries around his neck with the number of his unit on them.

" 'Oooh'—I hear a deep groan near me. The young Amur Cossack Sazonov has dropped his rifle and grips his stomach; his face turns grey, lips bloodless. . . .

"The Japanese are moving up; their fire creeps nearer and nearer. The enemy dead have been stripped; it is high time to retreat.

"We double back, carrying two seriously wounded. The Japanese have quickly occupied the ridge where we had lain and are firing as fast as they can. Crouching and availing ourselves of every small cover, we make our way back, and overtaking our flight, bullets whine and hum like a beehive. Stumbling and sweating profusely, several Cossacks carry the severely wounded master sergeant. His broad face, with sweat-streaked hair and rumpled beard is wreathed with agony. He has put his arm around the neck of one of his carriers, shakes his head and moans huskily. 'Don't leave me, boys. God will help you. Don't forsake me'—his voice drops as he begs his men for help. 'Don't worry, Ivan Petrovitch—have no fear. Who has ever heard of one leaving a buddy!' the Cossacks try to calm him as hurrying and stumbling, they drag him, paying no attention to the whine of bullets about them.

"Leaning heavily on his rifle, slowly, and stopping often to take breath, Lieutenant Vykrestov makes his way through the bushes—he is wounded, but he courageously refused any help.

" 'Bang Bang'—our volleys are now ringing out loud and heavy over our heads; our troops are giving us covering fire. The Japanese feel their effect—their fire slackens and soon ceases altogether.

"Breathless and exhausted, we reach our lines. From all sides happy, laugh-. ing faces surround us. Everyone tries to be helpful. Some run to get stretchers for our wounded; others draw cold water from a well. Lieutenant Smetzky gives one of the wounded a swig of cognac from his hip flask. All congratulate us, showering questions and more congratualtions. It is hard to describe the warmth one feels from those kind words, how close and dear these sunburned, hardened faces seem. . . .

"One looks about with happy, cheerful eyes, as if awakened from some ghastly nightmare—a feeling of intense well-being overwhelms, an animal feeling of security and comfort—the danger is behind; you are sound and well — the whole organism glows with unbounded happiness. . . ." (*End of Wrangel's letters from the Japanese War*)

Soldiering had become a vocation; Wrangel decided to stay on in military service. There were, however, difficulties; his Cossack regiment was a second-line regiment, a regiment made up of reservist Cossacks, who, once the war was over, disbanded and rode back to their villages.

Returning home, Wrangel had himself transferred to the 55th Dragoon Regiment based in Willmenstrandt, Finland.

Meanwhile, the 1905 revolution had broken out in Russia. The lost war was a pretext; the long-brewing dissatisfaction of the intelligentsia, the main reason and the spark that ignited the fire — thirty people killed during a manifestation in St. Petersburg on January 22, 1905. In parentheses, let it be said that in 1920, during workers' strikes, two hundred people were gunned down in Manchester, England, and in the disorders in Paris in 1934 some eight hundred people succumbed; however, the British and French people had sense enough not to destroy themselves as the masochistic Russians tried to do — and eventually succeeded in 1917.

The 1905 revolution in Russia spread to the Baltic countries, where it assumed a nationalistic tone — the peoples there having acquired ambition for independence. To quell disorder, Russia sent a detachment under General Orlov — a regiment of Guards Lancers, attached to which was Captain Wrangel. He had many friends in the Guards Lancers; besides, sitting in the barracks of a provincial Finnish town was hardly to his taste. General Orlov's detachment had no combat operations; there were no casualties, but the tedious patrol and guard duty lasted some six months.

Returning to St. Petersburg, Wrangel managed to get himself temporarily attached to the Horse Guards, pending examinations for entry to the Staff College. His former "sin" seemed to have been forgotten; the martinet Colonel Prince Troubetzkoy had left the regiment, which was then under the benign command of the Khan of Nakhichevan, a Moslem princeling from the Caucasus and an easygoing Oriental potentate.

The Czar was the honorary commander of the Horse Guards; he often visited the officers' mess and on the day of the regimental holiday always reviewed the regiment on parade. During the 1907 parade, when the Horse Guards were drawn up, resplendent in gleaming helmets and breatplates over white tunics, the Czar noticed a tall officer in the discreet dark green tunic of a line dragoon regiment, the sobriety of the uniform enlivened with several combat decorations. "Who is this officer?" asked the Czar. "Captain Wrangel, of the 55th Dragoons, temporarily attached to the regiment, Your Imperial Majesty," answered the Khan of Nakhichevan. Wrangel was a name familiar to the Czar as previous members of the family had served in the Horse Guards; the combat decorations were also duly noted, and the Czar said: "I want Captain Wrangel in my regiment." . . . And so it came to pass that without ballots or any further ado, Wrangel became a full-fledged officer in the Horse Guards.

It was not long before he became a member of the more turbulent group of "gay blades" within the regiment, and the life of its many parties. The gypsy orchestras in the better, more frequented cabarets soon got to know him, as did the musicians, guests, and attendants at society balls, where his good looks and dancing were in much demand. His taste for champagne, his favorite brand, being Piper Heidseick, soon earned him the name of Piper, by which name he became known to his fellow guard officers from then on and forever afterwards.

General Rodzianko, the famous horseman, remembered one such party:

"It was in the mess of the Chevalier Guards [the other regiment in the brigade] —some party! At the end the food ran out; someone offered to roast shashlyks over an open fire. No sooner said than done; furniture was smashed and a fire lit on the floor of the dining room. Unfortunately, it started getting out of hand, but before help could be summoned, Piper had seized some bottles of champagne and had the fire doused!"

However, some of the antics were of less innocent nature. In one restaurant a drunk, top hat on his head, staggered up to Wrangel's table and protested against someone or something. In a flash Wrangel had drawn his sword and cut off the top segment of the top hat. On another occasion, when the manager of the biggest department store in St. Petersburg was rude to Baroness Maria, Wrangel's mother, Wrangel grabbed the man by the scruff of the neck and threw him out of the window, which fortunately was on the ground floor. In the Horse Guards, decorum was a sine qua non; incidents were not often excused, and even under the "live and let live" command of the benevolent Moslem Khan, too loud a behavior cound mean transfer to a distant line regiment.

The influence of woman on man has been well known since Adam and Eve, but whether to benign or malevolent effect has remained a lottery — Wrangel drew a lucky ticket. He fell in love and married a girl who not only remained his faithful companion until his death, sharing joyfully the trials and tribulations of war, revolution, civil war, and exile, but also moderated and influenced Wrangel's impatient and turbulent character, enabling him later to view with equanimity the grins of fortune and the grimaces of misfortune. Olga Wrangel never interfered with her husband's decisions and yet was constantly at his side, a modest yet strong support throughout his eventful life.

Olga Ivanenko came from a family of rich Ukrainian landowners. Their ancestry could be traced back to Mazeppa, the Cossack leader who sided with Charles XII of Sweden against Peter the Great and whose very name had become through the ages in Russia synonymous with traitor. Small wonder that the descendents chose the innocuous name of Ivanenko, which allowed them to live and flourish in the southern steppes of the Lower Dniepr river. Olga Ivanenko's maternal grandfather was Katkov, publisher, friend of the Czar Alexander II and his enthusiastic advisor in the liberation of the serfs.

A beautiful girl with many suitors, Olga Ivanenko was twenty-four years old when she married Wrangel. Interested in medicine, she had already turned down several marriage proposals so as to devote herself to her studies; she had graduated as a full-fledged nurse and had practiced her profession in Moscow and in the village near the family estate.

Wrangel's decision to get married was as sudden, impetuous, and unalterable as all his decisions in subsequent life. General Rodzianko remembered:

"We were out for a cross-country ride; Piper rode up to me and said: 'I am going to get married!' 'Go ahead, you fool – you'll be sorry!' " Rodzianko was then married to his second wife (he had four altogether).

Rodzianko's advice was proved wrong, although Wrangel's wedding and the start of his honeymoon were hardly auspicious. First, the Staff College, where he was already enrolled, gave him only two days' leave. Wrangel told the authorities in no uncertain terms that he would resign if not given a longer leave. An ordinary officer would have received immediately his walking papers; however, Wrangel was a decorated combat officer and belonged to the Horse Guards. Mindful of these facts, the bureaucrats relented and gave him a week. After the wedding, as relatives and friends went to see them off at the railway station, it turned out that the train compartment reserved for the honeymoon couple had been taken; a passenger had given the train conductor a suitable bribe and had installed himself in the compartment, comfortable in the thought of the power of money. Beside himself with rage, Wrangel roared that he would throw the train conductor out of the carriage and that the passenger and his suitcases would follow suit. Impressed, the unknown traveler vacated the field of battle.

Back from the honeymoon, the couple occupied married officers' quarters at the Horse Guards barracks, and Wrangel settled down happily to domestic life, study at the Staff College, and the social activities expected of the St. Petersburg aristrocracy.

Although the curriculum at the Staff College was very demanding and included higher mathematics, engineering, astronomy, and other sciences, Wrangel had little difficulty; his past civil engineering degree made science, a stumbling block to many other officers, an easy subject. He even helped many of his classmates. On one occasion, during an examination, a Cossack officer and he received their assignments —the Cossack, a mathematical problem of considerable difficulty; Wrangel, a relatively easy question. Quickly substituting the slips of paper, Wrangel solved the mathematical problem, leaving his Cossack classmate the easier choice. Years later the Soviet Marshal Shaposhnikov, who was Wrangel's classmate, recalled the incident in his memoirs; however, in deference to the party line and to Stalin, whom Wrangel had previously soundly beaten at Tsaritsyn (Stalingrad), Shaposhnikov changed the roles, crediting Wrangel with "stealing" the easier question — a not very worthy way of recording history, even for a Communist field marshal.

Wrangel graduated among the top of his class; his final examination was, however, characteristic of the man. Having received a high grade in all subjects, Wrangel had still one last hurdle — the German language, which he did not know and had studied but little. To pass on a minimum grade, one had to read and translate a text; to get a higher grade, a written examination was mandatory. Knowing that he had need of only the minimum grade, Wrangel dutifully translated the German text. As the examiner gave him his grade and asked him to write the next assignment, Wrangel bowed and said: "Thank you, sir; the minimum is all I want!" So saying, he left the room.

To every officer graduating in the top half of his class in Staff College unlimited horizons opened for his subsequent career, the more so following the reforms in the aftermath of the disastrous Japanese War. To everyone's surprise, Wrangel, after a course at the Officers' Cavalry School, returned to the Horse Guards, turning his back on the General Staff. "I would be a poor staff officer," he explained. "Their job is to advise their superiors and remain contented when their advice is not taken — I am of too independent a mind!"

Wrangel threw himself into his domestic life with as much enthusiasm as he did into his military career. Three children were born — Helen, Peter, and Nathalie — and much later, at the end of the civil war, another son, Alexis, was born in exile. Miraculously, a pack of letters written by him to his wife between 1910 and 1914 survived the turmoils of two World Wars, a revolution and a civil war. These letters reflect great tenderness and concern for his wife and children.

Every year the Russian army pulled up stakes and moved to camp from May to September. For the Guards regiments quartered in St. Petersburg Krasnoe Selo was the summer bivouac. There, in the case of the Horse Guards, the men settled down in wooden barracks, whereas the officers rented rooms in the outlying villages; some of the officers' wives rented villas in the neighborhood. The Horse Guards had as the officers' mess a villa surrounded by a garden, a gift of a grand duke who had served in the regiment and, on leaving, presented the house for use as an officers' mess. A church, oddly enough built by the Moslem prince, the Khan of Nakhichevan, the Horse Guards commander, stood in the middle of the bivouac.

For the duration of the camp, the Wrangel family separated. Olga Wrangel and the children moved to her parents' estate in the Ukraine. Peter Wrangel wrote faithfully, two or three times a week.

"Darling, I miss you and the children terribly, but I think you did the right thing to move South for the summer. It is cold and rainy here; today, returning from the morning exercises, I poured water out of my boots. . . ."

The apartment and household in St. Petersburg preoccupied him: "Yesterday I went to the city. Nicholas the butler is drunk daily; I did not fire him as I have no time to find someone else. I even had to shine my own boots. I looked for your nightgown; the laundress thinks she may have delivered it to the wrong party — she promised to look. . . ."

His parents, their health and well-being, also preoccupied him: "Look in on the 'Old People'; Father feels much better; you should have seen with what enthusiasm they examined the photos of the children which you sent me. I miss you terribly and count the days when I shall have you again in my arms and kiss the children."

He wrote of his daily routine: "My day runs as follows; 7 a.m. we start off and are back around 11 after the morning exercises. I breakfast then with the Grand Duke Dimitri* and I school horses over fences. In the afternoon I take the squadron out for a ride. Usually in bed by 10; eat like a horse — an animal life, but I feel healthy."

He wrote of Olga's brother: "We got news that our officers won most of the prizes at the London Horse Show; Dimitri [Olga's brother] as individual got a 3rd. I feel so happy for him. . . . Dimitri fell during a steeplechase and was unconscious for two days. I visited him in the clinic; he feels much better and should be out soon."

And always he missed his home and family: "I look so much forward to my leave. Please see that I have plenty of No. 8 and 6 shot. I have been offered a very good bird dog, but if you think the one you have in mind is good, buy him anyhow."

So between duty in the city, with its numerous parades and court and social functions, and summer camp, with its troop, regiment, and division exercises culminating in maneuvers and a General Parade taken by the Czar, life went smoothly and happily for the family. In May of 1912 Wrangel was made commander of the 3rd Squadron.

During this period the only incident worth relating was a duel between Dimitri Ivanenko, Olga Wrangel's brother, and Alexis Panchulidzev, who many years later was to become aide de camp to Prince Bernhard of the Netherlands. The quarrel was over a woman; the duel was in Warsaw, and Wrangel was summoned as a second. In the same train compartment traveled an old lady, who to Wrangel's amazement produced a box with two dueling pistols which she proceeded to polish.

"May I ask you, Madam, what you intend to do with those pistols?" asked Wrangel. "My idiot of a son is fighting a duel; I ám taking the family's pistols to him," answered the dowager.

Wrangel refrained from commenting. The duel was duly fought, luckily with no casualties, and a great reconciliation party was thrown in Warsaw's Hotel Bristol, during which Wrangel used the dueling pistols to shoot out the dining room windows.

---

* Served in the Horse Guards and was a member of the Russian equestrian team in the Olympics of 1912.

1. NOTE: On Cossacks

The word *Cossack (Kazak)* is derived from the Turkish word *quazak*, meaning adventurer. As the Russian Muscovy kingdom developed in the thirteenth and fourteenth centuries, men seeking freedom, adventure, and booty settled on the frontiers in the southern steppes of Russia; they became, much like the American pioneers of the West, an advance guard in the expansion of their country. Fiercely independent, they formed military republics with elected chiefs (*Atamans*): they fought their own wars against the Poles, the Tartars, and the Turks, and acknowledged only in the loosest manner the authority of the Russian czars. Gradually, however, in the midst of rebellions, wars, and changes of alliance, the Cossacks became part of the Russian Empire, while still maintaining a form of self-government, with democratic principles and a kind of military socialist system wherein land was evenly apportioned to all male members of the Cossack communities.

Each Cossack was bound to serve in the Russian army: four years of active duty and twenty in the reserve, the service being performed in their own units, staffed by Cossack officers. Each Cossack came mounted on his own horse, with complete equipment at his own cost; only rifle and ammunition were government-issued.

Centuries of warfare with their neighbors — the Poles, the Tartars, the Turks, and the mountain clans of the Caucasus — had developed a military caste that accepted war as a way of living. Cossacks had taken part in every war of the Russian Empire. They had taken Berlin in the Seven Years' War, crossed the Alps with Field Marshal Suveroff, and fought in all the Turkish wars. Perhaps their greatest achievement had been the War of 1812, when they raided and harried the French Grande Armee from the moment it crossed the Niemen to the day when the last remnants of frostbitten Frenchmen stumbled back across the border. The pinnacle of Cossack fame occured in Paris in 1814, when Cossack horses were watered in the Seine as their owners sat around bivouac fires on the Champs Elysees.

There were eleven Cossack hosts, as they were called, stretching from the river Don to the Volga, thence down to the Caucasus, across the Ural mountains, east to the steppes of Orenbourg, the forests of Siberia, and the tundras of Trans-Baikal. The hosts were Don, Kouban, Terek, Astrakhan, Ural, Orenbourg, Ussuri, The Seven Rivers, Siberian, Amur, and Trans-Baikal.

Each host had its traditions, its uniform, and its organization, civil and military. The Kouban and Terek Cossacks wore a uniform copied from the dress of the Caucasian mountaineers, the people on whose borders they lived and with whom they waged ceaseless warfare for many centuries. A long woolen tunic with cartridge holders sewn on in lieu of breast pockets was bound by a narrow rawhide belt studded with ornaments from which hung a long dagger; a lambskin hat, breeches, and long glovelike boots reaching to above the knees were standard; a long sleeveless cloak of tightly woven uncarded wool (the *burka*) protected the rider and his saddle; and the *bashlyk* (a combination of hood and muffler) hung loosely from the Cossack's shoulders.

The other Cossack hosts wore uniforms resembling that of the Russian soldier except for the wide breeches with a broad colored stripe down the side, the color identifying the host.

Lieutenant Baron Peter Wrangel (center bottom) poses with fellow officers during the Russo Japanese War.

*Elements of the Trans-Baikal Cossack Brigade, in which
Wrangel served, cross a river under enemy fire.*

*Captain Wrangel (second from right) and Prince Ton Ti Kayo of Siam (third from left) join
the members of the Horse Guards in full regalia on Regimental Day.*

Captain Wrangel leads
the Horse Guards on
parade during the
Winter of 1913.

Colonel Wrangel commands
the Trans-Baikal Cossack
regiment from horseback.

Captain Wrangel and Horse Guards
squadron return from maneuvers.

Olga Wrangel, nurse at the Guards
Corps field hospital, stands in
front of her husband.

The charge at Kaushen, in which Wrangel captured German guns,
gave him a faith which paved the way for the great cavalry battles
of the Russian civil wars some five years later.

3
World War

THE CLOUDS OF WAR GATHERED SWIFTLY and unexpectedly; when the storm broke, Europe found itself in a war with no precedent, a war that destroyed three empires, millions of lives, and values that heretofore seemed immutable. .

Yet everyone believed that the war would last no more than six months, as the experts predicted, and the Horse Guards entrained for the front amid hurrahs, songs, and blessings. Disembarking on the German border, the regiment spent the next days in scouting forays and light fire fights with almost no casualties. The mood was one of a war picnic; Wrangel, among the most enthusiastic, kept repeating: "This is the life, not the dreary drudge back at the barracks!" But the days of reckoning were not far off.

On August 3, 1914, the Guards cavalry crossed the border; the next day they took the town of Pilkallen in a rousing cavalry charge, albeit with almost no casualties. On the night of the 5th scouting parties kept meeting the enemy; the Russian infantry was getting heavily engaged, and everyone felt that the game was getting earnest. On the morning of the 6th the large Guards cavalry column moved on, and soon the Chevalier Guard regiment became heavily engaged against enemy infantry and artillery. Dismounted, they advanced but soon were brought to a standstill against overwhelming German infantry forces. In those first days of the war the officers remained standing in the firing line, easily distinguished by their gold or silver epaulets. The casualties in the officer ranks of the Chevalier Guards soon became catastrophic. A cavalry charge by one of the squadrons ended in disaster as it came up against barbed wire and was shot to pieces. An urgent request for help followed; the Horse Guards regiment trotted up, dismounted, and went in to help its brother regiment. Wrangel was left in reserve to guard the colors.* The Horse Guards fared no better; in short order the major part of its officers were killed and wounded despite heroic desultory charges. However, the Germans them-

* In World War I, the Russian regiments carried their colors with them to battle.

selves were under heavy pressure; their battery, well camouflaged near a windmill, came under the blanket fire of the Russian Guards horse artillery and was finally silenced. They managed to pull two guns to safety, but two remained not quite within reach of the attacking Russians. The situation for the latter was gradually becoming desperate; they were being shot to pieces while within inches of success — a last final push was imperative.

In the meanwhile, back at division headquarters, Wrangel was beside himself; the constant inpouring news of casualties, the fight in which he had become a mere powerless observer, the need to do something, made him rage in helpless agony of suspense. An artillery lieutenant rode up and reported to the general that two German guns were almost within reach. Wrangel rushed up and literally begged for permission to charge; after a moment's hesitation the general assented. Led by the artillery lieutenant, who had reconnoitered the approach, the squadron galloped forward, availing itself of every possible cover and, deploying between twelve hundred and fifteen hundred paces from the enemy, charged. The German gunners rushed to their guns and opened fire. By some freak chance, the casualties in men were light, most of the fire hitting the horses. But when almost on top of the guns their last salvo killed the artillery lieutenant as well as two other officers and wounded more. Wrangel's horse fell, literally torn to shreds; he escaped injury and, grabbing a rifle, ran to the guns. Fighting desperately, the German infantry and artillerymen were cut down to a man.

To Wrangel, the charge at Kaushen was what Toulon had been to Napoleon. It gave him a faith which never forsook him and which paved the way for the great cavalry battles of the Russian civil war some five years later.

Just prior to the war the military experts precluded in their forecasts the chances of success of mounted cavalry against machine-gun and artillery fire; hence Wrangel's charge made headlines. He was awarded the St. George Cross, 4th class, the highest decoration a company grade officer could aspire to.

In September, 1914, Wrangel was made Chief of Staff of the Joint Guards Cavalry Division; its commander was General Skoropadsky, former commanding officer of the Horse Guards and years later Hetman of the Independant Ukraine. A perfectionist and meticulous man, General Skoropadsky was careful, restrained, whereas Wrangel was impetuous and impatient. A wit among the Guards officers remarked: "A bizarre combination of fire and water!" The marriage was not a success, and when the regiments composing the division reverted to their original formations, Wrangel was happy to return as Senior Colonel to the Horse Guards.

A young officer of the Horse Guards Lieutenant Belosselsky remembered: " 'Piper' was always on the move; when the regiment was not in the front lines and when most officers ate or slept, he would take his horse and gallop cross-country, followed by one or two (myself included) young enthusiasts."

His relations to subordinate officers and other ranks were reflected in the diary of one of the officers of the 3rd Squadron: "July 26, 1914, 1800, we received orders to march to Vilkovishki. . . . We reached it in compete darkness and under a downpour; it took a long time to find quarters and settle down. . . . As always Wrangel was the last one in bed, having first seen to the meals of all ranks and getting nothing to eat for his pains. . . ."

In April, 1915, Wrangel was again decorated, this time with the St. George Sword (the second highest decoration) for a successful action during which prisoners and trophies were taken. He also received the honorary rank of ADC to the Emperor and was promoted to colonel.

The prospect of commanding a regiment was now open to him. Of those available he could have taken his pick on the basis of his military performance and decorations. To everyone's surprise, he did not accept the command of one of the more fashionable line cavalry regiments but asked for the Nertchinsk Trans-Baikal Cossack regiment, those Cossacks with whom he had served in the Japanese War. He knew the men and had high regard for their bravery; the regiment itself had from the beginning of the war an excellent record. In peacetime it had been commanded in far-off Siberia by a Colonel Pavlov, a renowned steeplechase rider and a rich man, who on receiving the regiment had at his own expense mounted his officers on imported English thoroughbreds which he acclimatized to the forty-degrees-below-zero rigors of the Siberian climate. One of his officers subsequently won the Grand Imperial Steeplechase, the most coveted sporting trophy of the Imperial Army. This sporting renown had brought an influx of enthusiastic young officers to the regiment, so it was a good unit that Wrangel inherited in October, 1915.

With his customary enthusiasm and energy Wrangel proceeded to command the regiment. A series of successful engagements culminating in a spectacular attack in the Carpathian mountains earned new rewards; the regiment was awarded silver bugles* and as mark of special distinction the Czar's son Czarevitch Alexis was named honorary chief of the regiment. A group of officers and men from the regiment were commanded to appear in the Czar's presence in St. Petersburg to receive the honors.

It is difficult in our time to comprehend what it meant in 1914 for an average Russian to appear and talk to the Czar. In the eyes of a vast majority he was still God's symbol on earth. Officers and civilians endowed with a higher education were often speechless with emotion when addressed by the Czar. For a Cossack hailing from far-off Siberia it was an experience of a lifetime. Not so, however, for the officers of the Guards like Wrangel. These saw the

* A regimental combat award dating from the Napoleonic wars.

Emperor on many occasions; the Emperor knew many of them by name, dined often at their officers' messes and grand dukes of the Imperial family served in the Guards regiments (particularly in the Horse Guards). Court and political gossip was bandied freely, and though loyal and respectful, the Guards officers took a somewhat freer look at the throne and what went on around it.

In his memoirs Wrangel recalled the trip in detail, as if wishing to engrave the last days of a period about to vanish and never to reappear again. A keen and critical observer, he saw the cracks appearing in the thousand-year-old structure and sensed the forthcoming storm: "In accordance with an old custom, we had to offer the new honorary commander a horse and the uniform of the regiment which was to bear his name. Consequently I left for the capital at the head of a deputation from the regiment, taking with me a small Manjourian horse just big enough for the young Czarevitch.

"Scarcely two months before this I had been in Petersburg recovering from a wound. I had got it in the famous charge which had earned us the signal honor which was the cause of my returning to Petersburg today.

"Confusion was rife in all circles; there seemed to be a presentiment abroad of the nearness of the terrible events which destiny was preparing for Russia. In the Duma and the Imperial Council and in different political groups, a pretence of stern authority was reduced to a matter of public-speaking-matches and political debates; while in artisan circles and urban associations, there was subterranean propaganda at work, fed no doubt by Germans. Yet, at the same time, the majority of the population remained absorbed in its little daily cares; the queues lined up outside the shops, the theatres and cinemas were full, and the same old trivial conversations were to be overheard in the crowd.

"Court circles appeared to be paying no heed to the approaching storm. High society and the upper bureaucracy remained absorbed in their usual 'weighty' questions, such as the appointment of someone to some post, or the opinions held by the Grand Duke's or the Empress's party.

"Social life followed its usual course, and it seemed as if these people were merely to be the spectators and not the victims of the drama to come.

"Some days after my arrival, I entered the service of the Czar as his aide-de-camp. I had had many opportunities of meeting the Czar and chatting with him. He produced an impression of extraordinary simplicity and unusual kindliness on everyone who met him — the result of the outstanding traits of his character, his perfect education, and his complete self-mastery. He had an alert mind, was skilled in the art of innuendo, and possessed an amazing memory. He remembered not only events but names and dates. One day he spoke to me of the battles in which my regiment had taken part, although it was a long time ago and we had done nothing noteworthy; he even mentioned the villages in which the regiments of our division had been quartered.

"I began my service as aide-de-camp to the Czar one Saturday, relieving Duke Nicholas of Leuchtenberg. That day dinner was served in the Empress's apartments. There were only the Imperial Family and myself at table. Their Majesties kept me part of the evening for a chat. The Czar was merry and vivacious; the Grand Duchesses and the Czarevitch laughed together and exchanged badinage; but I was struck by the expression of suffering on the Empress's face. She had grown much thinner in the two months since I had last seen her, and I particularly noticed the expression in her eyes; it was sad, I might say absent-minded. She was especially interested in the organization of medical relief in the Army, and also asked me detailed questions about the new type of gas-mask.

"The next day being Sunday, I accompanied Their Majesties to church. The little temple, built in the old Russian style, was packed. Watching the Imperial couple at prayer, I involuntarily compared the Czar's expression of pious contemplation with the Empress's look of sorrowful ecstasy.

"Some days later I presented the deputation from my regiment to His Majesty. I little dreamt that this was the last time I was to see the Czar."

Military events now centered on Rumania, and the Nertchinsk regiment marched there within its division. Wrangel was recalled from St. Petersburg and had a narrow escape when the train in which he and his men were riding crashed into another train; several hundred people were killed or injured, and only the fact that their carriage was hooked onto the back of the train saved their lives.

Great masses of cavalry were concentrated on the Rumanian front for a projected breakthrough, which, however, did not come; regiments were pulled back, and Wrangel, who had just been promoted to general and brigade commander, took occasion to visit Jassy, where the Rumanian court had taken refuge.*

The Russian Grand Duchess Cyril, sister of the Queen of Rumania, invited Wrangel to tea. Although acquainted with her, Wrangel had never been a member of her intimate circle and was surprised when she kept him for over an hour, describing in detail all the court gossip and criticizing the Emperor and the Empress, going as far as to say that the whole Romanoff family was against them and that something must be done about it. Embarrassed and confused, Wrangel listened in silence and was glad when the audience was over.**

Although a monarchist and loyal to the Czar, Wrangel looked at Russia and

---

* The Rumanian Queen was a Russian Grand Duchess.

** During the Revolution Grand Duke Cyril, her husband, paraded decked out in red ribbons, a latter-day version of Philippe l'Egalité of the French Revolution.

the army with sober, and at times pessimistic, eyes as the 1916 winter came, covering with its white shroud the hundreds of thousands of war graves stretching from the Baltic to the deserts of Mesopotamia. His mood at that time is reflected in his own words: "Towards the winter of 1916 the bloody struggles which had been waged throughout the summer and autumn drew to a close. We consolidated our position, filled in the gaps in our effective forces, and reorganized generally.

"The experience gained from two years of warfare had not been acquired in vain. We had learnt a great deal, and the shortcomings for which we had paid so dearly were now discounted. A number of generals who had not kept pace with modern needs had had to give up their commands, and life had brought other more capable men to the fore. But nepotism, which permeated all spheres of Russian life, still brought unworthy men into important positions too often. Convention, routine, and fear of disregarding the custom of promotion by seniority still held sway, especially amongst the higher military staff.

"After two years of warfare, the Army was not what it had been. The majority of the original officers and men, especially in the infantry, had been killed or put out of action.

"The new officers, hastily trained, and lacking military education and 'esprit de corps,' could not make satisfactory instructors for the men. They knew how to die bravely for the honor of their country and their flag, like all the regular officers, but they felt that they had been uprooted from their normal and anything but military work, and had neither the mentality nor the spirit of the true soldier. They found difficulty in enduring the dangers, fatigue, and privations of life at the front, and war to them meant nothing but suffering. It was impossible for them to inspire the troops and put fresh heart into their men.

"Neither were the troops what they had been. The original soldiers, inured to fatigue and privation, and brave in battle, were better than ever; but there were few of them left. The new contingents were by no means satisfactory. The reserve forces were primarily fathers of families who had been dragged away from their villages, and were warriors only in spite of themselves. For they had forgotten that once upon a time they had been soldiers; they hated war, and thought only of returning to their homes as soon as possible.

"Before they were sent to the front these men were passed through the cadres and given some preliminary training, but it was very inadequate. There were not enough cadres, and the barracks allotted to them were too small to house all the men. Furthermore, the instructors, both commissioned and non-commissioned officers, were not up to their work. They were either disabled and worn out from active service, or else very young officers who themselves had much to learn.

"The infantry, whose losses were heaviest of any, suffered most from this arrangement. But nevertheless, in spite of everything, the Army was still strong and impressive. The morale of the troops was excellent, and the discipline perfect. I never once saw or even heard of the slightest expression of disaffection or disorder; indeed, before this could happen, the very idea of authority had to disappear, and the generals themselves had to set the example of breaking the bonds of loyalty which existed between officers and men.

"It is obvious that after two years of war the moral standards of the Army could not but have slackened, and respect for the law diminished. Requisitioning, an inevitable consequence of any war, had lessened the soldiers' regard for other people's property. Base instincts were aroused, but I repeat that they would not have been set in motion but for an external shock.

"A great deal of subversive work was being done, expecially in the rear of the Army, behind the lines, by a numerous class of people which was on the increase during these last months. The individuals of this class had been mobilized and were in perfect health, but they had an unconquerable aversion for the endless whining of bullets and the bursting of shells; and so, secure in the protection and support of a quieter atmosphere, they sat on all kinds of committees and occupied themselves with the organization of reading-rooms and canteens for the soldiers in the trenches.

"These men, dressed in absurd uniforms, all spurred and wearing divers insignias took great pains demoralizing the main body of the Army, especially the newly commissioned desk soldiers and those of the technical units recruited from amongst the intelligentsia. Most of the Army, rank and file as well as officers, took no part at all in politics: They had other things to do, and, besides, they lacked newspapers and information. One party amongst the officers echoed the gossip of the neighboring General Headquarters, au courant with events in the country, and prophesied that the disorder in the interior would finally react on the army and so lead to its defeat.

"We continually told one another that things would not come to this pass in Petersburg.

"Those of us who loved our country and the Army were very anxious about the continual changes in the Ministry, the conflicts between the Government and the Duma, the ever-increasing number of petitions and appeals adressed to the Czar by many influential organizations, each one demanding popular control, and, above all, by the alarming rumors concerning certain persons in the Czar's entourage.

"The patriots amongst the High Command suffered deeply as they watched the Czar making fatal mistakes whilst the danger grew and came ever nearer; they held mistaken views, but they believed in them sincerely; they contemplated the possibility of a revolution from within the Palace to be effected by means of a bloodless coup d'etat.

"There were other commanders who also agreed that things could not go on as they were, but they realized how inopportune a change in time of war would be, and saw that it would inevitably entail the collapse of the Army and the ruin of the country.

"Others, again, desired a revolution for purely personal reasons, hoping to find in it scope for their ambitions, or to profit from it and settle their accounts with such of the commanders as they hated. . . ."

In the meantime the cavalry divisions, among them Wrangel's Trans-Baikal Cossack Brigade, were sent to rest and recuperate in the town of Kishinev in Rumania. Olga Wrangel's field hospital had also moved to Rumania and she had occasion to spend a few days with her husband. A letter from her to her mother has miraculously survived the turmoil of the next years.

"Dear Mama,   Feb. 7

"After a harrowing trip in the Rumanian trains which either don't run at all or crawl along, I managed to hire a sled and rode the last thirty kilometers. I spent two days with Petrousha [Russian diminutive for Peter] in his peasant farmhouse, horribly cold. His soldiers had built a homemade stove which smoked atrociously. After two days the division moved on and I followed behind in a horse buggy. The division marched five days, covering fifty kilometers the first day in a snowstorm such as I have never seen before in my life. My buggy hopped over waves of snow. . . .

"Feb. 11. . . . Please send me some cold cream (Parke & Davis) for my face. . . .

"Feb. 12. Petrousha and I were invited over for dinner (blinis) at his former regiment, the Nertchinsk Cossacks. We had a great time; everyone was so nice and hospitable; the buglers serenaded us; it was cosy and fun. We stayed until dark and when we set off for my home seven kilometers away, we ran into a tremendous snowstorm and had to turn around. We barely managed to make it back to the regiment and spent the night on cots in the officer's mess.

"Feb. 13. Besides our division, the 12th Cavalry and the Caucasian division are quartered around Kishinev. The town is full of officers having a good time and being entertained lavishly by the local gentry. The young lieutenants dance and flirt with the local belles to the music of military bands. In spite of his General's rank Petrousha keeps up with the lieutenants and the other day danced and flirted at a ball and was the star of the evening. Burdened as I was with the sick (typhus), I have not been able to get away. I shall do so as soon as I can — Petrousha says that it's a beautiful town."

One of the officers of the 12th Cavalry Division remembers: "I saw Piper well in wine, having a great time. . . ." These were the last few days of the Piper as he was known to his fellow officers. Soon it was to be General Wrangel of the White army — and victories, success, sorrow, disillusion, fame, exile, glory with its attendant price and honor which was to remain.

But that was still to come. In Kishinev champagne flowed; pairs waltzed to the music of military bands and fun was had by all, all oblivious of the dark clouds gathering above them.

When the clouds burst, the storm came suddenly and overwhelmed all.

Food riots in St. Petersburg, mobs, revolt of untrained reserve troops crowded for some unexplainable reason in the country's capital; stormy sessions at the Duma (Russia's parliament), a deputation sent to the Czar at the front asking for his abdication. Abandoned by his relatives, the Czar turned to his chief of staff General Alexeiev, he in turn to the individual army commanders. These pale replicas of Napoleon's marshals — some for opportunistic reasons, others out of cowardice — turned thumbs down; the Czar abdicated in favor of his brother, who, feeling the burden too heavy, abdicated to the Duma and its Provisional Government.

Pandora's box was open.

A dictator is dangerous for a country; a demagogue in wartime is invariably fatal.

With labor unions in the military meetings at the front and hysterical speeches about the freest army in the world, the new premier lawyer Kerensky poured oil on the slope down which Russia slid towards the abyss.

In his book *The Unknown War*, Winston Churchill chose the appropriate epitaph: "The Russian ship of state sank as it was about to enter harbour."

4

The Revolution

GENERAL KRYMOV, WRANGEL'S DIVISIONAL COMMANDER, was a talented staff officer and a brilliant cavalry commander. He was also an ardent republican. Although of opposite political opinions, Wrangel and he became close friends; they often discussed their divergent views. On the evening of March 5, 1917, Krymov telephoned Wrangel and read the Czar's manifesto — the abdication, followed by that of his brother. The words barely uttered, Wrangel turned to his chief of staff and said: "This is the end of everything — this is anarchy."

Wrangel explained his reasons: "Certainly the very fact of the Czar's abdication, even though it was provoked by social discontent, would absolutely stagger the people and the Army. But this was not all. The danger lay in the destruction of the monarchical idea and the disappearance of the monarch. During the last few years many loyal hearts had become alienated from the Czar. The Army as well as the country realized that he had endangered his throne by his own actions.

"If he had abdicated in favor of his son or his brother, such an act would not have roused much painful feeling in the country. The Russian people would have sworn allegiance to the new Czar and continued to serve him and their country to the death, as they had always done — 'For the Faith, the Czar, and the Homeland.'

"But in the present circumstances,* with the disappearance of the Czar the very idea of authority and all the age-old obligations vanished, and nothing could take the place of either in the minds of the Russian people."

It did not take long for Krymov or the new Russian commander in chief General Kornilov to realize that in Russia the step from autocracy to mobocracy was but short; as the army disintegrated, they raised a cry of alarm, but it was too late — the momentum of history was not to be slowed.

* The Grand Duke Michael, in favor of whom the Czar had abdicated, had given up his power to the Provisional Government.

General Krymov, Wrangel's immediate superior and divisional commander, sent Wrangel to St. Petersburg to see what could be done at the government level. At one of the stations Wrangel met General Mannerheim,
Finland's future president and his friend through joint service in the Guards
Brigade. The news from the city was alarming: mob rule, murders of officers
and police; Mannerheim himself had spent three days in hiding.

In the train Wrangel had his first taste of the revolution. In the dining car a
disheveled soldier with a cigarette in his lips sat down next to a nurse and made
advances; when the lady objected, he broke into obscenities. Wrangel got up,
seized him by the scruff of the neck and, dragging him to the coach door, threw
him out into the corridor full of soldiers. There was some muttering, but no one
interfered. For much less than that officers had already been lynched by the
mutinous soldiery.

St. Petersburg produced on Wrangel the worst and most painful impressions. The Czar, Czarina, and their children had been arrested and abandoned by all their relatives as well as by the hordes of courtiers who in
peacetime had fawned for favor and who now sported red ribbons and had
nothing but slander for their former masters; the government issued decree
upon decree which no one obeyed; and a new menace was looming greater
with each passing day. The Soviets, led by Lenin and Trotzky and subsidized by
German intelligence, were working diligently at sapping the foundations of
the government, such as it was.

But the wheels of military bureaucracy still ground, even though most of
the time erratically. Wrangel was promoted to commander of the 7th
Cavalry Division.

General von Dreier, then a colonel and chief of staff of the 7th Cavalry
Division, described Wrangel's arrival as follows: "We were having dinner
together, Colonel Zikov and I; the colonel was acting commander of the division, expecting daily his promotion to general and confirmation of the division's
command. Zikov was taking a drink of vodka, humming to himself 'God Save
The Czar,' when the door opened and a tall, thin sunburned general walked in.

"Seeing Zikov, he said; 'Serge, how are you?' They embraced. 'What are
you doing here?' asked Zikov. 'Come to take over the division — didn't you
know?' And Wrangel handed him the orders. 'But what will happen to me?'
said the crestfallen Zikov. 'You will take over the brigade and we shall serve
together,' answered Wrangel calmly.

"Zikov, pleading sick, left the division and Wrangel proceeded to take
matters in hand, not a whit disturbed by his old friend's sudden departure.

"Wrangel immediately plunged into work. First the division's supply
officer was taken to task and the numerous discrepancies in his accounts given a
workover. Then report upon report flooded higher headquarters, requesting

this and demanding that. However, no answers were forthcoming from above as about that time the disintegrating army was rolling back, primarily the infantry, for the cavalry, which had suffered fewer casualties in the course of the war, had retained its cadre of officers and NCO's. It fell, therefore, to its unhappy lot to act as rear guard, while the masses of disorganized and mutinous infantry ran for the rear, raping and looting on their way.

"The retreating horde of demoralized soldiers plundered and burned everything that came to hand. Army depots, whole villages and in town buildings went up in flames with no rhyme or reason.

"One evening divisional headquarters had stopped to overnight in the Austrian town of Stanislav, through which streamed groups of haggard infantry. Wrangel, Zikov (who had in the meanwhile returned to the division) and I stood watching this sorry spectacle. Suddenly we saw several soldiers leave their ragged formation and go up to an office building with shops on its ground floor. The shop windows flew to pieces under blows from rifle butts and the soldiers started to set fire to the goods. Wrangel and Zikov rushed in, and oblivious of the mutinous crowd, proceeded to beat up the arsonists, Wrangel with his riding whip and Zikov with his fists. These fled, offering no resistance; the sullen multitude flowed past, menacing but cowardly. . . ."

Further remembering his days as Wrangel's chief of staff, von Dreier had this to say: "Serving with him in wartime was easy, but not always pleasant as he was the most restless person I had ever met. He always wanted to do something and never gave anyone a moment's peace, even during those days when we stood in the rear with nothing to do. Wrangel was very brave and totally self-sufficient, he really did not need a chief of staff drawing his own conclusions, once in a while only asking my opinion. He gave orders directly galloping from regiment to regiment, occasionally, however, losing sight of the whole. . . ."

Dreier's last remark notwithstanding, Wrangel managed to keep things together in the midst of chaos, eventually getting command of a cavalry corps — the 7th Division and the 3rd Caucasian. With these he earned the commander in chief General Kornilov's gratitude — a telegram of thanks for saving the army during its retreat.

Demagogues and dictators have the dubious talent of firing masses with their oratory. In peacetime they succeed, but in combat, when a veil of fear covers every man, whatever his rank or position, mere speeches and acting are not enough. Then a gesture, a word or two, personal example, and plain courage are the recipes to instill confidence and inspire men.

Wrangel had heretofore commanded a squadron and a regiment—from one hundred twenty to one thousand men. There he knew everyone and everyone knew him, whether in combat or on the march; he was there to see and a personal relationship developed. Now commanding a division and a corps from five thousand to ten thousand men, that personal contact became diffused. Something more—an intangible but indispensable wavelength—had to be found that reached the individual and yet molded the mass.

All great captains in military history had this quality; though it may be impossible to define, it is ever present and felt from the commander down to the lowly private. Wrangel had it, and in a great measure; it was one key to his success in subsequent battles in the civil war. He spelled out the recipe:

"I went down to one of my brigades which was resting in the forest. The officers were sitting at table near a forester's hut. I had scarcely dismounted when a shell fell not far away. A wounded man groaned; a horse covered with blood galloped off at top speed. Several troopers came out of the wood in great haste; others ran to their horses. There was nearly a panic. I gave the command 'eyes front,' sat down at the table, and picking up a fragment of a newly burst shell which had fallen quite near, I turned to the soldiers, saying: 'Who wants some hot rolls? Catch!' and I threw it to one of them. Their faces brightened, and a laugh ran along the ranks. They were no longer panicky.

"The firing soon ceased. We had only had two men killed and several horses wounded. The regiments set out for their bivouacs.

"Then afterwards I passed them at the gallop. I shouted a few words to them, and they cheered me enthusiastically. It was one of those psychological moments when officer and soldiers seem to be of one flesh. I have lived through other such unforgettable moments before and since—in Manchuria, in Eastern Prussia, in Galicia, in the Kouban, and in the Crimea. I do not know how these bonds are forged on the spur of the moment, always spontaneously and often without any apparent reason. One feels these things instinctively, though one cannot explain them. Without these bonds there would be no army. It is not enough to have your men well in hand; they must be yours, so that they will follow you, not only from a sense of duty, but because something stronger than themselves stirs in their hearts, and makes it impossible for them to do otherwise."

Generals Kornilov, Denikin, and Krymov, who had joyfully welcomed the revolution, now saw that unless drastic measures were taken, nothing but defeat and chaos were to follow. Kornilov demanded dictatorial powers and Kerensky seemingly acquiesced, only to double-cross his commanding general by outlawing him and having him and his generals arrested and put into jail.

The scene was set for Lenin and Trotzky to move in with the Communist dictatorship. By October they had succeeded. Kerensky fled, disguised as a sailor (less charitable sources say as a woman), deserting his colleagues, the army, and Russia.

General Krymov, Wrangel's friend and former commander, had marched on St. Petersburg to effect a putsch on General Kornilov's behalf. On the way he had stopped, hesitated, and asked for another conference with Kerensky. Returning from it, he had shot himself. His last words were: "I love my country too much."

Wrangel had had enough and asked for his discharge; the authorities refused on the grounds that there is no discharge in wartime. But in the meanwhile the Soviets had entered into negotiations with the Germans, asking for an armistice. Feeling no longer obliged to serve anyone anymore, Wrangel insisted, got his papers, and left for the Crimea, where his wife's family had a villa.

The Crimean peninsula's southern shore was and still is the resort area of Russia. Before World War I villas and palaces lined the shore where mimosas blossomed in early spring and grapes and fruit of all kinds grew in vast profusion. The population was partly Tartar, descendents of the Golden Horde of Ghengis Khan, Moslems long under the dominion of Turkey and under Russian sovereignty since the end of the eighteenth century. They were peaceful citizens, occupying themselves with agriculture and small-time commerce. Some of them did their military service in the Crimean dragoons, a regiment recruited from the local population. Wrangel's mother-in-law owned a villa near Yalta, not far from Sebastopol, a major Russian naval base. There Wrangel moved with wife and children. His wife's brother, a captain in the hussars, joined them.

The Tartar population elected to have its own government after the revolution, with its own army as well. Learning of Wrangel's arrival, they invited him to take command of their forces. Wrangel went to Simferopol, their new capital, took a look at their government, and, concluding that it was a mini-Kerensky government inevitably due to collapse, politely declined and decided to stay away from it all and await events. What followed were to be perhaps the worst days of his short but eventful life. He said later that these were his most frightening, and depressing, experiences.

At first life in Crimea seemed peaceful enough, but it did not last long! Sebastopol was a large naval base; as in all major cities, the Bolsheviks took over and armed bands of Red soldiers began terrorizing the population and wreaking vengeance on all forms of past authority.

Wrangel had always had an explosive temper; hearing the gardener insult his wife one day, he seized him by the scruff of the neck and threw him outside. Retaliation was prompt: That night a band of Red sailors broke into the house and Wrangel was hauled out of bed under the menace of a revolver. Outside, the gardener was exhorting the sailors to do away with the Russian general, the enemy of the people.

Wrangel and his brother-in-law, a captain of the hussars, were bundled into a car and were about to be driven off when Olga Wrangel rushed out and, clinging to the door of the car, insisted on going along. The sailors pushed her back and Wrangel implored her to stay, but she persisted and finally won when one of the sailors said: "Let her come—so much the worse for her!"

They were driven to the harbor, now crowded with a bloodthirsty throng. The cars drove up to a ship moored to the quay. As they got out they saw a horrible sight; bodies torn limb from limb were strewn about. Howling for blood, the mob of sailors and disheveled civilians screamed: "Here come the bloodsuckers. To the water with them!"

It appeared that besides the bodies on the pier, several people had been thrown alive into the water with weights attached to their feet. The group of sailors who had brought Wrangel, his wife, and her brother, proved to have retained some semblance of past discipline; pushing their way through the raging mob, they took the prisoners on board and locked them up in a cabin. All day they stayed there as drunken sailors tried to push in and lynch them. To their good fortune, the guard stood firm. At one point Wrangel persuaded his wife to go and try to get help from the neighborhood, where they were popular. He gave her his wristwatch to take back. It was only a few minutes before she was back: She had seen the crowd tearing an officer to pieces. Realizing that the wristwatch was only an excuse to get her away, she firmly decided to stay and share her husband's fate.

In the evening they were taken out to the customs house building, now turned into a vast prison where generals, officers, Tartars, common criminals, and hapless passersby were now united in common misery, sitting on the spit- and refuse-covered floor, listening to the shouts and obscenities of the sailors outside. All through the night the prisoners were interrogated by a student turned magistrate.

In the meanwhile, Wrangel's mother-in-law, an energetic woman, had canvassed the neighborhood, where she had many well-wishers, particularly among the poor, whom she had befriended over the years. Soon a delegation set forth to try and liberate the prisoners. It is highly doubtful if they would have succeeded in such a frenzied atmosphere had it not been for a fortuitous circumstance. The house laundress, it seems, had a liaison with a sailor who happened, again most luckily, to be the president of their revolutionary tribunal. She rushed there and in no uncertain terms demanded the prisoners' release, threatening otherwise to break off their romance.

The prisoners were sitting in the hushed gloom of the customs house. Turning to his brother-in-law, Wrangel said: "If they come to shoot us, let us not die like cattle at the slaughterhouse; let's try and grab a rifle from one of them and shoot until we ourselves are shot—at least we shall die fighting!"

A night and a frightful day had passed in suspense. At last, at eight in the evening, a group of men entered the prison, at their head the president of the tribunal, the sailor, lover of the Wrangels' laundry woman. The following dialogue ensued:

"Why were you arrested?" he asked.

"Probably because I am a Russian general," answered Wrangel. "It is the only crime of which I am guilty."

"Why are you not wearing the decorated uniform which you were probably flaunting yesterday?" And without waiting for an answer, he turned to Olga Wrangel. "And why were you arrested?"

"I was not arrested; I am here of my own free will."

He feigned surprise. "Then why are you here?"

"I have always lived happily with my husband, and I want to stay with him until the end."

With a theatrical gesture the sailor said: "Such women are not to be found every day. You owe your life to your wife—go!" He pointed to the door.

They were not liberated until the next morning, however, while all night long prisoners were led out and shot outside, their bodies thrown into the water.

The following days were spent in hiding among the Tartar population. Devout Moslems, they were enemies of the Reds and helped Wrangel and his family as best they could.

Wrangel had two dominating traits of character—determination and a thirst for knowledge. Spending the night in the hills, hiding from a possible rearrest, they saw a cow in labor; she seemed to have delivery trouble. Olga Wrangel had grown up on her father's ranch, but the general was strictly a city resident. They both proceeded under Olga Wrangel's direction to help the cow give birth. They toiled until daybreak, oblivious to Red patrols, and Wrangel was very proud of his veterinary experience.

Then, one fine morning, Wrangel saw German troops marching into the Crimea and the Reds departing. His reaction was mixed: "Deeply grieved as I was to see the enemy master of Russia, and my country disgraced, I was nevertheless happy at being free from the humiliating yoke of those blockheaded idiots."

The Germans brought with them an end to anarchy, pillage, and murders, but their military government forbade people to move in or out of the Crimea. Wrangel, however, succeeded in getting a pass to the Ukraine, also under German occupation, where he had some property which he wanted to check on. The Ukraine was governed by a German puppet government headed by Skoropadsky, Wrangel's former commander in the Horse Guards. This government, under the aegis of the Germans, was ultranationalistic, so only the Ukrainian dialect was to be spoken. Wrangel noted the comical side: Neither Skoropadsky nor his immediate entourage could speak the language.

Delighted at seeing his old friend and former subordinate, Skoropadsky asked Wrangel to serve as chief of staff. They spent many hours discussing the future and Wrangel became convinced that neither the Ukrainian State nor its army had any future. They were there as long as the Germans stayed; with their departure the card palace structure was bound to collapse. He summed up Germany, its goals and war effort, thus: "Germany had failed to conquer by force of arms, but had succeeded in corrupting her enemy. It is maintained that everything is fair in war. I admit it. But there are ways and ways—some honorable, some base. Quite often the end justifies the means, but the nation which uses unworthy means always gets a bad reputation."

He might have added "ends up badly," but then Hitler and World War II were not even on the horizon.

5

The Civil War

NEW EVENTS WERE STIRRING IN Russia. Generals Kornilov, Alekseiev, Denikin, and others imprisoned by Kerensky had broken out of jail and headed south into the land of the Don Cossacks, hoping to find there a suitable climate of resistance to the Red dictatorship. Reaching the Don Cossacks' capital of Novocherkask after many adventures, Kornilov and his group were sorely disappointed. The Don Cossacks had provided fifty-two cavalry regiments and twenty-two artillery batteries in World War I, a colossal effort which meant every able-bodied man up to forty-five years of age. After the three years of war, the Cossacks returned home war-weary, having lost the Czar to whom they had owed allegiance and unwilling to serve an amorphous, and to them incomprehensible, new regime. The cry of the soldier was: "Home, and let the Russians fend for themselves; whether Bolshevik or Republican—who cares!" The Cossacks had always had a democratic self-government, and although the Czar appointed the ataman (head of government), the individual villages, or stanitsas, as they were called, elected their own atamans and councils. In the climate of defeatism, war weariness, and revolution, the Cossack population elected to remain passive. General Kornilov's impassioned appeals and warnings went unheeded. Generals Kornilov and Alekseiev decided to recruit an army, foreseeing that the Reds would eventually swamp the Don region. Their initial efforts, seconded by a few Cossak officers and men, were hardly auspicious; 3683 men, all volunteers, joined this new army. In the Soviet literature, as indeed in some of the Western, this White army has been represented as an army of aristocrats—dispossessed, wealthy, and disgruntled former officers. The truth is different. In those 3683, there were hardly more than a half dozen people who could remotedly be considered aristocrats. Most were young wartime-promoted lieutenants and captains from all walks of civilian life—students, cadets from military schools, and Cossacks.

Finding no support among the wide spectrum of the Don Cossack community, this small army decided to head for the area of the Kouban Cossacks, neighboring the Don, a Cossack region that had already had a taste of the Communist regime: Red units of the disbanded army of the Caucasus that had fought the Turks during the war now flooded this region with attendant excesses of murder and pillage. The White army moved on in a column surrounded on all sides by large bodies of Red army troops heavily armed from the big supplies accumulated by the Czarist army at the time of the revolution.

The epic of this army of volunteers may well be compared to Xenophon's march: It marched 1050 kilometers during eighty days of which forty-four were in combat. All wounded were carried along in carts, for at first the badly injured, who had to be left behind, were immediately butchered by the first Red troops who came along. It became a custom for those who were severely wounded and could not move back in time during a retreat, to shoot themselves or ask their comrades to do it for them. Enraged by Red atrocities, the Whites themselves stopped taking prisoners, shooting all. Ammunition and medical and technical supplies were taken in combat—there was no rear from which these could be drawn. Food and fodder were provided by the Cossack villages through which they passed, often free, sometimes paid for. There was no need to requisition; the Cossack population sympathetically provided food and lodging as well as an occasional sprinkling of new volunteers, the number growing in proportion to the time during which the Reds had been masters in this or that Cossack stanitsa.

The army marched towards Ekaterinodar, the capital of the Kouban area. It tried to take the heavily fortified city by storm, failed, and the commander in chief, General Kornilov, was killed. General Denikin took over and in forced marches and daily combat fought his way out of encirclement and destruction. The army headed back towards the Don. There good news awaited them at last; the Don Cossacks, having tasted the Red regime, had risen in rebellion. Living as they had been over the last centuries in a paramilitary society, such a spontaneous uprising was not difficult, the more so as their officer corps had remained relatively unscathed, dispersed as it was through the different villages.

The Don Cossacks elected General Krasnov as their ataman, successful combat general in the World War and known also as a writer and historian. The armistice between the Germans and the Soviets having been signed, Krasnov had no compunction in dealing with the Germans: In exchange for wheat and cattle he received arms and ammunition and soon had assembled a combat-ready Don Cossack army.

The White army now joined forces with the Don Cossacks: it had left the Don region numbering just short of four thousand men; it returned five thousand strong, the addition being Kouban Cossack volunteers. It had lost four hundred men and brought back over fifteen hundred wounded. News of these events had reached Wrangel in the Crimea. He decided to try and join the White forces. It was not all that easy for the Germans, presumably under pressure from the Soviets with whom they had just negotiated an armistice and who made all sorts of difficulties for Russian officers to leave the Crimea. Wrangel made friends with a German professor in charge of military hospitals; he helped him and Olga Wrangel get through the German passport control. Leaving her children with her mother in Yalta, Olga Wrangel decided to follow her husband and start again as a Red Cross nurse, this time in the White army.

When Wrangel arrived at Ekaterinodar, the headquarters of the White army, he found the Volunteer army, as it was called, to number thirty-five thousand men and eighty guns. The infantry, artillery, and engineers were almost entirely composed of officers, as was the cavalry, with the exception of two regiments which were attached to infantry units. The remainder of the cavalry were Kouban Cossacks and Moslem Caucasians. The Don forces were operating on their own.

Arriving at headquarters, Wrangel presented himself to General Denikin, whom he had met once or twice during their military careers.

"Well, how can we make use of you," said Denikin. "I do not know what to offer you; as you know, we have but few forces."

With customary directness Wrangel answered: "As you may know, Your Excellency, I finished the World War as a corps commander, but in 1914, when we started out, I commanded a squadron; since then I have not aged that much and can start all over again with a squadron."

"Come, come now," Denikin answered: "How about a brigade?"

"At your orders, Your Excellency," and Wrangel received the temporary command of the 1st Cavalry Division, its commanding general being at that time on detached service.

Wrangel met also General Denikin's chief of staff, General Romanovsky. Wrangel's first impression was mixed: "He seemed to be intelligent and well-informed, but the favorable impression which he had made on me at first was somewhat modified, for he had a way of never looking straight at anyone, and would always avoid your eyes."

The next day Wrangel set off to join his division, which was operating somewhere in the Maikop area. Transferring from a train to a horse-drawn cart, Wrangel went looking for his division. They drove through the rich Kouban Cossack district where everything spoke of plenty: high wheat fields, orchards laden with fruit, the Cossack houses freshly painted with red-tiled roofs contrasting with the surrounding greenery. The gilded church domes stared into the blue sky; it looked like the land of peace and contentment.

Wrangel had the ability to speak to men of all stations of life. He soon was engaged in conversation with his driver, an old Cossack. Pleased to have such an audience, the old man told Wrangel much about the life and customs of the Cossacks and how this good life had been turned upside down by the arrival of the Red army. He described the plundering, shooting, and outrages to which the Cossack population had been subjected.

Driving along, they came upon a platoon of Cossacks; it turned out to be the escort of General Afrosimov, the acting division commander. The old general, his brigade commander Colonel Naumenko, and a staff officer were drinking tea in a farmhouse. No one expected Wrangel; no telegram from HQ had reached them. General Afrosimov reported that the division was in combat. Swallowing quickly a cup of tea, Wrangel mounted a horse and set off to take a look at his troops. Soon they trotted up to the deployed squadrons of one of the regiments.

The division was composed of six cavalry regiments, three horse artillery batteries, a small infantry unit, all totalling about twelve hundred men. A medical outfit consisted of one doctor and two nurses, with no bandages and hardly any drugs. The technical equipment consisted of one wireless; there were no field telephones. Later Wrangel obtained an old automobile which he made much use of, dashing about from regiment to regiment, often under fire. It was, one day, to almost cost him his life.

The daily ammunition ration for the whole division consisted of twelve hundred cartridges per day (this for the twelve hundred men in the division). The batteries received one to two shells per day. Opposing Reds numbered, according to staff intelligence reports, from twelve thousand to fifteen thousand with twenty to thirty guns and unlimited ammunition. The Reds were solidly entrenched around the village of Mikhailovka, with their left flank resting on the river Tchamlyk.

Lieutenant de Korvey, a young man serving with one of the batteries, remembered Wrangel's first day in combat: "We were lying on top of a Kurgan [the old Scythian burial mounds that dot the steppes of Southern Russia]; our cavalry was deployed in action and our guns silent as usual due to lack of ammunition. A group of horsemen rode up; a young lanky general in khaki uniform dismounted and climbed the mount — it was General Wrangel. We all stood up; occasional bullets were whining overhead. 'Please, gentlemen, remain at ease,' he said and remained standing, talking to our battery commander. We were impressed with his martial bearing, but also with his manners and polish of the Guards officer."

Another artillery lieutenant, Mamontov, also remembered Wrangel's first steps. "At first the Cossack soldiers resented Wrangel's appointment — 'Again one of the regulars, as if we did not have enough of our own officers.' The Cossacks were chauvinists, dividing the world into Cossacks and the rest. But soon their attitude changed. Each day Wrangel would ride out with a reconnaissance squadron, each day one from another regiment. The Cossacks perked up: it was highly unusual for a general commanding a division to ride out on scouting forays."

The headquarters demanded from Wrangel decisive action regardless of circumstances. Wrangel maneuvered, looking for a soft spot in the enemy's lines and not finding it. Despairing of finding it, Wrangel decided to make a sudden frontal cavalry attack. Personally reconnoitering the terrain ahead, he had two of his regiments at night cross the river in front of the enemy's position and with the first light of dawn hurled them at the enemy's lines. They came up to the village Mikhailovka, but met there with point-blank rifle and machine-gun fire; they turned back with losses. Although all killed and wounded were brought back, the operation was a failure.

Undeterred, Wrangel continued maneuvering across the enemy front. Most of the divisions officers were of young World War I vintage. After each action Wrangel would gather them together and discuss with them the day's action. Little by little he took the division in hand, dismissing the weak or incompetent, promoting the brave and able. One of the latter was the artillery commander General Belaiev. His career subsequent to the civil war bears relating. When the White armies finally left Russia, this officer made his way to South America and joined the Paraguayan army. With courage and ability he fought in the Chaco War against Bolivia and rose to high position in that small South American army. After the war he became interested in the unhappy lot of the local Indians; they were being exploited by the white population, who considered them no better than animals. Belaiev, using his prestige, went to work, making contact with the different tribes, cajoling the authorities, obtaining a budget for Indian relief. Gradually the Indians came to trust him and consider him their patron. Some would come half-naked out of the jungle and camp in his garden, seeking advice or help. In time the Indians became integrated as citizens of Paraguay, and when, sometime in the forties, General Belaiev died, the government built a memorial for him. To this date fruit and flowers are often laid at the statue by grateful Indians.

But this was to be many years later; in the hard days of the civil war Belaiev was firing the few shells he had at his disposal and Wrangel's division sought to pierce the enemy's lines. The divisions' losses show how intense this period of combat was: 260 officers and 2460 other ranks; in other words casualties of 200%. Only the influx of Cossack volunteers kept the division up to strength.

Headquarters sent the 3rd Infantry Division to help turn the enemy's flank; it wandered off course, coming unexpectedly from behind. Wrangel, who had not been notified of its mission, decided to work out a joint operation. The 3rd Division was to attack frontally; Wrangel with his cavalry was to turn the enemy's right flank and attack from the rear, cutting off the enemy line of retreat between the rivers Laba and Tchamlyk. Leading his column, Wrangel marched at night, aiming to cross the Tuapse-Armavir railroad line. An enemy armored train, searchlight sweeping, moved in to intercept the cavalry column. A battery unlimbered, firing at close range and damaging but not knocking out the train which disappeared into the night — the enemy was alerted. As dawn came, enemy infantry advanced from Mikhailovka and a regiment of cavalry tried to turn Wrangel's left flank. The division deployed, blocking the enemy's advance but unable to go further. Wrangel waited for news from the 3rd Infantry Division; they could hear the sound of battle, which reached a crescendo then died down around noon. New and ever stronger enemy waves of infantry again advanced from Mikhailovka. Wrangel was watching from the artillery's observation post. It came under fire; the battery commander lying next to Wrangel collapsed — a bullet through his head.

Now fresh Red infantry waves appeared, turning the cavalry division's flank; simultaneously an enemy cavalry column was seen trotting towards the Cossack division's rear. The situation was turning to critical. Wrangel still had four squadrons in reserve; he ordered them to attack the enemy cavalry. The squadrons deployed but came under heavy fire, stopped, turned, and started to retreat. If the enemy succeeded in seizing the bridge in their rear, the swampy Tchamlyk River would be difficult to cross — and this meant losing the artillery. Ordering his troops to retreat slowly towards the river crossing and the batteries to limber up, Wrangel saw that some of the squadrons were getting disorganized. Mounting his horse and drawing his sword, Wrangel sought to rally the retreating Cossacks. Some of them followed; others stopped. The enemy cavalry turned back. Shouting encouragement, Wrangel charged on; the enemy fire was more intense than anything Wrangel had seen in the World War. Bullets whistled overhead or hit the ground raising puffs of dust. The divisional fanion bearer fell wounded; Wrangel's ADC had his horse killed. Turning in his saddle, Wrangel saw that only a small number of the Cossacks were still following him, and these were pulling up. Cursing them, Wrangel turned back and, dismounting the Cossacks he had at hand, had them occupy a small hamlet covering the river crossing. The artillery managed to make it over the bridge. It was a narrow escape. Reports from the 3rd Infantry Division told of failure and heavy losses. Wrangel was sick at heart. The operation which looked to succeed imminently had ended in failure; the enemy became morally stronger; and his men had not followed him in the cavalry charge. The psychological bond which must exist between commander and commanded had not been forged.

However, on the night of October 1, 1918, scouting parties reported that the Reds were blowing up bridges in their rear and were preparing to retreat. In spite of their overwhelming superiority and the 1st Cavalry Division's failure to break through, their morale had nevertheless been broken.

The war now moved into open country, where wide maneuvers were possible. This was to be the prelude to great victories and eventually to the liberation of the entire northern Caucasus. Wrangel pressed on hard in order to give the enemy no time to make a stand. The division moved in two columns, one heading for the village of Urupskaya, the other towards Bezkorbnaya. As village after village was liberated, Wrangel came face to face with two evils which were to plague the White army as much as any typhus or casualties — massacres and pillage.

At the beginning of the civil war the Red army represented a huge armed horde laden with booty that raged over the countryside burning, raping and looting. The miniscule White army at first took no prisoners and equipped itself from what it had captured. The Cossacks, in particular, who had borne the brunt of the Red army's occupation, felt free to recoup their material losses by helping themselves wherever and whenever they could. Unfortunately, the White command closed its eyes on many wrongdoings, and worse, some commanders actually condoned it. Arriving at a village, Wrangel saw Cossack officers and men putting the place to sack. He ordered the men arrested; they belonged to the division of General Pokrovsky, an able but ruthless commander. He sent them back with the dire warning that next time they would be shot.

The Kouban region contained three types of population: the Cossacks, the peasant settlers, and the Circassians. The first, a military democracy, owned the land, parceling it out to each male member (twenty-two acres), elected its elders, and considered itself in perpetual military service. The peasant settlers, who had arrived much later, rented land from the Cossacks or engaged in trade or artisanship; they had no say in the local government. The Circassians, to whom the land originally belonged, had been conquered by the Russians but allowed to live in their own communities and to practice their traditions and religion, which was Moslem. The Cossacks and the Circassians opposed the Communists, the first because they saw their very way of life threatened, the latter because the Soviets menaced their religion. Both people had lived in peace for almost a century now and both had been brutalized by the Reds.

Arriving at the newly liberated village of Mikhailovka, Wrangel attended a *Te Deum* mass. He and his Cossacks had been greeted with great enthusiasm; new recruits flocked to their standards. In the marketplace, along with a detachment of Cossack recruits, he saw a large group of Moslem Circassians; a huge green flag, the banner of the Prophet, waved above them. A group of elders met Wrangel and described to him how the Reds had terrorized their villages. They demanded justice and had brought their younger men to join Wrangel's division.

Wrangel ordered a couple of dozen prisoners to be handed over to them; he assumed they would be tried according to their Moslem law, the Shariat. No sooner had the last squadrons of the division passed out of the village than the Circassian elders, forgetting the Shariat, drew their swords and massacred their hapless prisoners on the spot.

Wrangel immediately undertook to stop such outrages. As there was virtually no rear to which prisoners and booty could be regularly and safely channeled, he ordered that all plunder taken from the Red army be fairly apportioned among all the soldiers, and to this end he appointed regimental and unit committees to divide and rule upon the booty. Later, when a normal front became a reality, he insisted on the proper handling and evacuation of prisoners and spoils of war.

The enemy was rapidly retreating; having given further instructions for his cavalry to follow up, Wrangel visited a liberated Cossack village, worked on dispatches, then, getting again into his car, rode to join his regiments. He found two of them at rest —horses unsaddled and being fed in the farmyards, the men drinking tea. A report reached him that Colonel Toporkov with the vanguard was in action some six kilometers ahead. Getting into his car, Wrangel drove on. The car had come to be a useful auxiliary; it also came near to causing his death. The account which follows is a composite of Wrangel's narrative and that of the young artillery lieutenant Mamontov; both nearly lost their lives but lived to tell the tale, each very vividly.

Wrangel: "Col. Toporkov and his staff were atop a Kurgan, on which also was the artillery's observation post; the battery itself was behind the mound, and some two hundred paces back, the battery's cover: two squadrons from the Cossack Zaporoj regiment. Other deployed squadrons could be seen far ahead. The enemy's infantry was about 1½ kms. away; the occasional bullet whizzed overhead. I got out of the car and walked over to the mound with my ADC and another officer. . . ."

Mamontov: "I was standing by my gun, when Wrangel arrived in his car and, getting out, strode rapidly towards the Kurgan. Curious to have a look at the General and hear what the 'brass' had to say, I left my gun and followed him.

"One of the officers said in a surprised voice: 'Strange . . . Why are our squadrons turning back?'

"Everyone grabbed their binoculars.

" 'Yes, funny, now they are trotting. . . .'

" 'The swords are glistening in the sunlight.'

" 'But look, these are not ours.'

" 'Reds attacking!'

" 'Prepare for action!'

"The Red cavalry was now near; the horsemen picked up a gallop. Panic started on the hillock. I ran back to my gun; we had time to fire grapeshot over open sights and it dispersed the cavalry immediately to our front, but their flanks swept in towards us. We limbered up the guns and they moved off at a fast trot. The horse holders handed us our horses. I still had not grasped the situation and the danger we were in; the horse holders' hysterical shouts took me by surprise: 'Take the horses, take the horses or I'll let them go!' "

Wrangel: "I heard the cry: 'Cavalry.' The squadrons ahead of us were galloping back towards us, followed by a dense cloud of enemy cavalry that had appeared from a ravine. The battery commander ordered 'Rapid fire,' but our Cossacks came galloping on and it was clear that the enemy on their heels would overwhelm the battery. I heard the command 'limber up,' but it was too late; horsemen were already dashing past us. The squadrons covering the battery turned tail and fled. Toporkov, myself and the other officers tried to halt the flight in vain; the torrent of horsemen swept irresistibly by. Enemy horsemen were at the guns and one of the guns turned over. I saw an artillery officer fire at one of the attackers, but another cut him down. Surrounded by enemy horsemen, Col. Toporkov was slashing left and right.

"I ran to the car, but saw, to my horror, that the car, its engine still running, was stuck in the mud. In the distance I saw the chauffeur and his assistant running away. I ran for the cornfield; on my left and right, Cossacks galloped and artillerymen ran. Around the second gun hand-to-hand fighting was in progress; shots rang out and swords flashed. An artillery officer galloped up to me: 'Your Excellency, take my horse!' I refused; he insisted riding alongside me. 'I shall not take your horse anyhow; gallop on to the village and bring back the other brigade, also my escort and my horses.' He galloped off and I kept running. Looking over my shoulder, I saw three horsemen chasing me. They caught up with a soldier running behind me; he turned and fired point-blank; a horse fell and the other riders turned on him. I grabbed my revolver and to my horror felt only the empty holster: the day before a Circassian elder had presented me with an ornate dagger; in turn I had given him my revolver and had forgotten all about it. I had no sword and was helpless. At this moment I saw an ambulance cart galloping full blast; two nurses were in it, and a wounded artillery officer. With a last burst of energy I caught up with the cart and vaulted on. The Red riders faded back. Despair and rage seized me; the loss of the battery, the flight of the Zaporoj regiment, my vain efforts to halt them, and the feeling that I still did not have the moral ascendancy over my troops choked me with helpless anger and sorrow. I urged the ambulance cart on, looking ahead for the help that was not coming. We passed an artillery soldier with a team of horses. Mamontov, the artillery lieutenant, had managed to gallop off."

Mamontov: "Wrangel saw our gun team of horses: 'Soldiers, let me have a horse,' he yelled.

"Ranjiev [one of the teamsters] unhitched a horse and Wrangel vaulted on it. Again Red horsemen loomed up. Spotting the general, his tall figure, gold shoulder straps and blue breeches with the general's red stripe having drawn their attention, they came charging on. Fortunately the gun traces were still dangling behind the horses; dragging on the ground, they scared the horses of the pursuing horsemen who could not close in. Wrangel and the artillery soldier got away."

Wrangel: "Finally I saw the Line Cossack regiment coming up at a trot, followed by the Circassians. Deploying the squadrons, I led them on; the enemy retreated, having had time to take along our two guns, my car and their wounded. They left behind our dead, stripped naked. We lost seven officers and a few soldiers all cut down on their guns."

Reflecting on past failures of his Cossack regiments, Wrangel gambled with a bold change in tactics. Heretofore the deployed formations used were the Cossacks' "lava," a widely deployed formation undulating like a serpent — in accordance with the enemies' moves. Inherited from the days of Ghenghis Khan and his Mongol cavalry, the "lava" had been an ingenious and useful formation; it had in 1812 harried Napoleon's forces out of Russia. Now, however, it was not working well. The widely spread out horsemen were difficult to control. Much depended on the individual; the brave ones advanced, while the timid milled on the spot. The vast hordes of Red infantry were invulnerable to the shock of these loose cavalry formations. Wrangel decided to revert to the old style "stirrup to stirrup" attacks in close order. At first glance such a procedure seemed suicidal in the face of machine gun and artillery fire, but Wrangel gambled on correct timing and the morale factor. Covered by artillery fire and that of machine guns mounted on horse-drawn carts, the squadrons charged in close order, commanders in the van. Precise timing and élan were mandatory. Once the shock came, success was imminent. Wielding their curved swords with dexterity acquired from youth, the Kouban Cossacks literally slashed to pieces everything that stood or ran. It took much effort for Wrangel to persuade his Cossack officer to adopt these tactics, but once mastered it became a credo spreading to other divisions as Wrangel's subordinates moved up in the chain of command. Much later the Soviets adopted the same tactics and their cavalry improved accordingly.

The Red forces were now entrenched behind the Urup River. At the same time they exerted a strong pressure on the 1st Infantry Division of General Kazanovitch, to whom Wrangel's division was subordinated. This infantry general insisted, much to Wrangel's annoyance, that the 1st Cavalry Division stay close to his right flank, thereby limiting Wrangel's ability to maneuver in depth. The enemy, not content with passive resistance along the Urup River, crossed over precisely in the gap between the 1st Infantry Division and Wrangel's cavalry. Leaving a small covering force at the village Bezkorbnaya, Wrangel made a night march and on the next morning attacked the Red bridgehead. After a long and bloody fight the Reds were forced back over the river. Again using a night march, Wrangel immediately rushed two regiments south to join the two regiments he had left behind at Bezkorbnaya. Concentrating these four regiments under the command of Colonel Naumenko, he had them force a crossing of the Urup at Livonsk, sending them around and into the Reds' rear. He himself stayed behind, ready with the two remaining regiments to cross the river and attack head on.

Colonel Sokolovsky, divisional chief of staff, recalled: "We were standing on a hillock looking across the river at the enemy lines. The sun was setting and time was getting shorter — where was Col. Naumenko? A howling cold wind was blowing; we stood wrapped in our overcoats; the horses, heads down, tails between their legs, looked as frozen as we, Wrangel, his burka flapping in the wind, paced impatiently to and fro: he seemed to try and conjure up those missing squadrons.

"Suddenly we saw myriads of black dots covering the slope facing us: the enemy was leaving his trenches. In an instant all was action with us. Wrangel leaped on his horse, shouted commands, as our battery opened up and the squadrons filed over a ford in the river. We saw them deploy and charge up the steep bank. Now cannonade could be heard from the east, clear evidence that Naumenko had reached his objective. Taken on from front and rear, the Reds broke: the booty 3000 prisoners, guns and machine guns, of which 23 taken by one squadron alone of the Kornilov regiment.

"Wrangel with our staff and a small escort rode into Uspeskaya. Along the way endless columns of prisoners, wagon trains of booty and our wounded transports moved in the opposite direction. Bullets were still flying as dismounted Cossacks were hammering down the last Red barricades and shooting the men manning them. Squadrons were assembling, men mounting up, horses whinnying, commands ringing out. The Cossacks, on seeing the General's St. George's fanion, broke into cheers. It was a moving moment."

Wrangel subsequently remarked that that was the day his troops and he became one. From that day on they flew from victory to victory. Lt. Mamontov remembered: "I saw the 1st Zaporoj Cossack Regiment coming back from action. The men were singing a lusty melody. In front of the regiment, standing bolt upright on the saddle a man was dancing — it was Captain Pavlichenko, later to become General and corps commander."

Wrangel had received orders to send the prisoners and the war booty to Armavir where new units were being formed and arms and ammunition were needed.

On receiving the command of the division, Wrangel had inherited the cadres of an infantry battalion that had been decimated in the previous campaign; a few dozen men remained. Wrangel decided to fill the ranks from the horde of prisoners. Three hundred and seventy Red army men, the officers and NCO's, were lined up and shot. Turning to the rest, Wrangel offered them service in the White army. Arms were immediately issued to them, and strangely enough, the newly born 1st Rifle Regiment fought with great distinction through the remainder of the campaign despite great casualties.

Lieutenant de Korvey, the young artillery officer, remembered: "Three hundred and seventy men, officers and men of the Red prisoners, had been drawn up and [were] about to be shot. Wrangel called in officers from all units and told them to look over the lot and see if there was anyone to reclaim. 'Be fair, but no false sentimentality,' he said, and we went down the lines, picking this one or the other according to more or less encouraging looks. I came up to a good-looking, stalward man, looking like a former NCO of the Imperial army. I made my proposal; unfortunately, I had called on the wrong party: brave but a fanatic Communist, he sent me to hell. . . . I shook my head sadly and walked on. . . ."

The Reds retreated towards the town of Stavropol and a sizable force was surrounded by the different White army units converging on the city. On the strength of his success, Wrangel was liberated from the tutelage of General Kasonovitch and his division was on its own.

Captain Meller-Zakomelsky on the divisional staff: "I rode with Wrangel to look things over: A dense fog enveloped the city, which seemed dead. Only on the northern outskirts could we see flashes of guns and hear their dull booming, occasionally interspersed with the staccato of machine guns. We saw some fires and rode over to a small grove where a Cossack detachment had dismounted. The horses were tied to trees, the Cossacks drinking tea around fires. On seeing us one called out: 'Hey, your Excellency, how about a gulp of hot tea?' He stood up and offered his tin cup. The traditional democratic spirit of the Cossacks devoid of any obsequiousness appealed to Wrangel. Smiling and thanking, he took a few sips and passed the tin canteen to me. . . ."

Riding over to the German colony of Johansdorf,* Wrangel had a bite to eat and, exhausted, turned in. He was awakened at dawn, the news was bad: massive Red forces had broken out of the ring of steel surrounding them; the 3rd Infantry Division had suffered heavy casualties and was retreating. . . .

It was senseless to attack through the town with cavalry; dismounted action was precluded by a shortage of ammunition. Wrangel waited until night, then he took four regiments and moved off under cover of darkness and the wood.

At dawn, as the enemy poured out northward, Wrangel quickly moved the four cavalry regiments into their flank and rear and hurled them at the Reds.

* German settlements in the south of Russia dating back to the days of Catherine the Great.

The Cossack General Babiev routed the Reds and, on their heels, burst into town. Wrangel followed with a few squadrons that he had in reserve. Reaching the outskirts of town, they came to a convent held by the Reds; these were shooting at the attacking Cossacks. Men and horses fell. Drawing his sword, Wrangel charged at the head of his men. With a loud hurrah the squadron charged and broke into the convent's compounds, sabering the Reds.

Hard on himself, hard on others when necessity demanded, Wrangel, beneath his steely exterior, was a sensitive man, at times also emotional. The following scene which he left us leaves no doubt as to the deep sentiments awakened in him at the sights within the convent. Wrangel remembered: "Dismounting the squadrons, I ordered them to occupy the outskirts and lead the horses back behind the convent wall. Wounded were being brought in and bandaged in the yard. Suddenly the doors of the convent opened and a priest followed by several nuns walked out. Bullets were whistling and ricocheting off the convent walls; a wounded horse was thrashing about in its death throes, but unconcerned with this the priest walked on sprinkling holy water on the wounded, while the nuns offered them tea and bread; a stirring night forever engraved in my memory."

The dismounted cavalry led by General Babiev hung on as best it could but could get no further as the numerous enemy fought from house to house. Finally help arrived from the converging White infantry divisions.

Wrangel regrouped his forces and gave the order to clear the town. Convinced now of the supremacy of his forces and of the correct dispositions he had made, Wrangel returned exhausted to the convent and fell asleep. He was awakened at four in the morning with the news that after a fierce street fight the town had been cleared.

Lieutenant de Korvey remembered: "It was terribly cold; fighting was still going on in the streets; our battery pulled up near a large building; we thought of going in to get warmed up. As we opened the door a crowd of men and women, disheveled, incredibly dirty, surrounded us; some babbled incoherently, others stood staring into space, still others gesticulated and danced. The floor was a solid carpet of lice and human excrement. We had walked into a lunatic asylum from which doctors and nurses had disappeared, leaving the poor demented on their hopeless own. We rushed out preferring to freeze rather than view this horrible sight."

Mounting his horse, bugles blowing gay marches, Wrangel rode into town to be met by a joyous crowd, cheering and weeping, showering tobacco, money, and wine on the escort Cossacks.

The Reds had engaged in atrocities: mutilated corpses lay around. Fearing that the Cossacks and the civilian population would take the law into their hands, Wrangel appointed a town commandant, ordered civilians to hand in all weapons, and forbade anyone to touch the immense loot accumulated by the Reds. But before order could be restored, a few Moslem Circassians had broken into a hospital where lay Red army soldiers and massacred seventy of them, fleeing before they could be stopped. Wrangel had a Cossack officer arrested for executing Red prisoners who had been placed in the city jail.

From the beginning of his service in the White army Wrangel took very seriously any breech of behavior by his troops: looting and massacring were not permitted and were punished ruthlessly. Unfortunately, this was not the case in other commands, where lawlessness, looting, and drunkenness were looked on as ways of life.

As the Reds retreated from Stavropol, Wrangel's division maneuvered back and forth, sometimes pursuing the Reds, other times wheeling around to help out other White divisons. Often in the enemy's rear, Wrangel sometimes rode alone from one unit to another, a hazardous, almost foolhardy exercise. One such trip he remembered vividly; hardened warrior though he was, the sight must have shaken him: "I rode on towards Pelagiada. The moonlight was trickling through a thick mist. Villages, trees, and fields had all taken on the livid hue of corpses, which gave them a weird, dismal appearance. The road was not only strewn with the dead bodies of men and horses, but was also churned up by the rain. As I was splashing through a large pool, my horse reared. A grinning corpse was staring at me, its head alone was visible, for the water hid its body. My horse trembled, snorted with fear, and shied from side to side."

These marches and countermarches interspersed with combat were again almost to cost Wrangel his life. The artillery lieutenant de Korvey remembered: "We were staying overnight in the village of Konstantinovka; Wrangel and his immediate staff bedded down in a large farmhouse with a big yard and outer gates, which, as it happens, were fortunately closed. During the night suddenly machine-gun fire erupted in the village; Reds were swarming all over. Wrangel jumped out of bed, grabbed the file of division papers and rushed out in his underwear only to be confronted by a Red army soldier who had got somehow into the yard in the middle of which stood a large hayrick. Wrangel ran around the hayrick and tossed the papers on top of it; the Red army soldier ran behind him. Someone of the staff shot the Red army man. Cossacks were bringing out the horses, saddled in quick time. Vaulting on, Wrangel ordered the gates open and, taking his sword from an orderly, prepared to charge out."

Lieutenant Gricius,* then twenty years old, awoke to the rattle of machine-

* Many years later department head of the US Army Language school in Monterey, California.

gun fire and, getting a dozen troopers together, galloped towards the head-quarters. He remembers: "A crowd of Red soldiers were hammering at the gates — I drew my sword and ordered charge. At the same moment the gates flew open and Wrangel, followed by a few men, burst out slashing left and right with his sword. . . ."

Colonel Sokolvsky: "It was getting light; the headquarters personnel followed our corps commander as he led us at a sharp trot towards the eastern side of the village. Carts and supply wagons were tearing past us at a gallop, amongst them individual riders. A ravine separated the village in half and from the other side we were met with intense rifle fire. Bullets whistled overhead. I suddenly felt my horse go lame. My orderly, who was by my side, managed to halt one of the wagons and take one of the horses out of the shafts. We ducked behind a house and quickly saddled the horse. Moments later we caught up with the group.

"We saw a dark mass of cavalry moving to cut us off. Wrangel halted and, peering into the half-light, said: 'Hell! We are being cut off!' At that moment, from the opposite side of the village, a gun fired and a second later shrapnel burst over the cavalry formation. 'Those are ours!' said Wrangel. 'Ride over to them and get our wagons together — this must be our battery firing.'

"So it was. General Belaicv had gathered together troopers and his battery crew and had opened fire. Wrangel and his escort galloped off towards the nearest cavalry unit bivouacked some ten kilometers away. Less than an hour later he came 'flying' in at the head of the Zaporoj Cossack regiment. The Reds had fled, leaving behind the bodies of the Cossacks they had killed, including Red Cross personnel; some of the nurses were captured and taken away. It must have been a great relief for General Wrangel to know that by a stroke of luck his wife was not with the Red Cross unit; she had gone back to Stavropol to buy supplies.

"We had lost all our personal belongings, and Wrangel his decorations. It had been a narrow squeak!"

Lieutenant de Korvey: "The next day I walked out of my house; a cold wind was blowing, raising dust clouds in the village main street. I saw a man hanging from a telegraph pole, the wind playing with his ragged beard. The villager who had guided in the Red troops had stayed behind, hoping to go undetected; someone had given him away. He had paid the price. Giving the corpse an indifferent look, I walked on. Life was cheap in those days. . . ."

As news that Wrangel had been captured had reached the regiments of the division, the acting commanding officer had given the order to retreat. Wrangel met the messenger on the way. Taking a pencil, he scribbled on the report: "I have not been taken prisoner — order to continue advance — Wrangel."

Olga Wrangel had followed her husband as a nurse in a field ambulance. It is hard to visualize today what that meant. A doctor, a couple of nurses, a long line of carts piled with wounded, almost no drugs, bandages made from bed linen; at night unloading the wounded in the village where they had stopped and in the mornings loading again those who had survived the night.

One such night firing broke out on the village outskirts; the Reds had attacked. As the wounded were brought out and piled pell-mell into the carts, the horses hitched up, and confusion reigning, bullets came whining down the street. Being caught meant massacre of the wounded, torture and rape for the nurses, most of whom carried capsules of poison ready to swallow when doom was inevitable. Someone had galloped on to the next village where Wrangel and his staff happened to be. Taking his escort and whatever men he could find, Wrangel charged to the rescue.

Olga Wrangel remembered: "The Cossacks came charging down the street, Petrousha [Wrangel's diminutive name] reined in; bullets were flying all over. In French, so that the men would not understand him, he bawled me out, telling me in no uncertain terms that his responsibility was bad enough without having to worry each day over his wife's fate. This situation was so tragic that under stress I saw only the comical side: The Reds, the bullets, the wounded, the charging Cossacks, and my husband speaking French in the middle of the pandemonium. I burst out laughing. Furious, he turned and galloped off."

Under duress Olga Wrangel was forced to return to a safe area, leaving her husband to the business of war.

Wrangel's success as divisional commander, his bold actions at Armavir and Stavropol, had raised high his prestige in the White army. General Denikin appointed him corps commander. The ranks of the Cossack cavalry swelled from an influx of volunteers out of the freshly liberated Kouban Cossack territory. Several Wrangel-trained officers, captains and majors in the 1st Cossack Division, had come up in grade and command and were to become Wrangel's chief commanders throughout the civil war. Those were the years that were to mark the end of an era: the end of great cavalry battles, with their charges, long marches, and that partnership of man and horse, known from times immemorial through the days of Ghenghis Khan, Saladin, the European knights, and on to Napoleon's Murat and Lee's Jeb Stuart.

Toporkov, Ulagai, Naumenko, Babiev, all Cossacks, all served in the World War and entered as captains or majors into the turmoil of the civil war.

Colonel Toporkov had risen from the ranks, starting his career as a private in a Cossack regiment. He lived simply, slept and ate with his men over whom he had complete authority. No order was too difficult for him to execute: He complied, cost what it might even if it meant heavy losses; he himself rode always in the van and pushed himself and his men to the limit of human endurance.

Colonel Ulagai was a Circassian Moslem of noble family. His attitude and impeccable manners reflected his background. Brave, a born cavalry leader, he showed the same brilliance as Murat of Napoleon fame. A highly sensitive and nervous nature made him at times difficult to deal with. His moods (probably the result of wounds received in combat) could vary from unrivaled élan to complete apathy. Beloved by his officers and men, he was the image of a knight of the Middle Ages, with all the same qualities and some of the defects.

Babiev, Wrangel's Jeb Stuart, was perhaps the most colorful figure. Good-looking, brave, and debonair, he had finished the war as a major, wounded and decorated with the St. George Cross. In the very early part of the civil war he was making his way home, riding unarmed when he ran into a Red army patrol. Ordered to get off his horse, he leaned down and tried to grab a soldier's rifle; a shot rang out, the bullet smashing his right arm. Babiev fell, but strangely enough — for in those early days no prisoners were taken — he was not finished off and was even taken to a hospital where he recovered, albeit with a paralyzed right arm. He managed to get away and join the White army. Undeterred by the loss of this right arm, he wielded his sword with the left, holding the reins in his teeth. His feats of horsemanship surprised even his Cossacks. Just as did Jeb Stuart, he loved what the French so aptly call "panache": good-looking horses, smart attire, buglers blowing gay marches. With that he also had an amazing flair for cavalry tactics; his rapid marches and smashing attacks were to Wrangel's taste. When, in the last months of the civil war, a shell brought an end to his dashing life, he was mourned by all his men and most of all by Wrangel, who had lost his best cavalry general.

Pursuing the enemy, Wrangel's cavalry corps surged far ahead. Again, his habit of riding alone from unit to unit nearly cost him his life. This was only one such incident among many before and afterwards: Riding with a captain, Prince Obolensky, formerly of his regiment in the Horse Guards, they came at night through a village on their way to join Colonel Ulagai's division. As they trotted through, they were met by intense rifle fire. As bullets whizzed about them, they galloped on, crossing a bridge as bullets ricocheted off the parapets. Wrangel was on a grey horse, a particularly good target; in spite of his orders, Obolensky spurred his horse alongside him, shielding him from the fire. Somehow they managed to gallop off with no damage.

The village of Blagodatnoye was to be the scene of another spectacular victory. The corps had run out of ammunition; the Reds, reinforced, reorganized and, as always in possession of vast firepower, were planning a counterattack. The messenger bearing an order to commence the attack at 0600 of the following day was intercepted by a Cossack patrol. Wrangel decided to forestall the

Red advance. Distributing all the ammunition available to the dismounted units of General Toporkov, he ordered them to act as a holding force. All other regiments were given over to General Ulagai with the order to concentrate on the left flank and to charge the enemy at 0500, one hour before the Reds' planned advance. To provide the holding force of General Toporkov with more firepower, all ammunition was taken away from the mounted units of General Ulagai, who were to charge with swords only. As the sun rose, General Ulagai marched his regiments into position and charged the enemy's infantry as it was in the process of deploying for their advance. The Reds were routed, sabred, and driven headlong into the river Kalaus, where many drowned.

Meanwhile, General Kazanovitch's infantry was under hard pressure and had suffered big casualties. Gambling with his previous success, Wrangel decided to rush to his aid, baring completely his own front in the hope that the Reds would not have had time to regroup.

The approach march and the battle are ably described by the artillery lieutenant Mamontov, himself a small cog in the war machine, but as is often the case the small cogs can picture most graphically the events as they occur.

"The village of Petrovskoye at 1700. We receive our orders: Tomorrow — rest, no combat, no marches. It was high time, for we had been in continuous combat. Lt. Korenev and I caught a sheep and handed it over to a farmer's wife to roast. I had my laundry done.

"At 2100 a new order: Saddle up; march out in 15 minutes. Well, that was our rest. We took back the unroasted sheep and I stuffed my wet laundry into the saddlebags, God knows when and where it could dry. It was getting dark. Later, much later, we were to learn that the order to rest was a trick. The Reds, on learning through their intelligence that our units were resting, availed themselves of the opportunity to recover and regroup. When at last they learned that we were gone, they feared another turning attack and remained in passive defence. Forty-eight hours later we had returned after a resounding victory and 120 kms. there and back.

"We marched all night, trotting and walking alternatively; we had no idea where we were going and why. Before dawn we stopped in a small ravine. We had covered 60 kms.

'No smoking, no talking.' That meant that we were close to the enemy. It was getting light and to our amazement we saw, some 300 yards away, Red infantrymen walking about on the opposite slope. It was still dark in the ravine and at first they did not see us. As it grew lighter, they finally spotted us and shots rang out. 'Mount up. Walk.'

"Around us were drawn up several columns of cavalry; they moved forward at a walk, not answering the Red fire which at first increased in volume then suddenly stopped. Seeing a huge cavalry mass in their rear (anywhere from 4000 to 5000 riders, not counting the horse artillery and the machine-gun units), the Red infantry broke in a panic. We started trotting.

"Our battery was going up the slope ahead of us, behind the Kouban Cossack regiment. The men of that regiment wore red bashlyks; *these contrasting sharply with the black burkas** and the white snow underfoot presented an unforgettable sight. We kept going, oblivious of the masses of surrendering infantrymen and baggage trains. Here and there a short engagement, a brief charge by a squadron, and on we would go, past whole fields of rifles surrendered bayonet down into the ground. Never again were we to see such masses of prisoners: We were in a sea of them; it was even getting out of proportion and dangerous. But on we went, mostly at a trot, and 18 kms. further came up against the last Red divisions about to make a stand at the foot of some hills. Here our whole corps went into one great charge. The ground throbbed under the hooves of thousands of galloping horses. Our battery galloped forward, although it really had no business there; we were simply driven headlong by our own enthusiasm.

"The defeat of the Reds was total; few escaped: Several Red divisions had been wiped out. We stopped for the night at the village of Sergeevka. Worn out, we flopped down to sleep. Somehow I woke up during the night, really by pure force of habit, as I was used to feeding my horse myself. Walking out of the house, I startled: The whole street was one mass of Red prisoners. One Cossack dozed, leaning on his rifle — the guard.

"On the morning, the whole corps took off back towards Petrovskoye. Between the mounted regiments walked huge columns of prisoners, 1000 men or so per column. A regiment of cavalry, a column of prisoners, another mounted regiment and so on. We had to return soon to Petrovskoye and to our front line, so when the cavalry trotted, the prisoners ran. Somewhere along the march, the regiments halted and formed a huge square. Alongside our four guns, three captured guns were drawn up, with prisoners riding as teamsters. Into this square Wrangel galloped in and, reining back his beautiful horse, took off his fur cap. In a strident voice he called out: 'Thank you, Eagles!'

"A thunderous hurrah answered him. The Red army teamster on one of the captured guns had torn off his cap and was yelling hurrah at the top of his voice. Was he also caught in the grandiose spell, or was he simply insuring his future — who knows!'"

After this victory and subsequent ones at Nikolina Balka, Predtechi, and Vinodelny, the enemy retreated east to avoid being driven into the swamp area of the river Manytsh. Availing himself of this opportunity and pressed to resolve the corps administrative and supply problem, Wrangel requested permission to visit headquarters at Ekaterinodar.

Wrangel was not impressed by what he saw there. Although warmly

* Hoods worn as scarves.
** Sleeveless coats of uncarded sheep wool.

received by General Denikin, who acquiesced to Wrangel's numerous requests, he was referred to the chief of staff General Romanovsky. There, however, Wrangel was met with polite yes and no answers, as he moved through the different sections of an enormous top-heavy staff, indifferent to pressing demands, but very busy with trivialities such as review of old regulations and other red tape.

Wrangel was also critical of the unbridled license reigning in town. It was the eve of the Kouban Cossack elections of their ataman, and senior Cossack officers had ridden in — among them General Pokrovsky and Colonel Shkouro. Every evening a crowd of drunken officers would descend upon the town's main hotel — bands blared loud music, wine flowed, and Shkouro and his partisan escort would gallop screaming and shooting down the main street. To Wrangel's surprise, General Denikin did not seem to object. Wrangel noted the demoralizing effect such orgies had on public opinion.

General Denikin was a scrupulously honest man of ascetic habits, yet for some reason he closed his eyes on the behavior of some of his senior commanders: Generals Mai-Maivsky and Borovsky drank; Shkouro, first partisan leader, subsequently corps commander, looted lustily; General Pokrovsky, able but ruthless, was a sadist who delighted in watching prisoners being hanged and encouraged massacres. Disgusted at what he saw, Wrangel tried to cut short his stay at headquarters, chaffing at the staff's delay in solving his administrative problems.

In Wrangel's absence fighting had resumed and his subordinate General Ulagai had again inflicted severe casualties on the enemy, using maneuver and shock, the recipe for previous victories. On arrival Wrangel ordered the corps to bivouac, as after weeks and even months the horses needed reshoeing. They were not due to rest for long.

South of them the Red army had massed against the infantry units of General Kazanovitch who in a series of engagements had suffered very heavy casualties. Again, as previously at Spitzevka, Wrangel decided to go to his aid.

Meanwhile, Allied military missions, British and French, had arrived to negotiate military assistance to the White army. Denikin wanted to show them the White army in action. He had planned originally to take the missions to General Kazanovitch's units. These were the general's favorite regiments, the founders of the White army with whom the General had started out in the winter of 1918. However, they were now retreating under heavy pressure and with heavy losses. Clearly this was not the moment to show them off.

Denikin got Wrangel on the telephone and asked if he could bring over the missions. "What can you show them?" he asked. Never at a loss for an answer, Wrangel responded: "How we pound the Reds. Do try and arrive tonight so as to be able to march with the troops."

Aside from his military ability, Wrangel had a flair for showmanship — most talented commanders know how to play this card. In World War II Rommel and Montgomery outdid each other in showmanship, which added a measure to their successes.

At night Wrangel prepared the corps directive, had it translated into English and French, and had maps and explanations added to it. An honor guard of Cossacks met the commanding general's train; horses were ready for the staff and the visitors. Leaving Colonel Babiev and a small covering force at Petrovskoye, Wrangel marched out with Denikin, his staff, the Allied mission, and the column of cavalry. The advance guard of General Toporkov had preceded them.

A young, newly promoted Colonel Lebedev rode at the head of his regiment. "As the sun tried to rise among rain laden clouds and made the puddles glisten, set off against the dark oozing mud of the unpaved road, our regiment marched off. Draped in their burkas, their astrakhan caps covered by bashlyks, the Cossacks rode, looking from a distance like monks of some obscure order.

"The horses slithered about in the mud and I wondered how the plastounes* could possibly march through that deep going. Occasionally we would dismount and give a hand to push some machine-gun cart mired to its axle. I wished the French and English missions following somewhere behind a 'pleasant ride.' It was not long before we saw wagons and carts abandoned; evidently General Toporkov, impetuous as always and leading the vanguard, had taken the horses as extra 'horsepower' for his artillery guns pulled by teams of exhausted horses. We rode on . . . ."

After ten hours of marching General Denikin, his staff, and the Allied missions could hardly hold themselves in the saddle: They had not eaten these last twelve hours and by then were dead beat, but Wrangel still pressed on, marching around the enemy's flank.

Finally the stage was set: Placing Denikin and his entourage on a good observation post, Wrangel galloped off, marshaling the regiments into position ready to attack. Firing picked up as artillery and machine guns opened up on the advancing Cossack formations.

Colonel Lebedev: "My regiment headed towards the river bank, beyond which were the Red lines, and still further a village. We crossed the river and I saw the fanion of General Toporkov; he and a few of his staff were standing by the river crossing. As we rode up the long slope beyond the river,

* Cossack infantry.

I looked back and saw General Toporkov and another rider trotting towards us; the other rider — he turned out to be General Wrangel — put his horse to the gallop. We had topped the rise; the Red lines were in front of us and bullets flew. I heard Wrangel's hoarse voice call out: 'Colonel Lebedev, show us that you earned your colonel's epaulets — charge straight ahead!'

"Everything seemed to go blank. I heard myself yelling commands and felt myself drawing my sword. The squadrons deployed and off we went. The going was terrible and the fire intense: horses slipped, stumbled and fell, but we went on and after what seemed an interminable gallop we crashed into their lines; cutting our way through, we thundered into the village as the Reds fell, fled or surrendered. . . ."

Cut off, surrounded, the Reds yielded over a thousand prisoners, twelve guns, sixty-five machine guns, and an immense war booty. The forces of General Kazanovitch, which had been under pressure, were relieved; it was again a major victory.

Again after a long ride which left riders and horses exhausted, Wrangel returned to the railroad station to find Denikin, his staff, and the Allied missions at dinner. He was met by cheers. When finally the visitors' train had left and Wrangel had issued directives for the next day, he went to bed. He had been up forty hours and ridden over one hundred kilometers.

Denikin now ordered Wrangel to take over the command of an army group comprising 1st Army Corps, 1st Cavalry Corps, 1st Kouban Cossack Division, and a separate detachment under General Stankevitch. The mission was to pursue the defeated enemy who was retreating along two different routes, one east and the other southeast. Wrangel's lieutenants Ulagai, Toporkov, Babiev, now divisional commanders, operated on their own in a manner worthy of their commander and teacher. A series of engagements culminated in the capture of Sviaty Krest, the base of the Taman Red army. A great war booty fell to them.

It was at this time that a new general reported to Wrangel for an assignment. General Chatilov, who was to become Wrangel's most trusted assistant and close friend, had known Wrangel in the Russo-Japanese War where they had both fought in the same Cossack unit as young lieutenants. Subsequently their paths went different ways and they had only met briefly. Fragments of Chatilov's memoirs give an unusual and striking description of Wrangel.

"I spent only a few days in Ekaterinodar" wrote General Chatilov, who had made his way there from the Caucasus. "In the later part of December I received a cable from General Wrangel asking if I was interested in an assignment with him. A similar request had been made to Staff Headquarters. General Romanovsky gave his assent; I got my things together and headed through Stavropol for General Wrangel's headquarters.

"An assignment with my old war comrade and friend was good news. I left Ekaterinodar on Dec. 30 and reached Stavropol on the 31st. There I learned that Wrangel's headquarters were in Petrovskoye. It took us a long time to get there, although the village lay on the rail line from Stavropol. It took a whole day until a train was assembled for Petrovskoye. We traveled slowly, stopping for hours on end at each station until we finally reached our destination. I reported immediately at Wrangel's headquarters.

"I found him dictating orders to his young chief of staff Colonel Sokolovsky. This was our first meeting in many years, as we had been assigned during the War to widely separate areas of our enormous front. I had hoped in 1915 to see him again as I had been offered the command of a regiment in General Krymov's division where Wrangel already commanded the Nertchinsk Cossack regiment. However, nothing came of it as my turn in seniority had not yet come.

"Meeting my friend again, I did not even have a chance to take a good look at him. Finishing his dictation to Sokolovsky, Wrangel walked quickly up to me and embraced me. He said that I had arrived more than on time. Right then he started explaining to me the general situation at the front, his immediate objective and the orders issued to the individual units. Absorbed in studying the situation map, I followed on it the different steps outlined by him. He then told me that he was making me commander of the army group's central sector and giving me permanent command of the 1st Cavalry Division, which he himself had commanded only a short while before. He said that the advance was to be resumed the next day and that I should hurry and get to my new headquarters. Then Wrangel turned to Colonel Sokolovsky and started checking with him the prepared orders of the day. These were signed by him and mimeographed for distribution. I received my division's orders for the next day's action.

"I must admit that my head was dizzy from absorbing all of this within a few minutes. Meeting my friend, already a hero on the strength of his past victories in the last campaign, my complete surprise at the important assignment and the haste with which I was to take over this command all stirred me up considerably. I was rather baffled at not having had the opportunity to say even a few personal words to my old friend and presently my new commander — words that would serve as a hyphen in those years that we had not seen each other. Seeing my somewhat perturbed looks, Wrangel turned to me and asked what was bothering me.

"'Look,' he said, "you will have no trouble with your assignment. Both the divisions* are composed of first-rate units and among your subordinates you

* Chatilov was to be acting corps commander before the return of General Pokrovsky.

will meet extremely brave and capable commanders.'

"I answered that this was not part of my worry, rather the fact that I may not come up to his expectations.

" 'I know more about you than you think,' he said. 'Your record in the Caucasus and your work during the revolution are well known to me from accounts of people who saw you in action. I would not request you here and give you an important assignment on the strength of our past friendship alone. The only thing I caution you about is to keep in touch with me by all means possible. Communications are our weak spot.'

"Taking a look at his watch, he said that we had chatted long enough and that I had to hurry if I wanted to reach my headquarters by dawn. I said goodbye to my friend and, loading my suitcase and saddle into a cart, set forth towards my headquarters.

"This meeting with Wrangel was typical in that it showed facets of his character. Although we had been friends for many years and had much to recall, he was not to be distracted from his task; the next day's operation absorbed him totally. At other times, when his mind was free, he could be very talkative and always seeking to probe the mind of his conversation partner. He even had a mannerism of repeating 'what' as if he had not heard right, encouraging the other person to speak further on the subject. He respected other opinion and was far from being obstinate in his decisions.

"As I drove along studying my orders, I involuntarily lapsed into the details of my meeting with Wrangel. I was amazed at his attitude towards the junior officers in his staff. In front of me he queried them on matters of primary importance and seemed to listen with great attention to their answers. His remarkable friendly casualness with his subordinates was completely genuine. Frankly, I had expected to see something different. In his youth his frankness was reflected in very trenchant ways of expressing himself and in the present explosive and unruly times I feared that these would have evolved into harshness. I really expected to serve under a difficult commander and was pleasantly surprised to meet a sympathetic and extremely uncomplicated person. On the other hand, going over his directives I was struck by their clarity and conciseness. Nothing was superfluous, but nothing was omitted. Our brief meeting sufficed for me to estimate him fully."

Sviaty Krest having been captured, Wrangel sent Chatilov with the combined 1st Cavalry and 1st Kouban Cossack Division in twin prongs along the rail line Sviaty Krest-Georgievsky and in the direction from Novoselts towards Obulnoye. The 1st Army Corps proceeded from Alexandrovsk towards the station of Alexandria. General Liakhov pressed the enemy towards the Caucasian Spas (Mineralnya Vody). The enemy at Georgievsky was nearly completely surrounded. By January 8, 1919, Chatilov took that town, inflicting a crushing defeat on the Reds. The enemy retreated in complete disorder, pursued by the 1st Cavalry Corps of General Pokrovsky. In twelve days the corps marched and fought three hundred and fifty kilometers. Thirty-one thousand prisoners, eight armored trains, two hundred guns, and three hundred machine guns fell to the Whites, along with innumerable baggage trains with everything from loot to ammunition.

The Northern Caucasus was liberated.

A. Filimonov, ataman of the Kouban Cossacks: "The liberation of the northern Caucasus had brought Wrangel's popularity among the Cossacks to its zenith; village after village elected him as its elder. The Kouban Cossack Rada made him and his family permanent and hereditary Cossack citizens of the village of Konstantinovskaya. Wishing to identify himself fully with the Cossacks at his command, Wrangel moved there with his family.

"How often we saw Baroness Olga Wrangel with her children, riding back from her field or orchard in a plain farmer's cart in lively conversation with the old Cossack coachman. This natural and unfeigned ability to get along with the village neighbors soon made her popular and enhanced even further her husband's prestige."

Wrangel's son, Peter, aged ten, played with the Cossack children, dressed as they were in astrakhan hat and loose tunic. Each morning mounting his pony, accompanied by a Cossack, he would ride ten miles to the railway station and bring back the morning mail. Strapped in his Cossack uniform, dagger at the belt, he was in the eyes of the Cossacks one of their children.

The victories at Urupskaya, Spitzevka, and Stavropol were for Wrangel what Rivoli, Arcole, and Lodi had been for Napoleon in his initial campaigns. Where Napoleon charged in front of his grenadiers, French tricolor in hand at the Arcole Bridge, Wrangel galloped with drawn sword at the head of his squadrons bursting into Stravropol. Both Napoleon and Wrangel used maneuver and shock; long fast marches, then shattering blows.

During this campaign, however, a new enemy had appeared, an enemy that inflicted on White and Red alike crushing losses far in excess of anything that cannon or machine gun had been able to do. Typhus, which started in the disorderly and dirty hordes of the Reds, soon engulfed the White army. The epidemic reached unheard-of proportions. Whole trains of dead and dying clogged the stations. Men hopelessly sick wandered around in a daze, then lay down and died. Entering a signal box at one of the railroad stations, Wrangel saw in the small room eight men lying shoulder to shoulder; seven were dead and one was dying — clasped to his breast was a mangy, half-starved dog. Soon Wrangel himself was to fall prey to the dreadful disease.

At one of the liberated Terek Cossack villages Wrangel got talking to a few Cossack boys aged ten and twelve, all carrying rifles. "What are you boys up to?" asked Wrangel. "Shooting Reds," answered one little fellow: "There are lots of them hiding in the marshes — I bagged seven of them yesterday." Wrangel's reaction was one of horror. As he himself said later: "Never during the whole civil war did the whole horror of that conflict strike me so forcibly!"

6

The Seeds of Failure

THE GREAT VICTORIES THEMSELVES PUT the question: What to do next? General Denikin called together a conference to which Wrangel and his chief of staff Yusefovitch were invited. He proposed concentrating all main forces in the Don basin region and aiming the main thrust at Kharkov and subsequently Moscow. On the right flank only a covering force was to be left on the Manytsh river. This plan of action, subsequently known as the Moscow Directive, was eventually to lead the White army to disaster. Wrangel and his chief of staff both objected strongly. Their idea was to head towards Tsaritsyn (later called Stalingrad, still later Volgograd) on the Volga River, hence across the river east to join another White army under Admiral Koltchak. This army, which had started out from Siberia, was moving west. Joining hands, the two armies would act as pincers squeezing the Red forces.

All the way west, Poland, newly independent, was also fighting the Reds. Menacing these from the north was the smaller White army of General Yudenitch. A ring of steel was to crush the Communist menace, while the rear would be organized, law and order restored, land and judical reforms introduced, and a stop put to the violence, lawlessness, and marauding which threatened to offset the initial goodwill of liberated territories.

Denikin thought otherwise. Neglecting to see the problem as a whole, focusing his total attention on the faraway Kremlin walls, he left Koltchak's army to its fate and subsequent defeat. The result of that eventual defeat was the accumulation of new and still greater masses for the Red army which, though at first contained and defeated, finally crushed Denikin's forces.

The conference sowed the first seeds of discord between Denikin and Wrangel. Their two opposite characters were to clash in roles worthy of a Greek tragedy. Denikin was of humble origin; his father was a peasant who had risen through the ranks from private to major, no small feat in the Russia of the nineteenth century. Desperately poor, living off his small army pay, and supporting his family, Denikin struggled slowly, stubbornly, and painfully up the ladder of the military hierarchy. A good Japanese War record was followed by an outstanding performance in World War I as an infantry division commander. Of liberal leaning, he had welcomed the Russian Revolution, seeing in it dreams of social justice. It did not take him long to see the dream shattered and the evil genie leaping out of Pandora's box. He was one of the few senior officers to react and try to stop the abuses. When the Russian army disintegrated, he was among the first to join the White army. At General Kornilov's death it was he who led the White army on an epic march out of the Red encirclement. Unanimously he was chosen to be the new commander in chief, and then the chief of state of the liberated territories.

But as is often the case with self-made men upon whom power is thrust, the liberal Denikin became a die-hard conservative. His slogan was "Russia, one and undivided." Poland and Georgia, both of which had acquired their independence, were looked upon almost as enemies; and Cossacks, on whose territory the White army had fought and who provided a major portion of the combatants, were regarded as traitors and renegades when they insisted on their old rights of self-government. Denikin's conservatism, however, did not reach out to former aristocrats, Guards, or cavalry officers, whom he regarded with the distrust born of an inferiority complex.

Short, dowdy in a badly cut khaki uniform and down-at-the-heel boots,* he cut an unprepossessing figure. In an army where a good half were cavalrymen and each Cossack a born rider, Denikin rode badly and had been known to fall off a horse while walking on parade.** Burdened as he was with state duties and administration problems, he rarely visited the combat troops; many of these did not even know what he looked like. His main shortcoming, however, was the complete lack of that charisma which every great military leader from Julius Caesar to Napoleon possessed and used to fire men's hearts and stir their imaginations.

Lieutenant Mamontov, the young artilleryman whose diaries often provide vivid accounts of men and events, described one of Denikin's appearances. "We had been drawn up in a huge square; one side the regular cavalry, one side the Don Cossacks, the Kouban and Terek Cossacks making up the other facets. General Denikin had flown in and was giving us a speech. It was windy and we could not hear too well. What we did hear was long-winded and dull. What was needed was Wrangel in his Cossack uniform on his splendid mount, reining his horse in and shouting a few words, as he did then by Spitzevka. That would have fired the Cossacks, but not the dowdy, melancholy figure of Denikin with his long and incomprehensible discourse."

Wrangel presented a striking contrast. Tall, good-looking, with the casual polish of the guards cavalry officer, he presented a striking figure. An excellent horseman, always well mounted and wearing his Cossack uniform with the studied negligence of the Djiguit (the Caucasian rough rider), Wrangel iden-

---

* They can be seen in the museum Rodina in New Jersey.
** Major Elaguin, commander of Denikin's service squadron.

tified himself with his Cossack troops whom he commanded from the forward line as would do the German Field Marshal Rommel some twenty years later in the African desert.

How well he identified himself with his men can be seen from an account of two young lieutenants from a White infantry unit. "We had marched into a village and dead beat had fallen asleep in a farmhouse. As we woke up later in the afternoon we heard a commotion outside. Peering from the window, we saw to our horror Red infantry marching in. Our unit had gone and we had been left behind. Pulling on our boots, we rushed out of the back door and made our way through the garden into the fields beyond. It was getting dark. We walked a long way until we reached a road; there were cornfields on both sides. We heard the clatter of horses' hooves and presently saw a troop of riders. It was too dark to tell who they were. We crouched at the edge of the cornfield, ready to dash into it if the riders proved to be Reds. On they rode past us; we could distinguish the burkas and the sheepskin hats—Cossacks? Perhaps, but some of the Reds were Cossacks too. As the last rider filed past, one of us called out, 'Who are you? What unit?' Turning nonchalantly in his saddle and hardly giving us a look, the Cossack tossed out: 'We are the Wrangels!' "

Captain Meller-Zakomelsky on Wrangel's divisional staff: "It was in the windswept steppes around Stavropol. Our small staff was riding behind General Wrangel when we met a lonely Cossack leading a lame horse. Seeing us, he stopped at attention.

" 'Hello, Eagle,' called out Wrangel.

"No answer: either shell-shocked or upset about his horse, the Cossack stared sullenly ahead.

" 'Hello, Cossack!' repeated the General.

"Still silence.

" 'Hello, you dumb bastard!' roared Wrangel.

"The Cossack suddenly came to and answered according to regulations: 'Greetings, Your Excellency!'

"Wrangel burst out laughing, so did we all. Suddenly the Cossack's morose features broke into a wide grin. Wrangel rode up to him and engaged him in familiar conversation. . . ."

Along with this flair, Wrangel's international background, a liberal education, and an engineer's practical outlook allowed him to see problems over and above the immediate military situation. He knew that the White cause could not prevail on the strength of military successes alone. He saw that the slogan "Russia, one and undivided" could hardly satisfy the peasant whose immediate preoccupation was ownership of land and its peaceful exploitation. Nor could the worker be lured by such high-sounding phrases, living as he was in misery and incertitude. Expropriation and requisition had given place to pillage and marauding. To win, law, justice, and order had to march alongside military successes.

In contrast to Denikin, Wrangel had no complexes. He simply had neither reason nor occasion to develop any. A happy childhood, a liberal education, a rapid military career, a brilliant social life, a happy family life, had left him unscarred. Of independent and unfettered mind, he said what he thought to anyone who wanted or did not want to hear. His reports to headquarters, couched often in trenchant form, first baffled Denikin, then irritated him, and finally plunged him into a state of morbid suspicion. . . .

But this came later on. Right then Denikin did not know how to applaud enough Wrangel's meteoric successes. In the next few days he came close to losing his subordinate, who was felled by the all-pervading typhus.

Wrangel fell ill during one of his inspection trips and was taken to Kislovodsk where the best medical authorities available were called to his side. The sickness took a particularly acute form and his life was despaired of. While being given the last rites, he came to, but lapsed into unconsciousness a few minutes later. For sixteen days he hovered between life and death. His wife had come over from Ekaterinodar and, as an experienced nurse, tended him day and night. Then, on the seventeenth day, suddenly the temperature fell and Wrangel was on the way to a slow but complete recovery.

During his sickness and his long convalescence, from General Denikin to soldiers and civilians alike, all made every effort to help by showering gifts and attention on the popular general. Wrangel himself summarized his recovery by attributing it to their kindness and care as well as to the predominant and self-less role of his wife who had stayed by his side through the critical stages of the sickness.

While Wrangel was recovering, his dire prophecies were coming true. The Soviet 10th Army coming west from Tsaritsyn moved against the flank and rear of the White army and by mid-April was threatening Rostov.

On the night of April 13th Wrangel, still convalescent, was awakened during the night. General Romanovsky, chief of staff, and his quartermaster general were there to see him. News from the Manytsh front was disastrous; the enemy was now threatening to cut the White army in two. Romanovsky proposed that Wrangel take command of a number of troops hastily assembled and improvise his own new staff. Wrangel refused. He said the scratch pack of troops was insufficient for a major operation and that to improvise a new head-quarters with unknown quantity and quality was beyond his means. Wrangel pointed out how a strong force of cavalry could be put together from the units under his command and with his permanent staff.

Romanovsky said, "Your refusal will force the commander in chief himself to take the Manytsh command which he offered you." Wrangel replied that this would be all to the good as the commander in chief could move troops at his will, whereas he would have to make do with whatever was given him.

Romanovsky and his quartermaster general departed in a huff. Wrangel returned to his headquarters in Rostov.

Taking over command on the threatened sector Denikin soon realized that what he had at hand was not enough to do the job. Cavalry divisions were pulled in piecemeal from Wrangel's command and from the Caucasus: seven cavalry divisions, more than Wrangel had originally proposed, were concentrated on the banks of the Manytsh. General Pokrovsky and his cavalry corps had managed to force the Reds behind the Manytsh. General Chatilov crossed over twice but was forced back with heavy losses. The riverbed was swampy; there were no ways to cross over the artillery, and the one ford was strongly held by the Reds. The White operations were fragmented; a strong hand to govern the operations was lacking.

Still half sick and his legs swollen, Wrangel arrived at Supreme Headquarters. General Denikin complained bitterly that with all that cavalry nothing had been done. To Wrangel's question who commanded this mass of cavalry, Denikin replied that individual corps and divisional commanders reported to him, but that there was no one in overall command. No one was to be "offended." This weakness of General Denikin vis-a-vis his subordinates was always to appear as a dangerous crack in the edifice of the White army; he seemed to wink at the drunken orgies of General Mai-Maivsky, the looting of Shkouro, and the merciless massacres of General Pokrovsky.

Denikin asked Wrangel to take over the whole operation. Wrangel agreed and proceeded to make contact with the troops in action. First he drove over to the infantry units of General Mai-Maivsky, the original regiments that had given birth to the White army. Under heavy enemy pressure they were now barely holding their own and bleeding to death. Walking along the front line under heavy fire, stopping casually here and there to ask a question or to encourage a soldier, Wrangel lost one orderly officer and another was wounded. But morale went up, and a successful counterattack with the men of the Kornilov regiment walking upright into the teeth of enemy machine-gun fire restored the situation. Moving his headquarters to the Manytsh river Wrangel met the individual commanders and, having observed the enemy positions from atop a steeple, decided on an unusual and daring plan.

To force the river at the two available fords at Velikokniajeskaya and nearby at Baranikovskaya was impossible; heavily fortified with trenches and gun emplacements, it would have entailed disproportionate losses. At other places the Manytsh river, saline and swampy, offered no footing for artillery or passage for the machine-gun carts. On two previous attempts while fording it with his cavalry division Chatilov had lost a number of horses; dauntlessly he had charged the Reds and cleared the ford at Baranikovskaya, allowing him to bring over artillery and machine guns, but his forces were not sufficient to do the job and after two unsuccessful attempts he had to cross back. His losses were heavy.

In the Cossack villages the individual farmhouses were surrounded by picket fences; Wrangel decided to pull down the fences and build transportable shields which would rest in the mud of the river bottom and allow the artillery to ford the river. His immediate entourage doubted the feasibility of this plan, but Wrangel ordered an engineering company to build a trial shield, sink it in a nearby swamp, and have a trial run with guns and caissons—it worked.

Seven and a half White cavalry divisions were now concentrated on the Manytsh. Most of the regiments had fought under Wrangel's command during the previous campaign; his arrival was met with thunderous hurrahs, and as he inspected the troops, he stopped to chat with officers and men. The forcing of the Manytsh was planned for the night of May 4th. During the morning a piece of good news had arrived. One hundred twenty kilometers east the cavalry corps of General Ulagai had gained a smashing victory over a corps of Red cavalry. Six Cossack regiments clashed with six regiments of Red cavalry, the last massive cavalry battle in history, reminiscent of the battle of Mars Latour when Prussian and French cavalry divisions fought it out in the war of 1870. In our age of jet aircraft, rockets, and pushbutton warfare, it is difficult to visualize such a scene: the steppe stretching out to the horizon, the clouds of dust raised by the multitude of galloping horses, the flash of thousands of sword blades; the screams and rage and pain, the thunderous hurrahs of the victors, the oaths of the vanquished; and in the midst of the confusion General Ulagai, the Russian version of Marshal Murat, mounted, sword in hand, marshaling his squadrons, deploying, charging, reforming, and charging again. Everything depended on him and he was everywhere at the right moment. The rout of Tovarishch Dumenko's cavalry corps with the loss of all its artillery earned the Circassian General Ulagai a place among the great cavalry leaders of all times.

The crossing of the Manytsh started that same evening. First crossed the scouting parties and supporting squadrons, and at dawn of the 5th the cavalry corps.

Lieutenant de Korvey riding with one of the batteries remembered: "We marched at night and by dawn had come to the crossing. The sun had risen, and as we topped a rise, I saw a huge mass of cavalry drawn up on this side of the Manytsh which itself was covered with a low bank of fog. Into this fog would ride one by one the individual regiments in long columns of twos. A band was playing gay cavalry marches. At the head of one of the regiments a commander rode standing up on top of his saddle; for an instant, as his horse disappeared into the fog, he could be seen towering above it, looking like a miracle man walking on clouds; then too he vanished into the milky mist."

The sight must have been unforgettable, for Wrangel also remembered it vividly in his memoirs: "I reached the ford when the 1st Corps was completing its crossing. The muddy, lazy flowing saline Manytsh glistened under the sun. On the other side, stretching endlessly, lay the steppe, dotted here and there with large salt licks. There squadrons could be seen deployed in Lava,* intermittent rifle fire was heard. Our cavalry regiments drawn out in a long column, like some black snake, were winding down towards the river crossing. Colored squadron fanions waved above them. The brass of the regimental bugles flashed in the sun. On the southern shore, grouped around smoking fires, Cossack horsemen in colorful uniforms waited for their turn to cross over.

"Kouban, Terek, Astrakhan Cossacks, Moslem Circassians, and Buddhist Kalmyks, units representing all the peoples of the Caucasus and the Don steppe, a mass of horsemen reminiscent of bygone eras; of Napoleon wars, or even much further back, of Ghenghis Khan's and Tamerlane's mounted cohorts."

Chatilov's corps followed the river bank, Pokrovsky on his right, on both sides of the road leading to Velikoknyajhevskaya. Again Chatilov charged and again he cleared the Baranikovskaya crossing, allowing further units to come over the the north bank. With batteries unlimbering and firing over open sights, the regiments charged over and over again. Chatilov wrote: "Wrangel's impulse and intensity of purpose could be felt everywhere. No sooner had we finished with one group of the enemy than an order would come flying in from him, directing us at another group."

The White army had a few aircraft, beaten-up Nieuports and Spads; Wrangel mobilized them into coordinated action with the cavalry, a prelude of World War II Blitzkrieg and air-ground combination of the German panzers.* Reconnaisance flights landed right on the steppes' smooth surface whenever they saw the St. George black and orange fanion of Wrangel's headquarters. They reported direct with no intermediate loss of time. Not content with reconnaisance, Wrangel had them also strafing the Red reserves as they concentrated for counterattack.

---

* Deployed cossack mounted formation.

* The German author Dzwinger wrote extensively about the cavalry tactics of Wrangel; his writings were not lost on the embryo of the German general staff post World War I.

Night fell on the battlefield; the regiments stayed where darkness had overtaken them. It was cold; it was impossible to light fires on the steppe devoid of all vegetation; horses could not be watered as the only water available was salty.

The next day the advance continued and by 1700 the final attack was to take place. A huge hayrick served as Wrangel's observation post, from which he watched Chatilov's and Pokrovsky's regiments move forward. But suddenly gunfire was heard from the extreme right and large masses of Red cavalry appeared, attempting to outflank Wrangel's forces. His only reserve was a mixed brigade of Astrakhan Cossacks and Moslem Circassians, weak in numbers and lacking experience. As this brigade deployed, it came under accurate and murderous artillery fire. The commanding general was wounded; the brigade stampeded and galloped back towards the river crossing, threatening to engulf other units in its flight. Jumping down from his haystack, Wrangel got in his staff car and raced towards Pokrovsky's corps, which was already on its way, attacking towards Velikoknyajhevskaya. Stopping the corps, he turned part of it against the Red cavalry. Pokrovsky's regiments, all old-time combatants under Wrangel's command, turned, reformed, and attacked, stemming the tide in a series of hard fights, but the final blow had again to be postponed in spite of Chatilov's success on the left.

Again the regiments spent the night in the open and in a precarious position; they were surrounded by the enemy with one narrow river crossing behind them. Wrangel's escort had occupied the river crossing where disorganized regiments of the Astrakhan brigade were gathering; they had orders to shoot on the spot any deserters or panic mongers. With dawn the battle resumed; the men had had no warm food in three days, and the horses, lacking water, could hardly move; with iron determination Wrangel drove his forces for the final effort.

By the afternoon he had enlarged his base and the final push had to be made, for it was getting late and only a couple of hours of daylight remained. The main thrust was to be directed along the river bank straight at the village. General Chatilov's forces included the 1st Cavalry Division with which Wrangel had started out. Wrangel personally inspected the regiments and addressed the men. "I shall watch my old division attack — I hope you will reaffirm your past glory." Hurrahs answered him.

The regimental colors were unfurled and buglers were ordered to play regimental marches. Everything was done to create the maximum psychological effect for the final showdown. Chatilov sent his batteries forward and ordered them to fire over open sights. The six regiments were drawn up in a staggered formation and at Chatilov's signal moved off at a trot. Turning for a final look, Chatilov saw Wrangel slowly riding off. After the battle he asked him why he had not stayed to watch the attack.

"It was enough for me to see your pattern of attack, the position of the different commanders and the formations of the regiments — I knew we had the enemy beat!"

Chatilov's Cossacks were now galloping. As they topped a rise, they were met by withering machine-gun and heavy, accurate artillery fire. Horses fell; men tumbled as shrapnel burst overhead, showering the galloping lines of horsemen. But there was no stopping; they rushed into Velikoknyajhevskaya, sabering all in front of them. Red infantry leaving their trenches sought safety in flight; artillery batteries surrendered or were abandoned as the crews fled in panic. Darkness only stopped the victorious squadrons.

As the attack proceeded, Wrangel, changing his horse for automobile, drove to Pokrovsky, whose regiments had met hard going, having to tackle simultaneously Red cavalry and infantry; he suffered heavy losses but managed to hang on long enough for Chatilov to achieve the victory. There again Russian aircraft helped by strafing the Red cavalry formations.

Fifteen thousand prisoners were taken along with fifty-five guns and one hundred and fifty machine guns.

Guarded by one or two Cossacks, whole columns of prisoners marched back. Wounded Cossacks were riding back, telling excitedly how they had won the day. The White losses were heavy, particularly on command level where regimental, brigade, and divisional commanders, following Wrangel's example, rode in the van of their troops.

Denikin, who had witnessed the final attack from across the river, said: "In all the war I had never seen such intense artillery fire."

Velikoknyajhevskaya was a large civilian center. Wrangel was determined that the troops would not get out of hand. That same evening five Circassians caught plundering were brought over to headquarters. Wrangel had them court-martialed. Convicted, they were hanged, and their bodies were left hanging several days both as a warning to other would-be plunderers and as a sign to the civilian population that it was to be safe from all excesses. As Wrangel and Denikin drove by the next morning, the latter, seeing the hanged, turned to Wrangel with a questioning look. "Caught in the act of plundering!" responded Wrangel. Denikin silently turned away; perhaps he felt a hidden rebuke in Wrangel's curt answer — a rebuke for his tolerant attitude to his own senior "marauders."

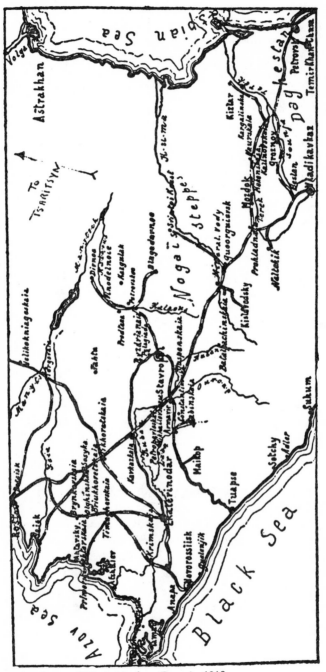

The Theatre of War in Northern Caucasia, 1918.

7

The Dash to the Volga — Tsaritsyn

THE ROAD TO TSARITSYN AND the Volga was open—three hundred kilometers over a steppe partly devoid of water. A rail line ran from Velikoknyajhevskaya to Tsaritsyn. The retreating Reds had blown up bridges and viaducts, making this line useless for transport. Wrangel was ordered to take Tsaritsyn. To Denikin's question how long it would take him, Wrangel answered that it would take him three weeks, but that without infantry and sufficient artillery he had no hope of storming the city. Denikin promised to have those forces available.*

Three cavalry corps—Pokrovsky, Ulagai, Chatilov—started out in pursuit of the Reds.

Wrangel had two options: One was to halt his troops; the other was to pursue relentlessly the Reds in the direction of Tsaritsyn. The first plan had the advantage of giving the troops a well-deserved rest after the strenuous fighting along the Manytsh as well as time to arrange the supply problem, but it also allowed time for the Reds to regroup and organize successive lines of defense.

Wrangel chose the first option, as he estimated that he could reach Tsaritsyn in three weeks, during which time the railroad could be repaired and the promised infantry, artillery, and technical equipment moved up.

The cavalry had to move across the steppe almost devoid of water** (in the area of Jutovochervlennaya there was no water at all and it had to be carried in barrels). Some days horses were not watered for two days and the Cossacks went without bread for ten days. Local supplies were nonexistent: whatever had not been taken by the Reds had been destroyed; cattle had been driven off, and supplies of hay burned. The enemy systematically destroyed the rail line,

* There were now three White armies in the south of Russia: the Volunteer army operating in the Don basin; the Don Cossack army; and the newly formed army of Wrangel, called the Caucasian army.

** In World War II, the Germans faced the same difficulties in their advance towards Stalingrad (Tsaritsyn), and when they were defeated and some units managed to break out of the Soviet encirclement, one man only was known to have made his way back—all others perished on the way.

not only blowing up the bridges but also demolishing the stations and water towers and shipping off whole segments of rails.

But the advance went on: Pokrovsky along what remained of the rail line, Ulagai on his right, and Chatilov in reserve.* Another corps of Don Cossacks was to swing left and, disposing of the Red forces active between the rivers Don and Sal, join up with the army of the Don, leaving Wrangel with the previously mentioned three corps of cavalry, a brigade of Kouban Cossack infantry, and a weak 6th Infantry Division. The only automobile available was a small, battered Ford. When the tires gave out, cord was wound around the wheels. Most of the time Wrangel rode his horses with the units of Chatilov's corps.

On May 15th Ulagai took Kotelnikova halfway to Tsaritsyn. Pokrovsky crossed the small river Aksai and routed the Reds at Verkhne-Iablochnogo. The Reds however reacted and for the first time counterattacked en masse. The 6th Infantry Division marching along the rail line was overrun by a strong force of infantry and cavalry and was almost totally destroyed, losing its artillery. The commanding general Patrikeef and his staff were cut down to a man. The Cossack cavalry division of General Babiev rushed to the rescue but had to withdraw also. At this moment General Ulagai appeared at the scene with his staff. Gathering whatever units were available, including his escort, he charged the Reds, himself in the van. He recaptured the guns and forced the Reds to withdraw.

On May 20th Pokrovsky and Ulagai reached the Esaul Aksai River. It was heavily fortified and strongly defended. Here General Pokrovsky proved his military qualities. Although he lacked the cavalry drive of Ulagai, he possessed a unique stubbornness in achieving his objective and knew how to handle infantry. Where Ulagai failed in his efforts to dislodge the enemy from his positions, Pokrovsky broke through, using combined infantry and cavalry attacks. Following up the breakthrough he drove the Reds for fifty kilometers until he came up again against fresh and strong Red forces. By then the condition of his horses was such that he had to turn back. Total absence of forage forced his men to cut grass in the steppe and feed it to the exhausted horses. Wrangel's last reserve, Chatilov's corps, was pushed into the gap between Pokrovsky and Ulagai. This last effort was successful and the Reds broke.

Wrangel called Headquarters: "Trying to keep in touch with my cavalry units, I set out in the only automobile available. Halfway I had to turn back as the car broke down. Neither at army or corps level do we have a single automobile. As we have no other means of communication, I am no longer able to control operations. Our successes bought with much blood will come to

---

* During subsequent operations the corps were regrouped: Ulagai along the rail line and Pokrovsky on his left echeloned forward.

naught and this while at Headquarters innumerable staff personnel drive around in cars. I request six automobiles for army headquarters and three for each of the corps, along with corresponding supply of parts and tires."

Neither Wrangel's nor his Chief of Staff Yusefovitch's requests received any answers. Headquarters, mesmerized by the prospects of easy victories on their way to Moscow, remained deaf to the requests of what they considered a secondary theater of operations.

The bridge of the river Sal was destroyed and could not be repaired under three weeks time. With Wrangel's blessing, a young officer organized a horse-drawn transport using the rails. Ammunition and other supplies moved up at the speed of walking horses. Wishing to stay in touch with his far-flung cavalry corps, Wrangel set out again in his much repaired Ford, accompanied by his chief of operations Colonel von Lampe and his quartermaster general. At the last moment a war correspondent asked if he could come along. He was taken on board and the Ford set out across the never-ending steppe in the direction of the cavalry corps.

Von Lampe thus described the trip: "It was a dangerous undertaking, Wrangel risking again to fall into the hands of the Reds. The little Ford gound forward slowly with no spare tires. When these were punctured, rags and grass were stuffed in. Anywhere along the far-flung front we could have met a Red scouting party that would have finished us off in no time.

"At the river Sal Wrangel examined the destroyed bridge; his engineer's experience aiding, he personally organized a detail of soldiers and Red army prisoners and set them to work. There was no one who could be put in charge; he could not detatch one or the other of his two staff officers, so acting with his usual determination and improvisation, he appointed the war correspondent as chief of the bridge repair operation and we drove off."

In answer to General Romanovsky's request to detach some of his troops to the Don front Wrangel called headquarters: "I have reached my forward units as the flow of our advance is beginning to ebb. The condition of men and horses after twelve days of marching and combat is pitiful. Our units are under strength: the whole of the 2nd Kouban Corps numbers about 1500 men. The other two corps are somewhat better. The 6th Infantry Division has ceased to exist. Our men have received no rations these past ten days. As regards detaching any units, not only can I not do so, but will not move forward another step regardless of orders, until the technical and other promised help arrives."

Finally, after numerous calls, Romanovsky advised Wrangel that the promised brigade of Kouban Cossack infantry could not be spared and that he would be getting a rifle regiment instead along with six tanks. The regiment numbered a few hundred men and the tanks could not reach Wrangel anyhow, as the Sal bridge needed another two weeks of work.

Nevertheless, the indomitable three corps pressed on, reaching the river Tsaritsa, the first line of defenses of the city of Tsaritsyn. The crucial battle for the city was about to take place.

May 29th. Wrangel called in Generals Ulagai and Chatilov and explained the situation. He warned them not to expect the arrival of the promised infantry and supplies. On the other hand, to stay and wait for them was even more dangerous. Intelligence advised that the Reds were pouring troops and artillery into Tsaritsyn from all sides; from Astrakhan, from Central Russia, and even from the front against Admiral Koltchak's White army. Extensive fortification work was proceeding on the approaches to Tsaritsyn and a flotilla of gun-carrying barges was cruising on the Volga. A great force of Red cavalry was also moving towards Tsaritsyn. It was unanimously agreed to wait no longer and to try and take Tsaritsyn by storm before the Reds could mass there an overwhelming force. Wrangel disposed of the same three corps, severely curtailed by losses and with the minimum of artillery and other technical aids. The cavalry army lived in the field; it ate, slept, and fought in the open steppe devoid of buildings, trees, or any form of shelter.

Wrangel: "I remember one night which we spent in the open, on the eve of a bloody battle. It was a beautiful night; the sky was covered with stars, the steppe with tents. I was lying on my cloak, my saddle for a pillow, and I could hear my soldiers laughing and talking, the horses snorting with fear in the mist and the firing in the distance. I felt that I was back in the times when the technique of modern warfare was still unknown —when telegraphs, telephones, motorcars, trucks, and railways did not exist, when the commander marched with his troops, slept on the ground as they did, and sometimes lacked water to quench his thirst, even as they."

The Reds had also brought to Tsaritsyn another weapon, one that could have spelled the doom of Wrangel's Cossack cavalry. Several Red units of fighter planes had appeared at the theater of operations. But in this instance luck favored the Whites: a new ally appeared simultaneously — a squadron of British RAF volunteers, flying their Sopwith camels and DH9's. Among the pilots were some of World War I best aces: Raymond Colishaw, sixty-eight kills; a New Zealander, Kincaid, with thirty-nine kills; and several other prominent "Knights of the Air," as they used to be called in the skies of the Western Front. There was even an American, a Texan, Captain Marion Aten who left an interesting and vivid account of the RAF over Tsaritzyn.* Again, just as over France of 1917–1918, planes looped, spun, and dived. The superior skill and experience of the British pilots told and several Red planes crashed in flames. With the mastery of the air, the RAF fighters went in against the masses of Red

---

* *Last Train Over Rostov Bridge.* N.Y.: Julian Messner.

cavalry converging towards Tsaritsyn, diving low and strafing the cavalry columns.

General Ulagai moving up to Tsaritsyn was met by heavy artillery fire from the Red barge flotilla on which field and heavy guns were massed. Hence it was decided to attack from the west.

June 1st. Chatilov attacked and took the station of Bassargino and the village of Voroponova; covering him on the left was Pokrovsky and on the right Ulagai. there was a fairly dense railroad net around Tsaritsyn; the Reds moved in armored trains at will. These and massive artillery fire made progress difficult. Wrangel came to Chatilov's headquarters to supervise personally the final attack. Pokrovsky reported that heavy Red concentrations were massing on the left flank. Notwithstanding, Chatilov attacked again on the next day but was met by concentrated fire from armored trains and artillery positions and had to withdraw.

The first attack on Tsaritsyn had failed. Sick at heart and sick physically with hepatitis, Wrangel cabled Denikin. "After three weeks of exhausting marches and combat the Army reached Tsaritsyn. The two-day-long assault of the city has failed against the overwhelming superiority of the enemy in numbers and material. Looking honestly at the facts I can state again that without artillery, infantry and technical aids the city cannot be taken by storm. It is to be assumed that in the event of a Red counterattack our army, bled white as it is, will have to give ground. The army cannot be blamed. During this operation some of the regiments have come to number a hundred men. Killed and wounded are 5 divisional commanders, 3 brigade commanders and 11 regimental commanders. June 2nd. Railroad siding Voroponovo."

The Wrangel tactics of command from the front were particularly costly on those who led. The above numbers show not only the intensity of fighting, but also the valor of individual commanders.

Hardly able to contain himself, Wrangel tendered his resignation, to be effective after the completion of the Tsaritsyn operation. Colonel von Lampe, bearing this letter, was sent to Headquarters. Intercepted on the way by Wrangel's chief of staff Yusefovitch, he was told to keep the letter until notified by cable. Yusefovitch and his chief of operations drove to Wrangel and persuaded him to withdraw the letter. The move was timely, for on June 4th Headquarters, suddenly awakened to the situation, called saying that the 7th Infantry Division (two regiments, five batteries, three armored trains, and six tanks) was finally on the way.

Captain Bulgakov, an officer of a line rifle regiment: "We came up to Tsaritsyn, our CO Colonel Tcherkassov was a great admirer of General Wrangel. As a gesture of honor for him he had a 'W' drawn on our shoulder straps and presented the regiment to Wrangel. A few days passed and we were deluged with cables and letters from Headquarters ordering the immediate erasing of the offensive letter. This we could hardly do, as it had been done with indelible pencil in fault of better material. So we had three options; the first, to erase, which we would not do; the second, to take off our shoulder straps, which would have exposed us to the first Cossack regiment who, viewing us as Reds or deserters, would have attacked us; and lastly, perhaps the simplest solution, to get wounded or killed, which, as a matter of fact, many of us were within the next few weeks. Were Headquarters as generous in rations, ammunition and reserves as they were with their own regulations, we would have been deeply grateful!"

In a letter to his wife dated June 9, Wrangel wrote: "Just as I foresaw, we failed to take Tsaritsyn with our forces. With heavy losses the Army was brought to a standstill at the very gates of the city. Now, as the old peasant saying goes, ' Only when it thunders does the peasant cross himself,' Headquarters has come to and is rushing reinforcements and supplies. ... Shortly the Army will recuperate and with God's help deliver the final punch ... but what a pity the heavy, useless losses due to Headquarters' incompetency."

For in those days there was much rejoicing at Headquarters. The White Volunteer army was advancing on all other fronts. In the headquarters at Rostov, army commander General Mai-Maivsky was throwing parties which degenerated into orgies with due negative repercussions on the civilian population witnessing the drinking and splurging of money. Supreme Headquarters paid little attention to organizing the rear: Individual commanders reigned as satraps, with power of life and death; requisitioning had turned into pillaging; army units started to regard war as a way of living. True, the old cadres of the Volunteer army had been decimated in combat; the old crusader spirit had been dampened by the mobilization of Red army prisoners into the regiments, as well as of officers who at the beginning had stayed on the sidelines; but Headquarters, eyes focused on the Kremlin walls each day approaching nearer, blotted out of its sight all that it considered superfluous.

Wrangel's requests and forecasts were met at Headquarters with open hostility: General Romanovsky speaking to General Naumenko, formerly a brigade commander in Wrangel's 1st Division and now president of the Kouban Cossack Rada (parliament), complained bitterly about Wrangel's tone in his dispatches. "Wrangel," he said, "does not request but demands, almost orders."

In contrast to the rear and to the Volunteer army, Wrangel kept his forces in an iron hand. The Cossacks, who had suffered much at the hands of the Reds, regarded loot as mere repayment for what they had lost, and it took Wrangel much patience and some violence to instill descipline and stop illicit requisitions. Money captured from the Reds was divided among the troops by special regimental commissions. All weapons and supplies were handed over to the appropriate commands: ordnance and supply. Generals Chatilov and Ulagai, the two corps commanders, strongly supported Wrangel in his measures. It was not so easy with General Pokrovsky, a remarkable and yet sinister personage. Pokrovsky had been a flier in World War I. During the revolution he had had his family massacred by the Reds. His hate for them and the lust for revenge turned eventually to sadism. Making his way to the Kouban Cossack territory in 1918, he formed a partisan unit, which gradually grew in size, and at the time Wrangel received command of the 1st Cavalry Division, Pokrovsky also headed a division. His troops took no prisoners; those who were not sabered or shot on the spot were subsequently hanged, a form of torture at which Pokrovsky took goulish delight. The White partisan Shkouro, himself by no means squeamish, remembered: "We took the village of Temnolesskaya — some war booty and a squadron of Red army prisoners. When I got there, Pokrovsky had all the prisoners, including those who had come over to our side, hanged. I had a serious encounter with him on the subject, but he simply laughed it off. Another time I called on him and we sat down to lunch. He suddenly got up and opened the door leading to the courtyard: Several hanged dangled before our eyes. 'To better your appetite!' he said. . . . "

Wrangel took such things not lightly, but at the same time Pokrovsky was a most competent commander; brave, stubborn, intelligent, and tremendously self-controlled, he could be relied on to hang on even in the worst of circumstances. His actions during the epic fight on the Manytsh proved him to be one of the toughest and most competent commanders.

Meeting him for the first time, Wrangel wrote: "General Pokrovsky called on me. I had a long talk with him; it merely confirmed my initial impression. Undoubtedly he was a man of great intelligence and much will power. I knew that he was aware that I was strongly prejudiced against him, and I valued the more his calm, dignified and independent manner. . . ."

Under Wrangel's determined dominance Pokrovsky was forced to mend his ways: Pillaging and masscres stopped, at least while he was under Wrangel's command.

By June 10th the Soviet forces in and around Tsaritsyn numbered sixteen thousand infantry, five thousand cavalry, one hundred nineteen guns, six armored trains, and an undetermined number of fighter planes. On the Volga cruised a flotilla of four squadrons of armored barges, nine gunboats and torpedo boats. All these forces were under the command of a former Czarist officer, General Kluiev. More reinforcements were under way from the Siberian front. The Reds' slogan was "Hold Tsaritsyn at any cost." By an ironical twist of fate, the same slogan was to be repeated, some twenty years later in 1942 in the same Tsaritsyn, then Stalingrad, as the Germans pounded at its gates.

8

The Storming of Tsaritsyn

THE FIRST ECHELONS OF THE promised 7th Infantry Division started to arrive on June 9th. The men wore British issue uniforms and steel helmets; the cadres were for the most part regular army officers of World War I. Six tanks and a few armored cars with Russian crews and British instructors followed. Along the repaired rail line came four armored trains. The stage was set for the final act.

The first assault on Tsaritsyn on June 1st had been launched in the direction of Bassargino-Voroponovo due east. There Chatilov's corps had met very heavy resistance, the enemy having fifty guns and the ability to move them along the rail lines skirting the city. This time Wrangel came up with a very bold plan. He completely bared his center (almost twenty-five kilometers) and concentrated three quarters of his forces on the right flank along the Volga. On his left flank Pokrovsky was to use his corps to cut off the enemy's line of retreat to the north.

From a tactical point of view the attack on Tsaritsyn from the south was not favorable; the enemy's line of retreat was to the north and the presence of the enemy's river flotilla with its heavy artillery added to the difficulty. Nevertheless, the assault had to be delivered from the south as the newly arrived tanks and armored trains were bound to the rail line Velikoknjajhevskaya-Tsaritsyn, the line coming up to the city from the south. Two cavalry corps — Ulagai and Chatilov — the 7th Infantry Division, the six tanks, and the four armored trains were to deliver the main punch. This force was put under the orders of General Ulagai. General Chatilov, corps commander, Wrangel's personal friend, and subsequently his chief of staff, left interesting memoirs covering this operation. These reflect Wrangel's great flexibility and intense use of psychology not only vis-a-vis the enemy but also in relation to his own subordinates.

"As I received my directives on June 14th," wrote Chatilov, "I was astounded by its contents. As I read the orders, I saw that Wrangel had put nearly the whole army under Ulagai's command, withholding not even a small reserve for his use. It seemed that he had simply handed over the whole operation to his subordinate, and this during the most crucial phase of the battle. Furthermore, I was amazed that Wrangel, at other times so sensitive to the capabilities of his subordinates, would appoint Ulagai, the least adapted of the corps commanders, for such an operation. As a cavalry leader Ulagai had no rival, but leading a combined arms operation was not his forte. I could not restrain myself and confided my doubts to Wrangel. He merely smiled and let me in on the secret of his resolution. He agreed with my appraisal of Ulagai's qualifications and even went so far as to say that at the present moment, using racing jargon, Ulagai was not 'in form.' Hence Wrangel had determined to take the operation in his own hands, while still giving Ulagai the illusion that he was 'running the show.' He would thereby revitalize his corps commander by making him feel the elation of a victory reaped by himself. Wrangel went on to say that he had sensed Ulagai's depression when during the first assault on Tsaritsyn he had transferred nearly all his forces to me, which, according to Wrangel, was a clear proof that Ulagai was in a period of temporary depression; otherwise he would have never relinquished any of the units under his command.

"Wrangel went on to explain to me his philosophy. 'In the civil war, the secret of success lies in choosing the right commander for the job ahead. Even when I commanded the 1st Cavalry Division, I never hesitated to regroup my brigades. If I needed stubbornness, I would appoint Brigadier Toporkov. If, on the other hand, maneuver and flexibility were required, the other Brigadier General Naumenko was called upon. This is why,' concluded Wrangel, 'The striking cavalry force will be under your actual command; I shall command the overall operation; and Ulagai will glean the laurels, which are indispensable for his morale.'

"Only Wrangel could come up with such a delicate operation: not losing the rhythm of the battle's development and at the same time sparing Ulagai's ego," concluded Chatilov.

On the night of the 16th Ulagai's army group formed for the attack: In the middle and leading, four tanks and three armored cars; followed by infantry (7th Division and the Cossack infantry brigade); in reserve, two cavalry corps; on the right flank along the Volga the 3rd Kouban Cossack Division and three armored trains.

On the eve of the assault the British instructors asked Wrangel for the honor of taking part in the battle. (The British sporting instinct was, as always, aroused on such an occasion.) Wrangel thanked them and gave the English Major Bruce the overall tank command.

A young cavalry captain Petrov remembered: "The grey light of dawn was beginning to take over the night's darkness; a blanket of fog was lying over the Volga. Our squadrons stood dismounted, waiting for the attack to begin. Whether it was the usual sinking feeling in the pit of the stomach before going into action or just hunger, I don't know, but I suddenly remembered that I had had nothing to eat the previous day. I saw some men pulling a boat ashore and wandered over to them. They were fishermen. Thrashing about in the bottom of the boat was a large sturgeon. 'How about some caviar, Captain?' one of the fishermen called out. Taking a knife he slit open the fish and a mass of black caviar oozed out. Spreading some over a piece of black bread, he offered it to me. . . . This was fifty years ago, but whenever I get to eat caviar, I still see before me the Volga, the receding darkness, the fishermen and the sturgeon; I almost feel again that mixture of hunger and fear that gnawed at me then, on the eve of the great battle of Tsaritsyn."

At 0200 the tanks rumbled forward in the direction of the village Kopany. Rolling over the barbed wire they spread out, machine-gunning the Red infantry. The enemy artillery met the tanks with concentrated fire. A shower of shrapnel and splinters came down on the tanks. Several crew members were wounded; one of the Englishmen, Captain Walsh, had his arm torn off. But this did not stop the tanks, which, enveloped in a veritable cocoon of barbed wire, moved on and on ahead of infantry.

By 0320 the enemy front around Kopany was broken and the infantry, followed by cavalry, rushed into the breach. The armored cars which had broken through wheeled left into the Red's rear, creating a veritable panic and allowing Chatilov's cavalry to take the railroad station of Voroponovo without losses.

The Red army's reaction was to throw a mass of cavalry against Chatilov; he wheeled around and, with the aid of the armored trains that had come up, repulsed them.

Meanwhile, on the extreme left Pokrovsky attacked after an initial artillery preparation. His attack ground to a halt. Undeterred, he started again and at 1500 pierced the enemy's front, taking eight thousand prisoners and eight guns. Had he at that moment wheeled right, the fate of all Red army troops in and around Tsaritsyn would have been sealed. The British air squadron helped mightily, bombing and strafing the Red cavalry formations.

Capt. Marion Aten, the Texan flying in the RAF, recalled vividly: "Five hundred feet above the ravine. The crowded masses of cavalry gazed up with white faces. I pressed the triggers, easing the joy stick back slowly so that my bullets would sweep the line of men; a horse reared, a man began to fall. The horse was still upright, the man still falling, when I shot upward out of the dive and my wing blotted them from view.

"I zoomed straight up into the brightening sky. Above me Kink cartwheeled into line behind Eddie's anchor machine as it passed him in its dive.

"The banshee wail of my wires subsided as my speed cut down. I could hear the roar of the motor. It was deep and smooth, and I blessed Charley and his mechanic's filthy hands.

"Then a cartwheel into line behind Kink again, and another start down the hill.

"We formed an endless chain of attack. Dive. Shoot. Zoom. Cartwheel. The Red cavalry was helpless. We came so fast they had no chance to defend themselves.

"A few raised rifles from pony backs. Some stampeded both forward and back, but Kink had concentrated the attack at both ends of the column, and the narrow gulley was choked with horses and men at entrance and exit.

"On my third trip around I saw an officer whipping his horse up the steep side of the gully toward the steppe. I pushed my left rudder slowly. Dust spurted from the dry, eroded earth; the bullets struck a few feet short. I pulled my stick back a fraction and the dust spurts traveled closer and closer in an ineluctable geometry of line until the horse reared and the man flung his arms upward and fell. I was so close I could see the scar on his cheek, the flash of a ring on his finger.

"I felt neither elation nor guilt but only a knife-sharp sense of concentration. In the air a man exists in a different element of action and response; he is detached from the earth and what he had learned on it of pity and hate; he is himself, and at the same time he is not quite human.

"The Cossacks had now charged the Reds before them. Kink signaled Bill Daley out of line, and the two of them raked the columns as the Cossacks galloped in."

Wrangel drove over to Chatilov at Voroponovo, told him to carry on the attack towards Gumrak, and went back to Ulagai. By then Ulagai was asking for a respite, which Wrangel refused, knowing, as he had said it on the eve of battle, that Ulagai's nerve was failing.

On the day of the 17th several hours were lost by Ulagai. Wrangel virtually took over, insisting on an immediate attack. The decisive action came on the extreme right flank. There the old Cossack General Mamonov, on his own initiative, sent forward three armored trains which opened fire on the Tsaritsyn railroad station, forcing out of action the two Red armored trains, *Lenin* and *Trotzky*, stationed there. Then deploying the 3rd Kouban Cossack Division, he charged in the van. Supported by machine-gun-carrying carts, the Cossacks galloped forward and, dismounting at the edge of town, forced their way in. A Cossack and Circassian cavalry brigade followed. In the meanwhile the 7th Infantry Division had fought its way into the southern edge of town and Chatilov's cavalry had taken the village of Gumrak, then, swinging left, reached the Volga. On seeing the river for the first time, Chatilov's Cossacks were beside themselves with joy; songs about the river Volga burst out among the regiments. They passed on towards Dubovka, meeting at first only scant resistance, but they had one last sharp engagement to ford the river Pitchuga.

By then the horses were utterly spent and Chatilov reported that for the next few days he could only send out a few scouting parties and set up pickets. But at last they had come into an area where forage, water, and food were plentiful and the war booty taken would hold them for quite a while.

Tsaritsyn, the Red Verdun, had fallen, leaving forty thousand prisoners, seventy guns, three hundred machine guns, several armored trains, and huge supplies. The march to Tsaritsyn and its capture covered a period of forty days.

On the morning of the 19th Wrangel entered Tsaritsyn and went directly to the cathedral. A huge crowd filled the church, the town square, and the neighboring streets. During the service many wept. The city had been subjected to a reign of terror which, combined with typhus, had played havoc with the population. In a ravine on the city's outskirts about twelve thousand bodies had been piled up unburied.

The commander in chief arrived the same evening. After reviewing the honor guard, he asked Wrangel and his chief of staff into his railroad carriage. "Well, how is your mood now? At one time it was not so good," Denikin asked, smiling. "Yes, Your Excellency, we had a very rough time," Wrangel answered. "Well, all right, now you can have a good rest."

Anticipating Denikin's arrival, Wrangel and his chief of staff General Yusefovitch had prepared a memorandum. In it they stated that it was preferable to stop the advance northward until the lower Volga region had been cleared, which would allow ships to come up the river, thereby resolving the supply problem, which was acute, as there were no suitable roads and no rear supply base.

The headlong advance of the Don and Volunteer armies had stretched the front to extreme limit, which in the absence of reserves and the total disorganization of the rear had developed a dangerous situation. Wrangel proposed to stabilize temporarily the front with the flanks resting on the two main north-south waterways, the Dniepr and the Volga, then detach some troops from the Caucasian army to clear the lower Volga region and concentrate a large mass of cavalry (three to four corps) and move it into the Red army's rear around the city of Kharkov. This cavalry army would in effect be operating on the shortest axis to Moscow, aiming its blows at the Red army's rear. Simultaneously the White army as a whole would deploy newly organized units, create reserves, and, bringing order to its own disorganized rear, create fortified centers of resistance in the areas behind the front.

Denikin read the report and said with a sly grin: "Of course, you want to be the first to enter Moscow!" Wrangel remained silent, deeming it below his dignity to reply.

The next day, after a *Te Deum* and a parade, Denikin again invited Wrangel

and his chief of staff to his railroad coach and read the general directives—
known subsequently as the Moscow Directive. It was in effect the death sentence of the White armies. Disregarding all principles of strategy, it simply
showed each army corps the route to Moscow. Spread in a thin spider web over
an eight-hundred-kilometer front, the White armies were to march towards
Moscow with neither strategic reserves nor a concentration of forces nor a
single operational axis with the capacity for maneuver.

It showed Denikin's complete self-assurance and a total neglect of the
enemy, and of its gigantic resources and capabilities. Denikin seemed to have
forgotten that the Red army's defeat of Koltchak's Siberian army (abandoned
to its fate in spite of Wrangel's earlier warnings) would liberate three to four
Red army groups which would sooner or later appear en masse, whereas the
White army, marching dispersed towards Moscow, had no strategic reserves of
any sort.

The resumé of the directive read: "The Caucasian Army (Gen. Wrangel)
was to march on Saratov and then on to Moscow via Nijninovgorod; the Army
of the Don (Gen. Sidorin) was to go to Moscow via Voronezh-Ryazan; the
Volunteer Army of Gen. Mai-Maivsky direct on to Moscow via Kharkov,
Kursk, Orel, Tula." To the consternation of Wrangel and his chief of staff,
Denikin remarked merrily; "We are going to advance on big lines now. I shall
have to use a large-scale map for this campaign."*

Immediately after Denikin's departure, General Holman, head of the
British military mission, arrived; he brought decorations for the Russians and
for the British contingent. Wrangel was awarded the Order of St. Michael and
St. George.

Holman was typical of his generation of British empire-builder soldiers. A
huge man, as tall as Wrangel, he was a sportsman who delighted in flying on
reconnaissance missions with members of the British squadron.

Wrangel gave a dinner in his honor; invited were the senior commanders,
members of the staff, and the officers of the British forces. In his book *Last Train
Over Rostov Bridge,* the Texan Captain Aten gives a graphic description of the
feast. Among the many toasts one was in honor of the RAF volunteers: "Silence
fell over the room as Wrangel got to his feet. He held up his glass in our direction and a smile of extraordinary charm lit his severe face with its high cheek-
bones and ice-blue eyes. 'To my new Cossacks,' he said in English learned for
the occasion. 'To my conquerors of Budenny**, to my Cossacks of the air!' The

---

* It is a remarkable coincidence that twenty years later Hitler also rushed
headlong for Moscow, believing that its capture would be the end of the
campaign.
** The commander of the Red cavalry dispersed by the RAF fighters—subsequently Marshal of the Soviet Union.

place became a madhouse. The Cossacks jumped from chairs to tables, sending the platters and other dishware flying. The bowls of caviar oozed their black treasure to the tablecloth. On the dais, next to Wrangel, General Holman good-humoredly wiped a blob of caviar from his eye."

At about this time important changes in personnel occurred in the Caucasian army. General Yusefovitch became a corps commander and Wrangel was left without a chief of staff. The next officers in line for the job were judged by Wrangel as inadequate by his standards, so he addressed himself to General Chatilov, who had heretofore been one of his most successful corps commanders and who besides had a long experience in staff work. At first Chatilov refused; he valued highly the regiments under his command, enjoyed the leadership, and remembered well the past, present, and future role of a chief of staff: "Generally blamed for anything that may go wrong."

Wrangel could be extremely obstinate when pursuing an objective; he wanted Chatilov as chief of staff and used all means of persuasion at his disposal. When all blandishments failed, he simply said: "Look, I know that what I offer you is not a promotion, but for our friendship's sake and the common cause you must accept." Then guessing Chatilov's thoughts, he added: "I am not a difficult commander and I promise you not to interfere in your shop!" Willy-nilly, Chatilov accepted. In his memoirs he said: "From that day started my work as his closest assistant; this partnership was to be broken only by his untimely death."

Chatilov also had interesting remarks about Wrangel's character and personality. "In all the time we served together, I knew that Wrangel valued my friendship and my work as chief of staff. But I also had the opportunity to estimate him fully. His military genius was exceptional, and I more than anyone else had the possibility of fully appreciating it. One of his most characteristic traits was his bursting energy, which sometimes forced me to carry an impossible burden. His care for the forces under his command was overriding. This caused his numerous and demanding requests to Headquarters and had much to do with the rise of Denikin's negative attitude towards him. His feelings were quickly aroused both positively and negatively. He took good care of his sympathies and goodwill, but at the same time was quick to forget a grievance or an offense. He did not know the word *suspicion*, never uttered it or felt it towards anyone. He judged people solely by their achievements.

"He was often harsh, a trait inherited from youth, but on the other hand was willing to accept criticism of himself.

"It is to be regretted that General Denikin did not deem it necessary to allow for Wrangel's characteristics in the way Wrangel himself allowed for those of his subordinates.

"It was easy to disarm Wrangel, and his at times highly explosive behavior; all one had to do was to call on his high sense of honor. Instead, Denikin's future responses were to be both harsh, petty, and, what is worse, totally undeserved. . . "

*General Wrangel sitting on his horse during the Civil War
of 1918 when he commanded the First Cavalry
Division of Kouban Cossacks and Circassians.*

Generals (left to right on foot) Romanovsky, Denikin, and Wrangel march in the victory parade in Tsaritsyn (present-day Stalingrad). Mounted at extreme left is Cossack General Mamonov, one of Wrangel's most gifted generals, killed in action a short time later.

Near this bridge over the river Sal, blown up by the retreating Reds, Wrangel with two officers and a war correspondent took a perilous ride in an old Ford in a no man's land.

9

The Turning of the Tide

DURING THE RED RULE IN Tsaritsyn the city's government had been totally destroyed; leading civic personalities had been killed; others had fled or gone underground. Until Higher Headquarters sent the necessary civil personnel, a temporary military governor was appointed. In his book *Yesterday** General Shinkarenko remembers his appointment and Wrangel's views on the subject of the ever suffering civilian population.

"This was a couple of weeks before the capture of Tsaritsyn, the army bivouacked in the open steppe. Wrangel was spending the night with my unit, sleeping in an open cart. It was a hot, sultry night, the sky shining with a myriad of stars, the steppe dotted with bivouac fires. A Kouban Cossack regiment was riding past, the men singing their Cossack martial songs. Some of them fired for fun a few verey lights. These rose like fireworks. Roman candles giving a weird look to the steppe, the bivouacs and the riders. Wrangel had stood up and was greeting the squadrons as they filed past. The men answered lustily.

"Wrangel walked up to where I lay and said to me, 'I talked it over with Chatilov; when we take Tsaritsyn you will be the commandant. All right with you? I give you plenty of advance notice, so you can give it some thought as to what measures to take in order to restore order until the arrival of permanent civil authorities.

"The next day I presented four hand-written sheets for his approval. I remembered the World War and Kishinew, Rumania, where the authorities had a military commandant with police, curfew, regulations — 'All forbidden what was not allowed.' I modeled mine accordingly.

"Wrangel read and, taking my pencil, put a large X over the text. 'Don't you understand we are importing FREEDOM, something these people have not enjoyed!' "

With all his goodwill towards the civilian population, Wrangel was not about to let the troops and the rear get out of hand and have the situation degenerate into the sort that existed behind the front of General Denikin's army. Shortly after the capture of Tsaritsyn an orgy took place in the city hall; furniture and windows were smashed, and silver, which by some miracle had remained untouched, was stolen. An inquest revealed as culprit some Cossack

vchera. Madrid: N. Belgorodsky, 1964.

junior officers and a captain whose past conduct had left much to be desired. Wrangel had them all court-martialed; the young officers escaped with light penalties, but the captain was convicted and sentenced to be shot. Wrangel rejected mercy pleas, even from the Cossack ataman, and the sentence was duly carried out. Posters advising the population of the court-martial and sentence were posted all over town. Further excesses ceased immediately.

Although Denikin had promised to give Wrangel's army a two-week rest, the order was rescinded a few days later and the exhausted troops and faltering horses ordered to drive on northward.

Meanwhile, the Reds were accumulating more and more troops liberated by their victory over Admiral Koltchak's army and rushed to stem Wrangel's advance. Soon fifty thousand men faced the few thousand horsemen of Wrangel's army. The losses during the storming of Tsaritsyn had been enormous; some cavalry regiments were reduced to anywhere from sixty to one hundred men. More and more troops were being transferred by Denikin to the central front and its headlong rush for Moscow. Not only did the promised replacements not arrive, but Wrangel was beginning to experience a shortage in the replacements within the Kouban Cossack regiments.

Denikin and his headquarters had quarreled with the Kouban Cossack parliament who had rather naturally demanded the same measures of self-government as were enjoyed by the Don Cossacks, who furthermore had their own army. Because of Denikin's total intransigence, the radical secessionist wing of the Cossack parliament grew stronger, and it had a direct effect on the flow of men, horses, and supplies to Wrangel's army, composed, as it was, primarily of Kouban Cossacks.

In spite of this, the exhausted and decimated squadrons of the Caucasian army rallied for one final effort and after hard fighting took the town of Kamyshin; the result, thirteen thousand prisoners, forty-three guns, many machine guns, and badly needed ammunition. The enemy rushed a cavalry corps under Budenny, the friend of Stalin and future Soviet field marshal. In three days of hard fighting the stubborn, tough General Pokrovsky defeated the Reds, forcing them back. Again the losses were heavy, including irreplaceable casualties among the senior unit commanders.

Eighty kilometers remained to Saratov, but the army had run out of steam. Wrangel's frantic appeals for reinforcements remained unanswered; the enemy's tenfold superiority made further advances suicidal.

To save the army from being bled white, Wrangel decided to retreat slowly back to Tsaritsyn, now two hundred fifty kilometers in the rear, and there base himself on a fortified line and an adequate railway net suitable for moving troops and armored trains. But before doing this he sat down and wrote a letter to General Denikin. It was a fateful letter written in anguish and anger, a letter that Chatilov, his chief of staff, vainly attempted to stop. The bitter truth was poured out in a manner not apt to mollify Denikin or make him change his mind, for which anyhow it was too late.

In the first paragraph of the letter Wrangel gave Denikin full credit for his exceptional role in getting the White army on the way. He went on to say: "Serving with you in our common cause and now for over a year serving under your command, I am bound to you as a soldier; as a man I am beholden to you for your warm friendship towards me, particularly during my almost fatal illness. As a person faithful to you, I would deem it dishonest not to speak to you of my doubts and of everything that weighs heavily on my soul."

Wrangel touched further on his operations on the Manytsh and Tsaritsyn, the difficulties in communications and supply. Regarding the storming of Tsaritsyn, Wrangel remarked on the late arrival of promised reinforcements which had come only after the bloody repulse the underequipped army had suffered at the first try to capture the city. He drew attention again to the fact that his essentially cavalry army had lost in the campaign from the Manytsh river to Tsaritsyn five divisional, two brigade and eleven regimental commanders, all in the space of some five weeks. After the capture of Tsaritsyn, regiments had melted down to squadron size. Then, instead of the promised rest and recuperation time, the army's remains were rushed forward again towards Kamyshin. While the enemy was pouring in new divisions and Wrangel's regiments were reduced from sixty to one hundred men each, Headquarters demanded the transfer of yet another division — the Terek Cossack division. Complaining further, Wrangel stated that bread rations were not coming from the Kouban region, that money transfers had been held up, and that ammunition was running out. Having returned the 7th Infantry Division, he was still waiting for the arrival of a promised Cossack infantry brigade.

"That is the bitter and undisguised truth," he wrote. Continuing his letter Wrangel spoke of Denikin's favoritism towards the Volunteer regiments of the central front, to which flowed all equipment and reinforcements, while his units—hungry, ill clad, and often without ammunition — were bled white in operations considered by Headquarters as of secondary importance.

Stressing the fact that although he may not agree with this or that decision of Denikin, notably some aspects of his dealings with the Kouban Cossacks, he felt as a soldier duty-bound to follow Denikin by obeying him implicitly.

Wrangel concluded with the question whether Headquarters' neglect towards the Caucasian army might rest on his, Wrangel's, personality. "My conscience is clear, but the thought that I may be driven to the role of executioner of my army gives me no rest — hence this letter, written with an open heart and leaving nothing unsaid."

The letter struck Denikin as nothing short of a breach of discipline and a way of discrediting him in the eyes of the army by divulging the letter's contents to other senior commanders in the form, as he saw it, of an inflammatory pamphlet.

Denikin's reply came more in the form of a polemic than of a reply from a commander in chief. Refuting point by point Wrangel's complaints, juggling with the numbers and times of arrival of promised but not-sent reinforcements, Denikin had to admit that his forces were stretched out thin over an eight-hundred-kilometer front, with neither reserve nor strategic maneuvering force, rushing headlong towards "new perspectives — Kiev, Odessa, Kursk, Moscow" and occupying new areas rather than defeating the enemy. This seemed to be the overriding preoccupation.

Analyzing Wrangel's letter and Denikin's reply, General Chatilov, Wrangel's chief of staff, had this to say: "I had tried to stop Wrangel from sending the letter, hoping that having said all that was boiling in him, he would simply consign it to paper for his record and, cooling off, would refrain from sending it. I sympathized and concurred with his feelings that Headquarters had neglected our army, but attempted to motivate this neglect by its wish to concentrate all available means in the pursuit of their main objective.

"I advised Wrangel to talk over personally the questions raised in his letter. But Wrangel was adamant and I managed only to get him to soften some of his sentences. When, however, I tried to persuade him to delete the expression 'that I be made the executioner of my own army,' he categorically refused, saying that he wanted to know exactly where he stood as army commander. In the extended conversation we had on the subject I saw clearly through his feelings. No thought whatsoever entered his head as to intrigue or discredit of Denikin. Knowing Wrangel so well, I realized that the harsh tone of his letter and that of previous telegrams accorded fully with the more turbulent aspect of his character. But he himself had often to deal with the same traits in his subordinates and bore their outbursts with tranquil forbearing, letting them first 'let off steam' and then in heart-to-heart conversation getting them to his, Wrangel's, point of view.

"Alas, in Denikin Wrangel did not meet a flexible or intuitive personality. Denikin's answer to Wrangel's letter was made in an ultraharsh tone, and included personal and disparaging allusions to intrigue on Wrangel's part.

"All who knew Wrangel could assent that intrigue was totally foreign to his character and below his self-esteem. The trenchant form of his letters and expressions is unquestionable; it harmonizes rather than clashes with his exceptional bravery, his willingness for self-sacrifice, civic courage and his straightforward judgments and sayings. As Chief of Staff I can ascertain that he neither divulged the contents of his letter to third parties and certainly did not disseminate it."

What, then, sowed the seeds of mistrust in Denikin's soul, seeds that grew to an impenetrable thicket forever dividing the two so different personalities?

Among Denikin's improvised organizations was a staff named Osvag — its mission intelligence-collecting, propaganda, and counterintelligence. In times of civil strife or internal disorder such impromptu organizations seem to gather the worst of human elements: those allergic to the whistle of bullets and the sound of explosive shells, mingled with the professional political intriguer and the petty bureaucrat. It is hard to estimate Osvag's value in collecting intelligence; its propaganda activity consisted of posting posters on newly liberated towns' walls. Unfortunately, its counterintelligence activity was not limited to searching for Soviet spies and infiltrators; rather Osvag occupied itself predominantly with editing and reporting to Headquarters on Denikin's subordinates — their correspondence, conversations, and gossip. Wrangel's trenchant reports, his free discussions with staff and subordinates, gave the Osvag agents unlimited material which, digested and edited to goad his susceptibilities and mistrust, was fed to Denikin. It is indeed less than surprising that with such "assistance" the breach between the commander in chief and his talented and explosive subordinate could no longer be bridged. As a sorry postscript to Osvag and its relation to Denikin came the fact that Colonel Siminsky, one of its chief officers, turned out to be a Red agent who defected later to the Soviets, taking along the White army's cipher code and an attaché case of secret documents.

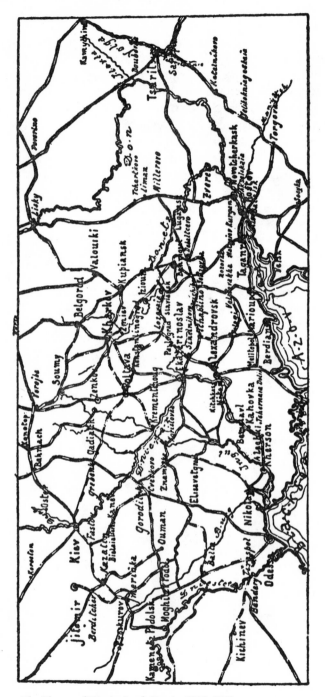

The Theatre of War in South Russia, 1918-1919.

10

Defense of Tsaritsyn — Cossack Revolt

ON AUGUST 1ST THE CAUCASIAN ARMY started to pull back towards Tsaritsyn two hundred fifty kilometers away. The retreat proceeded under conditions of extreme hardship, with heavy losses due to constant rear-guard actions.

It was tragic to see that the heretofore invincible Cossack cavalry could no longer stand up to the masses of enemy cavalry due to the pitiful condition of their horses. The Red cavalry men sat on fresh horses mobilized from all over Russia, whereas Wrangel's Kouban Cossacks' and Circassians' mounts were at the last stages of exhaustion after marching and fighting over six hundred kilometers with no interruption. Furthermore, the Soviets' Volga river flotilla sailed mostly unhampered — firing into the flank of the Caucasian troops and interfering with the movement of supplies and evacuation of the wounded.

Wrangel had forseen that sooner or later the tide would turn and that with the small and used-up forces at his disposal it would lead to disaster if he had no fortified base on which to fall back. Even as his troops were chasing the Reds northward to Kamyshin and towards Saratov, he had ordered extensive for-tification works to be erected on the north and northwest approaches to Tsarit-syn, encompassing the relatively developed railway net around the city.

Back in the Kouban the tension between the Cossack parliament, the Rada, and Denikin had reached catastrophic proportions; the left-wing separatist party had come to power with the result that neither reinforcements, horses, forage, or bread were reaching the Caucasian army. Wrangel decided to travel to Ros-tov and Ekaterinodar for consultation with Denikin and his former subordinate brigade commander General Naumenko who was now deputy ataman of the Cossacks and as such in the unenviable position of being between hammer and anvil. The head of the Kouban Cossack government General Filimonov, though well-intentioned, was weak-willed and in his relations with the Rada had let the left-wing radical faction get completely out of hand. This faction had also decided to enter independently into the field of foreign relations and had sent its deputies to the Inter-Allied Conference in Paris and propagandized the Cossack replacements due to leave for the front. Wrangel and other commanders had noted the deterioration in the fighting quality and discipline of these units.

Reaching Rostov, Wrangel was received enthusiastically by the popula-tion. Everywhere he appeared he was met with ovations, first at the theater, then in a restaurant. There a crowd gathered around his table; strangers sent him champagne and asked him embarrassing questions as to his views on future operations and his relations with Headquarters. Avoiding the publicity, Wrangel escaped back to the railway station, locked himself in his carriage and went to sleep — without having had his supper. The next day at Denikin's headquarters optimism was the order of the day. The fall of Moscow seemed only a question of time, but staff officers whom Wrangel knew from past World War service spoke critically of the handling of operations, warning that the White army was due for a shock. Some tried to get Wrangel to influence Denikin. "Can you not make him understand?" "Can you not explain to him?" came from many sober-minded officers.

The tête-à-tête with Denikin convinced Wrangel that there was no point in attempting to change his mind. Convinced that he was on the right track, Denikin measured only the kilometers between his advance units and the Kremlin walls.

Not so optimistic, however, were his pronouncements on foreign policy, and totally negativé his views on the Kouban Cossack question. He criticized the English, who wère supplying him with military hardware and who had tank and RAF units at his disposal besides. The newly independent countries of Poland and Georgia were in his eyes akin to enemies: "I have decided to break off negotiations with them; I have informed them that they will get nothing out of us, not so much as an inch of Russian territory!" The former liberal Denikin had become an imperialist.

On the subject of the Kouban Cossacks Wrangel expressed his views that the majority of the Cossacks were not in sympathy with the left-wing faction of the Rada, that while a certain firmness was definitely needed in dealing with them, everything could be settled by negotiations respecting the Cossacks' hereditary rights to their autonomy. Wrangel said: "We must respect the Koubans' right to autonomy, and yet concentrate the executive power in the hands of the ataman and his government, which will be responsible only to the local Rada. One of the deputies could propose this in the Rada, and I am certain that the majority would agree to it. As, however, the extreme left could make capital by stirring up trouble, I suggest that under some pretext or another the garrison at Ekaterinodar should be reinforced with thoroughly reliable troops."

Thinking it over, Denikin held out his hand and said: "I give you carte blanche."

In Ekaterinodar Wrangel worked out the details with generals Naumenko and Pokrovsky, giving the latter authority to act. However, knowing Pokrovsky's violent character and his more than resolute measures, Wrangel categorically enjoined him not to resort to force unless it became absolutely necessary.

A sudden telegram from Denikin was to foil all prearranged plans. It read:

> In July the Kouban government concluded an alliance treaty with the Medjilis [an assembly of mountain tribes], which is equivalent to treason to Russia. The Kouban armies were to be put at the disposal of the Medjilis. This treaty was signed by Bytch, Savitsky, Kalabukhov, and Namitokov. Order the arrest of any of these traitors you can find, and have them court-martialed for treason. — Taganrog, October 25, 1919

DENIKIN

Having given Wrangel complete freedom of action Denikin was now putting before him an accomplished fact, virtually ordering him to use force and, inevitably, bloodshed.

The Rada informed Denikin that the above-mentioned deputies had acted on their own and that they would have to answer to the Rada for their misdemeanor; therefore the Rada would judge them, not Denikin's headquarters. A complete break seemed inevitable. General Pokrovsky urged a coup d'etat: Dissolve the Rada; arrest the culprits and shoot them on the spot. Again Wrangel categorically forbade such an extreme measure. Again Denikin forced the issue by formally ordering immediate action. As it happened, the left-wing faction doomed itself by issuing separatist proclamations and vilifying its own Cossack generals and the army; it created a climate against which other members of the Rada objected and reacted.

Entering the Rada with a sergeant and a few Cossacks, Pokrovsky arrested four dissident members. They were court-martialed and their leader Kalabukhov hanged; the others were pardoned at Wrangel's intercession. Had Denikin not interfered by ordering the arrest and court-martial, the whole matter could have been resolved without loss of life.

Wrangel made a formal call on the Rada. Knowing the Cossack psychology and their love of martial display, he rode in with General Pokrovsky and his staff through the streets lined with Cossack troops. Welcomed by the ataman and the head of the government, he made a long speech, purposefully avoiding the thorny political question and dwelling at length on the successes and plight of the Caucasian army and its Kouban Cossack regiments. He knew how to talk to the Cossacks and his vivid descriptions of combat and privation stirred the members; even those whose political views were negative gave him a standing ovation.

With the hard-fought retreat towards the fortified positions of Tsaritsyn, Wrangel decided on the evacuation of wounded, civilians, and rear echelons. The staff's plan was the departure of seven trains per day from Tsaritsyn. In fact only three a day was the maximum achieved. Dissatisfied with the explanations of his staff officers, Wrangel proceeded to the station with a few Cossacks from his escort. Looking into the departing trains, he saw that they were loaded with furniture, grand pianos, mirrors, and paintings belonging to private individuals. Wrangel ordered the Cossacks to throw everything out and smash it to pieces. Going further, Wrangel noted several sealed carriages supposedly loaded with artillery supplies. Forced open, they revealed merchants with their goods. Questioned, the scared passengers admitted bribing the stationmaster and a couple of his assistants. Wrangel's action was quick; he arrested and court-martialed the railway employees who were convicted of activities favorable to the enemy and that same evening hanged two at the station itself and one in the town square. Posters apprising the population were posted all over town. Within the next days the train departures rose to eight per day.

As supplies from the rear were usually either delayed or not forthcoming and as in the rear the steppe was devoid of major population centers, Wrangel instructed General Vilchevsky, his chief of ordnance and supply, to arrange for a series of workshops which could provide for the needs of the army. Materials were brought in from the Kouban and Terek regions and everything from saddles to mess cans was manufactured locally in the army's immediate rear. The English General Briggs on a visit to Wrangel's front declared that such improvisation existed in no other army in the world.

The Reds had by now accumulated an unprecedented concentration of troops, their commanding general Kliuev had received two fresh army groups from the Ural district with massive infusion of artillery units. Knowing that the loss of Tsaritsyn would mean a disastrous retreat over three hundred kilometers of the waterless steppe that the army had so painfully conquered some four months before, Wrangel resolved to defend Tsaritsyn at all costs.

Disposing his infantry units in the center under the command of General Pisarev, Wrangel concentrated a large mass of cavalry on the left flank; its mission was to envelop the enemy and force them against the Volga river. Intelligence warned that the Red attack was to be on August 23rd. On the eve of the attack, the thin infantry lines of army and Cossack units occupied the trenches, and the cavalry, crossing the rail line Gumrak-Tsaritsyn, deployed some eight to ten kilometers northwest of the town.

As dawn rose, three huge enemy columns moved to the attack. Among the Red infantry were regiments composed of sailors reputed for their ardent Communist views, and mercenary regiments of Chinese, whose reputation was built on their extreme cruelty to prisoners and wounded and who in turn were mercilessly put to the sword by the Cossacks when they fell into their hands. The central column moving in the direction of the village of Razguliaevka was the first to deploy. Penetrating the lightly held White lines, the Reds fanned out but were immediately counterattacked by General Pisarev's reserves and routed; one thousand prisoners and some machine guns were taken.

The second Red column advanced along the main Tsaritsyn-Saratov highway along the Volga; it was mightily supported by the Red river flotilla. Meeting little resistance due to the relentless fire from its riverboats, this column also penetrated deeply into the White lines. But Wrangel, personally in command at this sector, quickly wheeled Pisarev's reserves to the right and hit the Reds in the flank, again with decisive success. The Red infantry was decimated; many drowned in the Volga.

At one moment of the battle a regiment of Red marines succeeded in reaching the edge of town. Wrangel had only his mounted escort. No other reserves were available. It also was thrown in and succeeded in stopping the enemy.

Dawatz, a war correspondent: "Wrangel said: Let's go to the corps of General Pisarev; he may have a serious situation on his hands today.' The little Ford grinds forward, as we reach the outskirts of town we see a commotion: Something of importance must have occurred on the banks of the Volga. More and more soldiers file past us, some with rifles, others without, a forlorn look about them. Wrangel's face looks grimmer; he seems to draw within himself. Suddenly he orders the car to stop and stands up. Immediately a crowd gathers around. 'Where are you from? What unit?' The voice sounded harsh with unfamiliar overtones. 'Machine guns to be posted — let no one by!'

" 'Your Excellency, the Reds have broken through!'

" 'Stay put — all women to get back to their houses; get the children off the road'. . . .

"The General's escort squadron comes at a full gallop around the corner.

" 'Your Excellency, General Chatilov has ordered . . .' starts to report the squadron commader.

" 'My horse,' thunders Wrangel.

" 'Pokrovsky [his ADC], wait for me at the bridge!'

"Vaulting on his horse, he disappears with his squadron in a cloud of dust. . . ."

Captain Bulgakov: "We were sorely pressed: Our thin line was in danger of being driven in. The Red soldiers were advancing in mass formations; we could now distinguish their faces and hear their obscenities. I glanced to the right and saw two horsemen coming up at a trot: It was General Wrangel and his fanion-bearer. The General trotted past me; I saw him draw his sword. A minute later he was charging at the head of his escort squadron. They burst into the Red ranks, sabering. Those sailors who could not get out of the way blew themselves up with hand grenades, still shouting obscenities as they pulled the grenade pins. Others ran for the Volga cliffs and threw themselves down to their death. Our depleted companies were saved."

During this action a happy coincidence changed a desperate situation to victory. During the initial Red attack the White Saratov infantry regiment, a regiment recently arrived and composed of former Red army prisoners, surrendered, shooting its officers and going over to the Reds. A Cossack battery, firing point-blank over open sights, was overwhelmed and the enemy poured through the open gap. Bivouacking a few kilometers away were two White cavalry divisions, one of Kouban Cossacks, the other of Circassians. These divisions were on the way to the rear to form part of the army's mobile reserve. Due to extreme fatigue of horses and riders, the divisions had stopped en route and, unsaddling their horses, rested in some ravines. Hearing the sound of battle approaching nearer and nearer, they saddled up and rode out of the ravines to see in their immediate vicinity the waves of Red infantry. On their own initiative the two divisions deployed and charged, cutting the Red infantry to pieces.

General Shinkarenko, the commander of the Circassian division, remembered: "At the conclusion of the attack I heard some firing in one of the ravines. I saw the Cossack infantrymen dividing the prisoners in two batches — one, the Red army soldiers in their Russian grey blouses; the other, the Saratov infantrymen in their English issue tunics. 'What's going on?' I asked a fierce-looking Cossack sergeant. 'Just dealing swift justice,' he answered. 'You see, those in Russian blouses are the Red army soldiers; they get a kick in the a... and are sent to the rear. As for the other traitorous bastards in the tunics who went over to the Reds, we shoot them, but before that we have them take off their new boots and tunics — no use ruining good material!' He seemed most content with a job well done. The regiments assembled and we rode back.

"On a hill ahead of us we saw a group of horsemen and a St. George's black and orange fanion — Wrangel and his staff. In our times one hardly has the occasion to see a commander on the field of action — for that you have to go to the Louvre and look at the battle scenes of Gros and Vernet. But there he was: Wrangel — tall, lean, in a brown Cossack tunic with rolled-up sleeves, the fur cap tilted back, the Cossack dagger at his belt.

" 'Thank you, Shinkarenko, a fantastic attack!' he stretched out his hand with long fingers. 'My escort also charged — they cut up the Red marines on the right flank. Thank you again. Bravo, a great charge. Don't forget to send in award recommendations and don't be stingy about them!' "

Wrangel knew how to "fire" his troops.

The enemy again tried a major attack on Tsaritsyn and again was beaten back with General Ulagai's smashing attacks bringing in over four thousand prisoners. But the Reds kept on coming. South of Tsaritsyn they had fortified a bridgehead on the right bank of the Volga at Tcherny Yar. From there they launched a sally against Tsaritsyn, moving in from the south. At first contained and defeated by another of Wrangel's brilliant cavalry lieutenants, General Saveliev, they continued reinforcing their units and eventually pushed back Saveliev's division. Savaliev himself was critically wounded.

Availing himself of the respite given him after the last victory, Wrangel rushed Babiev south with the 3rd Kouban Cossack Division. Again the Reds were beaten back and retreated into the fortified complex. But there was no time to reduce this bridgehead, as already the Red command geared itself for yet another drive on Tsaritsyn; this time a flotilla of forty artillery-bearing boats was in support. The RAF volunteer squadron went in bombing and strafing the boats. This time the Red command sent forward its elite troops with special Communist units, including a women's battalion moving behind with orders to shoot anyone who retreated. This fourth-repeated Red onslaught was also doomed to failure; again they penetrated the White infantry lines and once again were taken in the flank and rear by Ulagai's divisions and hurled against the barbed wire entanglements which they had just penetrated. There they were cut to pieces, some throwing themselves into the Volga to try and swim away from the merciless Cossack swords. This last victory enabled Wrangel to chase the Reds fifty miles north of the city. But there he had to stop; the little that was left of the Caucasian army was too weak to advance any farther. No supplies were forthcoming, the Reds being in firm possession of the lower reaches of the Volga; hence, the only way was by the one rail line from Tsaritsyn to Velikoknyajevskaya.

The Volunteer army in the center was still advancing victoriously, Headquarters having eyes only for its progress.

Denikin had finally taken Wrangel's advice to hurl a strong cavalry mass into the Red army's rear between it and Moscow. But instead of letting Wrangel do the job, he ordered the Don Cossack general Mamontov with a Don Cossack cavalry corps to pierce the Red lines and sweep into their rear.

Unfortunately, Mamontov was no Wrangel and his lieutenants no Chatilovs, Ulagais, Babievs, and Pokrovskys. Diligently avoiding major engagements, the corps moved north, looting and pillaging as it went, instead of smashing the Reds as Wrangel had done at Spitzevka, Manytsh, and Tsaritsyn. Although Mamontov's raid did create a panic among the Red command, it produced no tangible results and the Cossacks, returning laden with innumerable wagon trains of booty, thought only of getting it safely back to their villages. Wrangel's terse comment on this raid was that Mamontov should have been court-martialed instead of congratulated.

Commenting on Wrangel's successful defense of Tsaritsyn and his defeat of four successive Red army attempts to take the city with a never ending influx of fresh reinforcements, General Chatilov, his chief of staff, wrote: "The August and September fighting around Tsaritsyn brought to focus Wrangel's exceptionally talented handling of his army. Not a day went by without major regrouping and maneuvering, whole divisions shifting from one end of the front to the other, often using the rail network. Regiments and divisions would march at night and attack at dawn in yet another direction. He himself was invariably present at the point where the main blow was to be delivered. His presence electrified his subordinates, driving them to still greater efforts. Innumerable times divisions charged, knowing that their commander was right there watching them go in. He knew also how to thank the troops for their bravery and sacrifice. The battles for Tsaritsyn were among the brightest pages of his brilliant military career."

During one of his trips to the Don army headquarters for coordinating action Wrangel was cut off from his own army by an advance of Red cavalry. Anxious to rejoin his army during a critical stage of the battle, he took his battered Ford car cross-country with just his ADC and a machine gun on board. Risking any moment to drive into the Red army troops, he reached a railway station, boarded an engine, and rushed towards Tsaritsyn, arriving there at dawn. Later that morning he was already on horseback and marshaling his units at Voroponova twenty kilometers away.

The march to Tsaritsyn, its capture, the drive north, the retreat, and the repulse of four consecutive Red army assaults had taken its toll among the senior commanders as well as of the rank and file. General Mamonov, the gallant old Cossack general, was killed in action; General Saleliev was hopelessly crippled; one after another, Ulagai, Chatilov, and Pokrovsky came down sick from stress and fatigue. In his memoirs Chatilov wrote: "I also came down, stricken from fatigue and overwork; the doctors ordered me to bed. Wrangel called on me that evening and, seeing me the worse for wear, said, 'My dear fellow, you simply cannot die! How could I ever do without you?' He then proceeded to tell me so many funny stories that I laughed heartily and for a long time; this more than anything restored my frayed nerves."

Meanwhile, Wrangel's dire predictions were beginning to come true. The dark clouds which had been slowly accumulating over the victorious and badly overextended Volunteer army driving for Moscow on a thousand-kilometer front now burst into a storm. The Red army blocked by Wrangel at Tsaritsyn transferred its main effort against the junction of the Volunteer and Don armies. There also went the Red cavalry corps of Budenny, previously mauled by Wrangel at Kamyshin, and that was to play a major role in the breakthrough of the Red army and the subsequent disastrous retreat of the Whites. With the Whites at Orel, almost at Moscow's gates, the Red army drove a massive wedge between the Volunteer and Don armies and drove deep into the Whites' rear.

Denikin's spider web broke, and the hopelessly disorganized rear produced no reserves, hampered retreat, and eventually caused the complete breakdown of communications.

The four Red onslaughts against Tsaritsyn having failed, Wrangel decided to clear his southern front and try to open the Volga river in its lower reaches. He again sent General Babiev, this time with a Cossack infantry brigade and some artillery, south by rail. Brilliant as he was in commanding cavalry, Babiev, who in less than two years had come up from major to general, had trouble handling a combined arms operation. He failed to take the heavily fortified Tcherny Yar and incurred heavy casualties. A long time before, Wrangel had begged Denikin to send sufficient troops to clear the lower Volga to allow transports to move upriver from the Caspian Sea. Considering it of secondary importance, Denikin's Headquarters had done nothing about it.

Babiev, it has been said, resembled the Confederate General Jeb Stuart in many ways—among them was a love for parties and dancing. But whereas Stuart limited his dancing inclinations to waltzes and polkas with the Southern belles, Babiev preferred the more martial dance of the Lezginka, the Caucasian war dance. At a certain point during the dance revolver shots would be fired to accentuate the effect. Thinking the sonoric efforts to be insufficient, Babiev asked for rifle volleys, and when these paled had a '75 wheeled into the dance hall and fired out of the window. The effect was stronger than expected: The roof caved in, wounding some of the party, including his chief of staff, a serious, introverted infantry officer who had been appointed as a steadying influence on the somewhat exhuberant thirty-year-old general. The shaken staff officer asked for immediate reassignment. When Wrangel heard this, he laughed heartily but ordered his chief of staff Chatilov to reprimand Babiev.

Chatilov gave the cavalry commander a serious dressing down for conduct unbecoming a general officer. But that same evening, sitting down to dinner with his officers, Wrangel asked Babiev for tips about dancing to the sound of cannon fire. The whole table laughed and the incident was forgotten. However, outside of these gay idiosyncrasies Babiev, as all other of Wrangel's lieutenants, maintained order in his troops, whose discipline in and out of action presented a vivid contrast to other units of the White army outside of Wrangel's command.

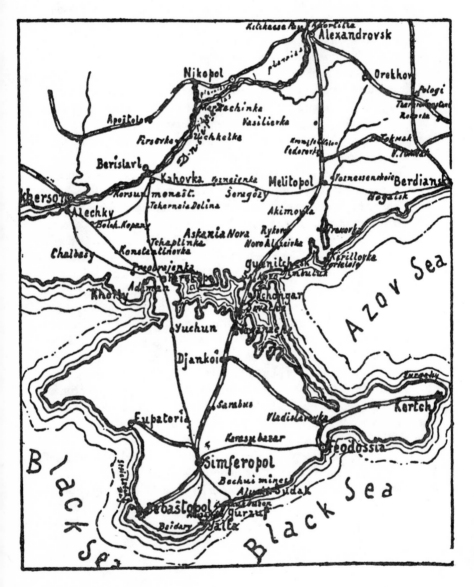

The Theatre of War in the Crimea, 1919–1920.

11
Retreat and Disaster of the Volunteer Army

AT THE TIME OF THE Red army's defeat on the river Manytsh in May, 1919, and Denikin's decision to drive on to Moscow, the command of the Volunteer army was given to General Mai-Maivsky, one of the old senior commanders of the Volunteer regiments which had given birth to the White army. A brave officer, intelligent and well-educated, Mai-Maivsky had unfortunately lapsed into alcoholism. Generally drunk, he would drive up to the front lines and, staggering out of the car, walk under a hail of bullets at the head of his troops. While such a state of affairs might possibly have been glossed over on the strength of past merits in a small command, the entrusting of a whole army, and of THE army aimed at the principal objective, was on General Denikin's part an unforgivable sin.

At the beginning, while the White army regiments of the Volunteer army marched forward on their victorious procession and city after city welcomed the liberators, unsatisfactory commanders relied on their chiefs of staff and senior operational officers. But when the massive Red counterattack took Orel and Kiev and the victorious march had ground to a halt, generals of the type of Mai-Maivsky and the looting Cossack General Shkouro no longer had control over their troops, which they themselves had demoralized by setting a bad example. The retreat was to degenerate into a rout. The autumn campaign of the Red army had begun with forces accrued from two fronts; the Siberian front against Admiral Koltchak and that of the northern front against General Yudenitch. By the late fall the Reds were on the move on a front stretching fifteen hundred kilometers. The cities of Orel, Kursk, and Kiev had fallen, and only Wrangel at Tsaritsyn stood firm, defeating four massive Red attacks and barring the enemy from access to the northern Caucasus.

Shattered against Wrangel's Caucasian army on its left flank, the Red army command sought victory in the central sector, concentrating everything there, including its cavalry corps of Budenny, which had been diverted from Tsaritsyn. Kharkov, one of the principal cities under the White army's control, was doomed. Everyone at the front and in the rear realized it except Mai-Maivsky, who remained optimistic and drunk. Every evening in the best hotel in town there would be drinking and carousing with the commanding general in the main role.

Whenever the question of evacuating the city and moving back the rear echelons came up, Headquarters would merely declare that panic mongers would be court-martialed. As a result, all was lost.

When finally Denikin resolved to dismiss Mai-Maivsky and called on Wrangel to save the situation, it was too late: "The building was burning; the walls were caving in."

The circumstances of Wrangel's appointment bear relating. Wrangel was recalled from Tsaritsyn. Arriving at Taganrog, the White army's headquarters, in spite of a recurrent bout of typhus and an attack of hepatitis, Wrangel called on General Denikin.

"I ask you to take over the Volunteer army," Denikin said, coming directly to the matter at hand. Wrangel replied that he doubted that he could be of use in that position, as everything he had previously suggested was no longer valid; that it was too late to effect the necessary regrouping; and that the city of Kharkov and its strategic position could no longer be held. Denikin interrupted him: "Yes, we all know that we shall have to give up Kharkov, but that will in no way affect your reputation." "I am not worried about my reputation," Wrangel replied dryly. "It needs no safeguarding. I do think, however, that I can hardly assume the responsibility for a job that cannot be done."

General Romanovsky put the matter in the light that Wrangel had the moral obligation to serve Russia by assuming the command. Wrangel asked for a day to think it over. The next day Romanovsky again called on him, pressing him to assume command. "General Mai-Maivsky is no longer able to cope with the situation," he said. "What did you think about before," answered Wrangel. "Everyone has known for a long time that Mai-Maivsky was incapable.* You know also that I was always at your disposal, but while things looked good, Headquarters felt no need for my advice. You remember last spring I urged you to concentrate on the enemy in the direction of Tsaritsyn and knock him out before he could concentrate against us. You did not want to

---

*Mai-Maivski's reaction to his dismissal was somewhat unusual, though symptomatic of the prevailing sickness. Meeting Wrangel sometime later, he complained that Wrangel's orders to the troops had offended him. "But why, General?" Wrangel asked. "I cannot remember a single derogatory word pertaining to you!" "How about the sentence 'drunkards and marauders will be mercilessly punished'? Is that not an indirect reproach to me?" He went on to explain his philosophy: "In wartime you have to utilize the positive and negative traits of your subordinates, especially in this hard war. If you ask your officers and men to live like monks, they will not fight!"

To Wrangel's astonished question: "What then would be the difference between Whites and Reds?" — Mai-Maivsky replied: "Well you see that is why they are winning!"

listen to me, and now when my forecasts have, alas, proved correct, you ask me to save the situation."

Appealing to Wrangel's sense of honor, Romanovsky prevailed, and Wrangel accepted to act in a situation that deep down he knew was hopeless. Wrangel did not waste time but, as was his custom, proceeded directly on an inspection of the troops and rear echelons now under his orders. What he saw was far worse than even he expected.

In its headlong rush for Moscow Denikin's army relied heavily on the rail network. Along the railway lines shuttled back and forth the White armored trains supporting the infantry; supplies were moved up; headquarters of different divisions, corps, and armies worked and lived on them; and there were even trains for rest and recuperation owned and operated by the Volunteer divisions.

Accustomed to the Spartan life of the Caucasian front, Wrangel was infuriated to see first-class Pullman carriages with armchairs and sofas, with grand pianos, and with officers relaxing over drinks and cards. As the thinly stretched front had burst and the hurried retreat begun, innumerable trains jammed the overburdened railway system. Red Cross trains carrying wounded or typhus cases remained standing forlorn on railway sidings, while trains loaded with goods bearing no relation to the war effort proceeded south, bearing refugees and often army personnel leaving the front under one pretext or another.

Preoccupied with its advance on Moscow, Headquarters had totally neglected the rear. The individual corps and divisions had set up their own systems of supply, bargaining in the rear what they requisitioned at the front. A whole system of buying and selling drained military manpower, clogged normal supply channels, and debauched the army, turning it into a business enterprise.

At one station Wrangel was met by two desperately sick men who had crawled out from an abandoned Red Cross train, where men were dying and where an officer had just hanged himself in despair. Getting together whatever personnel he could find, Wrangel set up a ward in an abandoned building, moving there the sick and the wounded, scraping together some medical supplies and purchasing food in town.

The British military mission, also lodged in a train stuck somewhere along the way, was rescued by Wrangel.

With great difficulty Wrangel established communications with the forward units under General Kutepov and ordered him to hang on as long as possible to allow an orderly evacuation of all the wounded and military supplies.

In one of the trains Wrangel found the headquarters of a cavalry corps. He immediately ordered it out of the train, onto horses, and into the field. The

Don Cossack General Mamontov, whose raid into the Red army's rear had brought another huge train of booty instead of military successes, was dismissed; General Ulagai was appointed in his place. Finding Cossacks of General Shkouro engaged in drinking and hell-raising, with the general himself on leave somewhere in the Kouban region, Wrangel cabled headquarters: "The army is falling apart from drinking and debauching; I cannot punish junior officers if senior commanders give a bad example by remaining unpunished. I demand the immediate dismissal of General Shkouro who has thoroughly debauched his troops. Wrangel."

Instead of complying with this request, Headquarters simply "advised" Shkouro not to return to his post.

Wrangel proceeded with drastic measures to bring order in the rear. Special command posts with generals or senior staff officers were set up at key railroad stations. All trains proceeding south were checked, superfluous freight thrown out, legitimate supplies allowed to proceed on. All military personnel capable of bearing arms were assembled in companies and sent back to the front lines. These command posts were authorized to court-martial any unruly elements, plunderers, and deserters. Those convicted were shot on the spot.

Wrangel's hope that General Ulagai could hold together a sufficiently strong force of cavalry and thereby thwart the Red cavalry of Budenny proved unfounded. The Don Cossacks, by now thoroughly demoralized, had given up all pretense of fighting and flowed back in a disorderly crowd, abandoning guns, machine guns, and supply trains to the Red cavalry. The Kouban and Terek Cossack divisions, pulled from the Tsaritsyn front where they had been bled white during their successful defense of the city, were of little use; even such a dashing cavalry leader as Ulagai could do nothing but report the chaotic withdrawal.

It must be borne in mind that throughout the civil war in the south of Russia the Cossacks — Don, Kouban, and Terek — had provided not only the major contingents in the fight against the Reds but also supplies and remounts. Over the period their losses were enormous. Though the Don Cossacks enjoyed autonomy and a separate army command, the coordination between them and Denikin's Headquarters was far from perfect.*

As regards the Kouban Cossacks, the previous pages have dealt with the unhealthy relations between Denikin's Headquarters and the Cossack parliament, their deterioration, and Denikin's orders to Wrangel for repressive

---

* The Don Cossack army constantly suffered from a shortage of officers; in the Volunteer army whole battalions were composed of officers only, with colonels standing in the ranks. No effort was made to change this situation. The Volunteer army suffered enormous casualties in officers who could have been utilized as cadres in Cossack regiments.

action in spite of the latter's reluctance and cautionary advice. With the retreat and military setback this sickness, which had been endemic but suppressed, burst out with a renewed malevolent force.

Returning from his inspection Wrangel drafted out a report, the complete text of which is reproduced below. It was strong medicine and bitter to taste: Wrangel, in his usual trenchant style, minced no words in denouncing the evils that had befallen the White army, characteristically providing also suggestions on how to remedy the almost hopeless situation.

DISPATCH TO THE COMMANDER IN CHIEF

YOUZOVKA   No. 010464   December 9, 1919

I arrived here November 26th, and having acquainted myself with the situation along the principal section of the front, I have the honor to make the following communications to you:

Our disadvantageous position at the present time has two principal causes:

1. A strategy diametrically opposed to the rudiments of the art of warfare.
2. Complete disorganization behind the lines.

In my dispatch No. 82, of April 4, 1919, I felt it my duty, whilst insisting on the advance on Tsaritsyn, to draw your attention to the impossibility of simultaneous action in several directions whilst we lacked the necessary forces. After we had taken Tsaritsyn, General Yusefovitch and I sent you two dispatches in which we indicated the necessity of occupying the short Tsaritsyn-Ekaterinodar front, which is defended on both its flanks by large rivers, and of concentrating three or four cavalry corps in the Kharkov area for operations along the shortest route to Moscow.

This plan, to quote your own remark at our interview in Tsaritsyn, was only dictated by "my desire to be the first man to enter Moscow."

When the enemy recently concentrated considerable forces near Orel and began to put pressure on the Volunteer Army, General Romanovsky asked me, on October 17th, for some troops to reinforce our front line.

I telegraphed on October 18th that "in view of the reduction in the effective force of the cavalry, the problem could not be solved by sending one or two detachments," and suggested a radical measure — "the sending of three and a half Kouban divisions."

My suggestion was turned down, and a hybrid measure was adopted: Only two divisions were taken from the Caucasian Army. Later events compelled a return to the measure I suggested; three and a half divisions have now been taken from the Caucasian army, but the time that has been lost is irreparable.

We wanted to do too much and make ourselves master of every position at once, and we have succeeded only in weakening ourselves and so becoming powerless.

The Bolsheviks, on the contrary, have held firmly to the principle of the concentration of forces and the launching of operations against our strongest point. When the Caucasian army's advance on Saratov threatened the Bolsheviks' eastern front the Red Command let our troops advance on Kursk and Orel with perfect equanimity, inexorably following the plan of concentration at Saratov, followed by a great mass attack which would shatter the Caucasian Army and throw it back to the south, weakened as it was by a thousand-kilometer march and the sending of some troops to other fronts.

It was only when the remains of the Caucasian Army retreated to Tsaritsyn, powerless now to undertake a fresh offensive, that the Red Command, uniting its forces for the defense of Moscow, began operations against the Volunteer Army which was advancing without reserves along an enormously long front, and turned it back.

In spite of the transport crisis and other difficulties, the Red Command have carried out the principle of the concentration of forces in its entirety.

We have been advancing continuously, but have taken no steps to consolidate our possession of the immense territories we have conquered.

We have made mistakes from the Sea of Azov to Orel; we have not a single fortified position or base of support. Therefore, if we have to retreat, we shall not have a single place on which to fall back.

The continual advance has reduced the Army's effective forces. The rear has become too vast. Disorganization is all the greater because of the reequipment system which Supreme Headquarters has adopted; they have turned over this duty to the troops and take no share in it themselves.

Headquarters ought to provide and distribute all necessaries, making use of all the spoils of war for this purpose.

The war is becoming to some a means of growing rich; reequipment has degenerated into pillage and peculation.

Each unit strives to secure as much as possible for itself and seizes everything that comes to hand. What cannot be used on the spot is sent back to the interior and sold at a profit. The rolling stock belonging to the troops has taken on enormous dimensions — some regiments have two hundred carriages in their wake. A considerable number of troops have retreated to the interior, and many officers are away on prolonged missions, busy selling and exchanging loot, etc.

The Army is absolutely demoralized, and is fast becoming a collection of tradesmen and profiteers.

All those employed on reequipment work — that is to say, nearly all the officers — have enormous sums of money in their possession; as a result, there has been an outbreak of debauchery, gambling, and wild orgies. Unfortunately, several highly placed officers have set the example of costly banquets and have spent money lavishly, for all the Army to see.

Our badly organized police and counterespionage systems are a great help to the Bolshevik agitators in their subversive work behind the lines. Each of these two systems works independently of the other; the officials are both underpaid and unsuitable.

As a result of the inadequacy of their salaries, the most indispensable of the railway officials quitted their posts when the Bolsheviks arrived, and went over to the enemy.

The population greeted our Army with wild enthusiasm; they have all suffered from the Bolsheviks and only want to be allowed to live in peace, and yet they have to endure the horrors of pillage, violence, and despotism all over again. Result: confusion at the front and risings in the interior.

When I arrived here, Kharkov had already been abandoned by the General Staff, and the Army was in full retreat.

The evacuation has been conducted disastrously, without plan or order. None of the institutions were given directions concerning their destination. Everybody merely wandered off anyhow. I found the railroads blocked by trains and abandoned ambulances without any staff but full of sick and wounded who had eaten nothing for three days. When I reached Slaviansk, a wounded officer had just hanged himself rather than endure the tortures of starvation. Crowds of refugees — mostly officers' families — are cramming themselves into all the trains and stations; no steps are being taken to evacuate them, and they are literally dying of cold and hunger. . . .

On the road between Zmiev and Izioum, behind the lines, local bands are destroying the railroads, molesting the troops, and robbing the ambulances and luggage vans.

I find that our forces have diminished; the 1st Corps has about two thousand six hundred men; the 5th, one thousand and fifteen cavalrymen; the Poltava group musters one hundred foot and two hundred horse; the cavalry force is about three thousand five hundred strong. Total: three thousand six hundred foot, four thousand seven hundred horse. The Kouban corps is a mere brigade; Kornilov's regiments are only battalions. Markov's two regiments and the "Special" brigade have only their cadres left, and are out of action. Of Drosdovsky's division, only three companies are left. The troops refuse to use the tanks because they are afraid of losing them. The artillery is no longer of any use.

The enemy have fifty-one thousand foot, seven thousand horse, and more than two hundred and six guns.

Behind the lines we have only the remains of Alexeiev's division, three hundred men all told.

The Army has been on the march for months, without respite or rest, and is utterly exhausted. The horses have gone sore; therefore we have been forced to discard guns and equipment.

The condition of the cavalry is simply lamentable. The horses have not been shod for a long while and have nearly all gone lame, whilst many of them are ill from exhaustion. Most of the units are out of action, as their commanders can witness.

The bitter truth is that there is no longer an Army. Measures are being taken to restore order to the interior; bases are being organized; all the available contingents are being mobilized — but all these measures have come too late, and it will take a long time to create a new Army.

The enemy realize this, and are doing their utmost to exploit their successes in every possible way.

We must have the courage to see things as they are, to look the situation squarely in the face, and be ready for fresh ordeals.

I consider it indispensable:

1. To adhere to a definite plan — that is to say, to choose one principal direction in which to concentrate our forces, and be ready to abandon part of the occupied area if it should be necessary.
2. To evacuate Rostov and Taganrog at once.
3. To choose bases behind the lines and fortify them.
4. To cut down the overlarge General Staffs and send the surplus and useless personnel to the front.
5. To provide the necessaries of life for the families of officers and employees who cannot do their work properly until they know that their wives and children are safely out of misery and danger, and to organize colonies immediately for the families of officers and officials, so that these families can be provided with food and shelter. Arrangements must be made to transport them to a place of safety in case of danger.
6. To take measures, ruthless if necessary, to put down marauding, drunkenness, and every kind of abuse; and to begin with the higher ranks, whose bad example is corrupting the troops, whatever their military worth may be.
7. To provide reinforcements of men and horses. To reequip the cavalry, or this branch of the Army will be worthless.

I have written many dispatches on this last point, but all in vain; the matter is extremely urgent. The enemy are using all their resources to create large cavalry units. Our cavalry was established and recruited without any kind of system, and it will soon fall to pieces altogether.

8. To put the counterespionage organization and the police force in order, to amalgamate them and to furnish them with sufficient credits.

9. To put the railways under military control, and to subordinate the head officials to the chief of Military Communications. At the same time to guarantee a regular living wage to the employees.

To sum up, unless the above measures are put into force, it is impossible to improve our situation. Moreover, unless they can be put in hand immediately, I must request you to transfer the command of the Volunteer Army to someone else, for without them I can accomplish nothing.

> LIEUT.-GENERAL WRANGEL
> CHATILOV, Chief of Staff

Accompanied by his chief of staff, General Chatilov, Wrangel delivered the report in person. General Denikin read the report, put it down on the table without a word, and looked up. Then he said dully: "All the same, we must go on with it."

Wrangel answered: "Of course, Your Excellency, and do our utmost to win the upper hand. But before we do anything else, we must come to a decision. The enemy are operationg between the Volunteer Army and the Army of the Don, and want to drive me down to the sea. Our cavalry is no longer capable of fighting. If you order us to retreat to Rostov and join the Army of the Don, we shall have to retreat with the enemy striking blows at our flanks the whole time. If, on the other hand, we retreat into the Crimea, where we still have troops. . . "

Denikin interrupted him: "I have been thinking it over for a long time, and I must follow the dictates of my conscience. I have not the moral right to abandon the Cossacks to their fate. We must retreat together. . . . "

Wrangel and Chatilov left Headquarters having received no further directives. They walked for a while in silence. "What is your opinion?" asked Wrangel.

Chatilov shrugged his shoulders. "They have lost their heads; they are no good for anything now."

Many personalities who had worked or fought together with Wrangel described him as chivalrous: Memoirs and even his obituaries constantly dwelt upon that word. He had no reason to like Denikin, many reasons to dislike him and, having delivered his report, nothing was simpler than to say to himself, "I told him so many times; now I wash my hands!" But such was not Wrangel's character: A fighter by nature, he was also imbued with the spirit of chivalry.

He could strike out in anger but was incapable of meanness.

Now as he pondered over his report and his meeting with Denikin, he felt compelled to express his sympathy and to repreat his feeling of loyalty. That evening he wrote Denikin:

"Your Excellency, at this moment, when luck is against us, when the ship which you are piloting between the rocks and the storm is in danger of submersion by the foul Red waves, I feel morally obliged to tell you that I understand what you must be suffering. If at this crucial moment it lightens the load with which circumstances have burdened you to know that you are not alone, please believe that I, who have followed you almost from the beginning, will continue to share your joys and sorrows, and will do everything within my power to help you.

December 10, 1919   P. WRANGEL"

The very next day Wrangel receive a cordial reply to his note. It was to be hoped that the strained relation between Denikin and him would improve — unfortunately this was not to be.

Wrangel's report was tantamount to a bomb at Denikin's headquarters: The sycophants, the incapables, the bureaucrats, and the intelligence operators saw in it an attack on their positions, a criticism of the immunity in which they had heretofore enjoyed. Working on Denikin's susceptibilities, they succeeded in awakening again his suspicions and mistrust. In Wrangel's proposal to retreat with a part of the army towards the Crimea, thereby saving it from a disastrous flank march, he saw the specter of Wrangel in a separate command.

The very same day that Wrangel received Denikin's cordial personal note, a circular telegram from Headquarters to all senior generals read: "... that certain generals have allowed themselves to express their own opinions in their dispatches in an inadmissible manner, threatening to leave the Service if their advice was not followed. In consequence the Commander in Chief demands obedience and forbids any future statement of conditions."

Attempting to coordinate action, Wrangel arranged for a meeting between General Sidorin, commander of the Don army, General Pokrovsky, commander of the Caucasian army, and himself. Headquarters reacted immediately with another circular telegram: "The Commander in Chief cannot permit the generals of the Armies to treat directly with one another, and forbids them to leave their Armies in future without his express permission."

By then key military and civilian personalities were beginning to raise questions about Denikin's capability to go on as supreme commander. It is an historical paradox that the man who openly and frankly criticized Denikin's strategy and measures would remain loyal to him despite suspicion and mistrust and subsequent direct accusations of disloyalty.

General Chatilov remembers: "During our meeting with the Don Cossack army commander General Sidorin and his chief of staff Kelchevsky, both the generals outdid each other in their harsh criticism of Headquarters, laying the blame evenly on Denikin and Romanovsky. Kelchevsky said with no equivocation that it was imperative to submit an ultimatum to Denikin demanding his resignation. I distinctly remember Wrangel's answer. Trying to pacify the two generals, Wrangel warned them against taking such a step. He recognized full well the errors of Headquarters, but said that Denikin's resignation could have positive effects only if he himself deemed it imperative to resign his command."

Seeing the enemy on their own territory, the Don Cossacks rallied; there were even moments of fleeting victory: General Pavlov and his Don Cossack corps defeated Budenny's Red cavalry army taking forty guns. The battle was fought on the lower reaches up the River Manytsh, the scene of Wrangel's successes during the previous spring. But in January the frozen steppe on the left bank of the river was covered with snow and offered no cover, food, or forage; an icy northwest wind increased the chill factor. Pavlov requested permission to move his cavalry along the populated right bank; Headquarters refused. Pavlov obeyed and lost more than half his force of men and horses, decimated by the intense cold. He was made the scapegoat but Headquarters' authority declined even further in the eyes of the Cossacks. The Volunteer army, forbidden to retreat towards the Crimea, completed a marathon flank march of five hundred kilometers, taking such losses that certain regiments simply ceased to exist. When Wrangel had taken over command of the retreating Volunteer army, there were only thirty-six hundred infantry and forty-seven hundred cavalry left; this was reduced to two thousand men at the end of the flank march. Intelligence estimated the Red army to number fifty-one thousand infantry, seven thousand cavalry and two hundred five guns.

The regiments that had been the foundation of the White army bore the brunt of this exhausting retreat. When the Volunteer and the Don armies were finally reunited, the former was, in terms of numbers, overwhelmingly inferior, though at this stage superior in quality. Nevertheless, as this was Don territory, Denikin found it convenient to unite both under General Sidorin, the commander of the Don army. Wrangel was left with no command.

It had now been the third time that Wrangel had got Denikin out of a difficult if not hopeless position: first on the Manytsh river in spring when the Reds threatened Rostov, then at Tsaritsyn, and this time during the retreat. He was to receive no thanks.

One of Wrangel's last acts as commander of the Volunteer army was to help evacuate the British military mission, which among others had been abandoned to its fate by Headquarters.

Generals Denikin and Romanovsky now asked Wrangel to proceed to the

Kouban Cossack region and raise there new forces by effecting a total mobilization. Wrangel went to Ekaterinodar and started to work on the mobilization plan. To his amazement and anger, Headquarters also sent there General Shkouro, whom Wrangel had recently dismissed from command.

Andrew Shkouro was a major at the start of the civil war. As a partisan he raided Soviet-held cities, organized Cossack uprisings against the Reds, and worked his way up from regiment to division and thence to corps commander. His popularity among the Kouban Cossacks was strong; unfortunately, it was based on the negative traits of the Cossacks: license rather than freedom, the urge to pillage, the quest for booty — characteristics developed through centuries of skirmishes against the Turks, Poles, Circassians, and other enemies, as well as in uprisings against the Russian crown.

Over the years order and discipline had replaced those "pioneer-outlaw" characteristics, which had lain dormant. The civil war had awakened them, and unscrupulous or debauched leaders put them to use. Though Shkouro's Cossacks did perform notable feats, the drunkenness, looting, and the bad example of their leader had reduced their effectiveness. As a senior commander Shkouro's use was minimal.

Wounded in his vanity by Wrangel's dismissal, urged on by Wrangel's enemies at Headquarters, Shkouro toured the Cossack villages and, instead of helping to raise troops, indulged in bitter propaganda against Wrangel. Returning to Headquarters, Wrangel presented his report and asked for reassignment, feeling that under the circumstances it was hardly possible to organize a new Cossack army.

The White army was rolling back towards Novorossiysk; the evacuation of the army by sea, if not imminent, was at least to be envisaged. Wrangel requested permission to proceed there and start planning for fortifications which would give the army a perimeter to fall back on. At first Denikin refused on the pretext that it would create a panic among the population; then changing his mind, he ordered Wrangel to go ahead. No sooner had Wrangel arrived at Novorossiysk that the orders were countermanded and the job given to General Denikin's assistant. As a result, again nothing was done and the White army was to suffer its greatest calamity.

In Novorossiysk a British member of Parliament, MacKinder, called on Wrangel and asked if he could speak with him on a delicate question. He then showed Wrangel a telegram he had received from London, notifying him that according to sources in Warsaw, a coup d'etat was to take place with the overthrow of Denikin and Wrangel's appointment in his stead.

Wrangel replied that while he differed with Denikin on questions of strategy, he was under Denikin's orders and would never, in any contingency whatsoever, act against him. To MacKinder's question if he could communicate this reply to his government, Wrangel replied positively and the same day sent a report of this interview and his answeres to General Denikin.

He received no answer: Sulking and suspicious, Denikin kept silence.

Losing all patience, Wrangel asked to be relieved from duty. General Chatilov followed suit. Headquarters issued the relevant orders and Wrangel and his chief of staff left for the Crimea, where Wrangel's wife had a house and where he decided to sit out and await developments. Fate prescribed differently.

12
Dismissal – Exile

THE CRIMEAN PENINSULA HAD BEEN defended by General Slachtchov. This young general had been left on his own and with minimal forces had successfully defended the Crimea, letting the Reds penetrate into the peninsula, and then smashing them with his small but mobile force. Left to his devices, bearing the stress of combat over a long period, Slachtchov had taken to drugs in order to keep going. Gradually his mind had become deranged; he assumed dictatorial powers, tyrannized the population, and issued decrees full of unbalanced fantasy. The unhealthy attitude which had come to permeate the White army through the series of military setbacks and disorder in the rear also infected the Crimea. Refugees had fled to the Crimea after the disastrous evacuation of Odessa, where scenes of nightmarish disorder and despair ranged from mass suicides to women and children being trampled to death as they sought to scramble on board the departing transports. General Schilling, blamed for the disaster, had also arrived in the Crimea. Feeling that he had lost all authority, he went to Wrangel and asked him to take over command of the Crimean peninsula. Wrangel answered that he could not do so unless he received a direct order from Denikin. Schilling and other senior commanders, including Loukomsky, Denikin's assistant, all cabled Headquarters and insisted on Wrangel's appointment.

To make matters worse, an adventurer named Captain Orlov, who had put together an armed band of deserters, malcontents, and bandits, advanced from the Crimean mountains down towards Sebastopol and other coastal cities. He issued a proclamation:

To officers, Cossacks, soldiers, and sailors! The whole of the numerous garrison of Yalta has come over to my side, including a company of several hundred men, complete with artillery and machine guns. General Schilling wants to negotiate with me, but I will not enter into any discussion with this man until he has brought to life again all those men whose deaths he had caused in Odessa. I hear that our new leader, General Wrangel, is in the Crimea. He is the only man with whom we can and will negotiate. He is the man in whom we all have complete faith; he will sacrifice everything in the struggle against the Bolsheviks and those who are corrupting the interior. Long live General Wrangel — the strong man with the mightly soul!

Orlov's appearance and his proclamation poured oil into the fire. Wishing to dissociate himself from Orlov and his proclamation, Wrangel sent a telegram with copies to General Schilling and local authorities:

I have noted the proclamation in which you declare that you submit to my authority, although actually I am holding no command whatsoever. Until recently, the Army has been invincible solely because it knew how to obey its leaders blindly. Having forgotten its oath of loyalty, it has come to civil war. We have renewed the struggle of our own free will, and of our own free will, which is equivalent to an oath, we have put ourselves under the orders of our superiors. Neither you nor I have the right to be disloyal to them. Speaking as an old soldier who has served his country loyally all his life, I earnestly beg you to put an end to your rebellion and submit to your immediate superiors.

Headquarters' reaction to this was unexpected. Wrangel, Chatilov, Denikin's assistant Loukomsky, Nenukov, Commander of the Fleet, and his chief of staff Admiral Bubnov were all cashiered with no further explanation. But worse was to come. From a Royal Navy ship off shore a message reached Wrangel.

From R.A., Second in Command to Marlborough

W.I.T. Cipher

Inform Wrangel destroyer will bring him to Novorossiyak at once. Following from Holman*: Holman guarantees his safety, and will endeavor to arrange meeting between him and Denikin, but he should not come unless he is prepared to abide by Denikin's final decision regarding his future movements. Wrangel should understand the whole future of Russia is at stake. He must be prepared to state publicly his adherence to Denikin's new democratic policy, and sternly discountenance reactionaries now using his name. Holman trusting to his loyalty as enough for length of coming to Novorossiysk. If Wrangel desires, send him destroyer to arrive tomorrow, Wednesday. Inform me time of arrival as soon as possible.

Angered, confused, and astonished, Wrangel sent Chatilov to Holman. Chatilov thanked Holman on Wrangel's behalf and told him that as Wrangel had committed no crime, he needed no foreign safe-conducts and as such considered it totally useless to vindicate himself to Denikin. Chatilov returned the next day without having received permission to land in Novorossiyak. He bore a message from Admiral Seymour, Commander of the British Fleet: It stated that Denikin was demanding via Holman that Wrangel leave Russian territory immediately.

Wrangel sat down and wrote Denikin a letter. This time it was not a trenchant report from a subordinate to his commander in chief, nor was it a

* General Holman, the head of the British Military Mission.

personal letter of discontent to a companion in arms; but rather it was a harsh indictment. The man who had forthrightly and loyally served under Denikin, saving the latter three times from defeat, the man whose warnings had been rejected and whose efforts to end misrule, plunder, and massacres had been met with surly silence, now poured out unrestrainedly against his former commander. The thoroughbred horse, spurred and clumsily abused, had taken the bit and was running away!

In his memoirs General Chatilov wrote: "How sad it was for me to see Wrangel's reaction to the message I bore. Pacing incessantly from one corner of the room to the other, he vented his feeling of outrage and anger. It was not so long ago that Headquarters invariably called on him to take over whenever things had gone badly. How many times he had staved off impending disaster and saved the situation, and now he was asked to go.

"It was late at night before we turned in, but early next morning he met me with his letter to Denikin. I implored him not to send it, but it was no use; the best I could do was to get him to soften some of the harshest sentences.

"Had Denikin had the capacity to deal with people and see their motivations, he would have had in Wrangel the most trustworthy and loyal subordinate. Denikin neither appreciated Wrangel's sense of honor nor understood his tempestuous character. Nor, again, did he wish to recognize Wrangel's military talent. I myself had so many times the opportunity to see Wrangel in the most crucial stages of battle: He was simply wonderful: fearless, calm, firm. Always looking ahead, forseeing difficulties and divining the road to success. Sure in his own strength, he naturally reacted strongly to Headquarters' incessant bungles. Headquarters' reaction to these outbursts were suspicion and the haunting illusion of a takeover of power."

Wrangel and Chatilov left for Constantinople.

There Wrangel received Denikin's reply:

Dear Sir, Peter Nikolaevich!

Your letter has come just at the right time — at the most difficult moment when all my spiritual strength must be concentrated on preventing the collapse of our front. I hope that you are satisfied.

If I still had a vestige of doubt concerning your role in the struggle for power, your letter has eliminated it completely. It does not contain a single word of truth. You know this. It brings forth monstrous accusations which you don't believe yourself. They are obviously brought forth for the same purpose for which your preceding pamphlet-reports were multiplied and circulated.

You are doing everything you can to undermine the government and bring on disintegration.

There was a time when, suffering from a grave illness, you said to

Yuzefovich that this was God's punishment for your inordinate ambition.

May He forgive you now for the harm you have done to the Russian cause.

February 25, 1920

A. DENIKIN

If Wrangel's letter to Denikin sinned by extreme harshmess, the latter's reply had lost all touch with reality: *Quem volent dei perdere prius dementant* (Whom the gods wish to destroy they first make mad).

13

Transfer Of Power — Crimea

DURING ONE OF HIS ARDUOUS campaigns Napoleon drew up projects for the French theater; on the eve of El Alamein Winston Churchill immersed himself in a book. Great men have the ability to dissociate themselves for a short time from reality, as if to force themselves to relax and draw new strength for further endeavors. Wrangel was no exception. Guidebook in hand, he visited Constantinople's mosques and monuments, commented in his memoirs on the beauty of the Bosphorus, the activity in the bazaars, and the bright colors.

But events in the south of Russia rolled on in their fateful course. Demoralized Don and Kouban Cossack regiments flowed back, avoiding combat; the Volunteer army regiments, bled white in their long retreat, marched among hordes of civilians, baggage trains, and driven cattle.

Wrangel's original suggestion of an orderly retreat to the Crimean peninsula (at that time it could have been easily done) had been spurned by Denikin; now it had become the only possible solution and that solution had to be by an evacuation of the army by sea from Novorossiysk. Wrangel had warned Denikin that the city had to be prepared as a base of defense; this too was disregarded. Now in the bitter cold, a howling wind blowing from the north, the human mass of misery streamed towards the port of Novorossiysk: Demoralized Don Cossacks, some of whom had thrown away their rifles; Kalmyk tribesmen driving their horses and camels; a never-ending stream of carts, some loaded with goods, some with sick and wounded, and some with helpless civilians; men, women, and children, terrorized victims of the civil strife. Maintaining their iron discipline, the remnants of the Volunteer regiments, many units of which were composed solely of officers, drove their columns through this disorganized crowd. Singly or in small groups Kouban Cossacks moved sullenly in the opposite direction, heading back towards their villages, no longer interested in the fate of their regiments or the fortunes of war.

The torrent of desperate humanity poured into the undefended city. The tonnage of ships available was totally insufficient; no evacuation plan or schedule had been prepared; it was "first come, first served." The Volunteer regiments, better disciplined and organized, seized ships and, posting guards, loaded only their own units, turning Cossacks away; later this was to lead to bitter conflict between the Cossack and the Volunteer units.

Young Lieutenant Mamontov had retreated with his battery; marching into Novrossiyak, they had unhitched their horses, spiked their guns, and pushed their way on foot towards the piers. Mamontov had bidden a tearful adieu to his horse. He remembered: "We waited all day on the pier; it was getting dark. The captain hailed from the bridge: 'I cannot take any more people on board!'

"Our captain Sapegin answered: 'You will take ALL my sixty men even if you have no place on board.'

" 'I can't — impossible; the ship will keel over.'

" 'You will take us even if we have to blast our way in!' And he unslung his carbine. We all followed suit; bolts were drawn, and we closed in around our captain. 'Three minutes to think it over and we open fire!' Captain Sapegin's voice was calm but determined.

"We would have fired; it was a matter of life or death. Furthermore, the ship was full of rear echelon personnel, cowards, deserters, and other bastards to whom we owed a large share of our defeat — and those SOB's were going to sail away, leaving behind the combat units — no way!

"After a moment of silence the ship's captain called back: 'All right, I'll take the artillerymen, but leave the saddles and all baggage.'

"One after the other we climbed down to a barge and moved across it towards the ship. I walked over a gangplank onto the barge which was so full of people that I had to stumble over their shoulders in order to get to the ship. Hands reached down and pulled me aboard; I was jammed against the railing and could only put one foot down . . . but I was saved."

Mamontov was among the lucky ones. The less fortunate crowded on the piers, shouting and begging to no avail. Horsemen dismounted and, giving their steeds a farewell pat, shot them, tears streaming down their faces. Some seeing no hope of getting away put guns to their heads and followed their equine partners to eternity. Cossack units which had maintained discipline but who saw that there was no hope of getting on board the ships turned around and headed for the Taman peninsula, hoping to reach the Crimea from there; others marched towards Georgia, now an independent but inhospitable haven.

Denikin and his staff watched the disaster from a destroyer anchored in the harbor. On landing in the Crimea, faced with open hostility, Denikin called a Council of War and announced his resignation. He requested an election of a successor to the command of the White forces. It is ironic that General Denikin, who at the start of the Russian Revolution had set himself resolutely against any elective command, was now offering his troops just that solution. Aside from violating a basic military principle, he was in effect offering the possibility of another bloody discord among its senior commanders.

Public and military opinion was strongly for the nomination of Wrangel, yet Denikin could not muster sufficient civic courage to appoint as his successor the man who had criticized his strategy and prophesied his failure.

Wrangel had decided to leave Constantinople for Serbia and there work on the eventual possibility of providing a haven for the refugees. On the eve of his departure the English High Commissioner in Constantinople, Admiral de Robeck, invited Wrangel for lunch. On the way to his luncheon Wrangel was handed a telegram from the British General Holman, head of the British Military Mission at Denikin's Headquarters. It stated that Denikin had decided to resign his command and had summoned a Military Council to elect a new commander in chief. Denikin requested Wrangel to attend. After having fired Wrangel and sent him into exile, this request seemed highly unusual.

During lunch on the admiral's flagship *Ajax* Wrangel could hardly keep his thoughts together and take part in the general conversation. After lunch the admiral invited Wrangel and General Milne, commander of the British occupation forces, into his study.

"I sent you a wireless message from General Holman," he said. "If you wish to go to Sebastopol, one of our ships is at your service. I am very well informed on the Crimean situation, and I know beyond a doubt that you will be called upon to succeed Denikin. I also know the state of the Army and the hopelessness of the cause; I doubt whether anyone can save it. I have just received a telegram from the English government; it aggravates the situation considerably. It is addressed to General Denikin, but I cannot conceal its contents from you. I do not want to deal treacherously with you. If you do not learn its contents here and now, it will be too late. Read this before making your decision."

He handed Wrangel the following note addressed to General Denikin:
SECRET

The British High Commissioner in Constantinople has been ordered by his Government to make the following communication to General Denikin: The Supreme Council (of the Allies) is of the opinion that, on the whole, the prolongation of the Russian Civil War is the most disturbing factor in the present European situation.

His Britannic Majesty's Government wishes to suggest to General Denikin that, in view of the present situation, an arrangement with the Soviet Government for an amnesty for the Crimean population in general, and the Volunteer Army in particular, would be in the best interests of all concerned. The British Government is absolutely convinced that the abandonment of this unequal struggle will be the best thing for Russia, and will therefore take upon itself the task of making this arrangement, once it has General Denikin's consent. Furthermore, it offers him and his principal supporters hospitality and a refuge in Great Britain.

The British Government has, in the past, given him a large amount of assistance, and this is the only reason why he has been able to continue the struggle up to the present; therefore they feel justified in hoping that he will accept their proposal. If, however, General Denikin should feel it his duty to refuse, and to continue a manifestly hopeless struggle, the British Government will find itself obliged to renounce all responsibility for his actions, and to cease to furnish him with any help or subvention of any kind from that time on.

BRITISH HIGH COMMISSION

CONSTANTINOPLE, April 2, 1920

After a short silence, Wrangel said, "Thank you for having warned me, Admiral. Until this moment I was still hesitating, but now I have no doubts. If I am chosen, it is my duty to accept the command." Admiral de Robeck, obviously much moved, wrung his hand.

General Chatilov tried to dissuade Wrangel from going. "You know that it is an impossible fight: the Army will either be killed off to the last man, or it will capitulate. You will be dishonored forever afterwards. You have already lost everything except your spotless reputation; it would be madness to lose that too." But when he was convinced that Wrangel's decision was unalterable, he told him that he was coming along.*

Wrangel and Chatilov set out for the Crimea on a British destroyer. Exiting from the Bosphorus into the Black Sea, they were hit by a violent storm. Wrangel, always subject to seasickness, became so ill that he suffered a heart attack. Climbing to the bridge, Chatilov saw the captain and several officers, some of them also seasick; not speaking English, he had great difficulties explaining. After a brief consultation with the British general Keyes who was also on board, it was decided to turn back. On arriving at Constantinople, Admiral de Robeck transferred Wrangel and Chatilov to the battleship *Emperor of India*, which finally brought them to Sebastopol.

While Wrangel went straight to the War Council which was already in session, Chatilov went looking for information on the status of those troops at the front, those recently brought over from the Novorrossiysk and those still stranded on the mainland. What he found out hardly inspired confidence. On

---

* In his book *White Against Red*, D. Lehovich, an admirer and apologist of Denikin, has left out the above facts, making Wrangel's return to the Crimea appear as a grab for power. Even the most casual observer would agree that with the battered remnants of the White army in disarray the mutinous corps of disgruntled Cossacks, the chaos in the Crimea, and the British ultimatum on top of it, only a hero or a fool would be tempted to return. Even Wrangel's severest critics, the Soviets, agree unanimously that he was not a fool.

the Crimean front everything was relatively quiet, the Reds having had no time to regroup their forces; General Slachchov, the mercurial and bizarre commander, was holding on with his small force. The situation of the Cossacks on the mainland was nothing short of catastrophic. Thoroughly demoralized, they had retreated to the seashore; some Don and mostly Kouban Cossack regiments with a mass of refugees now hugged the shore. The elected Kouban Cossack ataman Boukretov and the left wing element of the Rada (Cossack parliament) clamored for negotiations with the Reds and surrender to them. Boukretov had come over to the Crimea to state his demands.

The Volunteer army regiments had arrived by sea low in morale, having left behind their baggage trains, machine guns, and artillery. Now, quartered around the town of Simferopol, some units were no longer in hand. The cavalry regiments were horseless. The navy had neither coal or oil. Not one ship had the capability to leave port.

This was the military situation that faced Wrangel as he was about to decide on his further steps. The first thing Wrangel did was to state that under the present circumstances General Denikin did not have the right to simply step aside without appointing a successor. To this, General Dragomitov, presiding over the Military Council, answered that Denikin's decision was irrevocable and that in spite of further votes of confidence from some of the Volunteer army units he was throwing in the sponge.

The Council in the meanwhile was proceeding under tumultuous conditions; present were not only senior commanders but junior officers as well. Wrangling, shouts, and disorder ruled supreme.

Under those conditions no decisions could be taken and Wrangel suggested that the Council be limited to senior commanders only. The idea was accepted. General Chatilov, who attended the meeting, described it thus in his memoirs: "Wrangel again reiterated his opinion that in those trying times Denikin had no right to abandon the army. His statement was met by complete silence. Continuing, Wrangel said that if anyone was chosen to bear the cross of command, he should at least know what his subordinates were to expect from him. Again complete silence; everyone knew by now the contents of the British ultimatum, and no one could imagine how one could cope with the situation. The army remnants, devoid of supplies, demoralized, and uprooted, could no longer be considered a real military potential; evacuation was not possible due to lack of fuel, and even if such were available, where would they go? As the British categorically stated that no further supplies would be available, no one could even imagine what further action could be awaited from the High Command.

"Wrangel went on to say that whoever was chosen as General Denikin's successor must know what is to be expected from him by his electors, that even if victory was now out of question, it was incumbent on the designee to maintain to the end the honor of the army."

Having stated his views, Wrangel pleaded fatigue and asked permission to leave the Council.

Alone, deep in thought, and with a heavy heart, he walked through the streets of Sebastopol.

Wrangel's parents were not religious; his childhood and adolescence were not within the church's orbit, and as a student and later as a young officer, he was not a churchgoer excepting the obligatory attendances customary in Czarist Russia. His marriage changed that. Olga Ivanecho came from a deeply religious family; under her benign influence Wrangel became a churchgoer, his belief deepening with family life and the birth of the children. Perhaps, also, his explosive character was aroused by the revolution's desecration of the churches and by the massacres of priests.

During the epic battles around Tsaritsyn, Sergeant Koshul of the Kouban Cossacks remembered: "I was then a private in a Cossack regiment and my unit was on guard at Headquarters, a number of railway carriages where Wrangel and his staff lived and worked when not out in the field. I was on sentry duty and paced back and forth along the carriage where General Wrangel sat working behind a makeshift desk. Around 2 a.m, glancing through the window, I saw him get up, kneel down, and pray for a long time."

Now, wandering about Sebastopol, Wrangel had the urge to unburden his soul. Sometime before he had met Benjamin, the bishop of Sebastopol. He decided to call on him. The bishop was a man of immense drive, faith, and courage. He received Wrangel not only as a clergyman but also as a dynamic civic leader. Blessing Wrangel with a fifteenth-century ikon, the bishop laid before Wrangel several petitions that he had received from Orthodox, Catholic, and Moslem clergy, urging him to use his influence in securing Wrangel's nomination to Supreme Commander. Fortified in spirit, Wrangel returned to the Council, which had in the meantime unanimously elected him as Denikin's successor. Signing the Council's protocol, Wrangel wrote:

> I have shared the honor of its victories with the Army, and cannot refuse to drink the cup of humiliation with it now. Drawing strength from the trust which my comrades-in-arms place in me, I consent to accept the post of Commander in Chief.
>
> LIEUTENANT-GENERAL BARON P. WRANGEL

March 22, 1920

General Denikin's last order read:

EDICT OF THE COMMANDER IN CHIEF OF THE ARMED FORCES OF SOUTH RUSSIA

FEODOSSIA   No. 2899   March 22, 1920

1. Lieutenant-General Baron Wrangel is hereby appointed Commander in Chief of the Armed Forces of South Russia.

2. Sincere greeting to all those who have followed me loyally in the terrible struggle. God save Russia and grant victory to the Army!

LIEUT.-GEN. DENIKIN

Having signed this edict, General Denikin departed with his wife and chief of staff General Romanovsky. They left by ship for Constantinople, abandoning to its fate the army and the parcel of free Russia. On arrival in Constantinople General Denikin and his entourage were met by the Russian military attaché who brought them over to the Russian embassy. While Denikin conversed with the ambassador, Romanovsky walked out into the crowded lobby. An unknown man dressed in an officer's uniform walked up to him, drew a revolver, shot him dead, and disappeared into the crowd. Mrs. Denikin panicked, appealed for help to the British general Holman who had accompanied them. A unit of Ghurka soldiers occupied the Russian embassy over the protest of the ambassador and of the military attache.

In our days forceful occupation of an embassy has become almost a routine event and draws almost routine coverage in the news media. In 1920 it was still an act of unprecedented gravity. In spite of pleas from the members of the embassy General Denikin refused to ask the British to leave. Surrounded by foreign soldiers, he stood during the memorial service for his friend and former chief of staff. The next day, without waiting for the funeral, he left with his wife for London.

Thus ended ingloriously the career of a soldier and a sincere patriot, but a man too small for the gigantic task that confronted him. As the problems loomed larger, his stature diminished, and as his edifice built on faulty strategy and poor administration showed cracks and finally crumbled, he retreated behind the ramparts of his inferiority complex and thence lashed out at those who disagreed with him — and particularly at the one man who could have saved him.

On learning about the murder, Wrangel had the military attaché relieved, charging him with failure to protect Denikin and his entourage, also underlining to the British that Russia, or whatever was left of it, was still a sovereign state.

14

Against All Odds

THE BRITISH CABINET'S DECISION TO abandon the White army to its fate was by no means unanimous, although Lloyd George, the Prime Minister, had bluntly state on July 22, 1918: "Liberty means that the Russian Nation should have the right of setting up any Government they choose. If they choose a Republican Government or a Bolshevik Government or a Monarchical Government, it is no concern of ours." Some twenty years later another British minister excused equally well the advent of Hitler. But, just as he opposed the policy of Chamberlain in 1940 and the Prime Minister's acquiescence to the Hitler regime, so did Winston Churchill rise to the defense of any anti-Communist movement in Russia.

In a speech on November 26, 1918, Churchill said: "The Bolshevik system was from the beginning doomed to perish in consequence of its antagonism to the fundamental principles of civilized society. The Bolshevik regime has already deserted its system, but is separated by a gulf of crimes and miseries from the mass of the Russian peoples and can have no power in the permanent future of the Russian Empire. Sooner or later the system and regime must perish beneath the vengeance of the Russian nation. It was never possible for a civilized Government to establish normal peaceful relations with the Bolshevik Government. Even had it been possible from our point of view, that Government itself carried within it the seeds of its own destruction, so that the arrangement could only have been temporary and we should have been building on a perishing foundation.

"It is a mistake to suppose that we have a choice at the present time between 'a strong Russia' and 'a weak Russia.' 'A strong Russia' will certainly arise. The only doubt is when and how. The only choice open to us is to accelerate or delay that resurrection. By accelerating it we bring nearer to ourselves the problems inseparable from 'a strong Russia.' But we also place ourselves in the most favorable position for dealing with those problems, at any rate in the immediate future. By delaying that resurrection, we 'prolong the agony,' we keep an immense nation and an enormous branch of the human race and family in a state of poverty, misery and anarchy; and when, finally, revival takes place, we must be confronted by a new Russia and 'a strong Russia' animated towards us by sentiments of implacable and it may be thought not ill-deserved hostility.

"We have definitely chosen, and rightly chosen, to aid all the anti-Bolshevik forces. For more than a year we have pursued this policy, spending not only money but blood in their support. The anti-Bolsheviks are as much devoted to the ideal of a 'united Russia' as the Bolsheviks are to the ideal of 'world revolution.' These are the opposite principles which are now contending in Russia, and their adherents in each case must, in the nature of things, pursue them to their logical conclusion or perish.

"In this connection it is not perhaps unfitting for us sometimes to remember that the Russia of Kolchak and Denikin is the direct lineal successor of the Russia with whom we joined hands on the outbreak of the Great War and with whom we signed the Treaty of London of September 4th, 1914. Naturally the Russians, who will soon have their own country back again restored to the ranks of the great Powers of the world, who feel themselves the guardians of the principle of the Russian State, are sometimes tempted to think that their allies of 1914 have not used them too well. It is practically certain in a military sense that, but for the loyal and impetuous onslaught of Russia at the beginning of the war, Paris would have fallen and our cause would have been defeated. It may even be permissible to remember that the unhappy Prince, against whose atrocious murder with the entire family scarcely a voice has been raised, was absolutely loyal to the allied cause.* Russia fought stoutly for three long and terrible years against the common enemy in circumstances of appalling difficulty and with a loss of life exceeding that of all the other allies put together. At last she collapsed before the blows of the German arm reinforced by the poison of Bolshevism, which the Germans had known how to inject. From that moment there has been a dispostion on the part of some of her allies to treat her as dead, to deny her all share in the victory to which she was so great a contributor, and to divide her estates and disintegrate her Empire. Our Russian ally has, in fact, been treated as if she had been an enemy State and injuries of the most fearful character have been inflicted upon her. These facts constitute a formidable record."

In constant opposition to the Prime Minister, Winston Churchill, then Secretary for War, pleaded and thundered on behalf of the White armies, maintaining his views as one after another of their efforts failed.

Notwithstanding Churchill's persuasive efforts, Lloyd George loftily stated that Britian trades even with the cannibals, and the Cabinet decided: "It was highly important for the British Empire that trade with Russia should be resumed with as little delay as possible." The Russia meant was

---

* On 16 July 1918 Czar Nicholas II (who had abdicated in 1917) had been murdered in a cellar at Ekaterinodar by the Bolsheviks. Six other members of his family and four of their attendants were also murdered.

Soviet Russia, with whose representative Krassin and Lloyd George were busy negotiating. Lloyd George went on record to say that Britain would in no way support any anti-Bolshevik action by the forces of General Wrangel.

Wrangel's only hope was to stall for time. Time to reorganize the remnants of the White army, time to get fuel for the navy to save whatever Cossack forces were still to be saved from the mainland or to plan for an eventual evacuation, time to organize law and order in the Crimea, and, most of all, time to arrange for a breakthrough out of the Crimea; for bottled up within the peninsula, the army and the population were doomed to starvation.

His first act was to send a dispatch to the British government through the British high commissioner in Constantinople, Admiral de Robeck. Therein he stated the total impossibility for the White army to negotiate with the Reds. Capitulation should have meant massacre; besides which, the Bolsheviks, feeling superiority on their side, were in no mood to negotiate. Wrangel deftly laid the responsibility and the onus of negotiating on the British, knowing full well that such negotiations, even if doomed to certain failure, would take time — time, the most precious asset that he could only hope for.

His next move was the reorganization of the armed forces.

Hungry, armed, and desperate, the remnants of the White army had left behind them all armored units, aircraft, artillery, and, above all, horses — horses for the Cossacks, unaccustomed to fighting on foot, for the regular cavalry, for the field artillery, and for transport. In those days an army with no horses simply ceased to be an army. The Crimean territory could not supply the remounts. Abuse of authority, requisition, and pillage, born during the laxity of Denikin's command, had again blossomed out.

A.P. Albov, then a young soldier nineteen years old, had disembarked with his unit at Kerch; he remembered: "We landed in the evening: it was winter weather; a cold wind, the pavements wet from rain. We were brought to our 'quarters'; these consisted of a paved courtyard within a three-floor building. It was almost dark when we, mostly young boys, settled down on the wet cobblestones. We froze, were dead tired and hungry.

"Someone yelled: 'Look there is a wine depot in the cellar!'

"We all jumped up. Sure enough, over the door was the sign 'Wine Depot.' We decided to get at the wine, cost what may; wine just to warm ourselves. We knocked on the door, long and loud — no one answered.

"We decided to break down the door, and as we hammered at it, we heard a voice cry out: 'Don't break the door — I'll open up!' A key turned; the door creaked open, and before us stood a grey-haired, tired-looking old man. He looked us over and sadly remarked: 'But you are just a bunch of kids; I see that you are frozen and that you need the wine to warm you up. I'll give you a few bottles free and let you sleep in the cellar, if you promise to leave the rest of the bottles.'

"Ashamed and crestfallen we gave our word to the old man. We got our bottles and emptied them. We felt warmer and our spirits rose. We walked down into the cellar, lay down on the bare ground, and fell asleep."

Not all behaved as gently. There was pillage, murder, and drunkenness. With iron determination bordering on ruthlessness Wrangel took the demoralized units in hand. Court-martials and speedy executions brought a halt to lawlessness.

A Captain Manegetti shot and killed a sailor; both the killer and the dead man were found to have been under the influence of alcohol. Wrangel had the captain court-martialed; the press and the public were allowed to observe the proceedings. Manegetti was convicted of murder and sentenced to be shot. On appeal, in defense to his past service, he was reduced in rank to private and sent to the front, where shortly afterwards he was killed in action.

Such drastic measures soon restored discipline, and eventually morale. They also showed to the civilian population that marauding, illicit requisition, and debauching were no longer to be tolerated.

The bane of Denikin's armies were the enormously overpopulated staffs. Wrangel cleaned out the "Augean stables," ordering every nonessential officer back into combat units. Not all these measures were effective; the number of "hang backs" remained large until the very last days.

One day, walking down the platform of a station where his staff train stood, Wrangel saw a well turned-out cavalry colonel. Wrangel greeted him and asked him where he served. "I am assigned as liaison officer to General Slachchov, sir!"

Turning towards the railroad carriage where his chief of staff General Chatilov was standing by an open window, Wrangel called: "Paul, is there such a job?"

"Certainly not," answered Chatilov without even checking. "Another candidate for the front!"

Shaken to the core, the crestfallen colonel added with some hesitation: "I . . . I . . . I . . . am also attached to the staff of Bishop Benjamin."

"What?" bellowed Wrangel, "Bishop Benjamin? Well then, we shall have to give you an incense burner — so that you can officiate! Keeping yourself away from the front, are you? How dare you!"

A crowd of civilians gathered on the platform heard Wrangel's loud vociferations, generously laced with expletives. The colonel was arrested on the spot.

One of the first staffs hit was the counterintelligence, propaganda, and political unit Osvag, whose more than dubious activities had had much to do with the rift between Denikin and Wrangel. Besides that, its second in command, a Lieutenant Colonel Siminsky, had turned out to be a Soviet agent and eventually defected, taking with him classified papers and the army's cipher code.

The problem of the Don Cossacks loomed up. The Don Cossack army had had an independent status, subordinate to General Denikin only in an operational sense. The commander of that army, General Sidorin and his chief of staff General Kelchevsky were among the bitterest opponents of General Denikin and his policies. The Don Cossacks had suffered heavy casualties in the course of the civil war. When the Red offensive drove a wedge between them and the Volunteer units and large portions of the Don territory were lost, the Cossacks became demoralized; whole divisions retreated without a fight left in them; however, some individual units fought well (notably the Guards Cossack brigade whose discipline, combat record and losses in officers and men were among the highest in the White army) until the retreat engulfed them also and they headed for Novorossiysk expecting to be evacuated by sea. But the Volunteer regiments were there first; the tonnage was insufficient and major portions of the Don Cossack army were left to their fate. Some surrendured; others headed along the northern shore of the Black Sea and joined the Kouban Cossack division in the Taman peninsula; others managed to secure shipping and arrived at the Crimea in a state close to mutiny. The commander General Sidorin and his chief of staff General Kelchevsky, who had borne a large share of the blame for the debacle of the Don Cossacks, now availed themselves of this opportunity to engage in hostile propaganda not only against the Volunteer army but also against any further involvement in the war. The defection of the remaining Cossack divisions would have meant a final disaster. The propaganda involved inflammatory articles in the Don Cossack paper distributed to the troops. The ataman of the Cossacks, General Bogayevsky and other officers were loyal and not in accord with this separatist policy, but were powerless to act. Reading the articles, Wrangel ordered the editor of the paper arrested and an inquest made. This revealed that the editor was mainly a mouthpiece: the culprits were the commanding general of the Don Cossacks and his chief of staff. Wrangel moved swiftly; arrested and brought to trial, they were convicted and sentenced to hard labor. Wrangel corrected the sentences to dishonorable discharge and exile. The command of the Don Cossacks was taken over by General Abramov, a tough combat officer who soon had all his units in hand.

The army in the Crimea, united again, was rapidly becoming combat ready. Wrangel's worries, however, were far from over; one obstacle after another arose, and no sooner was one problem settled than another seemingly insoluble one loomed up.

Penned aganist the sea in the Taman peninsula were Kouban Cossack units along with some Don Cossack regiments. Wrangel's two best generals, his companions in the Caucasus campaigns and the battles of Tsaritsyn, Ulagai and Babiev, attempted to organize the Cossacks defense. They failed not because of the Cossack regiments' rank and file but because of their ataman, General Bukretov, and the left-wing members of the Rada, the Cossack parliament. These insisted on negotiations with the Reds which could only mean capitulation. Generals Ulagai and Starikov came over to the Crimea to report to Wrangel and recommend sea evacuation of the Cossacks to the Crimea. Along with these generals appeared Bukretov, the Kouban ataman. A stormy session took place: Present besides Wrangel and Chatilov were the atamans of the Don and Terek Cossacks, Generals Ulagai and Starikov; Bukretov, the Kouban ataman; and also the chief of naval operations. Ulagai and Starikov stated that the combat capable units were to be brought over to the Crimea and that due to the adverse propaganda of the Rada there was nothing that could be done further on the mainland.

"That's not true," said Bukretov, "I as ataman cannot condone any transfer of Kouban Cossacks from their national territory; they are perfectly capable of their own defense. It is only the Generals Ulagai, Babiev, Naumenko and others who are not willing to fight!"

The hot-tempered Circassian General Ulagai jumped up. "Is that so; then why does Bukretov not take over the command?"

Bukretov declined.

Wrangel: "Well, if you do not want to take the command responsibility, I cannot allow irresponsible persons to agitate against the High Command. You can go, but you will not leave the Crimea!" Turning to the admiral, he said: "See that no ship takes him on board!" Bukretov left; Chatilov and the other atamans tried to persuade Wrangel to change his mind, reminding him that according to the Cossack constitution to which Wrangel was a cosigner, the power of the ataman was inviolable and that any forceful action would further undermine morale. At first obstinate, Wrangel was finally persuaded and Bukretov in turn agreed to take over the command of the Cossacks on the mainland.

It was not long before Bukretov and another Kouban Cossack, General Morozov, entered into negotiations with the Reds and signed the capitulation. Bukretov himself fled to Georgia; those who surrendered, at least the officers, were promptly shipped off to Siberia, Archangel, and other places of doom.

But far from all let themselves be led off. Colonel Lebedev, whom we remember two years before charging at the head of his regiment during the visit of General Denikin and the British military mission to Wrangel's headquarters, was unwilling to surrender. He rode to the front of his regiment and told his Cossacks that he was riding down to the sea and was going over to the

Crimea — he was not going to let the Reds get him. "Whoever wants to can follow me!" he announced. The whole regiment turned their horses and followed him. Other regiments or parts of them made their way to the coast. Wrangel had collected all the fuel that could be found for whatever shipping was available. He appealed to Admiral de Robeck and the British Navy. In stormy weather, using lifeboats, the Kouban, Don, and Terek Cossacks were taken on board; horses, guns, and machine guns had to be left ashore.

Wrangel personally met the disembarking units, spoke with the officers and men. The ones who had come over were men that could be relied on in all circumstances; most had fought with Wrangel through the north Caucasus, on the Manytsh, and at Tsaritsyn. The weaker elements were those who capitulated: They were to regret it in the various concentration camps where they ended their lives. There was a lighter side to the Cossack tragedy. Some Don Cossack units under a Lieutenant Colonel Salnikov, fearing that they might not get away by sea, pretended to go over to the Red side, demanding only that they be sent to fight against Poland rather than against their compatriots. The Reds were having their hands full in the war with Poland and were short of cavalry, especially of the good Cossack variety, whose attacks they themselves had had opportunity to taste. They negotiated with the Don Cossacks, leaving their military organization intact and only appointing a heavy dose of Communist political commissars. The Don Cossacks marched off towards the Polish front. No sooner had they made contact with the Poles than they shot or expelled the commissars (presumably depending on their greater or lesser distaste for this or that commissar) and went over to the Polish side.

In order to survive it was imperative to break out of the Crimean peninsula into the rich Ukraine; bottled up within the peninsula, it was only a question of days before the army and the population would starve. Any military operations, however, necessitated supplies: Fuel, ammunition and food had to be obtained from outside and, until that was possible, hoarded carefully. A whole series of severe decrees were made public. Along with the prohibition of any willful requisitions by army units, decrees ordered three meatless days per week to conserve the dwindling supply of livestock and forbade army units to buy bread in civilian stores. Army bakeries were put into operation. Even the exact proportions of wheat, barley, and rye were prescribed in baking bread. All export of wheat, fats, meat, and fish from the Crimea was forbidden as was the baking of pastries and other confectionary. General Chatilov was sent post haste to Constantinople in order to get as much oil and coal as could be bought.

Learning that not far from Simferopol there was coal to be found near the surface that hence could be mined without major long-term engineering projects, Wrangel remembered his mining engineer's studies and gave detailed prescriptions as to its exploitation and ordered a rail line laid to the projected sites.

It was necessary that stocks of coal be laid up as reserves for emergency use in the event of an evacuation by sea. When the evacuation did take place eight months later all transport ships were fully provisioned and 140,000 people moved from the Crimea to Constantinople.

Wrangel (center) poses with Minister and President of the Council Krivoshein (left) and Chief of Staff Chatilov.

Leaders of the Southern Russia government meet in Sebastopol in 1920. Wrangel sits at center.

Every man, regardless of rank, brought a stone from a distant quarry to build the Gallipoli memorial to the dead.

Middle: *Men at Gallipoli make an immaculate turnout for a parade in spite of the fact that many were near starvation.*

Bottom: *The evacuation by ship from the port of Evpatoria involved 140,000 people and was the biggest naval operation prior to D-Day in WW II.*

Appalling conditions at Lemnos necessitated that twelve officers live in a single tent.

Wrangel's floating headquarters Lucullus, was sunk in the Bosphorus by the Italian freighter Adria, whose captain was bribed by Soviets.

After days of strenuous work, Cossacks assembled in evenings, here with Wrangel in their midst, for roll call and prayers in their uniforms.

The Kouban Cossacks put aside their rifles and swords and took up shovels and pickaxes to construct new highways in Bulgaria and Yugoslavia.

15
Forward Again

THE CRIMEA IS ALMOST TOTALLY surrounded by water; two narrow strips of land join it to the mainland — the isthmuses of Perekop, four kilometers wide, and Arbat, a narrow strip of land. In forcing these bottlenecks and emerging into the southern Ukraine, rich in food, livestock, and horses, lay the only hope for the White army, and the civilian population of the Crimea. Failure meant starvation. With most of the artillery, tanks, and aircraft abandoned during the Novorssiyak evacuation, the success of a frontal attack alone was unthinkable; Wrangel decided on a twin amphibious operation; simultaneous landings northeast and northwest of the peninsula combined with frontal attacks along the Perekop and Arbat isthmuses.

Wrangel was not going to follow the mistake of his predecessor and lose personal contact with the troops. He visited the different units preparing for the operation, addressed the officers and men, and was to be present when the offensive and the landings were to start.

The Volunteer regiments, as the most combat ready, were to be involved. The Reds, probably advised of Wrangel's intentions through their intelligence sources, tried to launch an offensive on the Perekop isthmus. They had intended to use poison gas, stocks of which were being prepared. On the 31st of March the 1st Red Latvian Division, supported by cavalry, attacked, but was met by the 2nd Don Cossack Division (the only mounted cavalry division in the White army, supported by a few tanks and whatever aircraft were still fit to fly). The Reds were routed and the exits of the Perekop isthmus secured. The next day the Reds tried again with an additional division and three thousand cavalry. Again they were beaten back with heavy losses. That same day an amphibious landing on the west coast was successfully performed at Kirilovica. Driving up the narrow neck of land, the infantry of General Angouladze seized the station of Sivash and repaired the bridge blown up by the Reds. With an armored train to back up, the station of Tchongar, at the head of the isthmus, was taken in a brilliant attack by cadets of the military academy — the last reserves.

Meanwhile, one of the elite Volunteer army divisions, the Drozdorsky, sailed forth towards its northwest landing area at a port called Khorly situated in an inner bay connected to a larger outer bay by a "canal" marked out by buoys and about a kilometer in length. Intelligence had reported no enemy presence in Khorly, When, however, at dawn the ships entered the inner bay they were met by heavy artillery and machine-gun fire. The ships withdrew first to the furthest part of the inner bay away from the murderous artillery fire, and then, under cover of darkness, back into the outer bay. A message went out to Wrangel, who insisted nevertheless a landing must be made.

It was decided to use a small trawler and rush the port with a battalion of infantry in the predawn half-light. Colonel Turkul, commanding the first wave, remembered: "We were jammed tight, six hundred men shoulder to shoulder, aboard the tug. I smoked a cigarette, hiding the light in the sleeve of my coat. We moved into the canal in complete silence; we could now see the hazy silhouettes of buildings on the shore. All was still — it seemed as though the Reds had gone. I ordered full steam ahead and the tug *Scythian* rushed ahead. We crashed into the quay, the ship keeled over to one side and we fell pell mell. At that moment the enemy's machine guns and artillery opened up. The first volley swept the captain off the ship's bridge. Oaths and groans from the wounded mingled with the staccato of the machine guns and the booming of the artillery. A captain with a Lewis machine gun stood next to me. 'Mishenko,' I cried, 'look!'" In the predawn fog we could now see a large stairway on top of which stood two machine guns around which flitted the shadows of the gun crew. 'Fire,' I yelled. Mishenko smacked the machine gun against my back; I leaned over, gripping the rails. Using me as a live mount, the captain opened fire. I felt the hot throbbing of the Lewis gun right into my bones. Mishenko fired a whole disk and the enemy's guns were silenced. Our infantry were rushing forward and in seconds had reached the top of the stairway. There mute stood two enemy machine guns and around the gun dead crews."

The landing force, aside from its infantry, had only eighteen horses, four light artillery pieces, a small Ford car and two motorcycles. General Vitkovsky, the divisional commander, decided to move ahead as planned towards the isthmus of Perekop. The wounded were loaded on board ship, and as the flotilla pulled out, the infantry prepared to march. But on April 3rd at 1 a.m. the Reds attacked, driving back the pickets. The slightest falter and the landing forces would be hurled into the sea. The general ordered the band to play and the White infantry attacked in serried ranks with the bayonets. The psychological impact was such that the Reds broke and the division, forming a column, drove forward towards the village of Adaman — there were sixty kilometers to cover before reaching the Perekop isthmus. A column of Red cavalry with artillery was spotted moving across the White's front. General Vitkovsky attacked in a cavalry charge with all of his eighteen horses and the Ford car. They took four guns and ten machine guns. These were to serve them in good stead.

The Reds had come to: masses of cavalry launched themselves from three sides (the fourth side was the sea), striving to crush the column. Allowing them to approach, the infantrymen opened up with all they had; the Red cavalry was beaten back, but new waves appeared, supported by machine gun carts and massive artillery fire. Again the iron combat discipline of the Volunteer regiments told: Steady, aimed fire sent the howling squadrons wheeling and galloping off.

On April 4th at 3 a.m. the column moved forward again — the last dash towards Perekop and safety. Red infantry now barred the way. Again the Drozdovsky regiments charged with the bayonet, forcing the way open for the rest of the column.

6 a.m., April 4th. Colonel Turkul remembered: "The air reverberates with echoes of firing. The column is on the march, no longer in quickstep but dragging along, as if weighed down. Haggard faces bathed in sweat; heaving breasts. The column moves along the rocky cliffs over stones covered with moss. The guns we captured are firing over open sights, serving us in more than good stead. On our right, below us, the sea: We can see the waves breaking and gulls frightened by the gunfire skimming over the water. A wounded soldier is crouched on the path, coughing blood. Gun flashes throw their yellow light on the young faces of the soldiers in the ranks.

"We are now attacked from three sides — surrounded, pressed against the edge of the cliffs. No way to retreat — but death better than capture and eventual torture. The column moves on to the frightful tune of a mixture of firing, yells of command, groans of wounded, the thumping of boots, and the harsh breathing — one ghastly chorus of misery.

"Colonel Peters, bareheaded, revolver in hand leads his battalion in a counterattack. They move in silence with no hurrahs: too exhausted. The Reds are driven off, but more waves come on from the left and from the rear. The column staggers on under heavy fire. I ride past, watching the darkened, sweatbathed faces, the open shirts, and bared breasts. The ranks are now being broken; the men move in a crowd carrying their wounded, by now several hundred. One final enemy onslaught and all will be over: If no superhuman last effort is made, the column will collapse.

"I rise in the stirrups and in a voice filled with frenzy and rage, a voice unknown to myself, I yell: 'Why is the leading company not marching in step? Get in step. Get in step! Count off.' The crowd, carrying its dead and wounded, with their last hoarse breath starts chanting one-two, one-two, as bullets whine and smack into their bodies. By some miracle the ranks form again and march in step.

"General Vitkovsky, with two horses killed under him, now has climbed into the Ford car. A direct hit; the car wrecked, the driver killed. Unhurt, the little general now walks alongside the column.

"The column marches on: Our regiment disposes of only two carts; both are now filled with wounded. Blood runs through the boards, leaving a track in the dusty road. Some wounded stagger along, leaning on their buddies; others are carried on crossed rifles or on blood-drenched overcoats.

"At last in the distance we see the park along the Turkish wall* of the Perekop isthmus. Have we broken through? . . God help us!"

The column had marched sixty kilometers under enemy fire, drawing off the enemy forces guarding the isthmus. Through some error of coordination the White columns storming the isthmus did not strike out to relieve the Drozdovsky division — they heard the firing far in the enemy rear but were in doubt as to its origin.

True to his policy, Wrangel was up with the troops during the battle. On the right flank one day he walked under a hail of bullets along the front line of the attacking infantry. He was followed by Bishop Benjamin, who, cross in hand, blessed the infantrymen as exploding enemy shells showered everyone with fountains of black dirt. The next day Wrangel was already on the left flank of the attacking troops and passed in review the Drozdovsky Division that had just broken through.

Again Colonel Turkul gives his colorful description: "To the music of the band whose many bandsmen were missing, killed, or wounded, General Wrangel watched the division file past. The regiments drew up in a field; Wrangel asked the command staff to step forward. General Vitkovsky, Colonel Harjecsky, and I walked up to him.

" 'General!' Wrangel called out. I looked around and stepped aside thinking that Wrangel was calling General Vitkovsky. — 'No, no, I mean you, Colonel Turkul,' Wrangel smiled. 'Congratulations on your promotion to general for the gallant action at Khorly!'

"I remember well his narrow face lit by the light of courage, his laughing green-grey eyes. I remember the smile playing on his chivalrous face!"

The Volunteer army, which effectively at the beginning of the civil war was composed only of volunteers, had outlived its men. In the course of the war, the decimated regiments had filled their ranks with mobilized peasants, captured Red army soldiers, and anyone they could find. Miraculously, with few exceptions, these units fought on with tenacity and extreme courage mostly because of their thoroughly dedicated and experienced cadres. Nevertheless, to the population at large, they had come to represent requisitions, repressions, and at times outright pillage. The "Holy Light" which illuminated the beginning was bound to become diffused in the two years of massacres, brutality, and sheer efforts to survive.

* Wall built in the 18th century to ward off the raiding Tartars.

With one stroke of the pen Wrangel renamed the Volunteer army the Russian army. New decorations and regimental battle awards were designed to lift the morale. Wrangel instituted the Order of St. Nicholas, equivalent to the Czarist Order of St. George, with corresponding colors and bugles for the units which distinguished themselves in combat.

Whereas before law was entirely in the hands of individual commanders, who dispensed it to their units and to the civilian population according to their own, and at times very hazy, comprehension of justice, Wrangel reintroduced the military legal arm, divorcing it entirely from the civilian judiciary.

Wrangel's only hope was to stall for time: time to organize a government creditable enough at least to be regarded as such by Russia's former allies, time to try to bring over to the Whites the inert and disenchanted peasantry, time to wean the workers from the Reds' promised paradise, and time to convince Europe that the threat of Communism was not only a Russian aberration but a formidable menace to the world at large.

This task seemed more like a succession of the labors of Hercules: The printing press was the sole source of money; credit abroad was limited to the funds held by Russia's former ambassadors, not all of whom wished to release the sums in their possession, some for political, others for personal reasons. Money was needed to buy food, guns, and ammunition; and ships laden with these, sailing under British auspices, were now being actually held up by orders of the hostile Lloyd George cabinet, while Winston Churchill protested in vain and thundered against the pro-Bolshevik line of his government. Answering sarcastically Lord Curzon's letter regarding some arms shipments from Varna which he had hoped were destined for the Crimea, Churchill wrote, "Thank you for your letter enclosing the telegram which shows that these arms were not after all intended for the 'wicked' Wrangel but only for the 'good' Armenians and Georgians!"

Presiding over his council of adminstrative chiefs, Wrangel realized that he had neither experienced administrators nor men of imagination and zeal, a zeal which in such desperate times had to be fired by revolutionary fervor: The old Czarist ministers and bureaucrats, hardened in their past comfortable routine, were unable to unravel the years of red tape surrounding their past administrations; the new heads of departments chosen by General Denikin from liberal circles were even worse — members of the intelligentsia, these were men of words but not of actions, men capable of delivering inflammatory speeches and writing theoretical articles imbued with unattainable idealism but totally incapable of meeting practical requirements.

Having no one at hand, Wrangel was forced to entrust the civilian administration to his chief of staff General Chatilov. This was a temporary appointment, for Chatilov, able as he was as a chief of staff in a military capacity, was hardly able to cope with the problems of putting together a new and complex system of adminstration. There were elder statesmen of experience abroad, but having escaped the whirlwind of revolution, they preferred the safer and more comfortable Paris, Berlin, and London, from whence they could observe events. Heroic exceptions, are, however, an historical rule in times of national stress, and such a civilian hero was discovered by Wrangel — a former cabinet minister, now president of a bank in Paris.

A small, frail-looking man, the very prototype of an elder statesman, Alexander Krivochein exemplified the politician and administrator who by dint of capability and hard work plus an instinct for correct timing had risen to the top in the Czarist administration, had survived the revolution, taken part in the Denikin government, albeit in opposition to the disorder and chaos that prevailed there, and having left Russia after the disastrous Novorossiysk evacuation had settled down to a lucrative job in Paris.

The grandson of a peasant, the son of an artillery officer, he was a man of the people and his past career was mostly involved with land reform, the sorest spot in the structure of Imperial Russia, a problem that the Russian cabinet minister Stolypin tried to eradicate by creating a process of land reform destined to build up a class of independent small farmers.* Working in that capacity, Krivochein had the opportunity to travel extensively through Russia, visiting Siberia, Turkestan, and the Caucasus. His aims were to raise the standard of living of the peasantry, to create a self-sufficient farmer class, and to develop modern agriculture. This brought him eventually to the cabinet post of Minister of Agriculture. Of liberal tendencies, he had been at times in the opposition sector of the Czarist government, but with innate tact and public relations ability had contrived to cultivate good relations on the left and right sectors of the political life. To Wrangel's request for help he answered in his usual careful way that he would come on a temporary basis to give whatever advice he could.

On arrival he was impressed by what he saw: Order had replaced chaos; the army had been reorganized and had achieved success, although it was in desperate straits; Crimea represented a model of law and order in comparison to the chaotic conditions prevailing in the south of Russia under Denikin's regime. Wrangel turned on all his efforts at persuasion, ending with a direct appeal to Krivochein's patriotism. Krivochein decided to stay as Wrangel's civilian assistant and to help him form a practical government. Both men were pragmatists, both uninterested in party politics, and both intellectually supple enought to deal with people on their personal merit only.

---

* These farmers, later named Kulaks by the Communists, were ruthlessly exterminated by Stalin in the 1930 purges.

The government thus put together was comprised of men varying from the ultraright to the ultraleft, including even a former Marxist. Someone coined it a "leftist government in rightist hands." Wrangel stated flatly to representatives of newspapers in an unusual press conference that he had convened: "I am not interested in monarchists or republicans. I need men of deeds, not words; their political orientation is of no interest to me as long as they are loyal and can function in these new and unusual circumstances."

At that time there were some twenty newspapers and periodicals appearing in the Crimea, representing every aspect of political thinking from neo-Marxist attacking the government and army to ultrarightist clamoring for pogroms. Censorship during Denikin's tenure was in the hands of the ill-reputed Osvag; its officers were totally incompetent in the field of news media — some forbidding the most harmless of articles, other allowing editorials with nothing short of sedition to appear unmolested.

Wrangel believed in the power and the freedom of the press; under freedom he did not include license, and this he made quite clear to the editors of the newspapers he had convened to his conference. Explaining that the Crimea could be compared to a beleaguered fortress, he explained that information detrimental to the national cause or of value to the enemy could not be sanctioned, and he offered two alternatives: one, the creation of a bureau of censorship to whose examinations material was to be submitted, or, two, complete freedom of the press with the cautionary advice that material of value to the enemy would result in military sanctions against the editors as outlined in the articles of war.

It is interesting to note that of the editors from the three most important papers, two opted for censorship (the left wing papers) and one (the right-oriented) undertook to write under its full responsibility. One of the correspondents has left us his impressions. "This was the first time I had seen Wrangel. Wearing the dark grey tunic of the Cossacks, tall, thin, exuding that military bearing that has made his characteristic image, the impression was one of total contrast to Denikin. If one can discern in Denikin's expression and demeanor an impression of calmness and of stubbornness not devoid of slyness, in Wrangel it is all movement, enthusiasm, boiling energy, and steel will power. I put to him questions pertaining to our military situation, the reason for our past mistakes, our national and foreign policies. I hardly had time to pose questions and had no need to look for words or expressions. Wrangel anticipated me and I wrote virtually under his dictation: 'After six days of uninterrupted combat we have secured the Crimea. The army is being reorganized and we are striving to do away with those negative aspects which previously had undermined our operations. Morale and discipline are to be given special attention, courts-martial within units will be allowed wide powers including that of reducing to ranks field grade officers.

" 'But along with army problems a series of measures are to be put into effect to resolve the most pressing needs of national existence. Three years of anarchy with a succession of governments each pronouncing promises with no hope of fulfilling them merely for the purpose of gaining popular support have left us with social and economic problems to which no immediate solution exists — as one example, land reform.

" 'I am seeking to solve the most pressing problems within, however, the limits of reality. The main task of the government is to provide for the population of southern Russia, an area occupied by our troops, with law and order to satisfy as far as possible their needs and aspirations.

" 'I have undertaken steps which will allot the greatest possible acreage of land as permanent possession to those who actually work the land themselves. The future of Russia rests on the small independent farmer; the days of vast landholdings are a thing of the past. The welfare and professional improvement of the working class is another matter of paramount importance.

" 'It is not by a triumphant march from Crimea to Moscow that Russia could be saved but rather by building here on this small parcel of the country a sound system of government and a living standard that will eventually draw to us the whole population presently groaning under the Red yoke.' "

One of the grave problems facing Wrangel was the suppression of anti-Semitism; in the Crimea there was a sizable Jewish population. Anti-Semitism had been a thorn in the flesh of prewar Russia. As second-class citizens the majority of Jews had welcomed the revolution in the hope of gaining full civic rights, but as often happens in national turmoil, a militant minority pushed itself to the fore of the Bolshevik party, acting as commissars in the Red army, as activists, and as propagandists. Such taken prisoners by the Whites were immediately shot. The Cossacks on whose territory the civil war raged and who suffered the most from Red army depredations went further, killing Jews whether they were commissars or recruits. From this to mass pogroms and massacres the step was but short.

General Denikin deplored anti-Semitism, but having little authority over his commanders, he closed his eyes to many of the excesses. Wrangel from the beginning took a strong stance. To a newspaper correspondent who queried him on the issue he said: "I consider any form of racial, class, or party strife as a calamity in this critical period of our existence, and I shall combat it by all possible means. Any form of pogroms lead to the moral disintegration of the army."

A series of edicts prohibited any forms of public discussions, sermons, lectures, or editorials aimed at racial, religious, or national strife. A certain priest named Vostokov specialized in sermons of ant-Semitic character. Wrangel invited the cleric to visit him at headquarters and with no further ado warned him that if his next sermon followed the same line he would be deported from the Crimea within twenty-four hours. The next Sunday the sermon flowed within strictly conventional channels based on the Scriptures.*

The blue-collar workers represented that segment of population where Communist propaganda was most successful, nor was their lot to be envied. Low wages, inflation, and the dearth of products made the soil ripe for the seeds of revolt. Strikes threatened and Wrangel chose to deal with the matter himself. He invited a delegation of workers to visit him. He proposed the following measures designed to improve workers' conditions:

1. Wages were to be immediately put on the same level as those of civil servants (minimum wages of both equal).
2. From army surplus sources, food was to be sold to workers at army purchase price.
3. Army surplus clothing was to be allocated to workers with the purchase price spread over twelve months.
4. Cooperative shops were to be organized to sell food and clothing to workers at special low prices to the amount of ten percent of their monthly pay.

This was in May, but in June Wrangel noted that bureaucratic lethargy had not yet implemented these measures and that army supplies earmarked for the workers had not reached them. Wrangel immediately ordered the army judge advocate to investigate the matter and prosecute the culprits for neglect of duty.

The measure of Wrangel's success in solving the workers' problems could be seen in the eight months of existence of the Government of Southern Russia: Not only did the Communist propaganda fail to find echo among the working class, but the unions actually helped maintain order during the days when 140,000 people prepared to leave the Crimea, some eight months later. Wrangel was enough of a pragmatist to realize that "cleaning out the stables" by restoring order amidst chaos and the initial military successes were only a delaying action to forestall doom, which was inevitable if three conditions were not met. First, the recognition and assistance from one of the former allies; England was not only out of the game but under Lloyd George's pro-Soviet policy even antagonistic; hence the only hope was France. Second, the exit from the Crimean bottleneck into the rich plains of the Ukraine where cereals and cattle would feed the army and the Crimean population while horses would again remount the cavalry, in those days of civil war, still the most

---

* The Crimean Jewish population was active with its newspapers, civic centers and a boy-scout organization named "The Maccabees."

important combat arm. Third, and most important, the lethargic peasant population despoiled from White and Red had to be gained. Without its support, no allied intervention, no military success, would suffice, and any venture would sink, without hope of emerging, into the morass of hostile indifference as it did with Denikin, Kolchak, and the other White Russian leaders. At the beginning of the revolution the shrill cry of Lenin and the Bolsheviks was "All land to the peasants!" However, beyond smashing the large estates of former landowners, nothing was done and the peasant driven into communes found himself no better off than a hundred years before in the days of serfdom. The arrival of the White armies in their day of success also did nothing to satisfy the aspirations of the bewildered peasantry; requisitions, if not actual pillage, remained their lot.

Wrangel's solution to this third problem was practical in the extreme. All land reform was to start at grass-roots levels by election within villages and redistribution of the land within each district according to its availability in acreage and according to the work performed by the purchaser on that land. For though given in permanent posession, the land was to be paid for; it was not land expropriated and given away free. The terms of the payment, however, were extremely generous: payment was spread over twenty-five years on the basis of twenty-five percent of the yearly harvest, which could be effected either in kind or in currency. The sums thus gathered were used to pay off those landowners whose large tracts of land had been taken over or absentee landowners who in effect did not work their own land.

The extreme right howled at expropriation and socialism, and the timid members of the new government procrastinated; but with Wrangel's characteristic decision and a stroke of his pen the new land edict came out, was formulated into law, and implemented into practice — all within six months.

The success was not immediate; too much had been promised by too many before, and none of the promises had materialized. Suspicious, the peasants waited to see the results. Driven by Wrangel's impetuous orders, agronomists and surveyors went to work, and gradually land elections at village level became a reality and the decisions of the local councils were respected and carried out. It is of interest to note that these decisions bore more often than not a conservative stamp: The initial thirst for land once assuaged, the peasant looked for order and security.

Realizing that mobilization of people and horses laid a particular onus on the population, especially felt during harvesttime, Wrangel issued orders enjoining army units to help the villagers during harvesting and gathering of crops. A captain of one of the Volunteer regiments remembered: "We received orders from army headquarters to assist the local population with harvesting as much as the military situation permitted. Everyone took these orders for granted; there was not enough land labor to harvest, what with the mobilization of men and horses let alone the void left by those who had left with the Red army and taken their horses with them. The Markovsky regiment settled down to its task with enthusiasm. With the first day of work a change of mood was felt by all ranks as well as among the villagers; everyone cheered up and even discipline seemed enhanced. The former Red army soldiers now serving in our ranks were particularly amazed at the fact that help was extended even to those families whose members had left with the Red army. 'The Reds don't act that way,' they would remark."

Through simultaneous amphibious operations from east to west Wrangel's army had secured the exits from the Crimean bottleneck. The Soviet command viewed with alarm the eruption of the White army into the rich territories of the southern Ukraine, the granary of Russia. White intelligence reported a constant flow of Red reinforcements, some divisions diverted from the Polish front where the Soviets were meeting with success in their war against Poland. Their arrival against the Wrangel army was imminent and the odds heavily in their favor.

Wrangel decided to act first. Two infantry divisions and one cavalry division under the command of the meteoric General Slachtchov landed forty kilometers northwest of Genichesk under extremely difficult conditions: a storm blowing and heavy seas. Concurrently with the landings the corps of General Koutiepov attacked the strongly defended Perekop isthmus, the final gateway existing into the Ukrainian plain. It was a coordinated attack using the few aircraft and tanks that had been scraped together.

An infantry officer described the scene: "May 25, 2 a.m., and all is quiet. Suddenly, up forward, rifle fire and two rounds of artillery: a Red reconnaissance party has stumbled upon one of the forward situated battteries. Again all is quiet. We strain eyes and ears to catch the signal: a round from a heavy artillery gun at 3 a.m. We hear a distant cannonade somewhere west. ... Then it came — a loud boom in our rear, and the night broke into a reverberating crash of guns, whistles of shells passing over us, and their crashes on the enemy position. The No. 1 regiment moves swiftly forward as tanks rumble past us, heading for the enemy's barbed wire."

The Reds rushed forward their reserves: three infantry and one composed of Communist Latvian volunteers. Defeated and pressed against the Sivash shallows, they either surrendered or were massacred. With the small mounted units available Don Cossacks pushed forward. Meanwhile, the units of General Slachtchov which had landed forty kilometers northwest continued to progress forward and, cutting the main north-south railway line, took the town of Melitopol.

An artillery sergeant Pronin remembered: "Our battery rode up to a mound from where, as far as the eye could see, stretched the saline marshes of the Sivash. Like small dots covering the glistening surface, men made their way through water. It was the remnants of the defeated Latvian division attacked from the rear by the Don Cossacks pressed from front and flank by our infantry. It seemed that their situation was hopeless and that all that remained was for them to give themselves up. But the desperate Latvians, waist-deep in water, carrying their cartridge cases around their necks, plodded on, shooting at our soldiers who yelled at them to surrender. The iron law of the civil war, 'We give no quarter and ask for none,' spelled the end of the battle of the Perekop isthmus: machine guns chattered and shrapnel burst low, sweeping the remnants under the water."

More and more Red units were pulled off the Polish front and sent to retrieve the situation; this time, from the east one cavalry and three infantry divisions tried to cut off Koutiepov's forces from the Perekop isthmus. The general, one of the Whites' best infantry commanders, allowed the Reds to push his center, then, rolling up his wings, encircled and smashed the Soviet concentrations. Part of the enemy fled across the Dniepr river; the rest retreated northeast.

Meanwhile, the enemy group in whose rear the White amphibious landings had been made, tried to break out, pushed from the front by the Don and the Kouban Cossack units, most of these acting as infantry due to the shortage of horses. Attempting to relieve the encircled troops, the Reds attacked Slachtchov, who found himself in his turn surrounded. His units exhausted by the difficult landings followed by incessant combat had difficulty in holding, but they stuck out long enough to let the enemy attacks collapse as Koutiepov and the Cossack units pressed north in a week-long pursuit and combat.

The small young Russian army had won its first major victory. The XIIIth Soviet army comprised of the 3rd, 15th, 46th, 52nd, 29th, 42nd, and the Latvian divisions plus two divisions and a brigade of cavalry along with many smaller subsidiary units had ceased to exist. The debris of this army was strewn through the Dniepr marshes; a few mounted units and small infantry detachments made their way out towards the northeast.

The trophies were ten thousand prisoners, forty-eight guns, six armored cars, two hundred fifty machine guns, three armored trains, vast quantities of ammunition, and, as a somber and ominous note, many containers of poison gas ready to be let loose at the Crimea—forestalled and mercifully not used by either side until the end of the civil war. Several million pounds of grain were seized, a welcome addition to Crimea's hungry diet.

All of the northern province of Tavrida was now in Wrangel's hands, his territory increased twofold. Wrangel had personally directed the combat operations while fighting was still going on. He was on hand to decorate the tank commander who had first breached the enemy's defenses.

Prior to his taking over, only the soldiers received decorations—the soldiers the St. George Cross, the old Czarist decoration—while the officers were upped in rank for conspicuous service. This led to a number of young, brave, but often inexperienced senior officers. Nor were individual units rewarded, many regiments turning over their personnel three or more times. The casualties in the civil war were appalling, many wounded dying due to lack of proper medical care. Wounded often shot themselves rather than be left on the battlefield as prey for Reds and almost invariable torture. As a morale booster Wrangel instituted the Order of St. Nicholas both for individuals and for units. The first to receive this decoration was the lieutenant tank commander.*

* During the whole Crimean campaign, 335 officers and other ranks received the St. Nicholas Cross.

16
Political and Military
Successes

THE SUCCESS OF THE RUSSIAN army in no way deterred the British Lloyd George's cabinet from doing everything possible to prevent these victories from blossoming out: Ships sailing under the British flag carrying supplies to the Crimea were stopped en route and diverted. Finally, the British military mission was recalled over the objections of its commander General Sir John Percy* and innumerable remarks and speeches by Winston Churchill in direct opposition to Lloyd George's pro-Soviet policy.

As Wrangel had predicted, the negotiations between Great Britain and the Soviets had come to nothing. Inebriated by their success against the Poles, who were in full retreat towards Warsaw, and hoping to crush the White army then still bottled up in the Crimea, the Soviet delegates scornfully rejected all British propositions to mediate. Wrangel's successes in defeating the Reds and emerging from the Crimean bottleneck had a direct effect on the Soviet Polish war. Over the Crimean period some forty Soviet infantry and twenty cavalry divisions were directed from Poland to the south of Russia.

If British foreign policy remained indifferent, or rather directly hostile, towards the Wrangel regime, the latter had, however, a happy windfall in a de facto recognition by France. France had traditionally been an ally of Poland (a French king, Henry III, had once even ruled over that country and Napoleon had striven to resurrect an independent Poland). The conservative French government viewed with alarm the Communist onslaught: A Communist Poland would be quickly followed by a Communist Germany, where the imperial rule had collapsed, the navy had mutinied, and the Spartacists had instituted a reign of terror. The French saw already the specter of a Red militant Germany arising on its border, just two years after the end of their history's most bloody war.**

France's answer was no less than the shipment to Poland of General Weygand, chief of staff of Marshal Foch, the Allied supreme commander in World War I, with a suite of two hundred officers, while ninety-five trains of

---

* Disgusted with his government's policy, General Percy left the service and retired to his farm in Canada.
** They had to wait twenty years to confront Hitler and his Nazi Germany.

arms and ammunitions followed. Reorganized, retrained, and redirected, the Poles stopped the Red tide at the gates of Warsaw. It was called the miracle of Warsaw and neither the French nor the Polish historians saw fit to mention that in fact Wrangel's victories in the Ukraine had brought about this "miracle." The Red's forty infantry and twenty cavalry diverted from the Polish front against Wrangel made up the major portion of the victorious recipe.* The miracle of Warsaw could well be called the miracle of Crimea. Nevertheless, while the war went on, France viewed with a benevolent eye Wrangel's endeavors in the Crimea.

Krivochein, Wrangel's assistant for foreign and domestic affairs, had several useful contacts in the French capital, not least Maurice Paleologue, former French ambassador to Imperial Russia and subsequently under secretary for foreign affairs in the Millerand cabinet. His consistent efforts on behalf of the Wrangel government were crowned with success. To this success contributed in no small measure Wrangel's emissary Peter Struve, a former Marxist turned nationalist, whose press and public relations campaign coincided favorably with France's panic at the news from Poland, where the Reds were rolling victoriously forward. The de facto recognition by France was no more than a moral victory but gave Wrangel's government a legal basis on the international scene. Practically it had but little effect: The Russian army was desperately short of guns and ammunition (there were only eight aircraft fit to fly); money was short, credit unavailable, while French bureaucracy and procrastination in government and military circles precluded a rapid and decisive aid. Until the very end, with few exceptions the Russian army relied on what it had or could capture.

The loss of the southern Ukraine, Russia's breadbasket, and Wrangel's military successes culminating in the complete destruction of the XIIIth Soviet army seriously shook the Soviet High Command. It was urgently decided to divert all the Red cavalry en route to the Polish front and, uniting it under one command, rush for the Crimean front.

The Soviets had learned much from Wrangel's successful cavalry campaigns in the northern Caucasus, the Manytsh, and Tsaritsyn. The value of cavalry formations maneuvering against the enemy's rear and supported by massive firepower had proved its worth, and with it in mind the Soviets concentrated a cavalry corps of seventy-five hundred sabers, with infantry support, a great number of machine guns carried on carts, artillery, and a squadron of ten aircraft. Its mission was to crash through the Russian army's defenses and race for the Crimean isthmus, thus cutting off the Russian army from its base

---

* Maxime Weygand in the biography of his father, *Weygand mon Pere*, does not even mention the existence of the Wrangel army!

and thereby sealing its doom. The victorious end of this plan would liberate major portions of three Red armies plus the cavalry corps for immediate action in Poland. On the Crimean front the enemy had twenty-five thousand infantry and twelve thousand sabers as its shock troops. The opposing Whites available to counter the Red attack numbered ten or eleven thousand; the whole White forces on all the front numbered a mere fifteen thousand infantry and sixty-five hundred cavalry. Some of the Cossacks fought as infantry due to shortage of horses. For them, unaccustomed to being on foot, it represented a severe disadvantage. Those cavalry units who were mounted rode horses that in peacetime would never have received a glance from a remount commission.

In spite of all these disadvantages Wrangel with his usual impetuosity decided to take the initiative and attempt to encircle the enemy. In order to make his infantry more mobile, he mounted it in horse-drawn carts—whole columns moving in long, snakelike lines with machine-gun carts and batteries in their midst. The initial objective of the Reds under the command of Comrade Jloba was the town of Melitopol; regrouping there, the next aim was the final rush towards the Crimean isthmus. On the 19th of June the partly dismounted units of the Don Cossack 2nd and 3rd Divisions received the brunt of the Red attack. Fighting desperately, asking for help and not receiving any, they retreated towards Melitopol. As darkness came, then all night long, the infantry divisions of the old Volunteer divisions, Drozdovsky and Kornilovs, some in horse-drawn carts (the forerunners of World War II mechanized infantry), the others on foot, marched encircling Jloba's corps, concentrated in the German colonies of Lichtfeld-Alexanderthal. On the dawn of the 20th they had reached their objectives. The scene was set for the final showdown.

At Wrangel's headquarters in the town of Melitopol, only one short cavalry march away from the enemy, a feeling of nervous tension prevailed. From Wrangel's headquarters train it spilled onto the station where crowds were beginning to gather, some carrying suitcases, others exchanging pessimistic rumors, as somewhere beyond boomed a lively cannonade—the Don Cossack divisions were slowly retreating almost at breaking point. As a last reserve there stood an infantry detachment of young cadets—beyond, nothing: The Crimea lay open.

Wrangel's ADC Captain Liakhov: "General Wrangel walked up and down the railway platform in his usual nervous style. Sensing the mood of the crowd, he said in a loud voice to one of the more pessimistic emissaries from the Don Cossack divisions: 'Splendid! We have the situation in hand and I am off to take a nap!' With this he strode towards his railway carriage as the crowd dispersed. At dawn of the 20th he had personally contacted by telegraph all the commanders of the encircling forces, repeated his orders, checked on their movements. They were now moving and could no longer be reached, Wrangel lay down and went to sleep."

General Chatilov, Wrangel's chief of staff: "Wrangel was still asleep as the morning hours went by and the encircling operations had started; my assistant General Konovalov was reluctant to wake him and did so only when the hard-pressed Don Cossacks' retreat was drawing near. Wrangel expressed surprise as to why he was being disturbed: He had complete faith in the outcome of the operation and unrevocable confidence in his subordinate commanders. As last an aircraft flew over the train, fired a flare, and dropped a message: Surrounded in a circle of steel, the Red army corps had been routed."

The operation had evolved like a well-staged peacetime maneuver. First the Kornilov division reached the village of Rickenau and, deploying its artillery, opened fire over open sights on the Red cavalry squadrons which were then just being saddled. A White armored car in an almost suicidal mission roared through the Red formations, spewing machine-gun fire. As dawn broke the last obsolete White aircraft came in flying low, machine-gunning and bombing the panicked cavalry. Splitting into two groups, the enemy rushed partly due east and partly northwestward. The first group of four brigades ran into the Kornilov infantry regiment. Met with point-blank rifle and machine-gun fire, the horsemen veered aside, only to be confronted by the Drozdovsky division. Standing with rifles at foot, they waited until the mounted horde was almost upon them, then, with deadly but orderly fire, dispersed the Red cavalrymen. Trying to find a way to the northeast, the demoralized Red squadrons came upon the cavalry of General Morozov, whose squadrons made short work of whatever cohesiveness still remained in the Red ranks. Rushing south they came upon the Don Cossacks, who, recovered from their hard-fought initial retreat, now rushed forward, anxious above all to seize horses so as to be mounted again. A group of six Red cavalry brigades led by Comrade Jloba and still in relatively good order came up against two regiments of the Kornilov division. The same scene was repeated: charging squadrons; the thin lines of infantry, cut here and there by horse-drawn machine-gun carts; the silhouettes of a few 75's pointed directly at the onrushing waves; hurrahs and yells of the galloping riders, silence from the White infantry ranks. Then a curt order, a pause, another order, and the crash of guns, chatter of machine guns and rifle salvoes. Horses turning over; others, their saddles empty, galloping wildly; the cries of wounded; and in a swirl of dust the remnants of the squadrons wheeling and galloping off.

Jloba rushed on towards B. Tokmak, hoping to find there a hole to escape. But drawn up on a railway line stood armored trains and lying on the embankment waited more infantry. From north to south, east to west, the bewildered Red squadrons bounced from one White unit to another. Soon the pursuit of the Reds turned into a general scramble: Cooks and orderlies rushed from the rear of their divisions to take part in the spoils. Two observers in a balloon let their machine down to capture a machine-gun cart. The sum of this brilliant operation, a modern Cannae* resulted in eleven thousand five hundred prisoners, sixty guns, three hundred machine guns, two armored cars, ammunition, rifles, and above all valuable horses to remount the Cossack divisions.

The defeat of Jloba was of great political importance. At a time when the fate of Poland hung on a thread Wrangel had drawn upon himself sixty-three Red infantry and thirty-two cavalry regiments, three quarters of which were already on their way to the Polish front and had to be diverted against Wrangel. Neither Weygand nor other French officers nor the massive help would have staved off the impending disaster and Red Poland would have been a prelude to Red Germany.

The successes of the Russian army in the spring and summer had positive effects on the army and the population. The city of Sebastopol was hardly recognizable. From a harassed port where the remnants of Denikin's army had landed—bewildered, angry, and in a state bordering on revolt—the town had almost acquired again the looks of its peacetime prosperity. Cinemas and theaters were open again; shops displayed even imported wares; army personnel on duty or on leave were disciplined and in uniform. Schools, hospitals, and government offices functioned normally. The occupation of the southern Ukraine had yielded vast quantities of grain, enough to feed the Crimean population and to allow for substantial export. The morale of the troops was very high; although lacking in everything, the army had complete faith in its commander. As law and order had superseded requisitions and pillage, the population looked favorably on the army. It was still far from an enthusiastic and self-sacrificing élan, but the peasant, worker, and civil service employee felt themselves sheltered by the law and encouraged in their enterprises. On the negative side was the small size of the freed territory in contrast to the enormous resources of Russia under Communist domination—the huge stockpile of arms from the World War; the vast, never-ending reservoirs of manpower upon which the Soviets could draw. Wrangel's victories were not won lightly: Who was to replace the killed and wounded? Soldiers, perhaps from prisoners taken; but the incomparable officer cadres in combat for more than two years were dwindling rapidly. As long as the Polish war continued, Wrangel could hang on—but then? . . . .

* Hannibal's defeat of the Romans.

17

The Kouban Expedition

WRANGEL'S THOUGHTS TURNED MORE AND MORE towards the Cossack lands of Don and Kouban, those areas that had made it possible for the White army of Denikin to exist, where the Cossack population had overtly espoused the anti-Communist cause and had given great levies of men and horses from 1918 to 1920.

True, Denikin's narrow-minded policies had alienated many of the Cossacks, the collapse of his army had led to massive desertions, and finally the catastrophic evacuation of Novorossiysk had the loyal Cossack regiments abandoned on the shores of the Black Sea as the White army units seized most of the ships bound for the Crimea. Some Cossack units fought their way through to the Georgian republic and were interned; others surrendered; and some were retrieved from the shores of the Black Sea by Wrangel's efforts when he took over the command. The Red army now occupied all of the Don, Terek, and Kouban territories and with calculated terror held the Cossacks in check. Nevertheless, the territories seethed with unrest, and partisan units in small groups continued to battle the Reds, seeking refuge in the marshes of the Kouban river or in the mountains of the Caucasus.

As a prelude to a major operation, a detachment of a few hundred Don Cossacks with one battery in support was landed between the cities of Mariupol and Taganrog. Led by a Colonel Nazarov, it met with initial success, fought its way through Red forces and made a dash for the Don Cossack capital of Novocherkask. It arrived within thirty-five miles of the city, but its expectations of a major Cossack uprising proved a disappointment. The Reds had mobilized vast numbers of Don Cossacks and had sent them to the Polish front. Their families were held hostage; repression was severe; and the Cossacks had lost heart after almost three years of civil war. Nazarov's detachment was finally surrounded and massacred. He was captured but escaped and, aided by the friendly population, made his way back to the Whites. It was an inauspicious beginning.

Undeterred, Wrangel decided to launch a major effort in the Kouban region. He had commanded the Kouban Cossacks in the victorious campaigns of the northern Caucasus, on the Manytsh and at Tsaritsyn. His name was legend among those Cossacks and rumours were reaching him that partisan units acting against the Reds were active in ever increasing numbers. Wrangel decided to act. He could avail himself of some five thousand men, with twelve guns, one hundred thirty machine guns, six armored cars and the same weather-beaten eight aircraft that were the sole resources of the White army's air force. This small force was to expand with the adherence of the Cossacks in whose land the landings were to take place.

Burdened as he was with the overall command, the running of the government, and his diplomatic efforts, Wrangel was forced to delegate authority. Just as Napoleon had failed in Spain by leaving that operation in the hands of his marshals, so also Wrangel was to experience his first major setback.

The command of the Kouban expedition was entrusted to General Ulagai, the "Murat" of Wrangel's previous campaigns. He had the same qualities, but unfortunately the same defects as the illustrious French cavalry leader: Unequalled in maneuver and attack, he was a poor organizer, made light of staff work, and was subject to meteoric rises and falls of morale. Wrangel's campaigns wre hard on the senior ranks: Generals followed his example and commanded from the front ranks; their casualties were extremely high. Of the senior generals, Mamonov and Saveliev had been killed.* Pokrovsky, the able but ruthless and sadistic commander, had been exiled; the younger generals lacked experience. So Ulagai, a Kouban Cossack himself, remained the sole logical choice. To compensate for his shortcomings, Wrangel looked for an able chief of staff. General Chatilov, who was charged with preparing the whole operation, recommended General Dratzenko: It proved then and again later a most unfortunate choice.

In examining the panorama of the White movement as a whole, one is impressed by one fact: The most successful generals were those who had come from the ranks of junior officers whose careers had started in World War I— lieutenants, captains, majors with no preconceived ideas, they had forced themselves to the top by their valor, imagination, and a certain daring verging on gambling. The successful senior generals of World War I were often lost in the bewildering kaleidoscope of the civil war. General Denikin was a glaring example; General Dratzenko was to be another. A good staff officer on the Caucasus front during World War I, he had been in General Chatilov's corps during the campaign of the northern Caucasus. Replacing General Chatilov when the latter was wounded, he commanded some mop-up operations. Wrangel accepted his nomination and ordered Chatilov to prepare the operation up to and including the landing, when Ulagai was to take charge and raise

---

* In general it must be noted that in the White army in south Russia no less than five senior generals (lieutenant general and above) were killed in action, the number of major generals exceeded twenty. In the Spanish Civil War, 1936, no officer of general rank was killed in action.

the standard of the Cossack rebellion. Busy himself as chief of staff, Chatilov delegated authority: Word of the projected landings got around as Wrangel brought into the secret the atamans of the Don and Kouban Cossacks. Soon, along with the military units, Cossack civilians, members of their governments, and even dependents crowded onto the ships. Coming to review the troops before their departure, Wrangel was angered and dismayed by what he saw. It was too late to disembark the burdensome elements and the flotilla set sail. The landings were successfully made and the first days gave rise to important advances. General Babiev, commanding the Cossack cavalry division, rushed forward and was soon within striking distance of Ekaterinodar, the Kouban Cossack capital.

But Ulagai, fearing for his base, hung back; two days were lost during which the Red command gathered all available troops. Ulagai asked for the navy to prepare for reembarking, then changed his mind, as harder and harder combats took place. He was at loggerheads with his chief of staff, who asked to be reassigned. Wrangel had General Konovalov, the quartermaster general, sent in by plane to retrieve the situation. In the meanwhile General Babiev with his cavalry was cut off and had to fight his way back in near desperate conditions.

Lieutenant Mamontov was along with his battery; he described it as follows: "All day we moved, encircled by the Reds. With another commander such a march would have been impossible, but we had Babiev, trusted him implicitly, gritted our teeth and moved on. Both our batteries worked in conjunction: One shot back while the other rushed ahead to the head of the column and opened the way by firing grapeshot over open sights. Sometimes Babiev judged the moment opportune and launched a counterattack. The Reds would be thrown back, but soon again the steel noose tightened around our necks. . . .

"As our battery moved to the rear, we would pass the ambulance carts with our wounded. To their queries on how the fight went on we answered gaily but averted our eyes. Some of the wounded asked us to shoot them, fearful of being taken prisoners. We tried to reassure them as best we could. . . . Towards evening a wide, boggy stream barred our way. A long dike half a mile long led to the village of Kirpili—the Reds held the village. We were blocked; there seemed no way out.

"I heard Babiev call out to one of the squadron commanders: 'Captain, you've got to take Kirpili; it is our only hope. Attack along the dike, Godspeed!'

"I heard with horror this command. Attacking along a half-mile dike— mounted. It seemed madness: Ten men could hold up a whole regiment. The captain seemed unperturbed: He simply answered, 'Yes, sir.'

"Babiev continued: 'We shall attack across the stream to divert their attention—seize that moment.'

"Turning to his men, some fifty of them, the captain commanded: 'By threes, column walk—Ho!' They moved off! We attacked and were beaten back—all seemed lost, then someone yelled 'Look,' pointing towards the village: The unmistakable figures of mounted Cossacks flicked to and fro among the courtyards and alleys of the village.

"A roar of enthusiasm engulfed us. As we moved with our battery along the endless dike, I simply could not imagine how they could have done it: Galloping two abreast against machine-gun fire. But they did it, and no one boasted about it—they just considered it a day's work! . . . ."

In cutting his way through the Reds, Babiev arrived in the nick of time to help the cadets of the Konstantine Officers' School from being annihilated: They were down to their last cartridges with orders to fire only point-blank, leaving the last shot for themselves.

As more and more Red troops were brought in, it became obvious that the Kouban expedition was doomed. General Chatilov was sent out to supervise the reembarkment. The spot chosen was fortuitous, as it was shielded on one side by almost impossible reed beds of the Kouban river. All troops, horses, and equipment, along with the many wounded, were loaded aboard and the expedition returned to the Crimea. The only positive side of this failure was the addition of ten thousand Cossacks fleeing from Red occupation and the acquisition of several thousand horses—enough to remount one of the Cossack divisions.

Wrangel blamed himself bitterly for the failure. Busy as he was with the fighting on the Crimean front and burdened with his civic and diplomatic obligations, he was unable to supervise and then direct the expedition. Chatilov, Ulagai, and Dratzenko, particularly the latter two, had let him down. The forces landed were too small for even the smallest margin of error. Wrangel himself would have gambled and probably won, but his generals, except for Babiev, lacked the spark that had fired the victories in the northern Caucasus, the Manytsh, Tsaritsyn, and recently the defeat of Jloba. The Crimean front left Wrangel no respite. No sooner had one concentration of Red troops been checked and defeated than the Soviets brought in new divisions: Red, Letts, and Hungarians; communist youth units and mobilized conscripts; also new divisions formed and officered by former Czarist officers under the vigilant supervision of Communist commissars taken from the almost inexhaustible reservoir of Russian manpower and armed with the enormous supplies accumulated during the World War. The quality of the Soviet army had improved: The great number of World War officers impressed into service by orders of the Soviet war commissar Trotsky were beginning to turn out more efficient combat formations.

In the days of Denikin's command Russian officers who deserted from the Reds had to pass a series of rehabilitation commissions. Their cases dragged out for months with no satisfactory conclusion; they became discouraged and word of it got back to those still in the Red army ranks. Still worse, some White commanders took justice into their own hands and summarily executed these unfortunates. With his usual imagination Wrangel issued a series of proclamations, offering amnesty and reinstatement of rank and pay to those willing to join him; the appeals were based on patriotism. Leaflets were dropped from aircraft or smuggled into Soviet army rear areas. It is hard to judge the success of these measures; it is certain, however, that what could have generated tens of thousands of applicants in 1919 now produced driblets.* Wrangel's efforts to wean away the anarchists and divert partisan units ranging from political groups to bandits had varying success. Makhno, the anarchist leader, simply hanged two officers sent from the White intelligence section. Wrangel left no stone unturned to increase his army which was steadily dwindling in incessant combat. Acting through French channels, he obtained the repatriation to Crimea of units of General Bredov which had been interned in Poland following their retreat from Odessa in the winter of 1919. They arrived in a deplorable state. The Poles had kept them in concentration camps, half starved, clothed in rags. Evidently it had not occurred to the Poles that they were meting out such treatment to their allies. Countering Lloyd George's efforts to convince Poland to make peace with the Soviets, Wrangel urged the French and Polish governments to keep the war going.

A memorandum to the French proposed the formation of a Russian army in Poland; Wrangel arranged for direct communication with the Polish government and a Polish military mission was sent to the Crimea. As a further step, Wrangel proposed the formation of a joint command under the French general staff with representatives of the Russian and Polish armies.

Finally a communication arrived through the Polish military attaché that the Polish government had agreed to form on its territory an army of eighty thousand Russians to be drawn from interned White Russian units, Red army prisoners, and deserters (many Don Cossacks who after the tragic evacuation of Novorossiyak had been abandonned by Denikin and his staff and later

---

* July 26, 1920 — on the front of the Markovsky Division a Soviet armored car drove into the White lines, driven by a Cossack officer who had been impressed into the Red army. He had killed the Red commissar watching over him and driven off through the Red lines. By cable Wrangel promoted him on the spot to major, decorated him with the new Order of St. Nicholas, and made him commander of the armored car.

impressed into the Red army). The army was to be commanded by a general nominated by Wrangel.

The favorable position of the French government was strengthened by the attitude of the United States. On the 10th of August, 1920, Secretary of State Colby stated that the U.S.A. firmly stood on its position to defend the sovereignty and territorial integrity of Poland and, while favoring any discussions leading to armistice, did not consider opportune the initiation of a conference, the evident net result of which would be recognition of the Soviet regime and the dismemberment of Russia. The note concluded that the U.S.A. would never recognize the Soviet government, as it negated the established principles of international intercourse, rejected the principles of democracy, and aimed towards world revolution under the banner of the Third International. . . .

On the 20th of August the American chief of mission, Admiral MacCully, presented to the South Russian government a list of questions.

For the information of the U.S. Government I would appreciate very much a fairly explicit and comprehensive statement of General Wrangel of his policy and aims. The following questions suggest the character of the information desired:

1. Is the policy of General Wrangel the restoration of Russia on the basis of a general expression of the will of the people and is pledged to the creation of a constituent assembly to be elected by the will of the people on the basis of general and direct national suffrage?

2. Does General Wrangel specifically disavow any intention to impose upon Russia any unrepresentative Government, ignoring the sanctions of popular assent and acceptance?

3. Is the interpretation of recent declarations of General Wrangel correct, recognizing the mistakes of the Denikin and Koltchak Governments, and profiting by their experience, he does not regard the establishment of law and freedom in Russia as primarily a military task; that he places first and foremost the organization of production and satisfaction of needs of the peasants, who constitute the great majority of the Russian people; that General Wrangel is organizing and training an organization not for pursuing extensive war against Bolshevism along the type attempted by Koltchak and Denikin, but would agree to protect against attack the nucleus of national regeneration; that, in short, his attempt is to create a center of political and economic order and consolidated effort, around which Russian groups and territories may gather freely and develop their own desired effect?

4. Information exists that General Wrangel is introducing behind the lines local self-government by means of popularly elected Zemstvos and other democratic agencies, and that, in particular, he is seeking to solve the

land problem in an orderly manner by constitutional methods and by validating the ownership of the lands by the peasants. Is this information correct?

5. Are there not a considerable number of refugees now dependent on General Wrangel's protection against the Bolsheviks? Approximately how many such refugees are there, and to what classes and groups do they in general belong?

6. Would it be justifiable to conclude that General Wrangel, although believing his movement to be the present center of Russia's efforts at self-restoration and recovery of unity and national life, does not at the moment profess or claim to be the head of an all-Russian Government; that he does not regard himself as authorized to make treaties intending to be binding upon any future Russian Government that may be set up, or to grant concessions or otherwise dispose of the national domains and resources?

7. Is the recent declaration of the policy of the U.S. Government satisfactory to General Wrangel, both as regards Poland and as regards the unity and integrity of Russia?

8. What are the safeguards which General Wrangel feels can be relied upon, and which may assure other nations that General Wrangel will be able to pursue the policy of building up the portion of Russia which comes under his jurisdiction without permitting its development into either a military adventure or a political reaction?

As definite and explicit a statement of his aims as General Wrangel may be good enough to make would be much appreciated.

N.A. MacCully
Rear-Admiral, U.S.N.

Admiral MacCully received the required answers;-

1. General Wrangel has declared many times that his sole aim is to enable the Russian people to express their wishes freely on the subject of the future government of the country. Today, therefore, he can but affirm once again his intention of establishing conditions which will permit the calling of a National Assembly based on universal suffrage, through which the Russian people can decide on the form of government for new Russia.

2. General Wrangel has not the slightest intention of imposing a government on Russia which would function without the cooperation of a national representative body, or the sympathy and support of the people.

3. The interpretation of General Wrangel's recent declarations in the

sense that he does not regard the establishment of law and liberty in Russia as preeminently a military task is perfectly justified. On the contrary, the series of reforms which have already been carried out prove that General Wrangel attaches primary importance to reconstructive work in the State and to the satisfying of the needs of the peasants who constitute the great majority of the Russian people. It is precisely because he wants to foster the peaceful development of creative government action that General Wrangel has refrained from bringing to the fore the question of the enlargement of the front on which his armies are fighting the Bolsheviks. He has rather tried to assure the integrity of the economic and political center which has been created by the Russian Army on occupied territory and in the Cossack regions with which he is in close alliance. The preservation of this healthy nucleus is indispensable, for it has to serve as a center of gravity for the free development of the final efforts of the Russian people for national regeneration.

4. The information concerning the reforms which General Wrangel's Government has carried out by creating district Zemstvos, and in agrarian spheres, is absolutely accurate. The first of these reforms anticipates decentralization and safeguards the local economic interests of the population who will deal with economic questions through their freely elected agencies. The law concerning the district Zemstvos will be followed at a very early date by one concerning the provincial Zemstvos; both laws are to serve as a basis for a representative organ of a more general character. The Land Reform will deal with the agrarian problem in a radical way by allowing the legal remission by redemption of arable land to its cultivators, who will become its owners; thus a strong class of small peasant proprietors will be created in accordance with the ideal of the Russian peasant.

5. The number of refugees who have sought General Wrangel's protection against the Bolsheviks is very high. It greatly exceeds five hundred thousand in the Crimea alone, and there are almost as many again scattered through the Near East, Egypt, and Europe. Most of them are old men, women, and children. All these refugees are benefiting in one way or another from the support and help of the South Russian Government. Should the integrity of the territories of the South Russian Government be guaranteed, General Wrangel thinks it is his duty to facilitate the return of these refugees to their country and to allow them to devote themselves to productive work. This body of refugees is made up of the most diverse elements. They belong to all classes of the population, for men of all classes found it equally impossible to endure the Bolshevik tyranny.

6. General Wrangel considers that the Government of which he is the head is the sole remaining depository of the idea of national regeneration and the restoration of Russian unity. He thinks, however, that only a Government set up after the National Assembly has settled its nature should have the power to conclude treaties affecting the sovereign rights of the Russian people, or of disposing of the national patrimony.

7. The declaration of policy which was made recently by the Government of the United States coincides in every respect with General Wrangel's political program. He is in complete agreement with the clauses dealing with the preservation of Russian unity and territorial integrity as well as with those dealing with Poland. General Wrangel would like to take this occasion to express his very deepest gratitude to the Federal Government.

8. General Wrangel realizes that if foreign powers accord recognition to the work already performed by his Government, they would like to be assured in some way other than by a verbal declaration that their fear that the South Russian Government's activities may degenerate into a military adventure or a political reaction is quite unjustified. As regards their fear of a military adventure, General Wrangel begs to remind you that he is ready to end the civil war as soon as the integrity of the territory under his authority and the Cossack regions is guaranteed effectively, and as soon as the Russian people, now ground down beneath the Bolshevik yoke, are given the means of expressing their will freely. General Wrangel declares, on his side, that he is ready to promise that they will be able to express their opinions. He is firmly convinced that this population will never pronounce in favor of the Soviets.

As for his personal affairs, General Wrangel has already declared openly that his object is to enable the people to express their wishes freely. He then will submit to the sovereign voice of the Russian nation without the slightest hesitation.

Sebastopol, August 24th – September 6th, 1920.

In his talks with Wrangel and with Olga Wrangel, who was intensely engaged in welfare work, especially with children, the number of orphans being particularly great, Admiral MacCully* felt sure that he could obtain relief in the form of food and clothing. Due to his unflagging activity and support, American relief became a reality: Generously given food, medicine, and clothing arrived in substantial quantities; this in contrast to the British, as Winston Churchill protested, "We have rigorously abstained from supplying

---

* Admiral MacCully personally took over thirty orphans who were brought up and educated in the U.S.A. at his own expense.

Wrangel with any assistance — even chloroform and antiseptics were denied
to his wounded!"

Had time permitted, it was logical to assume that a de facto recognition by
the U.S.A. of the government of southern Russia would have materialized.

It seems a miracle that tottering on the brink of doom in March, the government and the army had emerged triumphant in the solution of almost impossible tasks ranging from complete abandonment by the Allies, to bankruptcy,
famine, and an army consisting of defeated remnants which were disorganized,
unequipped and disillusioned.

Whether addressing the troops, meeting with his cabinet, talking to the
press or to foreign representatives, Wrangel maintained an optimistic enthusiasm that soon engulfed even earlier detractors. Shulgin, a prominent Russian
political figure, expressed it thus: "A high voltage current seemed to emanate
from his personality; his psychic energy seemed to change. his immediate
environment. This constant vibrant will power, his faith in his mission, and the
ease with which he bore the mantle of responsibility — all this made possible
the Crimea miracle."

As Regent of southern Russia he led a more than Spartan life. Up early in
the small one-storied pavilion that once belonged to a grand duke (he later
moved into the more spacious building, formerly the residence of the Black Sea
fleet commander), Wrangel received visitors and reports from eight o'clock
on. Lunch was one hour only and then, again, interviews, meetings, and
reports. From six on, special appointments with key personalities and, if time
was available, a stroll through town, accompanied by his ADC — what a contrast to chiefs of state today traveling in bullet-proof limousines to the accom-
paniment of howling sirens from a motorcycle escort! Nothing escaped his
attention: Whether an army hospital or a housing project, each would be
looked into; defects noted; inhabitants, wounded, or personnel conversed
with. Dinner was an informal affair in small company: his wife, mother-in-law,
a guest or two, and the duty officers. The meal was plain: one course; no drinks
except for a glass of wine. Conversation was on everything but politics;
Wrangel used that hour to relax. He could be an easy and engaging conver-
sationalist, his ironic sense of humor often at the cost of this or that individual.
"So and so came to visit me," he would say. "I listened to his long patriotic
speech which ended with a 'may I have a permit for grain export!' " Although
he was himself deeply religious, he would not miss the opportunity to poke fun
at some overzealous cleric. After dinner Wrangel worked until midnight. During his numerous and extensive trips to the front he lived with his staff in a train
under very primitive conditions.

A newspaper correspondent, A. Valentinov, reporting for the *Sebastopol
News* lived in this train and gave a graphic description of Wrangel and his staff.

"Doors in the train's compartments were generally open and he seemed to roam about at will, hearing much of what was going on.

"2-6-20, 1700. Wrangel's loud voice resounded through the train. He was haranguing his adjutant general. 'Where am I to find honest and capable workers —where are they, German Ivanovitch [General Konovalov, adjutant general]? Tell me where are they to be found!' Bitterness and anguish were reflected in his voice.

"During the tense moments of the critical operations against the Reds Wrangel was all motion and exploding energy. From senior to junior members of his staff, all admit that his scope of 'strategic fantasy' has no limit, and when the staff's dispositions do not conform to the directives, he explodes. 'You won't work as you should; then, please, off you go to the front. I'll find other staff officers; I'll get them from the combat units!'

"16-7-20, a.m. Wrangel, displeased with some action of the cavalry, blamed General Gxxxx of the general staff. 'He is not a general staff officer; he is an ass,' Wrangel said, addressing himself to the adjutant general. 'See to it that he is not to be allowed within a cavalry march of the nearest combat unit! If he insists on an assignment, let him work on the artillery positions on the Perekop isthmus well in our rear. This is an order, German Ivanovitch!'

" . . . After dinner Wrangel was walking back and forth along the platform, engaged in a heated conversation with his chief of staff. Suddenly drawing his Cossack dagger, he squatted down and proceeded to draw an operational sketch. Amused bystanders gathered to watch. Oblivious, Wrangel kept on sketching and explaining. . . ."

Wrangel's impulsive enthusiasm had an effect even on the foreign diplomats and military attachés. He had what is now popularly called a sense of public relations. As the negotiations with France and Poland proceeded, Wrangel decided to show his troops to the different diplomats, members of military missions, military attachés, and press correspondents. A trip to the front was organized. Different units who had just emerged from combat paraded or maneuvered before the visitors.

Captain Pronin, an artillery officer: "Friedrichsfeld, a German colony in the Tauride province. A bright sunny day, the end of summer. On the outskirts, an unusual group of people.

"In front, towering a head over the rest, lean, his long manly face lit by big expressive grey eyes—General Wrangel. Near him, officers from headquarters, the corps, and divisional commanders; a group of foreign military attachés—a small Frenchman with a gold embroidered cap; an even smaller Japanese; a Yugoslav officer, dark and sunburned; an Italian in tall headgear.

"In column of battalions the Drozdovsky division passes in review. The division has just been pulled out of heavy fighting in the Andreburg sector.

Immediately after the review the division will proceed to the north where heavy enemy pressure is again contained with difficulty.

"Our battery follows. What an unusual parade. We hear: 'Attention — Eyes Right!'

"The loud but clear tones of Wrangel's greetings: 'Hello, Eagles!'

"A pause—steps, and then one giant shout from the marching mass: 'Greetings, Your Excellency!'

"The 'Eagles' clad in dirty sweat-stained shirts. That morning each one searched his knapsack for something passably clean. Many wounded in the ranks, some with bandaged heads, the bandages grey with dust.

"Our battery passes at the trot: 'Attention!' We see Wrangel before us. Again, greetings, answers, and we pass by in clouds of yellowish dust.

"Scenes from ancient history come to mind; a huge yellow arena bathed in sunlight—the march of the gladiators. As they pass, they raise their arms in salute to the emperor and call out the traditional words: 'Ave Caesar, morituri te salutant (Hail Caesar, those about to die salute you!)'

"Wrangel was indeed our beloved leader. He personified for us our last hope in our fight for our country. We trusted him and loved him—our white knight—and yet the feeling of impending doom was upon us as we marched on north and saw on the horizon the white clouds of exploding shrapnel as the dull sound of a distant cannonade grew louder."

After the review a few obsolete aircraft patched up to the limit of possibility put on an aerobatic display. This unusual parade, where the martial tone of the troops contrasted so strangely with their complete destitution, produced a great effect on the foreign visitors: Favorable articles and comments began to appear in the world press.

18
Hopes, Plans, Exit of Poland

THE END OF JULY, 1920, saw the Russian army front stretching from the Sea of Azov at Berdiansk on to Upper Tokmak, Popovo station, and then on along the river Dniepr. All of the left bank of that river was occupied by Wrangel's troops except for a small bridgehead at Kahovka, very heavily fortified by the Reds. As the right bank of the Dniepr was higher than the left, it gave the Reds the advantage of covering their bridgehead with massive artillery based on the right bank. The bridgehead was occupied by elite Red army units. The use of this bridgehead was correctly evaluated by the Red army general staff. As long as it existed, it posed a threat to any advance of Wrangel's army north, as a constant danger persisted of a Red eruption from their bridgehead and the inevitable severance of Wrangel's communications with Crimea. Wrangel knew this and took measures to eliminate this bulge which was to prove a cancer in the Russian army's organism.

General Slachtchov had held the Crimea during all the campaigns of 1918 through 1920 and had greatly contributed to the new Russian army's success in breaking out of the Crimea in April, 1920. He was now ordered to eliminate the Kahovka bridgehead. Unfortunately, the moral and physical strength of that general, which had been on the wane for a long time, now broke down completely. Driven mad by drugs and alcohol, Slachtchov was no longer himself: His handling of the troops, sporadic and irrational, led to serious losses and the bridgehead remained Red. Slachtchov was recalled. Ruthless towards criminals and marauders, Wrangel was compassionate and full of consideration towards his associates. On Slachtchov's return to Sebastopol Wrangel visited him in the train where he had his headquarters. What he saw appalled him—a chaos, where arms, bottles, papers, lay in total disarray, as Slachtchov, dressed in a fantastic uniform, alternately cried and laughed while pet birds fluttered about the compartment. As gently as he could, Wrangel persuaded him to take a cure in a sanatorium.

General Vitkovsky took over Slachtchov's command and the elite Kornilov division supported by tanks attacked Kahovka. At first meeting with success they breached the barbed-wire defenses, taking three lines of trenches, but the Red artillery, massed in great numbers on the right bank of the Dniepr, pounded them mercilessly, and the Red counterattacks forced them eventually to withdraw, leaving behind many killed and the debris of tanks which could hardly be spared.

The Reds gave Wrangel no respite; more and more units en route to the Polish front were rerouted, attacking the northeast to relieve the pressure on the Kahovka bridgehead and to crash through to the Crimean peninsula. The odds rose from two-to-one to five-to-one. The Reds had learned from Wrangel's cavalry tactics of the previous years, and with an unlimited reservoir of horses at their disposal they put more and more cavalry divisions in the field. In a series of furious engagements supervised by Wrangel, two of his ablest lieutenants — the Don Cossack General Abramov and the veteran of the old Volunteer army, General Koutiepov — were able to rout the different Red offensives taking prisoners and war booty but suffering heavy casualties. Invariably Red prisoners were put into the White ranks, and strange as it seems, most of them fought loyally. But the precious officers, cadres diminished daily. In the forty months of the civil war the Kornilov division alone had lost 5,411 officers killed. During the summer of 1920 the military situation often demanded that units change front 180 degrees; such fighting and maneuvering with exhausting marches strained the army to the utmost. To students of military history, Napolean's 1814 campaign was perhaps the brightest page of his military career. Harried by the enormous coalition of Russians, Germans, and Austrians, Napoleon eluded them, standing them off and inflicting defeats, leaving to history the names of Montmirail, Champober, Montereau, Fère-Champenoise. Someday an impartial Russia will credit Wrangel with the battles of Upper and Lower Tokmak, Alekseevka, Konstantivovka, Uzku, and Kahovka, where the rapidly dwindling Russian army parried blows, maneuvered, and destroyed divisions and corps of the Red army.

Wrangel knew that unless the Poles continued the war, it would be only a question of time before all the Red army would face him in overwhelming superiority. Hence a dramatic move had to be made; hanging on the defensive meant only slow attrition. Despite further mobilization of horses, the quality of which left much to be desired, there were not enough to remount all the Cossack divisions, some of which continued to fight as infantry to their great disadvantage.

On the political front the situation was rosier. Krivochein was negotiating a loan from the French government. Aid in the form of tanks, guns, and ammunition was promised. The French Marshal Foch was very favorably disposed towards Wrangel. The harvest had been good and grain export had bolstered the desperately needed finances. Last but not least, all subversive Red activity had been almost totally eliminated, thanks to the work of a General Klimovich, a professional counterintelligence officer with great experience. It was no longer the improvised Osvag of General Denikin's days but an orderly, serious organization on the lines of all European intelligence organizations. A series of clandestine Communist groups were discovered and apprehended and, except for a few marauding bands hiding in the Crimean mountains, the territory of southern Russia behind the front lived a normal life. Shops were open again; movie theaters and cafes were full — and it was hardly possible to believe that a few months before Crimea was in its death throes.

Nevertheless, through diplomatic and intelligence sources rumors persisted regarding a possible armistice between Poland and the Reds. Furthermore, Wrangel's radio intercept unit had been receiving reports of the movement south of a whole cavalry army led by Budenny, a former cavalry sergeant and now a Red marshal. This great mass of cavalry was awaited on the Crimean front sometime around October 15. If anything dramatic was to be done, it had to be performed immediately, and Wrangel proposed a daring plan of crossing the Dniepr river, cutting off and eliminating the Kahovka bridgehead, and pushing westward to join the Polish army. This move would bolster Poland's courage and reinforce its desire to defeat the Soviets regardless of the pressure of Lloyd George and his cabinet for an immediate armistice.

19

The Trans-Dniepr Operation

IN ORDER TO SECURE THE CROSSING of the Dniepr and engage in a major operation it was imperative to clear the northern and eastern sections of the front. This was done in successive and brilliant combats by the corps of two generals, Abramov and Koutiepov, the latter having command of the overall operation.

Wrangel divided his small army (twenty-five thousand infantry and eight thousand cavalry) into two parts; the first under Koutiepov was to hold the Reds at bay, whereas the second under General Dratzenko was to force the Dniepr and cut off the Kahovka bridgehead.

Just as in the Waterloo campaign Napoleon made a fatal mistake in giving Marshal Grouchy the command of his right wing,* so in this case Wrangel erred in giving Dratzenko such a prominent role. Wrangel had become convinced that the failure of the Kouban expedition was due to General Ulagai's loss of nerve and that his chief of staff, Dratzenko, was in no way to blame. His World War I record and subsequent service made him seem a likely candidate. But as so often proved the case, the good World War I generals were not the ones fit for the civil war, where daring, improvisation, and sometimes sheer desperate gamble reaped rich harvests. The older generals, steeped in the trench routine of the World War, lacked the daring and that spark that sets off the fire of victory.

The proposed crossing sites were chosen very carefully and in complete secrecy.

The river Dniepr breaks out in a series of deltas heavily overgrown with reeds; at one point, an island called Khortiza separates the channel in two. Several fords were available to cross over to the right bank; they were carefully reconnoitered and marked. The island was held by elements of the Markovsky division.

Captain Pavlov described the situation: "The island, wooded; on the outskirts of the wood, a sandbank; then an even stretch of sand, a hundred yards of water — the other shore with a similar sandbank, then bushes and trees and a

---

* Grouchy wandered off in pursuit of Blucher, losing him and remaining stationary while Napoleon's main force was defeated by Wellington and Blucher.

very steep bank. The enemy held the opposite sandbank, which was defended by barbed wire. On top of the high bank were trenches with machine-gun emplacements. Their batteries were zeroed in on the ford. We could clearly make out this ford: it was sandy, about waist-deep at its shallow width, for to the left it dropped considerably; we could see the dark, swirling water. To the right, however, it did not drop off so abruptly.

"Previously a pontoon bridge had been erected on the left side of the island. On the night of September 24, as soon as darkness fell, the different army units filed across the bridge: the Kornilov infantry division, the Kouban Cossack division, the 3rd, the Markovsky regiment and its two mounted squadrons, the machine-gun carts and the guns — all crossed silently in pre-scribed order and melted into the darkness of the surrounding woods. There was no talking; the bridge creaked and swayed, the dark water swirling below: Here and there sappers kept watch on the anchors. Everyone was tense.

"September 25. All quiet, not a shot. Never have the Reds been so quiet. Are they expecting the attack? But if it was so would they not be raking the woods where three thousand infantry and fifteen hundred horsemen were quietly waiting?

"A dark, cold night; no fires, no movement on the banks, only whispers among the group of officers crouching in the bushes. Then three scouts led by Lieutenant Zadera walk out to the edge of the water; they carry stakes and walk in single file at intervals of ten yards. Zadera sticks the stakes to mark out the edge of the ford; a rope stretches from stake to stake — still no sound from the enemy. . . .It was decided to attack without artillery preparation, banking on a sudden effect.

"4:30 a.m. Two files of men walk silently out of the wood and head for the water. The sand crunches and a dull murmur seems to fill the air. Then the splash of water under foot as more and more men enter the river. The going is difficult because of the current and the fact that arms have to be stretched high to keep rifles and cartridges dry.

"Suddenly a rifle shot rings out, then another and another; machine guns chatter and bullets come whining. Someone has his cap blown off; another gets a bullet in the cartridge belt held above his head, loses his balance, and falls — his neighbors fish him out. Instinctively all bend down and rush forward. 'Hurrah' — the sound of exploding grenades, and the firing gradually dies down. We tear down the barbed wire as firing resumes from the top bank.

"Only when the leading companies had breached the trenches did the Red artillery open up. The shells splashed to the left and right of the wading files, luckily with no casualties. One man kept ducking in; someone wanted to help him, but he spluttered, 'My rifle,' and diving once more triumphantly retrieved it."

Availing themselves of other fords the different units crossed over the

Dniepr. The Cossack cavalry of General Babiev helped the infantry across by giving them a ride on the croups of their horses, the Cossacks laughing good-naturedly as the infantrymen climbed on and clung clumsily to the saddles.

Wrangel had staked his hopes on a hard punch and fast movement, the latter entrusted to the desperately brave, always successful one-armed General Babiev with his Kouban Cossacks securing the right bank of the Dniepr and leaving the Markovsky division to guard the crossings. The Kornilov division and the Kouban Cossacks swung south and ran into a whole cavalry army under the command of a certain Comrade Gay. Desperate fighting followed, often at close quarters with generals fighting hand to hand. A Red cavalryman seized General Babiev's* red bashlyk with the shout "I've got you!" — but the one-armed general, holding the reins in his teeth, whipped around and in an easy stroke lopped off his assailant's head. In all, the Cossack division repulsed thirteen successive attacks while the infantrymen standing shoulder to shoulder fired into the charging masses. Further downstream a Cossack corps under General Naumenko crossed over the river, attacked Red infantry taking over three thousand prisoners and several guns. Uniting with Babiev, they were to swing behind the Kahovka bridgehead and facilitate the attack of Kahovka. Despite these intial successes the advance became more and more difficult as the Reds threw in fresh troops on the northern front, where the small numbers of the Whites under General Koutiepov could hardly contain them.

All hinged on how quickly and how strongly General Dratzenko would deliver his punch enveloping Kahovka and allowing General Vitkovsky's tank-supported infantry to burst open the Kahovka fortress.

But despite Wrangel's imperative orders Dratzenko moved with desperate slowness. Soon he was to report that he could make no progress due to overwhelming opposition.

Air reconnaissance indicated that the Reds were evacuating the bridgehead (the report was inaccurate), but led to the order to attack. Following the tanks, the White infantry rushed forward only to be met by point-blank fire of guns stationed in the village streets. The tanks fared even worse, doused with petrol and ignited; this was the first use of what became later known as Molotov cocktails. The attack failed.

To Wrangel's dismay, Dratzenko reported that the Cossack cavalry was streaming back in disarray. What had happened to negate the initial successes? A night passed with no further explanations; then in the morning came a cable, the answer to all: "General Babiev was killed yesterday."* The soul of the whole operation was no more; the leadership assumed by the capable General

---

* Babiev, the Jeb Stuart of the Russian army, had the same dashing characteristics, the courage and élan that characterized most great cavalry leaders. They were both of the same age when they fell.

Naumenko lasted but a few minutes, as he himself was wounded. The otherwise staunch Cossack regiments broke and streamed back towards the crossings. Dratzenko lost control of his troops and only the brave Cossack infantry of General Tsyganok guarding the bridges held fast until the different units passed over in confused, disorderly masses.

An operation carefully planned, albeit with insufficient forces, and correctly, even brilliantly, executed in its initial phases, had come to naught — the death of the bravest of generals and the indecision of another accounting for the final reverse.

The Kornilov division which had marched, fought, and countermarched on the right bank of the Dniepr, recrossed again. General Skobline, the divisional commander, was met by his chief of staff who silently handed him three telegrams.

The first read: "The Poles have reached an armistice with the Reds, who have started major troop transfers against the Russian army. The forward elements of the Red cavalry and two infantry divisions have reached the station of Apostolovo."

The second telegram read: "General Babiev was fatally wounded and died without regaining consciousness. Units of the 2nd Army have recrossed the Dniepr with heavy losses in men and equipment, having had no time to destroy the pontoon bridge."

The third telegram read: "A Red Kouban Cossack division approximately five thousand men, has made a deep penetration on the northeast front, reaching our rear areas in the area of Major Tokmok where it seized and destroyed all our ordnance and supplies. The enemy continues its raid deep in our rear."

Wrangel now had to reach a decision whether to continue fighting in the plains of the southern Ukraine or retire to the Crimea and base his army on the fortified positions of the isthmus. This, after the unsuccessful trans-Dniepr operation, was tactically the most sound, but it would have meant the starvation of the army and the Crimean population — all the grain, cattle and other agricultural produce were in the Ukraine, their export the only source of revenue. Furthermore, the Russian army maneuvered better in the field than fighting in the trenches, where it would eventually be overcome by the unlimited numbers of Soviet infantry supported by massive artillery. Wrangel gambled on strategic advantage to which the more favorable tactical solution was to be subordinated. However, the moral and physical strength of the small Russian army had reached its limit: The heavy losses, the failure of the last campaign, and especially the knowledge that the Poles were withdrawing from the war and that the next combat would be at odds of ten-to-one could not but affect the morale of the army. Basing his tactics on intercepted Red plans,

Wrangel regrouped his forces, his plan calling for General Koutiepov's army corps to allow the enemy to cross the Dniepr at Nikopol; then to annihilate that body, throwing the remnants back across the river, and then, leaving a light screen in that area, to concentrate all efforts on the Kahovka bridgehead from whence Soviet infantry and the whole cavalry army of Budenny were to emerge.

Wrangel's intelligence had correctly estimated both the enemy's intentions as well as their timetable.

Unfortunately, Koutiepov was unable to contain, let alone defeat, the heavy Red attack from Nikopol; the Soviets, engaging new and fresh divisions, were pushing their way south. At the same time the whole cavalry army of Budenny emerged from Kahovka, supported by thirty thousand infantry comprising no less than six divisions. This overwhelming mass pushed the weak corps of General Vitkovsky, which retreated to the safety of the Perekop isthmus fortifications; the Red cavalry, in the meanwhile, moving in two columns, moved straight towards Salkovo cutting the Russian army's lifeline — the rail line Melitopol-Simferopol. The left Red column was intercepted by General Barbovitch's cavalry corps, but the right column moved unopposed and on the 15th of October occupied Salkovo and Genitchesk, the two centers where grain was being loaded in ships and barges. Cutting this rail line, Budenny moved on south and occupied the Tschongar peninsula.

This daring maneuver had dire consequences: The major portion of the Russian army was cut off from the Crimea; telegraph communications between Wrangel and Koutiepov and Abramov's troops were interrupted and the overall control of the army lost.

Wrangel had left Sebastopol for Djankoy in anticipation of the military operations. The sudden, fateful turn of events did not render him helpless. Every man he could scrape — convalescent wounded, cadets, rear echelon personnel — was rushed to the Sivash station to stop the Red cavalry from erupting into the Crimea. Meanwhile, Wrangel finally got in radio contact with General Abramov and ordered him to turn around, rush south, attack Budenny's cavalry and force it against the sea. The weather had turned for the worse. The mild Crimean climate was suddenly overrun by a cold wave of great intensity: Water froze in the pumps; snow squalls impeded vision. The Don Cossacks of General Abramov attacked the Red cavalry, taking trophies and prisoners; the Red Marshal Budenny hardly made good his escape. However, it was not possible to encircle and destroy the whole of the Red cavalry, as was the case with Jloba and his divisions a few months before. General Koutiepov's troops, with the Reds on their heels, had to sustain heavy rearguard actions while moving south to close the circle on the Red cavalry. Moving at times in squares reminiscent of Waterloo and Napoleonic campaigns, firing simultaneously in four directions, the exhausted remnants of the Volunteer divisions — Markovsky, Kornilov, and Drozdovsky — marched on through snow and sleet, while cart-borne machine guns careened between the squares, sweeping away the lines of attacking cavalry. Occasionally a White unit would break ranks; then it was all over: Red cavalrymen engulfed the thin line sabering everyone and all. Carrying their wounded, leaving their dead, the regiments marched south, but not fast enough, and parts of Budenny's cavalry slipped safely out of the Tchongar peninsula — but at least communications with the Crimea were restored.

Visions of the retreat were recounted by Captain Rebikoff of the 7th Howitzer Battery: "From the observer's position, the roof of a village house, I saw the Red cavalry overwhelm a battalion of the Drozdovsky division. I could see the cavalry sabering the infantry. General Mastein [commander of the division] threw in the 3rd Battalion and an armored car. Our battery opened rapid fire. The cavalry withdrew. The 1st Battalion was almost entirely annihilated (it was then already reduced in numbers to about a hundred and twenty men). On the field where the battalion fell lay a nurse who had been cut down. Next to her lay a dead Red cavalryman: A White infantryman about to die had had enough strength to fire and avenge the fallen 'angel of mercy.' "

The decisive battle on the fields of North Tauride had ended. To the enemy fell a large military booty: five armored trains, eighteen guns, one hundred carriages laden with ammunition, ten million cartridges, trainloads of supplies, and several thousand tons of grain ready for shipment.

Some military critics assailed Wrangel for taking a gamble in the open field. According to them, the army with its supplies could have withdrawn safely into the fortified positions of the Crimean bottleneck, to wait for better times. But what better times could be expected: The Red army was growing in strength on a daily basis; peace with Poland concluded, whole armies were on the march south. All the cities of Russia were placarded with posters calling : "All against Wrangel!" The numerical superiority from three-to-one would rise to ten and better.* The small Russian army, partly Cossack cavalry, adept at maneuver after having practiced it successfully over three years, would be a different proposition when it came to trench warfare for which it had not been trained. Finally, exit from the southern Ukraine meant slow starvation and the loss of Free Russia's sole source of income, the export of grain and meat.

Wrangel, his chief of staff Chatilov, and the senior field commanders unanimously agreed to gamble: the odds were too great and the gamble failed.

---

* In the second half of October 1920, the 4th, 6th, and 8th, plus two cavalry armies, and four partisan units were pitted against the Russian army: They comprised no less than fourteen infantry and twelve cavalry divisions.

20

The Agony and the Evacuation

DURING THE EARLY SUCCESSFUL OFFENSIVES Wrangel had but little illusion of the heavy odds against him and understood well that were things to go against the small Russian army, two missions were to be of primary importance — one, a strong defensive line on the Crimean isthmus upon which the army could fall back; the other, the evacuation by sea from the Crimea of the army and all those civilians whose lives would be threatened by the advent of the Reds. Work on the fortified line barring access to the Crimean peninsula was started in early spring: The best technicians, General Usefovitch and General Makeev, were assigned to the job. Trenches were dug, barbed wire stretched, machine-gun emplacements built, artillery guns sighted, and even a rail line laid which allowed armored trains to move in support of the defense positions. Banking on the mild Crimean climate and due to a shortage of timber, they delayed the building of dugouts and shelter for the defenders, which were not ready when the Russian army moved in after its retreat in winter conditions that had never before been felt in the Crimea — blizzards and hard frost such as the inhabitants of the peninsula had never experienced. The right flank of this defense system was anchored on the Sivash, a saline, shallow sea that never froze but was too deep to ford.

General Koutiepov was given the overall mission of defense and he chose to regroup his forces accordingly. The first and major line of defense was assigned to the old Volunteer divisions: Kornilov, Drozdovsky, and Markovsky. Koutiepov had fought with these "iron" divisions during the entire civil war and his absolute confidence rested on them irrespective of the extreme heavy losses these units had taken, especially in the command echelons. The guard of the Sivash Sea was given to Kouban's Cossack units, poorly armed and only recently formed.* When the Sivash Sea suddenly froze, the Reds advanced across it with two infantry divisions and two cavalry

---

* General Fostokov, a Kouban Cossack, had started yet another Cossack rebellion and fought successfully until surrounded by large Soviet forces. Forced to retreat to Georgia, he had with great difficulty gotten in touch with Wrangel in the Crimea. The White navy was able to save these partisans, transporting them to the Crimea where they were in the process of being formed into regular Cossack units, but they were short of officers and equipment.

regiments and found themselves deep behind the Perekop defense line. Driving before them the small Cossack force they outflanked the whole defense system. Instead of fighting on the first line of defense, the best divisions of General Koutiepov had to fight their way out. Wrangel threw in his last reserve, the cavalry. After a fleeting success they themselves were set upon by large formations of Red cavalry that had been steadily pouring into the Crimea, supported by massive artillery fire. The counterattack failed and the Russian army retreated to its last line of defense, the so-called Ushin line, a secondary defense system with shallow trenches, no dugouts, and no gun emplacements. This defense line had only subsequently been started and lacked almost everything needed for a strong defense.

Lieutenant Mamontov: "The defense line was good, even well protected by barbed wire. But again our headquarters seemed to have forgotten that they dealt with human beings: no dugouts, no supplies, no wells. Our savior was a huge haystack prepared by the local inhabitants. This haystack shielded us from the wind and partly from the cold. We fed our horses from it and even used some of it as fuel. It served us also as an observation post. There was no water: Horses and men had to eat snow and there was little of it around. I stuffed straw into my English overcoat, covering my chest and back, and drew my belt tighter. At night we crawled into the haystack, slept for some twenty minutes, then jumped out and danced about to warm our numbed bodies; then, exhausted, we would creep back into the haystack . . . and so on all night."

The Reds threw in new divisions in ever increasing numbers. Heavy artillery and over one hundred medium caliber guns constantly pounded the White lines. After twenty-four hours of unabated bombardment the Red infantry advanced in dozens of parallel lines with the elite Communist and Lett divisions in the van.

The White defenders fought back fourteen successive attacks: Huge mountains of enemy bodies lay among the partly destroyed barbed-wire entanglements. It became impossible to conduct aimed fire due to these heaps of bodies, but the Reds poured in division after division.

The inevitable happened and the last line of defense fell. Long before these events, at the height of his successes, Wrangel had decided to prepare just in case, for an orderly evacuation: Never again was the disgraceful evacuation of Novorossiyak under Denikin's mismanagement to be repeated.

It would have been catastrophic to let the armed forces and the Crimean population know about it: The first would have lost heart; the latter, panicked.

So it was in complete conspiratorial secret that Wrangel, his chief of staff Chatilov, and the navy commander Admiral Sabline started their plans early in May. Fuel began to be stockpiled, including the coal mined in the Crimea which had been one of Wrangel's first civilian administrative measures. All ships available were to be made seaworthy, including barges and dredgers. More fuel was ordered from Constantinople. As these measures developed, it became obvious that sooner or later people or the newspapers would start commenting on it. The intelligence department, under General Klimovich, started to leak out news about another impending landing in the Cossack lands. The hint was taken and no one bothered further about the intensive work on the wharves. Loading facilities of the different ports — Kertch, Feodossia, Yalta, and Sebastopol — were also taken into consideration and the access routes to these ports planned for the different army units.

When the coal ordered arrived from Sebastopol, it came on two ships; these had to be unloaded and the coal apportioned among the three loading ports. Always for heroic measures, Wrangel assembled details which included officers and civil servants and put them to the task, as the dry docks work on repair and refilling of vessels was accelerated. Whereas before workers under the influence of Communist agitators would often strike or slow down, this time they worked hard and willingly; Wrangel's reforms and his interest in their well-being had conciliated a milieu where traditionally the Communists had made heavy inroads. As it became clear that the last defenses of the isthmus were to fall, Wrangel took the train to the front for a meeting with the field commanders. Remembering Novorossiysk, they were naturally apprehensive, but Wrangel's calm and determined, positive outlook soon reassured them.

General Chatilov: "It was a great burden of General Wrangel's soul, that all that he had achieved in such a short time under such conditions had come to naught, but precisely here his fortitude manifested itself fully; he was as composed as in the days when he had achieved his last great victory over the cavalry army of Jloba. Whence did Wrangel draw this moral help? Primarily from his innate character, where the determination never to give up was always paramount!"

But what were his innermost feelings, those that he did not dare express even to his closest collaborators. Valentinov, the news correspondent, overheard Wrangel's monologue: "The C and C walked in. His drawn face expressed immense fatigue. Slowly he walked over to the window and looked for a long time at the lights of the ships in the harbor. I heard a hardly audible whisper: 'Oh, what a burden; what a terrible burden!' He turned and just as slowly walked back towards the door. I heard him pacing back and forth in the now empty reception hall. ...."

Now he asked General Koutiepov to hold on for five days, which would allow all rear echelons, hospitals, schools, and civilians to be loaded, the army units then withdrawing along routes prescribed to them, each towards its port of embarkation.

The Red army units were also exhausted after the bloodletting against the

Perekop defenses; they moved slowly on the heels of the retreating Russian army. However, a few days later large masses of Red cavalry were again on the move and the Guards battalion and elements of the Markovsky division were severely mauled. Captain Dudkine of the 1st Markovsky Regiment: Waves of Red cavalry came up against our battalion from the west and southwest, cutting us off from our other units. The battalion halted. Letting the cavalry come up to two hundred paces we opened up with all our machine guns. The loose horses did not gallop all over the place, but strangely halted and slowly turned back. The attack was beaten off, but at this moment another massive wave appeared over the hill. Again letting them come up, the companies opened fire. The center of the Red cavalry broke, but the wings lapped over our flanks. Simultaneously a new wave appeared and this one swamped us. Sabering started . . . a frightful sight. Firing died down except for individual shots: this or that infantryman firing point-blank at the Red cavalrymen."

The whole battalion was annihilated with all its officers except those three or four like Captain Dudkine who in the last moments had torn off their officer shoulder straps and found themselves among the few survivors taken prisoner. The Red cavalrymen galloped about, waving their swords and yelling: "Hand over the officers." In spite of the fact that most of the soldiers were ex-Red army men, not one betrayed them — a testimonial to the loyalty of the Russia soldier to his own officers.*

The other Russian units moved unmolested towards the embarkation ports. The inevitable confusion of a long march and many units led to some willful changes in itinerary, some units moving to ports other than those to which they were assigned.

Wrangel had issued a proclamation read to all the army and posted in all the towns; it read: "People of Russia! Alone in its struggle against the oppressor, the Russian Army has been maintaining an unequal contest in its defense of the last strip of Russian territory on which law and truth hold sway.

"Conscious of my responsibility, I have tried to anticipate every possible contingency from the very beginning.

"I now order the evacuation and embarkation at the Crimean ports of all those who are following the Russian Army on its road to Calvary; that is to say, the families of the soldiers, the officials of the civil administration and their families, and anyone else who would be in danger if they fell into the hands of the enemy.

"The Army will cover the embarkation, knowing that the necessary ships for its own evacuation are ready and waiting in the ports according to a pre-

---

* Captain Dudkine later escaped and made his way to freedom across the Rumanian border.

arranged plan. I have done everything that human strength can do to fulfill my duty to the Army and the population.

"We cannot foretell our future fate.

"We have no other territory than the Crimea. We have no money. Frankly as always, I warn you all of what awaits you.

"May God grant us strength and wisdom to endure this period of Russian misery, and to survive it."

This proclamation was read to the troops. Who were these troops and what thoughts turned over in their minds as they marched or rode towards the embarkation ports and exile? few were left of the original 3,683 who had started the White army; those who were still alive must have looked back with sorrow and bitterness on the three years of ceaseless combat always against overwhelming odds; wrapped in their burkas and bashlyks rode the Cossacks who had not surrendered, thinking of their ravaged lands over which a great deal of the civil war had taken place. Caucasian mountaineers, speaking their guttural dialects, rode gloomily but defiantly: To them it was the order of the Koran to fight the infidel who had defied God. Towards the sea marched or rode the Kalmyks, Mongols, the last heirs of the Golden Horde of Ghenghis Khan, now peaceful settlers in the Don plains. Their great herds had been dispersed, their Buddhist temples razed; they also knew that they must go. But there marched and rode also many men who had been at some time or other Red army soldiers. Taken prisoner, they had been retrained and had fought loyally alongside those same officers whom in the past they were exhorted to massacre on sight. What were their thoughts now?

Captain Pavlov: "Evpatoria, port of embarkation: two ships, a tug, and two barges moored. The wounded of the Don Cossack corps and their rear echelons have already been loaded. A Markovsky regiment comes marching up, singing. The company commander, Colonel Friede, reads General Wrangel's proclamation and says: 'Ten minutes to think it over — those who want to go, ten paces forward.' There were about two humdred who started to board. Addressing himself to the remainder Colonel Friede thanked them for their loyal service and wished them luck. He advised them to get rid of their arms and wait for the arrival of the Red army. 'Godspeed Colonel,' they answered in chorus."

Captain Statzenko; Sebastopol, November 1: "Markovsky and Drozdovsky units, corps headquarters, and some minor units were assigned to the large transport ship *Kherson*. Everything proceeded in orderly fashion: Special detachments directed the troops to their assigned places. Finally loaded to the gunwales, the *Kherson* slowly pulled away. But new troops arrived; a mass of about a thousand arrivals now massed themselves on the quays. Who will take us or will we be taken at all? Not all mastered their nerves. I saw an officer ride up and dismount. He patted his horse, then deliberately pulled out his revolver, shot the horse and then himself. A few shots rang out; then someone called out: 'Wait! There always will be time to shoot yourselves; other ships will be coming in to pick us up.'

"Around twelve, shouts of 'Hurrah' resounded on the quays, the hurrahs getting louder and louder; it was General Wrangel touring the harbor in a motorboat. 'Hello, my dear companions!' he called out, his loud voice articulating distinctly each syllable. Never before did I hear a mass of a thousand people return in such unison their greeting. 'Do you know where you are going? Or what awaits you in exile? I can promise nothing, as I do not know myself. But one thing I do promise; bad as it may seem, I shall take you out with honor. I can promise to those who want to follow me that I will get them out. Ships are on the way to pick up all of you!'

" 'Hurrah! Hurrah!' followed, never ending. Twenty minutes later several ships pulled in. . . ."

Arriving from the front, Wrangel had broken into feverish activity: Military rule was proclaimed in the cities, with detachments of cadets from the military schools patrolling. Wrangel gave a press conference in which he outlined both the course of events and the measures he had taken. He warned the world that the Russian army had fought for the preservation of liberty and Western culture. Another conference brought together all foreign heads of missions or attachés. Wrangel requested them to query their governments on the question of assistance from foreign shipping.

The British position had been made clear: The Secretary of the Admiralty had written to the Commander of the Mediterranean Fleet. There was not much to hope for from that quarter,* as can be seen from the British Foreign Office dispatches:

Secret
From the War Office
To:GHQ Constantinople.
86889 ciper H.I.R. Desp. 18.35 12.11.20
As regards General Wrangel, Policy of HM Government to observe strict neutrality. No action for the evacuation of refugees other than those of British nationality should be undertaken by British authorities. Admiralty have instructed C-in-C Mediterranean to this effect.

---

* In actual fact, in accordance with British naval tradition and in that feeling of "fair play" which so often motivated their actions, several ship commanders disregarded their orders and helped as best they could.

Urgent — Foreign Office

Sir,

With reference to previous correspondence regarding the evacuation of refugees from South Russia, I am directed by Lord Curzon of Kedleston to point out that, as a result of General Wrangel's retreat, there may be a further exodus of refugees from Southern Russia.

Lord Curzon is anxious that no more refugees should become a charge on HM's Government, already overburdened in this respect, and he would therefore be glad if instructions could be issued to the Commander in Chief Mediterranean, to the effect that no assistance should henceforward be lent by British ships to Russians attempting to leave South Russia. The guaranties given to General Denikin by Sir Halford McKinder on Jan. 10 last was fulfilled on the collapse of the Volunteer Army at the end of March last, and HM's Government have no further obligations towards the Russians at present in the territory occupied by General Wrangel, their efforts to protect whom at an earlier stage were indeed frustrated by the action of General Wrangel himself.

I am Sir etc.

J.D. Gregory

(The Secretary of the Admiralty)

In the meanwhile the French cruiser *Wladeck Rousseau* arrived from Constantinople. On board was the acting commander of the French Mediterranean squadron, Admiral Dumesnil. From their very first meeting the old, staid admiral and the young impulsive cavalry general understood each other and their first acquaintance ripened into a deep friendship. On Wrangel's death eight years later Admiral Dumesnil wrote: "Wrangel died without having for one moment betrayed the principles that motivated him, his thoughts ever directed towards his country, which he loved above all. He passes into History and will someday be an example to his country when it will be reborn. His name then will be ever present in the minds of Russia's children, when these will again be brought up as civilized people motivated by honor and morality." The admiral was appalled at the magnitude of the evacuation, the lack of available tonnage: Never before in history was such a vast enterprise contemplated;* Wrangel's unshaken determination convinced him, however, that it could be done.

Wrangel and Dumesnil exchanged letters, the former pledging as guarantee the Russian ships, the French in return promising food and care for the

---

* It was surpassed only on D-Day, the Normandy landings of World War II.

arriving multitude in Constantinople.

During the day Sebastopol's local authorities called on Wrangel. They asked if they could take over the city's security with detachments of local workers to whom arms were to be issued. Wrangel agreed and it was perhaps one of the great testimonials to his regime of eight months that workers — the very workers on whom the Soviets based their hopes and to whom they constantly appealed to massacre the Whites — insured the safe embarkation of the Russian army and civilians.

Shortly afterwards a telephone call was received from a Revolutionary committee in the port of Evpatoria; they asked for Wrangel, who took the receiver.

"We wish to report that we have taken over the local government. The army units and all those civilians who wanted to leave have embarked and the ships have sailed."

"Any sign of the Red army?"

"No, there are no military units in the city."

"Thank you for the news. I wish you the best."

"All the best to you!"

There, also, no enmity, only cooperation.

Wrangel toured the loaded ships on a motorboat as these gathered outside of the harbor. The crowded decks echoed with never ending hurrahs. History had seldom if ever seen a defeated army leaving for exile while greeting its commander with such unabated enthusiasm. Many years later a student of Russian military history, the Italian General Guillet, described it as "the twentieth century Xenophon and his Anabassis."

As embarkation proceedings were going on — the last troops boarding and the last security units drawn in — Wrangel, wearing the uniform of the Kornilov regiment, the first regiment to have raised the banner against the Communists and now, in Wrangel's person, the last to leave, walked down the quays. A group of local citizens, among whom Wrangel saw to his astonishment several prominent members of the left-wing opposition, came to wish him Godspeed. "Your Excellency, you were right when you said that you could leave with your head high, confident that you have fulfilled your duty. May we wish you a safe journey!" Nearly losing his composure, Wrangel shook hands. Walking down the marble steps leading down to the motorboat waiting for him, Wrangel turned, took off his cap, crossed himself and bowed to his homeland which destiny never allowed him to see again. . . .

The epic struggle had ended: two and one-half years; innumerable lives and enormous sacrifices; not all in vain, for some one hundred fifty thousand people were to find freedom, although far from home and often in miserable conditions.

The Soviets are not apt to shower their opponents with laudatory comments. They prefer to follow the precepts of Fouché, Napoleon's chief of police: "Smear, smear; a little will always stick!" In the mass of abuse heaped on Wrangel by the Soviet propaganda media, two voices, though most disparate, paid him a compliment.

The Soviet commander in chief Frunze wrote in his memoirs: "In the person of Wrangel and his army our motherland had without a doubt a very dangerous opponent indeed. ... In the various operations Wrangel demonstrated in most cases both outstanding energy and complete understanding of the situation."

The other was the Soviet futuristic poet Mayakowsky, a forerunner of the present-day Evtushenko. In his poem, "Well Done" he wrote:

We were advancing: their ships under fire
The last echelon was boarding pell-mell
Slamming the door of the empty headquarters
Wrangel strode out straight as a wire
The city abandoned, forlorn the pier
The General knelt as before a bier
Thrice he kissed the ground
Thrice blessed the town
Bullets whining, his army afloat
He jumped in the waiting naval longboat
— General, shall we push off? — Row on!

Mayakowsky's poem shows considerable poetic license: The embarkation of the White army and dependents had never come under fire; the Red army, exhausted by the fierce rearguard actions of the Russian army, had paused to gain breath; nor did Wrangel engage in any histrionics. But the sentiment was there, and by some miracle the poem escaped Soviet censorship ... at least for several years.

One hundred and twenty-six craft* varying from cruiser to a simple barge set forth. By Providence's grace the sky was clear, the sea an icy calm. Wrangel transboarded to the Russian cruiser *Kornilov* and sailed past his armada. Again a never ending hurrah greeted his tall ascetic figure standing on the captain's bridge. As they sailed out, the big transport *Don* loaded to the gunwales with men hove into sight. Climbing aboard a motorboat, Wrangel reached the *Don* among unending hurrahs. What he heard from the commanding general, Fostikov, did not please him: At Feodossia embarkation did not proceed as

* They carried 145,693 men and women excluding the ship's crew.

smoothly as elsewhere — the 1st Kouban Cossack Division was not loaded and was rerouted to Kertch. Wrangel called the port of Kertch, ordering General Abramov to embark the Kouban Cossacks — cost what may. A destroyer set out to check that there orders were complied with. Soon a cable confirmed that there also everyone was saved.

The fleet set forth; as the French cruiser *Waldeck Rousseau* fired a twenty-one gun salute, the Russian cruiser *Kornilov* answered. Lieutenant Wrangel (a distant cousin of the general): "The sun was setting over the high ridges of Sebastopol when we set sail. Our eyes riveted to the fast-receding shore, we saw, sharply etched out against the red sunset, a Red cavalry patrol on a hill overlooking Sebastopol."* Farewell, Russia. . . .

This time Providence was again on Wrangel's side; the sea remained calm for three days, permitting the armada to reach the Bosporus. However, in the night of November 8th to 9th the wind freshened and the old destroyer *Zjivoy*, towed by the ship *Holland*, capsized and went down with all its two hundred crew and passengers. This was the only casualty.

Commander London, U.S. Navy, on board the *USS St. Louis*; November, 1920: "Making 14 knots; approaching Sebastopol, Crimea; preparing to take abroad Russian refugees.

"As we approached Sebastopol we met many vessels loaded with troops leaving the port. Also leaving was a tow of four vessels, one an old Russian battleship whose deck was crowded with troops. In the outer harbor were several large transports — all crowded with troops. Admiral MacCully is on the *USS Overton*. After anchoring for four hours we were ordered to proceed to Yalta. We finally anchored there. Next day (November 15th, 1:15 p.m.) we sent boats ashore with a beach guard and took refugees aboard. Their passports were signed by the Red Cross. We had taken eighty-three passengers with a small amount of baggage — pitiful cases. General Wrangel is aboard a French cruiser. We sailed for Constantinople at 4:30 p.m. on the 15th.

At 9:30 a.m. on the 16th. we sighted the Russian transport *Rion* flying a distress signal — out of coal, food and water. We took them in tow sixty miles from the Bosphorus, speed 4½ knots. Just then an ice breaker towing an old Russian battleship came along. That night (9:30 p.m.) a tug from Constantinople met us and took the *Rion* in tow.

"An officer (Lt. Hoyt), whom we had sent aboard the transport with four men, signaled: 'Send bandages for two hundred wounded men. There are

---

* Lieutenant Leonid Wrangel and his platoon of the Horse Guards regiment was taken aboard the British destroyer *Seraph*. The captain, disregarding the orders of the Foreign Office and the Admiralty, preferred the orders of his own conscience as a British naval officer, gentleman, and humanitarian.

about four hundred sick children without food and water, etc. . . . '

"Our crew collected $500.00 to send the refugees food and other necessities."

The last ship to struggle in was a barge, the *Hrisi*. Its passengers were cadets who had not been loaded, as originally planned, on a transport, that, at the last minute had been requisitioned for combat units. Their situation would have been tragic, but quite "in extremis" the barge was found and allocated to them. The captain of the barge and his motley crew of Russians and Greeks tried to sail the barge to Odessa into Red hands. A couple of the cadets familiar with navigation noticed that they were on a false heading and, threatening to throw the captain overboard, took the barge over and sailed towards Constantinople. They just managed to make it, being the last arrivals of the nearly one hundred fifty thousand evacuees.

21
Hopes and Disappointments

WRANGEL WAS DETERMINED TO KEEP the army intact. For one thing, he hoped against hope that the turbulent events inside Russia and Europe's fast-changing politics would create a climate where the army would again be called upon to fight Bolshevism. Constant revolts inside Russia were sparks that one hoped would kindle the fire that was to consume Communism. But there was also another consideration. Only army discipline would keep this vast multitude of people — hungry, cold, and on the verge of despair — from becoming a menace to the security of Constantinople and Turkey. Men who had been fighting for three years in a climate of violence made even more formidable by its civil war horrors could hardly be let loose to fend for themselves.

The French military, Admirals Dumesnil and de Bon and General de Bourgogne, understood this only too well and agreed wholeheartedly with Wrangel's opinion to keep the army organization intact pending emigration to countries of asylum. These were primarily Bulgaria and Yugoslavia — the latter grateful for Russia's intervention that had started World War I and resulted in that country's total independence; the former, in spite of its enmity in World War I, still on the whole strongly pro-Russian, and grateful for its freedom as a result of the Russo-Turkish war of 1877-78. Besides these two countries, Greece and Rumania indicated that they would take in refugees. Wrangel had sent emissaries, including his chief of staff General Chatilov, to accelerate their response and work out its implementation.

In the first days the French help bordered on the miraculous. The multitude was fed, the sick brought to hospitals, the French military and naval authorities working hand in hand with the Russian army headquarters. Wrangel reorganized the Russian army into three corps: the 1st Army Corps under General Koutiepov was to camp in Gallipoli; the Don Cossack Corps under General Abramov, in Chatalgi, and the Kouban Cossack Corps under General Fostokov, on the island of Lemnos. The fleet was directed to the French base of Bizerte in Tunisia.

The French at first insisted on the handing in of all arms; Wrangel refused and the French did not insist. This later was to prove a factor of major importance in subsequent developments.

While the civilians settled temporarily and in most primitive conditions in and around Constantinople, the tireless and successful efforts of the American

Red Cross in allaying their condition must be noted: Food for the children, blankets, clothes, all efficiently handled and distributed, saved many a life and rekindled hope in many a heart. Active in welfare was the wife of a young American embassy secretary, Mrs. Allen Dulles, whose husband years later was to become the director of the CIA, brother of Foster Dulles, Secretary of State during the presidency of General Eisenhower.

The 1st Army Corps was to camp on the Gallipoli peninsula, the site of the British landings and fierce combats of 1915. The corps commander General Koutiepov was given a horse and rode out to inspect the site with a French officer. As he rode over the crest of a ridge, he saw below a barren, muddy valley at the bottom of which flowed a murky, small stream almost covered over by bushes of wild roses:* no trees, no houses; a desolate picture. "C'est tout?" asked Koutiepov. The French officer answered with an evasive gesture.

It is true that the French found themselves providing for the many thousands of refugees — army and civilian. Nevertheless, they had made no bad bargain. For the scant army rations surplus of World War I which they issued they had received 45,000 rifles, 350 machine guns, 60,000 hand grenades, 330,000 shells, 12,000,000 cartridges; 300,000 kilograms of wheat, 20,000 kilograms of sugar, 17,000 kilograms of tea, 50,000 kilograms diverse food products; 200,000 uniforms, 340,000 sets of underwear, 58,000 shoes (40,000 of leather), 140,000 blankets, 810,000 meters of cloth. Of the 126 ships, some had to be scrapped, but many continued in French service for years.

Twenty-six thousand, five hundred and ninety-six people, army units, and some dependents landed at a small cove on the northeast of the Gallipoli peninsula near the half-demolished small town of the same name. Some of the dependents found shelter in the ruins of houses often under open sky.

The troops were issued tents by the French, but neither means of transport nor instruments were issued; muscle and ingenuity replaced these. The men slept on the bare ground; heating consisted of Stone Age hearths heated by whatever scrub or driftwood could be gathered. There was no lighting, as the French had not issued kerosene. Empty ration cans, with wick and melted fat from the canned rations, made up the modern "Roman lamps." The same army ration cans provided for eating utensils and for primitive cooking. Furniture was, of course, nonexistent: beds were made up of seaweed or branches; benches were knocked together from empty army ration crates. The French food ration was minimal for the sustenance of life: five hundred grams of bread, some army canned rations, no vegetables or meat. To prevent starvation, the corps command managed to buy flour from its scant resources and set up some army bakeries. Here again, as in Constantinople, the aid of the American

---

* Known as the valley of roses and death, due to its large snake population.

Red Cross was invaluable: Tools, blankets, food and clothing for the dependents were blessed additions to people existing on virtually nothing.

The army corps of engineers performed miracles. On landing they had neither instruments nor materials to work with. Russian ingenuity, know-how, enterprise, and will power helped to overcome these deficiencies. Materials were found in the German and Turkish army dumps, including unused shells and barbed wire. Workshops were set up and the needed tools manufactured. A list of their achievements reads like a list of miracles. All repairs of buildings in the ruined town were done under their direction; a small rail line was laid from camp to town to provide access for the food supply. Saunas, kitchens, bakeries, and hospital units were set up and equipped. A dock for unloading in-bound supplies was built and a Roman viaduct repaired: It served to bring water to the town. The sanitary conditions in the camp — drainage, hygiene, malaria control — were worked on. Arms were constantly checked into and repaired; even an old automobile was reclaimed and put to use.

There was no such thing as rank when it came to work: general and private put muscle, knowledge, and brain together.

The stern General Koutiepov stated in one of his Orders of the Day: "No labor can be beneath one's dignity for a Russian officer." General Koutiepov realized that for twenty-five thousand men living on the bare minimum and still under mental shock from the fighting and evacuation, homesick and depressed, radical measures only could maintain the cohesiveness and esprit de corps that had brought it along so far. He insisted on discipline; hard as it was to keep up appearances, the army men must still appear as soldiers, the formalities of military courtesy maintained, and activity deployed not only in fighting for survival but also in training, learning, and even physical exercise.

Gallipoli became one big school. For the few devoid of elementary education, courses were given to raise their standard. Tactical and strategic study groups were arranged for the officer corps; a newspaper was edited, even a theater built and plays performed.

The church had traditionally played a strong part in the life of the Russian soldier, so in Gallipoli churches soon rose in tents, the icons and altar decorations either hand-painted or cut out from the same cans of food. Excellent church choruses were assembled.

Tuberculosis and typhus, the two dreaded diseases of the civil war, had to be fought. Here again the American Red Cross came forth with help: A sanatorium was set up on the seashore. The Russian Red Cross and the corps' sanitary units cleaned up the valley and its malaria-breeding mosquitoes; delousing stations and saunas were organized.

Parades played an important part not only in maintaining esprit de corps and morale but also in showing to the French, to other foreigners, and to newspaper correspondents that the army continued to exist and had not degenerated into a horde of helpless refugees.

It had been the custom prior to World War I for all European ambassadors in Constantinople to maintain a yacht at their disposal, at that time the best means of transport around the Golden Horn and the Bosporus. Wrangel organized his life on the Russian yacht *Lucullus*. This gave him the opportunity to visit the troops and maintain a liberty of action. A small crew, a few Cossacks from his escort, an ADC, and his wife became the residents of this mini-headquarters.

On the 15th of Februrary, 1921, Wrangel, accompanied by foreign military attachés and journalists visited the 1st Army Corps in Gallipoli. Colonel Riasniansky: "It was a grey, cloudy day. The army units were drawn up in line on the huge field. Wrangel, the foreign officers, and newspaper correspondents drove up in automobiles. No sooner had Wrangel walked up to the right flank of the army on parade than the clouds broke and sunshine lit the field. Two eagles were seen circling high. To the men this seemed an omen from above, a thunderous 'Hurrah!' burst forth from the multitude; many hardened veterans were crying. To Wrangel's customary salute, 'Hello, Eagles,' the answer came as a spontaneous and unending 'Hurrah.' After reviewing the troops, Wrangel harangued them in his loud hoarse voice. 'Hold on,' he called out. 'Hold on; do not be shaken; do not bend to any false blandishments!' "

The march past followed. Serried ranks marched past in columns. It produced a colossal and totally unexpected impression, particularly on the foreigners. It was evident that the spectacle had strongly affected them and one of the military attachés was heard to remark: "We were told that we would see refugees, but this is a real army!"

It was to be the same among the Cossacks on the isle of Lemnos. Different from the regular army in their democratic way of life, which permeated even their military units, the Cossacks broke ranks, running behind Wrangel's car and finally bearing him on their shoulders in triumph. No general in history received from his troops such an ovation in the midst of defeat and misery.

But dark clouds were already gathering on Wrangel's political horizon. A wit once said that postrevolutionary France existed in perpetual motion of totally contradictory governments. The right wing government of President Millerand had recognized "de facto" Wrangel's government in Crimea, and its military representatives did all they could to help in the evacuation and the early days in Constantinople. Millerand's cabinet went, and in came the left-wing cabinet of Herriot, a socialist, friend of Lloyd George, conciliatory to the Soviets, and in a great hurry to disperse and forget the Russian army, Wrangel, and all they stood for. Admirals Dumesnil and de Bon and General de Bourgogne were recalled and replaced by General Charpy, a narrow-minded, petty "political" general whose mission was to liquidate as soon as possible the "Wrangel army."

The solution he brought gave a choice of three: One, repatriation to Soviet Russia under a pseudo-amnesty given by the Soviets; two, resettlement in Brazil; three, dispersion as refugees. The first gave no guarantees whatsoever, as the French could not possibly supervise any sort of amnesty. The second solution offered vague prospects as settlers in Brazil, but in reality they would be more like white slaves on the big estancias. The third solution gave no indication as to how, where, or by what means the refugees were to disperse. The stick over the heads of Wrangel and the army was the cutoff of food rations — hence starvation.

To Wrangel's answer that negotiations were already under way with Yugoslavia, Bulgaria, Greece, and Hungary, Charpy observed that these presented no immediate solution and that his choice of three remained as the real answer. The first test was soon to come. The commander of the Senegalese battalion and the French commandant in Gallipoli invited General Vitkovsky, Russian acting commander (General Koutiepov being absent on sick leave), to headquarters.

Colonel Thomassen — wiry, small, a monocle riveted in his eye — spoke briefly, dryly, and to the point. "The commander of the French occupation forces in Constantinople has the following instructions for the Russian army units in Gallipoli. The Russian army evacuated from the Crimea is considered no longer an army but rather a body of refugees. General Wrangel is no longer its commander but a refugee like the rest. In Gallipoli there is no army corps, no commanders, but just refugees. Finally that all arms must be immediately handed over to the French, and that he, Colonel Thomassen, is to be viewed as the sole commander, acting as the French commandant."

The dimunitive, calm, and brave General Vitkovsky listened patiently and answered: "The Russian army even after evacuation remains an army. General Wrangel was and remains our commander in chief. Army units and not refugees are quartered in Gallipoli. I happen to be the acting corps commander and my orders only will be obeyed by the troops. As regards the French commandant, I consider him the commander of an allied unit garrisoned in Gallipoli and finally I have no intention of giving up any arms."

Loosing his composure, Thomassen threatened to arrest General Vitkovsky; to this the Russian answered that his troops will act as ordered. General Vitkovsky withdrew; the army corps was put on alert. Thomassen's Senegalese battalion dug in behind barbed wire. The standoff lasted a couple of weeks. This time it had a happy ending. It was Christmas and mass was being served in Gallipoli's Greek cathedral, Russians and Greeks praying together. Suddenly there was a movement in the crowd: Colonel Thomassen and his officers, in dress uniform and wearing arms and decorations, entered the cathedral and, upon completion of the service, walked up to General Vitkovsky and wished him a Happy Christmas.

The incident was closed: The Russians had rejected the ultimatum, the French estimated correctly the Russian force and determination. On Lemnos, however, things were to take a nasty turn. The French General Brousseau had been an exchange student at the Russian Staff College and had served one year in a guards artillery brigade where he had met nothing but the most widespread Russian hospitality; he was about to thank in reverse proportion. An ambitious career man, he was ready to do all he could to help his superior General Charpy to force through his tough measures. For these measures the soil on Lemnos proved more fertile than that of Gallipoli. The Cossack troops had a much greater men-to-officer ratio, with many officers promoted from the ranks. The commandant General Fostokov, a brave partisan leader, was culturally below-standard, a prey to the higher intellectual level of the French command.

It is a mistake for today's historian to call the Allied-enforced repatriations of post-World War II as unique in human rights history. Perhaps slightly more subtly, the French measures on Lemnos equaled those of 1945 and 1946. All possible efforts — posters, communiqués, and personal intervention — were put to use. Junior French officers, speaking Russian, arrogantly brushed off senior Cossack officers to harangue the Cossacks, the latter's officers being forced to stand aside. The Cossacks were promised full amnesty in Russia under French guarantee.

As a result of this propaganda and brainwashing 5,819 chose to return to Russia. They boarded the transports *Reshid Pascha* and *Don*. Some of their buddies went on board to bid them good-bye. The French refused to let these get off the ships. As a result several threw themselves overboard and swam ashore. A group of Kalmyks, who spoke little Russian and certainly no French, were directed to board also, under the guise that "everyone is going to sail somewhere else." Picking up their scant belongings, they trudged along towards the wharves. Some of the Cossacks warned them at the last minute; dropping everything, the Kalmyks turned around and fled back to the camps.

Desperate letters by Wrangel to General Pellé, the French High Commissioner, to the French marshal Foch, and to General Weygand made no headway: The first was firmly committed to the measures of the French cabinet, the latter as military powerless to act against the government's decision.

Meanwhile, the transports bearing the Cossacks and some civilian refugees sailed for Russia. The fate of these hapless people soon became known. As the transport *Reshid Pascha* returned to Constantinople, an inscription was found in one of its holds. "Comrades: 3,500 Cossacks reached Odessa; 500 were shot on the spot; the rest are being sent to camps and forced labor. I am Cossack Moroz of the village of Gnutovsk; I do not know my fate."

Caring little for such "details," Charpy, Brousseau, and their command worked hard on the Cossacks. They availed themselves of the help of some of the Cossack politicians responsible for the Cossack surrender on the Black Sea in the early days of the Crimean odyssey.

Echoes of this tragedy and the repressive measures of the French military command reached France; articles appeared in the press, condemning such practices; the question was raised in the Chamber of Deputies.

Wrangel had a certain freedom of action as long as he was on board his ship. It had not taken him long to make contacts with prominent members of the diplomatic corps. Among his friends were Admiral Bristol, the U.S.A. High Commissioner, and General Harrington, the commander of the British forces of occupation. Almost in the first days of the Russian fleet's arrival at Constantinople General Harrington called on Wrangel. "General," he said, "this is a personal call; as you know, His Majesty's Government does not recognize either your government or your army, but as a British citizen and officer I have the right to come here to voice my admiration for your unequalled fight and for your brilliant evacuation." This was a prelude to a long friendship. Whenever he could, General Harrington was there to give help. Disregarding Charpy, the senior Fench naval commanders, as well as the British, continued to show their respect to Wrangel as commander in chief. As their ships sailed past the diminuive *Lucullus*, naval courtesies were inevitably shown. Wrangel's freedom aboard the *Lucullus* was soon to have a tragic end.

On the 15th of October, 1921, the Italian freighter *Adria* sailing from Soviet Russia passed through the Bosphorus. As it drew alongside the *Lucullus* moored in front of the French embassy, the *Adria* veered at right angles and rammed the *Lucullus* amidship, hitting exactly Wrangel's cabin. Within a minute the *Lucullus* sank; the duty officer Lieutenant Sapunoff went down with the ship, as did the cook trapped in the galley and another seaman. The rest of the crew swam ashore or were picked up by Turkish boats. Wrangel and his wife had come ashore minutes before. Arrested, the Italian captain pleaded guilty to negligent maneuvering; the Allied tribunal preferred to close the incident.

Having lost whatever small personal belongings they had, Wrangel and his wife moved into the Russian embassy. The American High Commissioner Admiral Bristol wished to signal his sympathy to this last tragedy: He gave a reception in honor of Wrangel and invited the diplomatic corps. As the different ambassadors and consuls filed past, each had a word of sympathy, expressed his condolences on the loss of the ship and the lives of the sailors. The Italian High Commissioner bowed silently.

Wrangel had now lost his freedom of action; no longer was he able to visit the troops and keep up their morale. The French offered no means of transportation and Wrangel became a virtual prisoner in the confines of the Russian embassy, into which he now moved with his wife, one ADC, and twelve men of his escort, reduced from its previous two squadrons.

About this time a Soviet representative, Serebriannikov, came to Constantinople, called on General Charpy and offered him on behalf of the Soviets an amnesty to all the Russian army, providing General Wrangel personally issued the orders for repatriation, as he knew that without orders from Wrangel, neither his immediate subordinates nor the bulk of the troops would move.

General Charpy knew that if he broached such an "invitation" to Wrangel, he would meet with an indignant rebuttal, so he called on the Russian ambassador, Neratov (still maintaining his office), and warned him that if Wrangel did not proceed with the required orders, he would have him arrested. He added that he would come the next day to have an answer.

Charpy appeared on the very next day, and as he was sitting in the ambassador's study, Wrangel walked in. Seemingly not noticing Charpy, Wrangel said: "Mr. Ambassador, my apologies for disturbing you at this moment, but I have to show my escort where the machine guns have to be sighted — it seems that there is a rumor that certain foreign elements may have designs on the commander in chief." Giving the room a quick glance, Wrangel walked out. Of course there were no machine guns and the escort consisted of twelve unarmed men plus his aide, but the effect produced on Charpy was enough for him to desist from his plan.

The commander of the British forces in Constantinople, General Harrington, by then a firm friend of Wrangel and his cause, decided to do what he could to uphold Wrangel's prestige, this is in obvious contradiction to the dictates of the British cabinet. He arranged a reception, inviting the Allied high commissioners and members of the diplomantic corps. Standing next to Wrangel at the reception, he personally introduced the guests. When the turn came for Charpy, who walked up with outstretched hand, Wrangel coldly withdrew his, and turning to General Harrington, he said: "General, it is indeed painful for me to abuse your most kind hospitality by refraining to greet this gentleman, but he knows exactly the reason for my behavior and he must know that I am ready to offer him satisfaction wherever and whenever he wishes!" A stunned silence followed, happily broken by the appearance of Mrs. Harrington carrying a large goblet of champagne and wearing a traditional Russian dress. Walking up to Wrangel, she offered him the goblet with a Russian greeting. Charpy availing himself of the interruption slunk away. His answer was a further cut-down in the starvation ration of the troops on Gallipoli and Lemnos. It became evident that further and more drastic efforts by the French could be expected.

The army corps on Gallipoli prepared itself for a desperate venture — to break out of the Gallipoli peninsula and seize Constantinople. It seems hardly imaginable that an army of half-starved and unequipped refugees could even contemplate such a plan, but this army was led by desperate men who in the past had confronted greater odds than the Allied occupation forces. The Allied navies would hardly dare cause an international scandal by bombarding and setting fire to Constantinople. The Turkish dictator Kemal Ataturk was already the virtual master of Turkey and the Greeks viewed the Russian army more as allies than potential enemies. In secret negotiation they promised to provide help in such an event.

To all appearances, the breakout of Gallipoli was for the army corps to march towards Bulgaria, where negotiations were then being carried out for resettlement of part of the army. Heading north until it reached the latitude of Constantinople, it was to suddenly veer east and in forced marches reach the outskirts of Constantinople, joining forces with those Cossack units still camping at Chatalgi. The plan called for a sudden attack and subsequent disarmament of the French garrison in Gallipoli. Exercises, night alerts, and maneuvers preceded the operation with the different units gradually brought to combat fitness, all this in spite of the starvation rations and the well nigh impossibly difficult living conditions.

Fortunately, two events precluded this daring and almost impossible adventure: First came the news that Bulgaria and Yugoslavia were at last, after long negotiations conducted by General Chatilov, Wrangel's chief of staff, ready to accept a major portion of the army; then there also appeared in the French press articles deploring the official French attitude and throwing light on the Russian plight in Lemnos and Gallipoli. Questions were raised in the French Chamber of Deputies and as a result Charpy, Brousseau, and Pellé toned down their persecution. Scant though they were, rations were not totally cut off and an uneasy peace reigned between the French forces of occupation and the Russian army in exile.

22
The Army in the Balkans

BESIDES YUGOSLAVIA AND BULGARIA, a third country, Hungary, had offered asylum. Hungary, formerly a part of the Austrian empire, was on the list of the defeated countries of World War I and hence had to defer to the decisions of the Inter-Allied Commission. Hungary had just emerged from a bloody coup staged by the Communists under Bela Kun and was ready to welcome parts of the Wrangel army, viewing them as a stabilizing influence in the country. The Inter-Allied Commission's answer came late and came as a surprise. Signed by an Italian aristocrat, Italy's High Commissioner, Prince Castagnetto, the document stated: "The entry of the army of General Wrangel into Hungarian territory would not fail to excite commotion and facilitate anti-Bolshevist intrigues which are contrary to the true interests of Hungary and all of the civilized world." "The civilized world" had opted for Communism. . . .

Bulgaria and Yugoslavia were in a state of total disarray. Underdeveloped countries initially, they had suffered during the war, which had further divided them as opponents. Highways, railroads, and the little industry that existed were in dire need of repairs and development. In a series of complex agreements Russian army units were put to work: The skill of Russian military engineers and the muscle and brawn of the Cossacks were put to the test.

So the Kouban Cossack division built a new highway linking Yugoslavia with Bulgaria. The army's technical units were detached to reorganize the Yugoslavia railways. The cavalry division took over border security, saving the government 3,110,931 dinars in detained smuggled goods. Officers were detached as instructors to the gendarmerie; they lectured in the staff college and founded the country's air corps. In Bulgaria army units worked in coal mines or became lumberjacks in the mountain forests.

It took great restraint and inner discipline to discard the sword for the shovel and the rifle for the wood axe, but the iron discipline brought in by Wrangel in the Crimea was such that, surviving the vicissitudes of Lemnos and Gallipoli, it remained intact, though by now entirely voluntary in the Balkan countries. Working stripped to the waist, in clouds of dust digging tunnels or hacking down trees, the men assembled for evening roll call and prayers, washed, and dressed in their uniforms as if in peacetime in their own country. Regimental and other national holidays called for parades and march pasts, particularly impressive when Wrangel visited the army units. The army's budget had long ago reached an irreversible low, with no hopes of help from the large funds impounded, and alas often spent for their own use, by Russia's ex-ambassadors abroad. Means had to be found to keep sanatoriums for the many TB patients, to facilitate liaison between the different headquarters, to keep the military and civilian schools going, and finally to provide for some form of social security. To this end a small portion of each man's pay was deducted and went into a regimented fund—one part to keep the organization going, another as a form of insurance against sickness, loss of employment, or other calamity.

Gradually, as Bulgarian and Yugoslav government contracts became scarcer, individuals or groups sought self-employment while still retaining their military associations.

Some of the experiences on new jobs were not devoid of humor. A young twenty-year-old lieutenant, Karateev: "A group of four of us undertook to lay tiles on the roof of a house in the outskirts of town. The owner left for the day, leaving us a ladder and the tiles. None of us had the slightest idea on how to go about it, but we went to work with vim and vigor. As evening came, the owner returned and, casting a glance at our unfortunate endeavors, broke into a stream of four-letter words. Seizing a huge stick, he rushed towards the ladder. One of our group, a smart Cossack, had the foresight to pull up the ladder and a regular siege ensued. We waited until he had exhausted his expletive vocabulary and entered into negotiations. One of us, Krylov, proved a true diplomat. He suggested to the enraged owner that were it not for the Russian army of 1877 which liberated Bulgaria, the owner would now be sitting on the roof instead of us, while a Turk would be waiting below, armed with a yategan. This proved a conclusive argument and the Bulgarian allowed us to come down unharmed and even paid us a few coins for having brought the tiles from ground level to roof."

So, spread through the Balkans, the army worked, maintaining its structure and gradually phasing out to the self-employment of its individual members, but before this could come about, still new thunder clouds were to gather over their heads.

The Bulgarian Agrarian Party under Stamboulysky had, for reasons of political advantage, made an alliance with left-wing elements, leading to the recognition of Soviet Russia and a subsequent mass flow of Soviet agents to Bulgaria. The Bulgarian Communist Party raised its head and government employees bribed by Communist agents started to make a case against the presence of the Russian army in Bulgaria. A bought press raised hue and cry, and falsified documents provided the equally bribed police with a case to start persecuting the Russians. First came a demand to deliver all arms. This was partly executed, but as in the case of Gallipoli, only part of the arms were handed over—Again, as events proved later, the instinct for self-preservation proved correct—and many of the arms were hidden, some even with the help of Bulgarian anti-Communist officers. Orders forbidding the wearing of uniforms followed. In short order fifty-eight senior officers were expelled from Bulgaria. Attacks on individuals by groups of Communists soon grew to threatening proportions. Still Wrangel's strict orders were to remain neutral and under no circumstances to let the army engage in political activity incompatible with its guest status in Bulgaria. However, here again as in Gallipoli contingency plans were made for a mass exodus to Yugoslavia, with the scattered units fusing together for self-protection. As senior officers were expulsed or arrested, junior ones took over; again the discipline of Wrangel's Crimea triumphed over the Bulgarian political mischief and chaos.

It took eleven months for Bulgaria to get rid of Stamboulysky's government and a few months to put down Communist uprisings. On June 11, 1923, the Bulgarian army staged a coup; Stamboulysky was killed, a democratic government installed, the constitutional monarchy under King Boris maintained, and the plight of the Russians ceased with the expulsion or arrest of the Soviet agents. During the Communist uprising, with the tacit aproval of the new Bulgarian government, certain Russian units, particularly the Markovsky division, took part in armed intervention. Small in scope, they were however of strong psychological value both to the Communists whom they defeated in short order and to the Russian army in exile, proving to it, if indeed further proof was needed, the value of discipline, cohesiveness, and esprit de corps.

As the last major contingents of the Russian army left Lemnos and Gallipoli, Wrangel left Constantinople on board a French destroyer, his ship the *Lucullus* having previously been sunk. He first visited Gallipoli where a "rear guard" of twenty-five hundred men waited their turn to move to the Balkans. These last units to leave gave Wrangel an enthusiastic reception, unabated by the fact that they still had months to wait before leaving the "Valley of Roses and Death." Proceeding to Greece, Wrangel visited the five hundred refugees, mostly wounded and invalids. Their physical well-being was, as in all its previous work, admirably taken care of by the American Red Cross. The Yugoslav government sent a special train and Wrangel entered Yugoslavia as an honored guest of the nation with diplomatic privileges. In Belgrade the train was met by a large crowd. The Yugoslav king sent his personal representative, as did the prime minister. On hand was the Russian diplomatic mission headed by Ambassador Standtmann, who offered Wrangel the hospitality of the embassy. He was, however, soon to regret it. The tranquil and orderly diplomatic life of the embassy was turned upside down. Hundreds of people crowded in the waiting room to be received by Wrangel, some on political grounds, others for personal reasons. Military personnel flowed in and out, aides-de-camp flitted about, throwing into turmoil what had been a haven of quiet bureaucratic institution. The staid and dignified Standtmann, too polite to renege on his hospitality, turned to Wrangel's chief of staff, General Chatilov. On this latter's advice a villa was rented in the Belgrade suburbs and Wrangel and his staff moved there.*

*There on July 7, 1922, was born the author of this book.

23
Wrangel and the Russian Emigrés

BESIDES THE HUNDRED FIFTY THOUSAND who left the Crimea with Wrangel, several hundred thousand Russians had emigrated from Russia during the revolution. First came the members of Kerensky's Provisional Government, those who having opened Pandora's box were unable to close it and with the advent of Bolshevism had fled Russia, some with considerable funds. Now haunting the lobbies of Europe's democratic parliaments, they claimed the right to speak on behalf of Russia and its emigrés. To them the three-year civil war was but an unpleasant incident, the White army a reactionary force, Wrangel a would-be Bonaparte on whom no amount of rebuke and criticism would suffice; their newspapers heaped abuse and their leaders had much on their conscience for the ill treatment of the Russian army in Gallipoli and Lemnos. But if these elements reflected the left side of the spectrum, the right was represented by a small but vocal monarchist party clustered around the Grand Duke Cyril, who, having forgotten his role as the Russian version of Philippe L'Égalite* during the revolution, now proclaimed himself emperor in exile and demanded the allegiance of the army.

Though Wrangel by his background and personal conviction was a monarchist, he realized what a disservice it would be to the monarchist cause if he lent his prestige and authority to an exile institution which at its best would be a sad farce of a glorious past, a turning back of the irreversible process of time, and a source of discord within the army in which monarchists and republicans had fought shoulder to shoulder, an army whose unity and cohesiveness Wrangel had tried so hard to preserve.

His negative answer to the Grand Duke Cyril made him an implacable enemy in the ranks of those who "had learned nothing and forgotten nothing." Assailed from left and right, Wrangel's prestige remained intact within the ranks of the army as it engaged in the process of turning swords into ploughshares, settling in the Balkan countries, and moving in large groups westward to France and Belgium where postwar industry required labor and the living conditions and pay were considerably better.

Wrangel's constant preoccupation with keeping the army whole in exile

* The brother of Louis XVI, Philippe turned Republican during the French Revolution.

had two reasons. First, he still hoped that internal conditions in Russia might lead to violent changes, at which time the army would play its role: then, also, always practical, Wrangel realized that it was a necessary tonic to keep up the morale of individuals. To the officer turned taxi driver in Paris, to the steppes-bred Cossack now toiling underground in the Belgium coal mines, or to the young cadet who had lost parents and home, a feeling of belonging to something was a necessity; without it the daily drudge in a kind of work for which they were not brought up meant despair. Knowing the Russian propensity for factional squabbling, Wrangel firmly decided to keep the army out of politics and united within itself. To this end he founded the Armed Forces Union, an organization somewhat on the lines of the American Legion. Divided into chapters within the different countries where its members lived and worked, it was registered officially in those countries and conformed strictly to its host country's laws. Members paid small duties which served both for administrative purposes and as a relief to those unemployed or sick. The soundness and durability of this union was proved by its existence up to and through World War II. Its danger to the Soviets, by virtue of its mere existence, was enough to warrant the kidnappings of Wrangel's two successors* and the more than probable murder of Wrangel himself.

Another of Wrangel's preoccupations was the fate of the youths who had fought in the civil war: Their education had been brutally interrupted and their future seemed bleak indeed. With the agreement and some help from the Yugoslav government, three cadet schools were organized, which, while preserving the military aspect and maintaining the Russian army traditions, prepared the young men for civilian life. While some joined the Yugoslav armed forces upon graduation, others went in for higher studies in the universities of Czechoslovakia, France, and Belgium.

A whole generation of engineers, doctors, artists, and businessmen who were graduated from the cadet schools contributed to the economy and culture of their host countries around the globe.

Not all combatants of the White army had emerged healthy and unscathed from the incredible hardships of the civil war. Besides the invalids, the scourge of the army was tuberculosis, the end result of hunger and privations. In those days when X-rays and anti-TB drugs were nonexistent, the only remedy was rest and an abundance of healthy food, something that for most existed only in the realm of dreams.

---

* Generals Koutiepov and Miller were kidnapped by the Soviets in Paris in 1930 and 1939; their ultimate fate was never known.

Wrangel's visits to the cadet schools produced great furor. Here Wrangel is carried in triumph by a group of cadets.

Cossack honor guard stands at attention as carriage carrying coffin of Wrangel passes. Cossacks loved their commander as a fatherly figure.

Riderless charger was led in the funeral procession by two sergeants, a Cossack and a Guardsman, both decorated with the Cross of St. George.

The funeral was a tribute that united Yugoslavs and Russians. Here the caisson with the coffin is flanked by Russian and Yugoslav officers.

Cossack veterans stand at attention as a final mark of respect. Soldiers came to the funeral from all over the world, some donning ancient uniforms.

Over two hundred wreaths were laid on Wrangel's grave. Of the funeral, the Metropolian Antonias said, ". . . it reminds us more of a triumphant march than a laying to rest of an ordinary mortal."

24
The Angel of Mercy

A MUCH USED IF NOT ALWAYS true axiom states that behind every successful man has stood a woman. Certainly Sarah Churchill contributed much to the success of Marlborough and Napoleon's fortunes waned when he forsook Josephine. Wrangel was fortunate in having a wife who never left his side but unobstrusively helped in those realms where often, in the rigors of war, her husband had not the time or the possibility to act.

A nurse in World War I and the early phases of the civil war, Olga Wrangel came to the Crimea from Constantinople to join her husband in spite of the latter's formal injunctions not to come and expose herself to what then was thought by all as the beginning of a catastrophic end.

In contrast to Mrs. Denikin who had appointed herself as a political and most unfortunate mentor to her husband, Olga Wrangel devoted her activity to the care of the wounded and to the welfare of the thousands of orphans, products of the civil war. A prominent Russian political figure, Serge Paleologue, wrote this of her: "In April, 1921, I came on business to Constantinople, then a city filled to overflowing with Russians. Everywhere where Russian was spoken you heard these fragments of conversation: 'Why don't you see Olga Milhailovna* . . ' 'Olga Milhailovna will arrange . . .' 'Olga Milhailovna will write . . . will ask . . . will get . . . will go . . . will help . . .' And this is what she did — wrote, begged, helped; always willing, invariably cheerful, she did things quickly and with no fuss. . . . No one could talk so intimately and with so much heart with the simple Cossack, the rank and file soldier, the invalid officer, or with their forlorn mothers and widows. Her heart went out to the children and these reached out for her."

As a nurse she realized the ravages of tuberculosis and saw the need for sanatoriums for which no money was to be had from the depleted army accounts. One day, after placing her children in Belgian schools, she was returning to Belgrade and stopped over in Paris to see friends and relations. She was invited to lunch by Prince Youssoupoff, member of the conspiracy that had murdered Russia's bad fortune, Rasputin, in 1916. Youssoupoff had managed to bring out of Russia his family's jewels; they represented a fortune. He was on his way to the United States to sell them.

*According to Russian custom Olga Wrangel's patronymic.

"Why don't you come along?" he said. "You know how many friends and admirers of your husband have asked you repeatedly to come to America so that they can help you raise funds for your sanatoriums."

"Easy to say, Felix," answered Olga Wrangel. "But I have hardly enough money to travel third class to Belgium with my children, let alone go to America!"

"Look!" said the Prince, "I have enough money to back your trip; let that be my contribution to Wrangel!"

"When are you leaving?"

"The day after tomorrow, on a Cunard liner."

Rapid decisions were something that life had taught her over those past years: A cable went out to her husband, asking his permission. A few hours later the answer came back: "Think you are crazy, but good luck and Godspeed! Signed, Peter." A trip to the U.S. embassy produced a visa; a call at the Cunard office, a cabin reservation. Olga Wrangel set sail to America.

During the Constantinople days following the evacuation, several Americans, notably Mr. Whitemore, Mrs. Allen Dulles and her sister, Admiral and Mrs. Bristol, Admiral MacCully and others, had given their energy, influence, and means to help the evacuees. Since then they had often written to Olga Wrangel, around whom most of the welfare work had centered. They now promised to help form a committee to raise funds. Mrs. Vanderbilt, then New York's most prominent socialite, promised her patronage and gave a reception during which Olga Wrangel was asked to speak.

"Make it short," she was advised, "people don't like to hear long speeches!" Olga Wrangel had never spoken in public: Her mouth dry with stage fright, she faced the audience composed of strange people, mostly only vaguely interested. What could she say in ten minutes? How could she describe in such short time the vicissitudes of her country, the massacres, the sufferings, the fate of orphans, the tears, the despair of the sick for whom no hope existed?

Grimly she started: The ten minutes stretched to a half hour and then to one hour. When she finished, the audience stood up and gave her a rousing applause.

The next day there was no reaction to her plea for help and sadly she made arrangements for her return trip. But the very next day the postman brought in a bag of mail: All the letters contained checks — some small, some very large. America knows how to give — it gave unsparingly. Twelve thousand dollars, then a huge sum, was used to organize two sanatoriums, one in Yugoslavia, the other in Bulgaria. Several thousand sick passed through these sanatoriums during their existence from 1923 to the mid-thirties. Irrespective of rank or background anyone with TB in initial stages was admitted. The shock of rest and good food was often enough to arrest the dreaded disease: 32 percent were pronounced cured; 59.4 percent were released as sufficiently improved to return to normal life — high percentages when one considers that the patients would have been on the way to a slow and painful death. As the flow of patients decreased in proportion to the betterment of the general standard of living of the army in exile, the funds raised in the United States were diverted to scholarships for the Russian students in the universities of Belgium, France, and Czeckoslovakia. Belgium, in particular, proved responsive, and many graduates of the universities of Leuven, Gembloux, and Brussels owed their future careers to the generosity of the American donors and to the unflagging energy of a woman who, traveling the length and breadth of America, managed to strike a chord in the responsive heart of its citizens.

Sometime in 1924 Wrangel became convinced that it was time to hand over the leadership of the Armed Forces Union to someone else, someone who would have the prestige and authority acceptable to all members. Was it premonition of an early death or irritation at the pinpricks directed against him by the left and ultraright, or was he pushed towards some form of monarchist connection by his senior lieutenants? Perhaps a combination of all three directed his choice towards the Russian Grand Duke Nicholas, uncle of the late czar and commander in chief of the Russian army at the outbreak of World War I. It was the Grand Duke's decision to push two Russian armies into the depth of east Prussia in 1914 in response to frantic pleas from France, which forced the Germans to withdraw two crucial army corps from the western front and let their weakened right wing suffer defeat at the battle of the Marne. Russia paid a heavy price: General Samsonov's army was surrounded and destroyed at the battle of Tannenberg.* A six-foot six-inch giant, the Grand Duke had retrained Russia's cavalry after the Japanese war, raising it to a high standard of efficiency. His methods were not devoid of brutality vis-a-vis his subordinate officers, but his prestige had remained high. Early reverses in 1914 and 1915 led to his appointment to the secondary Turkish front. There, as on the Austro-German front, he let himself be directed by his staff, and when General Youdenitch, under his command, in deep snow stormed the Turkish fortress of Erzerum, he did it at his own responsibility, almost discouraged by the vacillating Grand Duke.

After the Russian Revolution the Grand Duke retired to France, where he was granted a marshal's pension by the grateful French government. He kept out of politics and lived modestly with a small entourage of Russian generals and admirals of Czarist vintage. The Grand Duke had the highest consideration and esteem for Wrangel, but not so his entourage. To them, Wrangel, who had started World War I as a major, was an upstart, even more so his lieutenants,

---

* Still in the process of mobilization it was rushed into Germany as Russia's whole strategic plan was changed to save France.

junior officers at the start of the civil war (there was even a Cossack lieutenant general who had been an ex-private at the start of World War I*). To those senior officers, the civil war, in which they had not taken part, was an unpleasant interlude and its participants interlopers.

Grand Duke Nicholas had important connections in the French government and among France's marshals and generals, and as a major portion of the Russian army had gravitated to France, Wrangel probably saw the Grand Duke's influence with the French as an asset to the general welfare of his men.

The Grand Duke at first declined to assume the responsibility of the overall command and finally consented only under pressure. But having assumed the leadership, he fell into his old habit of letting his advisors run policy. It took all of Wrangel's efforts to maintain the nonpolitical aspect of his child, the Armed Forces Union; the pressure to force it into a monarchist party was the work of the Grand Duke's entourage, as he himself kept out of any direct pronouncements. Twice Wrangel presented his resignation as acting commander only to hear the Grand Duke refuse to accept it and promise Wrangel his continued support. But one aspect of policy was acted on against Wrangel's strong objections. General Koutiepov, the brilliant commander of the original Volunteer divisions and the stubbornly successful commandant of the exiled army in Gallipoli, was given the authority to conduct partisan and subversive activities in Russia. Koutiepov was obsessed with the idea of "penetrating" Russia; he had no previous intelligence training, knew nothing of guerrilla or partisan warfare, but burned with zeal to continue the fight against the Soviets. Wrangel was just as strongly opposed. He maintained that only with immense money behind them could such an operation be even envisaged, alternatively only with the backing by an Allied power with unrestricted means. Neither was available: The army's coffers were empty; no Allied nation interested. Wrangel maintained that terrorist activities directed against the Soviets, operations carried on a shoestring, would mean only a useless waste of young and dedicated lives. As in the past he was proved right. Koutiepov was given the go-ahead; within a short time his operation was penetrated, and many young officers who had volunteered were caught and killed, while Koutiepov himself was kidnapped in Paris in 1930.**

* Lieutenant General Pavlichenko, who ended the civil war as a cavalry corps commander.

** Wrangel's words were prophetic. In our time such organizations as the Viet Cong, PLO, and Red Brigades operated successfully only by virtue of massive aid from sympathetic countries whether Arab or of the Communist world, Russia or China.

A small house some miles from Belgrade had become Wrangel's headquarters. A mini-staff included five to six officers, among them his chief of staff and close friend, Chatilov, and his secretary, Kotliarewsky; a few Cossacks from the ranks of his former escort and his batman were all that remained of the military establishment. The staff under Wrangel's guidance ran the far-flung and dispersed army, arranging for greater groups to move from the Balkans to western Europe, financing their trips, maintaining the three cadet corps, soon to be fused into one,* the sanatoriums, and other institutions. The orderly process of disbanding the army while keeping it united in a spirit of cohesive esprit de corps was no small undertaking and could be regarded as one of Wrangel's major political achievements. Around the army the civilian Russian emigration had broken out, as Wrangel had predicted, into small party squabbling: ultramonarchists against monarchists, socialists versus other brands. Even the Russian church was not spared and entered a schism engendered by two of its leaders within the ecclesiastic hierarchy. No amount of supplications from Wrangel moved the obdurate prelates, whose schism, a lasting monument to religious fanaticism and human foolishness, has endured to this day by passing even World War II.

Many political personalities, Russian and foreign, came to visit Wrangel, and he himself visited his men whenever possible. In Yugoslavia, where the wearing of the Russian uniform was permitted, these meetings assumed the form of parades with officers and men in uniform, battle standards flying, and bands playing. The Cossacks, who a few hours before plied pick and shovel, stood now at attention in impeccable uniform and cheered loudly as their commander passed them in review. The clouds of dust and heaps of stone to which they were now assigned by fate dissolved into dreams of the past, as in their minds they charged again in serried ranks against the Reds and saw galloping before them the tall lean figure of their General in his invariable Cossack tunic and astrakhan hat.

In France Wrangel met his troops in more austere and even plebeian circumstances. Captain Orekhov, an army officer: "Paris, civilian clothes, rented hall in some cheap restaurant; those were the sites of Wrangel's meetings with his 'Eagles.' However, when Wrangel entered, it seemed that the very doors opened of themselves to let him in; such was his commanding appearance, his moral authority, and ascendancy. . . . In those moments it seemed that there existed no one stronger or mightier than he. These rare visits instilled in us an unbelievable influx of faith and comfort."

But it was perhaps in the cadet schools that Wrangel's visits produced the most fervent furor. The children and youths, flotsam of the civil war's tide, had

* Which existed until World War II.

taken Wrangel to their young hearts with that instinct that motivates children and animals, a movement of the heart where the grown-up's reasoning plays no part.

Cadet Vorobiev: "The unforgettable day when our last commander in chief General Wrangel visited our school, we were drawn up on parade in the lower courtyard and before us stood General Wrangel in his usual pose, hand resting on the Cossack dagger. His loud, hoarse voice, accustomed to addressing mass formations, now called on us to have faith, to be patient. Hundreds of young eyes stared, hypnotized by his face, uniform, and manner. I doubt that the venerable walls (the school was lodged in an old Austrian fortress) had ever before reverberated with such frantic hurrahs. Seized by the cadets the General was lifted to their shoulders and borne in triumph."

Besides the small administrative staff, the unpretentious house not far from the river Danube housed also Wrangel's wife Olga, his aged parents, an old nurse who cared for their infant son born in exile, and during the summer the three children on holiday from their schools in Belgium. There were no horses and Wrangel had to forego his favorite sport, riding, but as a young man he had always liked hunting. Someone presented him with a shotgun and, accompanied by his son Peter, now aged twelve, and a Serbian friend, he would set off before dawn to shoot ducks along the Danube banks or wander through the cornfields in quest of partridges and hares. Sometimes taking a boat he would row the children across the Danube and they would bathe and sun themselves on the sandy beaches. But the hours of leisure were scarce; a driving obsession to bring his work to a successful end, to see his men resettled and, though spread apart, united in spirit, forced him to long hours behind his desk or in lengthy consultations with staff and visitors. Time and inaction were his worst enemies.

As the Grand Duke Nicholas had assumed the role of commander in chief of the Army in Exile and his immediate advisors and entourage demanded an absolute control of the rest of the diminutive funds under which the All Services Union functioned, Wrangel was forced to liquidate his small administrative staff. The Grand Duke offered to pay Wrangel a salary from the funds at his disposal, which Wrangel refused, as he did the offer to receive a pension from the dues paid by all the Union's members. His principle at the time he founded the Union was that none of its sums were to be assigned as pay to senior commanders; each had to pay his way. The lack of funds precluded also liaison with the Grand Duke and with the administration of the different chapters of the Union, whose center of gravity had shifted to the west and to France, the residence of the Grand Duke.

Two times Wrangel had offered his resignation; both times the Grand Duke had refused. He felt that only Wrangel's prestige and authority could hold together this mosaic of men spread over most of Europe, and yet his entourage pushed him steadily on the road of party (monarchist) politics.

Wrangel's mother-in-law had bought a small house in Belgium with the sum realized by the sale of a villa in Austria which had been bought by her husband prior to the World War. There she lived with her invalid son and a nurse. There also Wrangel moved in in 1926 with his wife, an old nurse, and their four-year-old son. His batman with wife and a cook completed this crowded household. Without the assistance of his secretary,* Wrangel was forced to write by hand his voluminous correspondence. To this man whose life had been a ceaseless adventure, on whose shoulders had rested the fate of thousands, and whose nervous energy in combat and disaster had never been abated, a quiet existence in an overcrowded house in Brussels must have been a cruel cross to bear. His sole exercise was walking daily to visit his old mother, who was living in a rented room in another quarter of the city. He faced his fate with equanimity.

Writing about him after his death, his chief of staff and his closest friend Chatilov, thus described this period of his life: "Recalling Wrangel's personality as I saw it the last years of his life, a change in his traits forces itself upon my memory: His character, his habits, and his attitude towards others had altered. He avoided company and sought satisfaction in conversations with persons close to him; invariably these talks had bearing upon the cause that he served.

"Brought up from childhood in affluence, he now had no use for the past luxuries of life: He not only did not regret them but considered them useless. His former sharp and at times devastating judgment of people had given way to an unusual degree of tolerance and patience. A man of immense all-round talent, he now contented himself to see in his associates those qualities only which suited this or that person for this or that job, disregarding personal sympathy or the overall make up of the individual.

"In the last year of his life I noted particularly his tolerance vis-a-vis his detractors. Although healthy and energetic as always, he seemed to live in a world of the beyond."

A Russian journalist and political figure, N. Chebyshev, wrote thus about Wrangel's foreign connections: "He had a few staunch friends among foreigners; they were those who saw and felt as he did,** but what is amazing is the

---

* Kotliarewsky later joined him in Brussels and was responsible for preparation of the Wrangel archives now in the Hoover War Library in Palo Alto, California.

** Among them two British generals, Percy and Harrington, the French Admiral Dumesnil, and two American admirals, Bristol and MacCully.

number of foreign average citizens with whom he was popular. They followed
with interest his activities, wrote in their newspapers in his defense — small
people: shopkeepers, waiters, passersby from the anonymous multitude,
watched and greeted him in the street." They were interestd in this general
with a phantom army, this politican who gathered no votes, this statesman who
had no country!

It is therefore not surprising that Wrangel's sudden illness attracted notice;
no less than forty-nine newspapers around the globe from Belgium to Argen-
tina commented on it, some hinting, and not without grounds, at poisoning.

What was thought at first to be a simple flu turned out to be an unknown
and vicious malady with high and undulating fever. Doctors called to his
bedstead could not diagnose it. His strength ebbed away daily. General
Chatilov: "When I learned of my friend's and commander's serious condition I
came over from Paris. I was struck by his appearance; haggard and drawn, he was
already very weak. On seeing me, he broke down and cried, embracing me
warmly. Pulling himself together, he told me that he had confessed and taken
communion; then calmly he proceeded to discuss with me matters pertinent to
the army and its welfare."

Wrangel died a few days later; his last words were, "Lord save the Army,"
and moments later, "I hear the church bells."

News of his death struck the army like a thunderbolt. One officer wrote:
"For me it is the end, his death a verdict that we shall never see Russia again."
Then, drawing a revolver, the man shot himself. Requiem masses were sung in
every country where Russians had settled, from major centers—Paris,
Brussels, Berlin, Sofia, Belgrade—to obscure villages in the Balkans and grimy
coal mines in Belgium and France.

During his life and tenure of office many European newspapers wrote
critically of his activities, particularly during his efforts to save the army
following evacuation from Russia. Now at his death, with the exception of the
Communist press, left and right joined in giving him his due.

"A man with authority," wrote Sir Samuel Hoare in the London *Times*.
"Let us remember with the greater sympathy a brave officer who loyally served
the cause of the Allies and a leader of men who was only defeated by the tragic
sequence of irresistible events."

The Daily Telegraph wrote: "Personal magnetism, his honesty of purpose,
his clean living, and his ceaseless energy won for him the admiration of the
army and of the masses of the people from the Caspian to the heart of Ukrania.
To his military achievements he attached a free but firm civil government, in
which he displayed the same eagerness for reform and the care of the
lowly."

The Belgian newspaper *Nation Belge* concluded Wrangel's obituary: "A great Russian nation has come into being outside of Russia. Now it has experienced its greatest catastrophe, for General Wrangel represented the symbol of union, honor and hope."

Wrangel's last wishes were to be buried in the Russian church in Belgrade, whose walls were lined with the colors of the regiments which had left Russia. A constitutional crisis in Yugoslavia, bureaucratic delays, and the absence of funds prevented an immediate funeral there. Temporarily he was buried in Brussels. A year and a half later the ground was paved for the return of his body to Yugoslavia and burial there in the Russian church. King Alexander of Yugoslavia who had just ascended the throne, himself Russian-educated and a strong sympathizer of Wrangel, personally ordered a state funeral and the full cooperation of Yugoslav military and civilian authorities. In the meanwhile committees set up to gather funds canvassed the "phantom army" and the Russian emigration at large. Funds came pouring in, sometimes in minute sums donated by some soldier or Cossack toiling for a few pennies in the western coal mines or cutting timber in some forsaken valley of Bulgaria. A sample letter written on a scrap of paper sent from an obscure village in the Ardennes: "I, Don Cossack, am sending herewith 5 francs for my commander in chief Wrangel for his burial in Serbia or to be given to his children."

On the 28th of September, 1929, a special railroad carriage attached to the *Orient Express* left Brussels carrying the coffin of General Wrangel. Upon arrival at Yugoslavia's frontier the carriage was detached and taken over by the Yugoslav Department of Railways. This department arranged for the carriage to stop at intermediate stations on the way to Belgrade, at towns where there was a sizable Russian colony. At such stops requiem masses were held, an honor guard in uniform posted at the head and feet of the deceased.

An eyewitness account at the town of Subotitze: "A great confluence of people, an honor guard of Russian Cossacks, and a company of a Yugoslav infantry regiment with its band. The Yugoslav mayor and city council, the commander of the local garrison, senior Yugoslav officers, priests, choirs, Russian and Serbian civilians, and school children crowded the station. The carriage had arrived the previous evening and the requiem mass took place the next morning. All through the night the sentries of the Cossack honor guard stood at attention like statues, drawn swords glistening in the light of candles. Their stern faces reflected their feelings. Eyes straight ahead, perhaps they stared beyond the crepe-drawn walls of the carriage and looked beyond, into the past: the steppes of the Kouban, the burning farms, the lathered horses, and they themselves charging behind their beloved leader. For the Cossacks loved and honored their commander, not only as a general, but as a fatherly figure who knew many by name, worried about their well-being, and pitied their fate." So it went on until the train arrived in Belgrade.

By personal order of King Alexander of Yugoslavia the state funeral was to be jointly Yugoslav and Russian, and the Yugoslav military commandant of Belgrade had been given the responsibility for its arrangements. All Russian military delegations attending the funeral were given free passage on Yugoslav railroads; this privilege extended also to Russian students and school children. Fifteen percent of the military garrison of Belgrade was detailed for the funeral, as was a field battery to render salutes and a horse-drawn caisson to carry the coffin.

The Russian "phantom army" sent delegations from the four corners of the world. Those who still had their old uniforms donned them; others had new ones tailored for the occasion. Remembering that day, General Chatilov wrote: "A year and a half had passed since Wrangel's death; the poignancy of this loss had lost its sharpness. The funeral was more of a solemn tribute to our commander in chief, a tribute which united the Yugoslavs and the Russians. His soldiers had arrived from all over the world; it was a day of meetings with old war comrades, the sharing of memories, and Wrangel's name was on everyone's lips."

As the train bearing Wrangel's body pulled up at the Belgrade station, it was met by the Yugoslav defense minister, General Hadjich, and by Wrangel's senior officers. These carried out the coffin and laid it on the artillery caisson. Drawn up on the square facing the station were the Russian and Yugoslav military units. Two Yugoslav army aircraft flown by Russian officers flew overhead and dropped a wreath. The procession wound its way through town towards the Russian church. Preceded by a boy carrying a cross came a Russian sergeant carrying the Russian national flag and flanked by two officers, then a group of officers bearing Wrangel's decorations, followed by wreaths, the foremost from King Alexander, borne by two Yugoslav soldiers. In deference to the Russians, their military units were given precedence over the Yugoslavs. Wrangel's charger* marched, led by two sergeants, a Cossack and a guardsman, both decorated with the Cross of St. George. Behind the caisson walked Wrangel's family, followed by representatives of the Yugoslav government and those diplomatic missions whose governments wished to pay Wrangel a final tribute, among them the American minister Prince and his wife. Three hundred and sixty-three delegations of all kinds took part in the funeral; over two hundred wreaths were laid—from the one of King Alexander to a withered bouquet of flowers sent clandestinely from Russia. The air reverberated from the artillery and rifle salutes of the Yugoslav army as the coffin was lowered into the grave by Cossacks. In his sermon the Metropolitan

---

* As Wrangel had no longer a horse of his own, a charger belonging to a Yugoslav officer was made available.

Antonias said: "The funeral which by its grandiose solemnity transcends even those of royal personages is in a way the reward which the Lord had chosen not to give him during his life of valorous achievements. But if his life was not rich in triumphs, but rather in toil and disappointments, this funeral reminds us more of a triumphant march than a laying to rest of an ordinary mortal."

Wrangel's associates and lieutenants discussed what inscription the marble plaque of his grave should bear. Unanimously they agreed on just two words, GENERAL WRANGEL—any other words were superfluous.

But if indeed an epitaph was needed, then surely *"Rumpo non Plecto"*—I break, I do not yield—the Wrangel family motto, would have served the purpose.

April 1, 1986

Brownstown Lodge, Navan,
Co. Meath, Ireland

Bibliography

Books

English

Aten, Capt. Marion, and Arthur Ormont. *Last Train Over Rostov Bridge*. Julian Messner, Inc.

Lehovich, Dimitry. *White Against Red*. New York: W.W. Norton & Co.

Luckett, Richard. *The White Generals*. New York: The Viking Press.

Wrangel. *Memoirs of General Wrangel*. London: Williams & Norgate Ltd.

Russian

Belgrad, V. *Perenesenye Prakha Generala Wrangelya.* Belgrade, 1929.

Belogorsky, N. *Vchera*. Madrid: Private Edition, 1964.

Bugvraff, M. *General Wrangel*. Los Angeles: Special Edition of the Society of First Campaign Combatants, 1972.

Dawatz, V. *Gody*. Belgrade, 1926.

Drier, V. von. *Krestnyi Put vo Imya Rodiny*. Berlin: Private Edition, 1921.

————. *Na Zakate Imperii*. Madrid: Private Edition, 1965.

Karateev, M. *Belogvardeytsy na Balkanah*. Buenos Aires: Private Edition, 1977.

Kvitka, A. *Dnevnik Zabaikalskago Kazachiago Offitzera*. St. Petersberg, 1908.

Lampe, A.A. von. *Wrangel–Sbornik Statei.*Berlin: Verlag Mednyi Vsadnik, 1936.

_____. *Puti Vernykh.* Paris: Private Edition, 1960.

Mamontov, S. *Pokhody i Koni.* Paris: YMCA Press, 1981.

Opritz, N. *Leib Gvardii Kazachiy Polk v Gody Revolutsyi i Grajdanskoy Voyny 1917-1920.* Edited by Siyialsky. Paris, 1939.

Pavlov, V. *Markovtsy v Boyakh i Pokhodah.* Paris: Private Edition, 1962.

Riasniansky, Col. *Gallipoli.* New York: Private Edition, 1970.

Russ, N. *Wrangel v Krymu.* Frankfurt: Posser Verlag, 1982.

Turkul, Gen. A. *Drozdovtsy v Ogne.* Edited by Iav i Byl. Munich, 1948.

Vitkovsky, Gen. V.K. *V. Borbe za Rossiyv.* New York: Private Edition, 1963.

Voronovich, N. *Vsevidiachee Oko.* New York: Private Edition, 1951.

Composite Authors. *Kornilovskiy Ovdarnyi Polk.* Paris: Private Edition, 1936.

Sedmaya Gavbitchnaya (Seventh Howitzers). Yonkers, NY: Alekandrovsky.

Vospominanie Generala Barona P.N. Wrangelya. Frankfurt/Main: Posser Verlag.

Unpublished

Chatiloff, Gen. P. *Zapisky.* Paris, 1957.

Valintinov, A.A. *87 Dney v Poezde Gen. Wrangelya.* Sebastopol-Crimea, 1920.

Government Dispatches

British:

Admiralty
Foreign Office
War Office (Military Mission South of Russia Situation Reports and Instructions)

Periodicals
Russian

"Nashy Vesty." *Magazine of Russian Combatants*. Monterey, Ca.
"Otechestvo." *Patrie* (June 1928). Paris.
"Pravosudie v Voyskah Generala Wrangelya" (1921). Constantinople: Babok & Sons.
"Tshasovoy." *La Sentinelle*. Brussels.

Newspapers
Russian

Novoye Vremya (May 9 to July 18, 1928). Belgraqde.
Rossiya (May 5 to 26, 1928). Paris.
Vozrojdenie (April 29 to June 8, 1928). Paris.

British

Daily Telegraph (March to November 1920, April 26, 1928).
The Times (April 27, 1928).

Belgian

Indepenance (April 26 to May 10, 1928).
Nation Belge (April 26 to May 10, 1928).
Soir (April 26 to May, 1928).